FILE UNDER FIDELITY

Geraldine Wall

Books in this series

In memory of my mother, Edna,
with gratitude, apologies and love.

3

'Written on the deep pages of the heart'

S. Longfellow

1

Anna squeezed her eyes until the sunlight through the leaves of the sycamore tree turned to flickering spangles. She could feel the chill of the lounger between her shoulder blades and reached out to touch the grass with her fingertips. These days, hot summer days, her nerve endings were vibrating with possibility – her senses overwhelmed by light and heat. Maybe her dad was right. She could love both men. She forced herself to imagine it. She would always be fond of her husband – more than fond, she would always love him. A quiet love, full of memories, a love in the past tense. He would never know. As he was now would he even care? She felt herself give permission for the smallest tilt in the axis of her lifetime's fidelity to Harry. An infinitesimal turn of the shoulder away from him and towards Steve. She felt the thrill snake down through her nerves in a hot penetration.

Last night Steve had cooked for them all at his house to thank them for having Alice for the weekend while he'd been in Norway climbing. He had been sunburned to brick red by his hours on the mountain so that his eyes were a lighter, brighter blue. His movements around the kitchen were quick and competent and he had frequently glanced at her, sitting with her knees drawn up in his basket chair, while he talked. She imagined how it would feel being made love to by Steve. She thought of his hands. She had sipped her wine and let herself go very slightly loose. Dangerously slack.

Something was licking her toes so she opened her eyes and twisted her neck to see Bobble trying to get her attention. He bounced up on to his huge paws and shook his shaggy head joyously, spraying her with wetness. She scrambled off the lounger and leaped up.

'No!'

He barked, thrilled with the success of his invitation and shook again, his body rolling down in segments until the tail twirled round. 'Bad dog!' She grabbed him by the collar and twisted her head up to the bedroom window. 'Ellis! Get down here! He's been in the pond again.'

She dragged him over to the tool-shed and found a length of rope hanging inside the door. She looped and then knotted one end round his collar and looked round for something to tie the other end to. Having been subdued for a second Bobble recovered his high spirits and grabbed the rope in his jaws, pulling and growling and rolling his eyes. She let him drag her across to the heavy wooden bench and tied him firmly to it. She stepped back. He bounced on all fours shouting with excitement. She noted that he was now strong enough to rock the bench in its footings. And not yet fully grown. She mentally cursed the allure of animal sanctuaries in general and Safe 'n' Sound in particular.

Pulling the stinking shirt away from her chest she ran past George's writing shed and through the narrow passage into the utility room. Ellis appeared at the other end.

'Sorry, Mum.'

'Can't you do something, Ell? This is the third time!'

He edged past her holding his nose. 'What, like aversion therapy by taser, you mean?'

'Or sticking something in the gap in the fence.'

As he passed, Ellis put his finger to his lips. She stopped. He mouthed, 'Who's that?' and jerked his head towards the kitchen.

'Who?' she mouthed back. He shrugged, grabbed a bucket and left. She went through the kitchen door to find that sitting at the table was a very large young woman with purple hair. Anna halted. 'Can I help you?'

The woman stood up and became even taller than she had appeared seated. She put out a hand. 'Rosa Kelly.'

'Um.'

'Helping Hands.' The woman smiled down at her. 'I think your husband let me in. He said to wait in here.' She paused. 'So I waited in here.'

'Oh, right. I'm so sorry. I was expecting you a little later.' Anna picked at her shirt again. 'I have to get changed – the dog's just showered me with stagnant pond water. I'll only be a minute and then I'll get you a drink and we can chat.'

Rosa Kelly sat down and lifted a large patchwork bag on to the table. 'Take your time.'

Anna washed quickly at the bathroom basin and picked at her hair. It seemed not to have been splashed enough to make a fuss about. While she was pulling on some fresh clothes she thought about the other two women who had applied for the job of being Harry's carer. The first one had been very interested in everything. She examined photos, commented on the garden, expressed herself willing to do a little light housework for extra pay and asked Anna far too many questions to which she didn't need to know the answers. She was squirelly in her movements. The only thing she didn't show any interest in was Harry. The second one had been a much older woman with a cynical look in her eye. She had announced before even sitting down that she needed fixed hours with regular breaks and would not be willing to lift anything or anyone. Perhaps this one, the third in the sequence, would be 'just right'. Anna smiled to herself remembering reading the story of Goldilocks and the Three Bears to Alice last weekend. Alice had been unimpressed. 'Don't eat *my* porridge!' she had ordered Anna, an imperious finger raised, as if the story might have set a bad example.

As Anna went back down the stairs Faye appeared in the hall, closed the kitchen door behind her, and muttered 'What's with the purple-headed mountain in the kitchen?'

'Don't be rude. Interviewing for the carer job.'

'Really?'

Anna pushed open the door and went in with Faye to find Alice already there.

The little girl was entranced. She had climbed up on to a chair and was sitting on two extra cushions with a piece of squared graph paper and a red felt-tip in front of her. 'Like this,' Rosa was saying. 'Then you make a pattern.' In Rosa's other large hand was an exquisitely fine piece of cross-stitch. It was a design of roses and ivy leaves set in a loose wreath on a ground of unbleached linen. A needle threaded with pink silk was poised while she watched Alice.

Anna smiled and went to the kettle. 'I see you've met Alice.'

'Lisha,' corrected Alice without looking up. 'Faye calls it me.'

'Your daughter?'

'No! I'm not *hers*, I'm Steve's.' Alice made another large cross more or less inside a square.

'Her uncle is a neighbour and a work colleague,' Anna said, getting down the mugs. 'My daughter Faye here has more or less adopted her.' Faye got out the biscuit tin.

'Make one for me, Mum?'

'Tea or coffee?' Anna asked Rosa, 'or something cold?'

'Tea – milk, no sugar, please.'

They settled round the table after Faye had poured a juice glass of milk for Alice. Rosa put her sewing away in the bag. When

Anna protested she said that she never mixed snacks and sewing since she'd once almost ruined a nearly-complete cushion cover.

'You're really good. What do you do with them?' asked Faye, dunking her ginger biscuit.

'This one's for the National Trust to re-cover a lady's bedroom chair. They give me the design.'

'Impressive,' said Faye. 'Do they pay well?'

'Faye!'

Rosa smiled, quite unoffended. 'I like doing it and it helps to get paid for it.' Anna heard something soft and comforting in Rosa's vowels. Black Country?

Ellis appeared looking harassed and very wet. 'Can anyone help? I'm trying to wash Bobble and he's being a pain.' Immediately Alice slid off her seat and ran to the back door. Faye stood up.

'Put a plastic bag over her,' Anna said, pulling one out of from under the sink. 'Just make some neck and armholes.' Faye took it from her. 'Does Steve know she's with us?'

'Yep. Ellis needn't think I'm going anywhere near that minging animal,' Faye said. 'He's got to take responsibility.' The utility room door slammed.

When Anna turned back to the table the pad of graph paper and the red felt-tip had gone and Rosa was replacing her bag on the floor. She sat down. 'Have they told you about Harry's illness?'

'They said it was Picks. Like Early Onset Familial Alzheimer's but not inherited.'

'Yes. Do you know anything about it?'

Rosa frowned. She was large but not fat. She looked like a Georgia O'Keefe succulent - firm, fresh and full-bodied. 'I looked it up. I didn't understand all the medical words but people can get a bit over the top, can't they? I mean as well as the usual.'

'Exactly. Harry rarely does but we have had a few incidents. It's when there's a highly charged atmosphere so we try to avoid that. Not a problem usually. This is hardly Party Central.' She was impressed. Neither of the other applicants had made a distinction between Harry's condition and the Alzheimer's disease they usually dealt with. She smiled at Rosa and noticed how clear and bright the woman's hazel eyes were and that her cheeks dimpled when she smiled back.

It seemed that Rosa was happy to be flexible with her time as long as she could be sure of twenty hours a week so Anna told her briefly about the other member of the household, her father George, who had been for nearly two years Harry's prime carer but now, as Harry deteriorated further, needed both help and some respite time.

'If you notice a sort of absent-minded elf of the human variety scuttling around, that'll be him. He's been great, but he needs more time for his own stuff. He writes poetry and edits magazines and all that. Thankfully, not in here. He's got his own shed outside.' Anna re-read Rosa's reference from the agency and asked a couple of questions. She wasn't quite sure what to do next. 'Do *you* have any questions?'

'I'd like to meet Harry properly.'

He wasn't in his usual chair in the front part of the knocked-through living room. He was at the back watching the children wash Bobble on the grass and picking out a tune with one finger on the piano. Suddenly Anna wanted to push Rosa out of the front door. What on earth was she doing bringing strangers into Harry's life? It seemed like a betrayal. She sat down beside him on the piano stool. He loomed over her and she felt the familiar peace which everyone feels in the physical presence of someone they love and trust. A small smile appeared at the corner of his mouth for a second and was gone. A flare of anger ignited her. His hair should be white, his skin should be lined, he should be old, not like this, still handsome and lean with those same sloping green gold eyes she had fallen in love with so long ago. He should have had so much more life to live.

'Harry, this is Rosa.'

He turned and looked at the tall woman and then went back to picking out sounds. Only a couple of months ago he would have greeted anyone with a handshake or a word just out of habit. She had been told that often these marks of early social training were the last to go. Please, thank you, hello, good-bye. She imagined the old Harry leaping from the stool and greeting whoever it was warmly with a pleasantry. She fought back the desire to tell Rosa – he didn't used to be like this.

Rosa looked around and pulled a wicker chair towards the piano. She sat down and began to sing softly in harmony with Harry's random notes. He stopped and stared at her. Then he started playing again but this time it was recognisable – Happy

Birthday. She sang and Anna joined in. This was not new. Harry did play from time to time, fragments from melodies he remembered or were there in his fingers not needing to be thought about. What Anna was seeing as extraordinary were not Harry's actions but how Rosa had responded to where he was, neither bossing nor praising nor making a fuss of any kind. She responded to him adult to adult, enjoying making music.

When Harry had had enough he looked back out into the garden and then stood up and tried to open the doors to the patio. They were kept locked. 'Can I see your dog?' Rosa said, moving towards the hall door. He followed her.

'Minging animal,' he said cheerfully.

Two weeks trial for all parties to feel comfortable, Anna decided, but Rosa did seem to be 'just right' if anything in this bloody horrible situation could ever be.

Within a week it became unthinkable that Rosa would not be part of their lives. The first day she was there was eagerly reported by George when Anna got home from work that night. He had introduced himself when Rosa arrived that morning and had stayed to make sure she knew where everything was and to be a general support. At breakfast as he went to get Harry up and dressed, Anna had sensed his anxiety about this stranger coming in to his son-in-law's life with so much responsibility but by dinner he was a convert.

'Rosa and I had a very interesting chat about the medicinal properties of honey and garlic,' he said, as Anna walked into the kitchen that evening. He was making salad at one end of the table while Anna sat down gratefully and sipped iced tea at the other. It was cool in the kitchen and she slipped off her sandals to let her feet rest in sweaty patches on the tiles.

'So the first thing she did this morning,' George said, slicing carrots into matchsticks, 'was sit Harry down and lay out on the table the wildflowers she'd picked from the side of the canal on her way here.' He scooped the carrots into the wooden bowl and pulled some tomatoes towards the chopping board. 'Then she picked one up and got him to really look at it, the colours, the shapes, the smell and then she encouraged him to tell her back and talk about it. Then she told him the name, put it down and picked another one up. I haven't seen him so focussed for ages!'

'That's really good.'

'Then she got Bobble on his lead and we all went to the park so she'd know where it was and we pottered round there a bit. When we got back she made him a cup of tea and he had a rest for half an hour or so and she and I had a bit of a chat. Spinach.'

'Left hand fridge drawer. So, then?'

'She asked me for our photo albums so I got them down for her. Lucky that you were so good at labelling because I couldn't remember half the places, let alone Harry.'

'Can't take the librarian out of the girl.' Anna's toes were getting cold and she tucked them up on the cross-bar of the chair.

'Right. So she didn't ask him questions, she just said things like, "It looks hot here," or, "You were having a good time," you know, and he really got into it. One photograph he actually said, "St. Ives." I couldn't believe it.' George straightened and frowned. 'Have we got any cheese?'

'Don't know. I can go and get some.'

He backed out of the fridge holding the packet. Anna noticed that he was wearing a not just different but new shirt. Diane's influence was slowly but surely tidying him up. His previous practice had been a trip to the charity shops when the seasons changed to refresh his wardrobe. 'Found it. Then she made him some lunch, she'd brought her own – something healthy-looking in a tub, and afterwards she sat with him at the piano for at least half an hour. Well, of course, by the time she left he was ready for a nap but seemed more contented than I've seen him for a while.' He smiled at Anna. 'I think you got a winner there.'

Anna stood up and scratched her head, lifting the hot hair from the scalp. She felt odd, irritable, unsettled. 'That's brilliant, Dad. And of course we'll all be popping in from time to time while she's here. Did she walk here then, from the canal? Did she mention where she lived?'

George was laying the table for five places and glanced at the clock. 'Yes, she lives on a narrowboat moored by the university, you know, near that new aqueduct. She told me her family were boat people before and during the Second World War. Not sure whether to put the garlic bread in now or wait till they get here.'

'She walked here from there?'

'No, she keeps her van behind a friend's shop in Selly Oak.'

Anna turned away. 'I should wait a bit, Dad. Ellis will be here in a minute but I can't get Faye to answer her phone and it's early yet.'

'Maybe I'll just go and have a quick look at today's post, then,' and he was gone out of the back door to his shed to look through the poetry magazines that were sent almost daily to him for review.

Anna thought Rosa would probably approve of George's shed. Years ago he and Faye had painted the inside walls with colourful cartoons and abstracts which livened up the dim interior. George's huge partners' desk was always heaped with papers and books and the dipped shelves held more. Rammed into the corner by the power socket was an ancient printer and scattered about were an eclectic mix of seating options including a car seat and an ancient rocker.

Anna looked in on Harry, fast asleep on the sofa, and slowly climbed the stairs to get changed.

It was brilliant that Rosa had fitted in so well, that Harry was so happy, so why was there this tight little knot of nausea in her stomach? She peeled off her damp clothes and lay down on her own single bed. The window was open and a breeze ruffled the nerves of her bare skin. Surely she wasn't jealous? Maybe she was, but more than that she felt guilty. How often had she inwardly condemned parents who used the television or the computer to child-mind for them? Wasn't that exactly what she had done sometimes with Harry? When she was tired at the end of the day and George was off duty it was so easy to put on a DVD, one of his favourites, or to switch to a pre-recorded documentary. Then she could either sit with him, which she had done less and less lately, or she could leave him staring at the screen, just assuming he was fine. Rosa's careful, sensitive stimulation of the little mental capacity Harry had left was an unintentional rebuke to her, his wife. She groaned and rolled upright to get a shower.

'I have so had it with Boz,' Faye said, stuffing a huge forkful of salad into her mouth. 'I hope he fails all his exams.'

'Faye.'

'I do. It's the last 'A' level tomorrow and it's Psychology and if he keeps up that snorting and sighing that he does I'll tell the invigilator that he's putting me off. I really glared at him in the

Business paper and then Mrs Waters glared at me for looking at him! As if I'd get any help from that cretin.'

'You only go on about him because you fancy him,' Ellis said. 'Ow!'

'Idiot child! Of course I don't!' Faye spluttered bits of lettuce at him. 'He's disgusting! He had this pathetic shirt on today with a button off it and actual chest hair was poking through – I almost vomited.' Because of the heat Faye was wearing her hair in a loose pony tail these days and it really did look like an especially glossy and beguiling horse's tail. A chestnut Morgan, like Beauty, Anna thought. Kimi was educating Anna about horses and although she was still scared of them she agreed that they were sometimes wonderful to look at.

'When I was a young man…' George began.

'In the dear, dead days of long ago,' Ellis chipped in.

'When I was a young man, chest hair was very much appreciated by the women. In fact we were all very hairy - including the women.' George took a last bite of garlic bread. 'They didn't have it on their chests, of course.'

'Gross.' Faye frowned at her grandfather.

'Yes, the preferred amount was curling over the top of your collar as I recall, meeting the hair coming down, so to speak.'

'Pops! Some of us are still eating!'

'Hair today and gone tomorrow,' said Harry, and they all burst out laughing and Faye gave him a hug. He sometimes did this, contributing a fragment from some lightly moored memory bank. Sometimes it made sense, sometimes not, but just to hear his voice was a pleasure. Anna looked from Ellis to his father and back again. They were so alike, lean and coppery and golden-eyed. Faye's creamy skin and chocolate eyes harked back to Harry's mother who had been three years younger than Faye was now when she had given birth to him and then, obedient to her appalled parents, handed him to strangers never to see her son again. It was Anna's secret that she had searched for Harry's birth parents and uncovered the all-too-common story.

Anna's phone buzzed and she saw that Kimi was calling. After a few moments' chat she turned it off and groaned. Faye and Ellis had gone and her father was making a pot of coffee.

'What?'

'She's remembered that it's my birthday soon and wants to do it up big, as they say.'

'Well, why not?'

'She wants to book a spa for a bunch of us.'

George glanced at her face. 'Not a good idea?'

'What do you think? Can you see me subjecting myself to a hot wax treatment? But she says I've got to come up with something or she's going to book it anyway and ask Michelle and Suzy from work and Briony, for God's sake. Why Briony, I don't know. She's never met her – in fact, she's only heard of her through Joan. What an unholy combination that would be! It would end up more like Cluedo than relaxation. Briony Clark with hot mud in the changing room.'

'Ok, well, what would you like? I've been meaning to ask. What do you really want to do?' Anna bent down to rub Bobble's ears to hide her hot face. What did she really want to do? As soon as the question had been put she had known exactly what she really wanted. To be with Steve. Not with the family and not with 'the girls' but with Steve. 'That new Mike Leigh film is on next week. Great reviews. Why don't you go with Steve?' It was as though her father had read her mind. Anna's heart thumped uncomfortably. 'You both deserve an evening out without family worries. Faye will be happy to see to Alice, I'm sure.' He set the coffee cup down by her elbow. 'You could have dinner first.'

'I'll think about it,' Anna said. 'Go on, go back to your mags, I know you want to. I'll do the dishes.' When he had left the room Anna went over the sink and started to rinse the plates for the dishwasher. Could she really ask Steve to go for dinner and then to the cinema? Why not? And yet they had never done such a thing before. He and Alice moved easily in and out of their family events and he often took Ellis climbing or Faye would have Lisha for the day. At work she and Steve would sometimes go for a pub lunch or a coffee in town but this felt different. It would sound like, look like, and maybe even feel like a date. What a dangerous and exciting thought that was. She angled the tap to swill hardened bits of mayonnaise from a bowl.

She thought back over the few years that she and Steve had known each other since she started work at Harts Heir Hunters and had turned to him for help with a difficult case. Briony Clark's case, in fact. They knew their attraction was mutual. There had even been kisses, at moments of crisis usually, that was all. They never kissed socially. But there had been careful words spoken and she remembered every one. What could they do? To betray Harry had always been unthinkable, completely unthinkable for her, until a month ago when George had said quietly, 'You can love two men.' Those few words had burned through her deliberately smothered senses like a red-hot iron through silk. Now he had suggested this date with Steve. She could almost feel the ground sliding away from beneath her feet.

It wasn't hard to remember why her father had said those five explosive words. Only a few weeks ago, it seemed like years now, she had been at the point of a violent death from a criminal gang and had survived through a mixture of comic coincidence and authentic heroism. Life had felt very precious and its transitory nature had never been more appreciated. Conventions had temporarily melted away. As the physical crisis had passed she had felt gouged clean of the clutter of everyday anxieties and her father, seeing everything that mattered to her as usual, had chosen that time, that brilliant spring sunset, to throw his grenade. If anyone else had said those words they wouldn't have made a dent but her father had been loyal for forty years to the woman who had left him with a small child and disappeared. Lena, Anna's mother. He knew about commitment. He also knew Anna and, she had to admit, he liked and respected Steve. But, he had only been able to turn to Diane when her mother had died.

Harry was not dead.

2

It was a little too cool in the air-conditioned office so Anna kept a jacket on the back of her chair which she now put on. Most of the researchers were out but Suzy was busy at her terminal, Anna noticed. Steve was, as usual, perched in front of the bank of screens in his own office and his door was open but Anna was not ready to talk to him today. She had a job to get on with and putting off making a delicate invitation was irresistible.

It was a common event for the Coroner's Office to contact Harts probate research company because someone had died intestate. It was their bread and butter work. In this case, William Dawkins had not only left no will but also appeared to have no family. It had been the work of an hour for Anna to discover that he did have a brother, Kenneth, but apparently no children or any other close relative. The brother had been listed on the electoral register until 1961 and had then, annoyingly, disappeared. No death was recorded. Anna remembered that at this time Australia was offering £10 assisted passages for people interested in immigrating so she had trawled their records no effect. In fact, he had not turned up in Canada, the USA or New Zealand either. Today she would search military records and those of the merchant navy.

At four o'clock she picked up her phone. It was Ted on the internal line. 'Come to see me in my office,' he barked. 'Make it quick.'

He was dressed in his golfing outfit and she tried not to smirk at the little tassells on his shoes. She decided to get in first. 'I need to visit Mr Dawkins' home and look for letters and so on, I've tried everything else.' He pretended to think about it.

'Don't tell me he lived in the theatre district of London.'

She rolled her eyes. 'Wolverhampton.'

'Just a bit of petrol money, then. Ok.' Ted rocked from side to side studying a scrap of paper in his hand. 'Quite an interesting job just came in. You might like it.' Anna remembered very clearly the last time that Ted had given her an interesting job and raised her eyebrows at him. 'Oh, not like that. No problems with this one.'

She was not reassured but she was intrigued. 'Go on, then.'

He pulled a folder towards himself and checked some details. 'It's an American called Maxon Blake. He's here for a few months doing a pud school course, owns some sort of eaterie in Philadelphia, but he'd like to use the time he's here to look up some ancestors in – er – Shropshire, Shrewsbury. Well, around there.'

'The Records Office in Shrewsbury, Shropshire Archives, could do that. He doesn't need to pay for us.'

'You're always trying to give work away! No. He's got money, there's family money apparently, and he just wants help to do everything smoothly. I think he'd probably like to find old family homes – you know, the usual. Basically he doesn't want to waste time going down blind alleys.'

'I don't know, Ted. It would involve quite a bit of travelling over there and there's Harry.'

He put the file back on his desk. 'Well, let me know. He wants to get started in a couple of days ideally.'

'Ok.'

Mr Dawkins' house turned out to be a neat semi on a 1930's estate. She had picked up the keys from his solicitor and was feeling hopeful from the orderly and well-maintained exterior that his papers would be easy to find inside.

It was a feeling that she never got used to, that moment when she, a stranger, entered a dead person's house with the full intention of going through their private things. Sometimes her heart sank as she entered, smelling the mildew and fustiness and seeing piles of stuff on every surface. In one house there had been mouse droppings all over the carpet and fleshy mould in the bathroom and bedroom. The neatness or otherwise of the house bore little relation to the wealth of the owner. In one remote Worcestershire cottage she had had to search through heaps of jumbled rubbish picking over stained clothing and decades old newspapers to discover snail trails of family connections. Ted had given her a small bonus for that distasteful work because Mrs Lowry had been worth a fortune. She had looked in all the likely places first – anything resembling a desk or bureau, boxes under the bed, tins up high on kitchen shelves, but nothing. Finally, after three days of wearing a decorator's onesie, rubber gloves and a mask and disturbing nests of rats and mice and troughs of slugs, she had found a metal box in the outside loo rusting under a heap of broken garden chairs. It contained photographs, birth, marriage and death certificates, the deeds of the cottage, some premium bonds worth £5 and a Will, witnessed and dated. It was the work of a couple of hours to trace and contact Mrs Lowry's son and tell him that he had inherited over a million pounds.

Mr Dawkins' house did not smell. She walked slowly through each room noting possible places to search and looking for family photos but, unusually, there were none. Anna opened the door of the third bedroom. It had been set up as a workshop and she gazed up, admiring the models of early aeroplanes hanging from the ceiling. They were not Air-fix kits but made exquisitely from balsa wood and wire and then painted. This was Mr Dawkins' shed, man-cave, whatever. Mrs Dawkins seemed to have left no trace – she had been tidied and dusted away. On a shelf were stacked dozens of books about the two world wars. She would find nothing here.

In the dining room there was a G-plan teak bureau. She dragged across a matching teak dining chair and pulled down the lid. She went through paid bills, statements and receipts and then she found it. A letter. It was in a plain white envelope and on the front was written: 'For Ken, in the event of my death.' She opened it and read:

December 2007

Dear Ken,

I don't know where you are so I hope this finds you. I want you to have everything but I knew I couldn't give them an address so I didn't bother to make a will. That's not what this is about.

There's something I want to tell you, I've wanted to tell you for years, well, decades I suppose. I don't blame you going off when you did. Janet was your girlfriend before she chose me and I know you really cared for her. You told me you were going to ask her to marry you after she'd met the family and then the next thing she wanted to marry me. I was flattered , she was a very good-looking girl and I let that come before loyalty to you, my own brother. To be honest, I think I felt a bit puffed up that she wanted me when you were the one who could always get girls and I couldn't. I believed her when she said it had been love at first sight and that all she'd felt for you was a flirtation.

She lied, Ken. The truth was that you were a penniless art student and I had just got that job at Rolls Royce as a draughtsman. It wasn't me she wanted, it was the meal ticket, but I couldn't see that for years. So we got married in a hurry like she wanted and moved to Derby. You left right after the wedding and you and me didn't even say goodbye. It broke mum and dad's heart you disappearing like that. But it was my fault, not yours.

Well, I got my comeuppance. I won't go into it but she was a bitch to live with. I'm sorry to use a word like that but it's the truth. She cared nothing for me, didn't want to have children or work or do anything other than shop and watch telly. After a while the rows started and then she got a better offer and left with some chap she met. I didn't bother with anyone after that. I hadn't the heart for it.

When all this family history stuff started to get easier with computers I tried to find you but I couldn't. I even hired someone for a little while last year but no luck.

Anyway, I just want to say if you do read this that I was wrong to marry Janet and let you go. You were well out of it as it happened but it was me that did you wrong. I'm sorry Ken. Before that we were always good brothers and got on well and I've missed you ever since. I hope you're happy and things have worked out for you. I just wanted you to know.

Your affectionate brother,
Bill

Anna sighed and folded the letter away. There was nothing else of interest in the bureau and she left, closing the front door quietly behind her.

Steve spun round on his swivel chair as she tapped on his door. 'Hi. Come on in.'

'Fancy a coffee while I pick at your brain?'

He glanced at his watch and jumped up from the chair. 'Lead me to it.'

They clattered down the green glass staircase and out through the lobby into a dry, hot afternoon. The tow path was clotted with a party of school-children being shown a lock but they pushed through and swung into a good pace past the expensive apartments and canal-side offices until they came to Brindley Place and their favourite Café Rouge.

'Inside or outside?'

'What do you think?'

For a moment they both sat silently gazing around and smiling. On every side hanging baskets and tubs were overflowing with colour and greenery. The arch over the canal and the brightly painted narrowboats on it made a cheerful sight and as people passed them their mood seemed to be as sunny as their surroundings. Anna felt loose, free, almost tipsy with it. So what that she was a bit floaty, a bit untethered? The redoubtable Rosa was with Harry, Ellis and Faye were fine, George was happy, surely it was ok to let go just a little bit after the years of tension and worry? She lifted her chin and closed her eyes.

'Can I get you something?' She almost ordered wine in her unfamiliar state of relaxation but settled for a double espresso and Steve ordered a latte.

'Ok, then. Brain open for business.' They discussed the letter she had found and where Ken might be. 'You can't go through the records of every country in the world, Anna, but I do have one suggestion.'

'Mm?'

'This guy Kenneth Dawkins must be, what, sixties, seventies even? People often come home when they're old. Partly instinct and partly it makes sense – we have better facilities for older people than most countries and he may even be entitled to a British pension unless he's taken a new nationality.'

'It's possible. So what are you saying?'

'I know you've checked the electoral register up to 1961 but why not go to the latest one and work back? It's easy and worth a try.'

'Ok. Good idea.'

The coffee came and they sat and sipped. Anna put on her sunglasses and turned her face to the light resting her chin on one hand. She let her lips curve into a smile.

'You look relaxed, Anna. Actually, you look happy. It's good to see. You've had a tough few years with one thing and another.'

She smiled lazily. 'Mm. I do feel much calmer. Rosa's helped such a lot and Kimi's dad's money will pay for her which was so lovely of him. I often smile at him wherever he is now and thank him. Whimsical, eh? I feel that at this particular moment I am marooned in a lacuna of peace.' She pushed up her glasses and fluttered her eyelashes at him affectedly.

'Right,' he snorted. 'Well, before you drown of inertia in that lacuna, a little bird has told me you've got a birthday coming up.'

'Yes indeedy. No-one will let me forget it.' Could she really ask him out on a date? Could she find a way to ask him without it being a date? He never wore sunglasses so his eyes were slits and only a flash of blue was visible. Why not? That lassitude which felt so good, so rare and seductive, winked at her.

'So, any requests? Like maybe having Alice for the day while I go climbing or weeding my garden, I know you've been desperate to. I might even let you clear the gutters if you're really good.' He touched her hand lightly.

'Dad suggested something. Not really a birthday thing – just a treat.' Her heart began to pound but she kept her face tilted to the sun and her voice easy. 'He thought that you and I should have a break from our families and maybe go to that new film at the Odeon. The Mike Leigh one. Maybe get a bite first?' She waited. He withdrew his fingers from her hand. The seconds went by. She glanced at his face and saw that it was registering nothing. Was it was carefully registering nothing?

'Ok. Good idea.'

'It was just a thought.'

'Why not?'

But as they walked back to the office she felt that there was that old tension back between them. No casual brushing of arm against arm or teasing glances or easy insults. She felt excited and alarmed. So much for the lacuna of peace, then.

She found she didn't want to go home when everyone left the office. She phoned her father who told her that Harry was asleep on the garden lounger and he and Ashok were busy in the shed. No sign of the others, no need to hurry home if she had work to do. She didn't have work to do, but staying here was preferable to fighting through the traffic in the heat and then having to deal with whatever was waiting or her. She recognised this as unusual. Normally she would be trying to leave early to get home, Steve always left early to pick Alice up from nursery, so what was different? She got up and crossed to the window.

'Hey! What are you doing still here?' Suzy was a vision. Her blonde hair had been pushed to one side and pinned with a comb and her mouth was scarlet. Anna had not realised what a huge bust she had, propped up and almost bare as it now was for inspection. She tottered forward. 'Too high?' They both looked at the five-inch chrome spikes.

'For what?'

'Getting in and out of taxis, what do you think?'

'You look like a patisserie trolley.'

'That's good. I'm thinking of cashing Rob in for a sportier model.' Suzy peered at her cleavage and tugged her dress down.

Anna smiled. 'That's what I love about you – your feminist world view!'

'We're meeting at Hughie's and then going on somewhere. Do you want to come?'

Anna laughed. 'That sounds so 1920's. I forget how posh you are, Suzy.' She indicated her own limp cotton top and heavily creased polyester trousers. 'Give it a miss I think.'

Suzy waggled a finger at her. 'If you would let me give you a make-over, Anna, you know I'm dying to. Ok, I'm used to the short hair now, but *definition*! Not caught-in-a-hedge! If I had your looks I'd be wearing draped, figure-hugging stuff, not this cheaper-by-the-dozen look.' She indicated Anna's work wear with despair. 'And don't think I've forgotten your birthday's coming up. Girls' night out is definitely in order! It's time you let go a bit.'

'Right – I'll think about it.' Anna turned back to the window. 'Have fun and don't be mean to Rob – he's ok.'

'If you say so. Bye.' And off she clattered.

Steve had come to her desk that afternoon. He'd looked up the cinema listings and told her they would have to go before her birthday to catch that film. They would have to go this Friday, the day after tomorrow. What kind of restaurant would she like, Italian, Thai or what? She had opted for a Moroccan place within easy walking distance of the cinema. He had gravely agreed and then returned to his office.

It was already going wrong. Normally, having suggested an arrangement, she would have done the organising if any needed doing. She tried to think what that might have involved. A Saturday morning trip to the Sports Centre with Harry and Joan? Quick phone call. Taking Alice with Faye to the Wacky Warehouse for an hour of hectic excitement? Ditto. Somehow, despite her casual invitation he had immediately labelled it as a date and as such he had taken on the responsibility of setting it up. He could have been arranging a funeral. Again she felt a throb of alarm and excitement and remembered that this was exactly how she had felt when Kimi had first hoisted her on to one of her horses only three weeks ago. Another rash opportunity for total loss of control. She would wear her lemon cotton dress which he'd often seen before to counter any suggestion of a heavy emotional evening and banter him into relaxing.

Beyond the double glazing of the office the sun was beginning to sink and the colours of the canal boats glowed. Two teenagers danced along, pushing at each other and squealing, and an office worker in a sharp black suit strode by, his jacket held by one finger by its loop over his shoulder and his other hand to his ear. She picked up her bag and keys and went home.

Harry was sitting glumly at the kitchen table when she went in. The back door to the shed and the garden were open and she could hear George's printer clacking and then it stopped. Bobble leaped up at her and took no notice as usual when she said, 'No! Down!' It wouldn't be long before he would be able to put his paws on her shoulders and look her in the eye. Not a comforting thought. She wrestled him off her.

'Hi Sweetie,' she said to Harry and opened the fridge door to see what there might be for dinner. He didn't reply. She closed the door and went to him, lifting her hand to stroke his hair. He made an irritated gesture and stumbled to his feet. 'Harry? Are you ok?' He flapped a hand and disappeared into the hall. She went out to the shed.

'Dad?' He was on his hands and knees by the ancient printer doing something with a toner cartridge. His face was raspberry pink and running with sweat. 'Do you want any help?'

'I can't remember which way to put the blasted thing in. I've been doing it for twenty years. Just leave me to it, Anna.' He looked contrite. 'Sorry. Didn't mean to snap at you.'

'Harry seems a bit out of sorts as well.'

'It's the heat, we're not used to it. He's been a bit off all day.'

'Hasn't Rosa been?'

'Oh yes. She did her best but he couldn't seem to concentrate on anything.'

Anna turned away.   It was ridiculous, irrational and superstitious to think that Harry had intuited his wife floating away from him, floating dangerously close to someone else. As she had asked Steve to go out with her while they sat in the sunshine of Brindley Place, had he paused at their kitchen table, lifted his head, looked away from Rosa's colouring book or whatever and for a second felt that movement in his heart?

'I'll get the tea on in a minute – it only needs putting together. You just have a sit-down, ok?' Since Rosa had taken over most of the day with Harry and freed George, he had picked up the duty of the evening meal and she appreciated it.

'No hurry, Dad. It's too hot to eat just yet anyway.'

She went through the open shed door and up the short path to the kitchen. Harry was not in the living room so she climbed the stairs wondering whether to shower before dinner and where Faye was.   She took her phone out and checked it but there was no message.

Now that exams had finished, Faye and her friends had joyously given in to sleeping during the day and socialising most of the night.   They popped into school some days to flaunt their freedom to the younger pupils and wail at each other about how much they would miss it all. Sometimes they saw her for meals, usually they didn't. She'd worked hard and soon she'd be starting her apprenticeship at Mecklins toy company and Anna didn't begrudge her the freedom of these few short weeks.   Ellis now almost lived at the tennis club when he was not at school. Wimbledon had given a fresh boost to their junior membership and he was considered an old hand on the youth programme even though he was only eleven. She didn't mind, she was pleased he had found something for himself outside school, and he was good. They were talking about county level already.

Again that inexplicable weariness welled up in her. Everything was fine and yet something scratched and tugged at her as though she was missing something important that needed her attention. She was tired of constantly scanning for it like a sniper on look-out.

Harry was lying on his bed with his eyes closed. The room was stuffy and she went over to the window and unlatched it. When she turned round he was looking at her but there was no softness in his expression.   She sat down on the bed, on the side that used to be hers before she had moved out to the single bedroom so he could stretch in comfort, and picked up his limp hand. He turned his eyes towards her.

'Can I lie beside you for a minute, love?' He nodded abruptly and closed his eyes again. She lay back and swung her legs up and then reached sideways and touched his hand but that reminded her of Steve touching hers and she let her fingers fall. 'I saw a heron fly over the canal today, Harry,' she said, after a pause. 'I think it was going to the reservoir at Edgbaston. It might be the one we saw that day at Earlswood Lakes.' She had almost asked him if he remembered. Of course he didn't. 'I miss the clouds, Harry. I know everyone loves the sun and I do, too, but I miss the clouds. There's nothing to look at.' She chuckled softly. 'The Cloud Appreciation Society slogan – you know – Help Stamp Out Blue Sky Thinking. Ha.' It was peaceful lying on this big comfortable bed which she so rarely did these days and looking out of the window at the ivy, even though it did need trimming, and she began to breathe more shallowly and her eyelids started to droop.

'Switch it off!' Harry said loudly. She sat up, her heart banging.

'What?'

He looked at her fiercely, his eyes burning into hers. 'Switch it all off!'

'Harry. What do you mean?'

He made a hopeless gesture with his other hand. 'I just want you to switch it all off.' She turned on her side to stroke his face and saw that there were trails of tears around the mounds of his cheeks and running down the creases beside his mouth. She stroked them away and kissed him but he shuddered and closed his eyes and turned his head away. She got up slowly and stood looking at him for a long time until she could see that he was sleeping. She walked into the bathroom and stared at her own reflection in the mirror.

'Ready!' George called from the foot of the stairs.

'For what?' Anna whispered to herself.

3

Steve's idea worked out. She found Kenneth Dawkins almost immediately on the 2011 electoral roll. At least, someone with that name and date of birth was living in Handsworth. She went back through the records but nothing before that. She made a note of the address – couldn't find a telephone number - and emailed Ted to say that she would be attempting a contact that morning. As she drove, she yawned. It had not taken long to trace Kenneth but it had been done in desperation when sleep was still eluding her at 5.00 a.m. Again, she saw Harry's fierce eyes and his command to her. 'Switch it off!' What did it mean, what did he mean? Was it just the random firing of damaged dendrites or was some deep instinct at work within him? She felt nauseous and jaded.

It was another hot day but they were promised a break on Friday. Scattered showers. The traffic was not too bad now that the rush hour commuters had been swallowed by the city so she found Kenneth Dawkins' road within twenty minutes of leaving her house. His flat was on the top floor of a Victorian terraced house, its woodwork picked out in mock-Elizabethan beams painted cobalt blue. She pushed the bell and waited. In the small front garden was a pink tricycle ribboned in purple and almost immediately a woman came out of the front door and retrieved it, scolding someone inside. Anna smiled at her. 'Kenneth Dawkins?' she asked.
'Never answers his bell. Just go on up.'

The lower stairs were thickly covered in a bright floral carpet but as she climbed the second set there was only scuffed wood. At the top there was a tiny landing and three doors but she could see that two of them were sealed shut with duct tape so she knocked at the third. She could hear a television chattering so she knocked again, louder. The door was unbolted and yanked open. The man facing her had the most lined face she had ever seen but set among the fissures were two very pale, very bright eyes.

'What?'

'Good morning. My name is Mrs Ames. I'm from Harts Heir Hunters.'

'What, police? You? A bit titchy aren't you?'

'No.' Anna got out her business card. 'I'm a probate researcher. We try to find missing relatives. We think you may be related to William Dawkins.'

'What's he done?' The man was wearing a threadbare but clean T shirt and loose grey sweat pants. His hair, which she had taken to be sweaty, she now saw was wet from a shower.

'Can I come in?'

He held open the door and when she was inside turned off the television. There was a very pleasant smell coming from a corner of the room and Kenneth picked up a cafetiere and waved it at her. 'Coffee?'

'That smells great. Yes, please, spot of milk if you have it but no sugar.'

'It's Jamaican. Blue Mountain. I know where to get it cheap.' He poured two mugs and she sat in the only armchair while he perched on the bed. 'So what's our Bill been up to?'

'You've not been in touch, then?' He shook his head. 'I'm sorry to tell you this, but he died two months ago.' Ken put his mug down and lowered his head. She waited. The room had minimal furniture and no personal effects except some calendar photographs of a tropical holiday resort tacked to the wall with drawing pins.

'Bugger.'

'Yes. Sorry.'

'I looked for him when I came back. In Derby. I looked in all the records.' He wiped his mouth.

'He came back to this area when he retired from Rolls Royce. He was living in Wolverhampton, not far from where you both grew up.'

Ken slowly shook his head from side to side and then looked up sharply. 'How did you find me?'

'The Coroner's Office asked us to try to find any relative when it was discovered that he had died intestate. I found out that he had a brother, you, and no children but you were hard to trace.'

'I was overseas.'

'So I worked backwards from the last census to see if you had come back and found you that way.'

'Janet still alive?' The pale eyes had a new, sharp focus.

'I don't know.' Anna gave him a moment and then added, 'William left a letter for you in his bureau. I'm sorry but I read it – I had to.' Ken waved a hand dismissively. 'I can take you to the house so you can read it.'

'So he was there, back home, for years?'

'Yes.'

'Bugger,' he said again.

'He's left you everything. The house is fully paid for and there are savings.'

Kenneth raised his head and looked straight at her. 'How much?' Many heirs fudged this question pretending not to be interested in the money so his directness was refreshing.

'Assuming the house could be sold for the market price it would all amount to about £250,000.'

He looked round the bed-sitter and then at her. 'That's a fair amount. He always was a steady chap. But no children? That's a surprise.'

'I think you'll understand when you've read the letter. You'll need to sign some forms, anyway, so if you like I can take you to the solicitor's office and then to the house. If you have your passport or other identification it would be a good idea to bring it. But I don't want to rush you.'

He shrugged and glanced round his room. 'I'm not doing anything.' He bent to reach beneath the bed and brought out a pair of bruised leather flip-flops. Then he tugged open a small drawer and took out a plastic pouch of documents which he pushed into a canvas shoulder bag.

'You don't need to tell me,' Anna asked, curiosity getting the better of her, 'but where were you? I tried Australia and New Zealand and Canada and - '

'Trinidad mostly.'

'The Caribbean. I didn't look there.'

Ken laughed and stood up, running his fingers through his sparse hair. His arms were bundled cords of muscle and sinew; he looked as though he had worked hard for many years. 'Well, if I'd gone to Jamaica you would have found me if you'd looked, they've got the best records in the area, but Trinidad and Tobago – well, a bit patchy to say the least I shouldn't be surprised. Didn't want to be found. Not then.' He held open the door for her.

They clattered down the stairs and he got into the passenger seat in Anna's car. She had to tell him to put on his safety belt and from his fumbling attempts she wondered how many cars he had been in since he had come home. As she drew away from the curb she couldn't resist asking, 'Why did you come back?'

'Pension Guarantee Credit.' He peered out of the window. 'I met an English fella, a tourist, and he told me they'd brought it in so if you're a Brit even if you've never worked here you can still get this. It's better than nothing. Where I was, well, I'd not been able to save and I could see the time coming when I might be too old to work, so.' He paused. 'And I wanted to see Bill.'

'I'm sorry,' Anna said again.

'It grieves me that he was around and I didn't know it.'

'He made aeroplanes. Model ones. The spare room is full of them hanging from the ceiling. I can take you there. You'll want to see the house since it's yours.' She smiled at him to soften the harsh implication of her words.

He was absorbed in his thoughts for a while as Anna negotiated the tangle of motorways out of town. 'So you don't know where Janet is? Did they split up?'

'Best if you read the letter, Mr Dawkins.'

At the solicitor's he was subdued and monosyllabic and when they got to William's tidy house he seemed reluctant to go in. Anna waited with him on the path. 'Would you rather leave this to another day? The news of your brother's death must be a shock.'

'It is. If I'd been a bit more switched-on, you know, thought more about how I could find him. If I'd maybe asked someone like you. I feel gutted that we could have had some time together. I've wasted so much of my life putting things off, getting by, not bothering.' He turned to her and unexpectedly grinned which changed his face completely. 'I'm an idle rascal. I always have been.' As he said this there was a lilt of West Indian in his voice that she had not noticed before.

Anna smiled at him. 'You look as though you're no stranger to hard work.'

He shrugged. 'Yeah, but that's easy isn't it? Labouring, doing this and that, sliding off when any responsibility gets offered. Living light with no-one asking questions.' He snorted. 'Do you know what it says on my passport for occupation?' She shook her head. 'Artist, it says. That's a joke, isn't it? All the time I was working on the docks or for a fella delivering fruit and vegetables and, oh a thousand other nothing jobs, I thought I'm only doing this so I can paint.'

'And did you?'

'A bit. Nothing any good.'

'Are you sure?'

'Yes. Are we going in or what?' Kenneth may be an idle rascal, she thought, but he saw himself clearly and without self-pity.

She sat quietly as he read the letter. For a moment he was silent and then he burst out laughing. She had heard that kind of laughter before and didn't smile herself. When he began to weep she went into the kitchen and got a glass of water for him.

Half an hour later they left and drove back to Handsworth. 'What will you do, do you think?' Anna asked eventually for something to say.

'Don't know. I miss the company I had in Trinidad. Always something happening, always someone to have a word or a joke with – pass the time of day. It's lonely here. Maybe I'll go back now I don't have to worry about money what with this and the pension. Find something to do.'

At his apartment building she turned off the engine. It seemed cold to simply drive off. They sat for a moment in silence and then he turned to her and in a quick movement gently grabbed her arm. 'You're young. Don't waste time regretting and putting things off. Squeeze the fucking orange for all it's worth.' He loosened his grip. 'Sorry. Sorry for swearing. Thanks for everything.' And he was gone.

In the kitchen Rosa was sitting at the table sipping a cup of what smelled like mint tea. Harry was sorting buttons from the button jar into colours, his fingers clumsy and slow. Anna looked away. In the fridge was a large glass jug of lemonade and Anna lifted it out carefully.

'George has been busy.'

'Yes.'

She poured a small beaker for Harry and a glass for herself noticing an unusual emotional tension in the room. She was just about to ask if everything was all right when the light from the garden coming in through the open utility room door was blocked. It was Len.

'All right?' He sat down at the table, placed his large red hands on it and stared at them. Rosa said nothing and Harry finished the blues and started on the brass. She recognised one from a navy winter coat she had been fond of. What had happened to that?

'Do you want a lemonade, Len?'

He swung his huge head from side to side continuing to stare at the bare table. 'Can of beer would go down.'

'There's one in the fridge. I'll get it for you.'

'No, you're all right.'

He pushed back his chair and stood up. Len was rarely free from the pungent odour of mildewed laundry and stale cooking smells but the heat of this summer and the fact that he was still wearing his winter coat caused a rancid burp of trapped air to erupt from his sudden movement. Both Rosa and Anna involuntarily jerked back their heads. She must speak to him again. Rosa stood up.

'Will it be all right if I get off now?'

'Yes, of course.' Anna stood up, too, and followed Rosa out to the hall. She was always both amused and slightly discomforted by the difference in their stature. It was odd to have to crane your head back to speak to someone of your own gender. 'I did just want a word about Harry, if that's ok?'

Rosa stopped with her hand on the door knob and turned. 'Yes?'

'Has he seemed a bit out of sorts to you? I mean, a bit fed up?'

'I think he sometimes finds things a bit frustrating. He's bound to, isn't he?'

'But you don't think he's unhappy?'

Rosa let one handle of her large bag drop from her arm and fished inside it. She brought out a crumpled piece of paper and gave it to Anna who smoothed it and looked puzzled at what she was seeing. Heavy scribble in black felt tip concealed something brighter underneath. It reminded her of when Ellis was a small child, before he had learned to write, when he would draw a story. As he drew he would narrate it: 'Here's the ship on the sea and here's the bomber and whoosh, the bomb's hitting the ship and the ship's shooting the plane with supersonic laser spray and now another plane is coming and...' By the end of the story all that could be seen was an incomprehensible scribble. She looked at Rosa for an explanation.

'Harry did it. He was doodling with big felt tips, not really drawing anything, just messing about and then suddenly he picked up the black one and did this and then screwed it all up and walked away.' Rosa smiled down at Anna's anxious face. 'Ten minutes later he was picking flowers in the garden and humming *Fly Me to the Moon*.'

'He used to sing that to me.' Anna didn't add - when we were in bed. 'So, what, just random moods you think?'

Rosa compressed her lips as if to say, who knows? She turned to the door and then back again to Anna. 'Can I ask you? Who is that person, that man, in the kitchen?'

Anna burst out laughing and it felt very good to release tension. 'Of course, you don't know, I'm sorry, I should have introduced you. It's Len, my half-brother. My mum left George and me when I was just a toddler and didn't turn up again until a couple of years ago. Len is hers by a different father. He lives in his own flat but he just sort of turns up when he feels like it. He's not bad on the flute – there's a kind of band he belongs to. Well, that's rude, it *is* a band. Did he not say who he was the first time he came?'

'No. He's been twice - just let himself in - and I didn't like to ask.'

'So does he know who you are?'

'George said.'

'Sorry he's so smelly. I'm going to have to have another word with him. He's oblivious.'

Rosa rolled her eyes and opened the door. 'See you tomorrow – I'm on till five aren't I?'

'Yes, please. I'll make sure I'm back on time.'

'No worries.'

Tomorrow. Friday. Anna suddenly wished it wasn't happening, that she hadn't pushed things like this and that she and Steve could go back to being frustrated and noble. But nothing had to happen between them, did it? She was lashing herself with imaginings and fantasies needlessly. They would have a pleasant meal, chat about the kids and work, watch a good film and go home back to their separate houses. It would be fun, it would be pleasant, it would be innocent.

The rain held off all morning but there was a discontented feel to the yellowish stratus clouds which didn't cool the ground and only made people sweaty and gloomy. It wasn't until they were out in the field and Anna was circling slowly under Kimi's intense scrutiny that the rain started.

'Straighten your back! Heels down, knees in.'

'It's raining!'

'So?' Kimi paced round her own small circle in the centre of the paddock, her hay-coloured hair springing out in corkscrews. 'Refreshing!'

'Bloody hell,' muttered Anna, feeling Maisie stutter beneath her as the rain hit harder. 'She doesn't like it!'

'She's just sensing your fear. Show her who's boss!'

'She is!'

'Get a grip. Now then, trot on. Squeeze with your knees and lean back a little.'

Maisie immediately broke into an energetic canter interspersed with little rushes towards the gate every time they passed. Anna took two circuits to stay in the saddle having lost one stirrup and then hauled desperately on the reins and the horse halted, rearing a little. It was terrifying. Kimi strode over to where horse and rider were trembling under a steady downpour. 'You're too heavy handed. She thought you meant for her to canter, you only needed to lean back slightly and squeeze just a touch. You're going at it as though she's a cart-horse. She's a bloody thoroughbred!'

'Just let me get the fuck off.'

Ten minutes later Maisie was tucked away in her stable to their mutual relief and Anna and Kimi made for the farmhouse. 'If you do feel you're losing control or that she's going too fast, what did I tell you last time?'

'Bring the reins down her neck, not pull them back,' mumbled Anna.

'She's got a very soft mouth, you wouldn't like it.' Kimi got a bottle of wine out of the fridge and poured two glasses. Outside the forecast shower was turning into a storm. It was so dark they had to put on the electric light and every now and then there were flashes of lightning.

'Can't you just teach me on some old nag? I feel guilty all the time – it's like I'm a clog dancer waltzing with a ballerina.'

'No, if you learn on a dull horse with a hard mouth, you'll never be able to handle a horse like Maisie. Just stop being such a wimp – you'll get the hang of it. Does wonders for your adductors and quads. Now then, what about this birthday do that you're supposed to be coming up with ideas for?' Kimi grinned and stuck her tongue out.

'Still thinking.'

Kimi strode across the kitchen to where her expensive leather work bag had been thrown into a rocker and pulled out her laptop. 'We'll do it now.'

By the time Anna drove home the summer storm was over and the lanes gleamed black under a sky strewn with racing clouds. The wet hedges and verges glittered in the late afternoon light and Anna felt her heart lift with anticipation. She was going to have a night out. Friday night out with Steve. How thrilling was that? She could almost hear Faye groaning and saying, 'Mum, you're going to the pictures - how sad are you?'

It was also George's poetry night. She thought back to when he had come to live with them to help with Harry and had treated himself to his study/ office/ publishing company known as 'the shed'. Ever since, he had been running these Friday evening sessions with whoever wanted to come. He and Ashok were always there and Harry came along, no longer to read but to be with them and doze a little. Anna normally loved these times, the magic of the spoken word taking them all off their hamster wheels and into a wider, freer space. Stacks of newly published collections and small press magazines made a city skyline of George's old desk. George would, like Father Christmas in his bristling white beard, hand out poems he thought people would enjoy reading and hearing.

When she walked in he was rushing about the kitchen. 'Sorry I won't be there tonight, Dad.'

'No. I'm glad you're having a break from routine. Enjoy the film.' They avoided each other's eyes.

'Thanks. Won't be late back.'

'Doesn't matter.'

'No, but I won't.'

'Faye's just getting chips to go with the quiche. She'll be back in a minute. Are you hungry?'

'No, I'll be eating soon myself.'

'Right.' George stopped scurrying and stared at her. 'You got wet.'

'Kimi made me go on in the rain. The horse didn't like it any more than me I can tell you.' She put the kettle on. 'I'll have a quick shower in a minute. It's nothing special tonight. It's not like I have to dress up or anything.'

'Right.'

'I'll take Harry a cup in and then go up and get ready.' Her father was still looking at her with maddening empathy. 'I'm all right, Dad, just don't make this a big thing, please.'

'Make what a big thing?' Faye bounced in with a greasy parcel which she threw down on to the table. 'Starving, Pops, where's the quiche? We're not waiting for Ell are we? I'm ready to faint with hunger.'

'Chips! Yeah!' So then there was Ellis as well and the kitchen was full of people and a large dog and she left Harry's plate on the table and went to get him to join them and then slipped away to shower and get ready for whatever the evening would bring.

4

Steve wasn't helping. She had chosen a simple cotton dress worn many times and just a touch of make-up so she didn't look as though she hadn't slept the night before, which was more or less the case. But Steve was in a cream linen jacket and some black trousers that looked new. He dropped Alice off in the kitchen and they both went out to his Yeti. He had washed it and cleaned the mud from the carpets at the front. She was so nervous that she tried to get in on the driver's side.

'I got soaked at Kimi's this afternoon,' she said after they had been driving for a few moments. 'I thought the horse was going to bolt the rain was so heavy. Lucky we got in before the lightning struck or I'd be lying in a ditch somewhere and the horse would be in Wales.'

'Mm.'

Ok, so it wasn't that funny but she was trying. Steve was staring grimly ahead at the traffic making no effort to break the tension. She found she was becoming angry. He was making a simple night out a high-pressure date, not her. 'You didn't have to dress up, it's not like we're going to the theatre.'

'Sorry.'

Oh, bloody hell. She folded her arms and looked out of the side window at nothing.

At the restaurant it was so early that they were the only diners and they were placed in the window, presumably to encourage others in who could witness how much fun they were having. After they had ordered she tried again, almost aggressively. 'Yesterday a client told me I should squeeze the orange tills the pips pop out. What do you think?'

Steve stared at her in bewilderment. 'What?'

The waitress came with their drinks and she decided to just stop all this, stop being nervous and on edge and excited and over-thinking and over-feeling everything. He had been a good friend to her through all the shocks and danger of the last couple of years and not only that, a good friend to Ellis and to Harry, who thought of him as a brother, and even to her dad. She looked him full in the face noting how miserable he seemed. 'What's the matter, Steve?' she asked quietly. If being alone with her for an evening was distressing him this much it wasn't worth it.

He had the kind of blue eyes that could darken or lighten with his mood - which was nonsense, of course, it was the surrounding skin colour that changed, but now in his tense face they looked almost grey. 'I've had an email from Cathy,' he said.

She picked up her drink. This was probably the very last thing she could have imagined. So, Steve was not riven with sexual tension or hyper-awareness of the potential significance of this 'date', he was thinking of his ex-wife. The rapid ebbing of adrenalin almost left her light-headed.

'What did it say?'

'Things are not going as well as she'd hoped in the States. They'd told her she'd be sure to get tenure this year because she's published so much and the teaching's gone fine.'

Anna felt dull and empty. 'So what went wrong?'

'The professor who was her mentor has decided to retire and a new dean has been hired who doesn't rate her field. Says it's draining money but not bringing in the students. Ridiculous, of course, because she's doing cutting edge work that would really enhance the university's reputation but she says the dean is an Arts person. Doesn't understand.'

'So what will she do?' Anna felt barely able to summon up enough interest to listen. Cathy had left Steve after it was clear that Steve would put his responsibility to Alice first. Following the traffic accident which had killed her parents he had given up his own academic career to raise his little niece but for Cathy, the brilliant physicist as Steve had described her, that had been too high a price and she had taken a post-doctoral position in a prestigious university in Boston. Now, Anna thought, she was moaning about what was surely a mere set-back to her ambition.

Steve sighed deeply and cracked his knuckles. 'She wants to come back here.'

They held each other's gaze for a long moment until the waitress placed their tagines in front of them. Anna felt stone cold sober.

'How do you feel about that?' The world stopped turning as she waited for his answer.

'I don't know.' He had picked up his fork and was pushing the savoury mounds of chicken and prunes round the plate. Wrong answer.

Anna didn't even pick up her fork. She felt furious and reckless. 'Well, this evening has not had many laughs so I'll give you one now. Do you know what I thought would happen tonight? I thought that we would have a lovely romantic meal and cuddle up in the cinema and go back to yours and screw each other's brains out because I am so messed up with wanting you all the time and not being able to have you. So, what a joke, huh?' She stood up.

Steve looked at her in astonishment. 'You thought *what*?'

She almost broke the door on her way out. Half-way back to the car park he caught up with her and grabbed her arm. 'Anna, please, stop! We have to talk. Stop this!' So she stood weeping and cursing in full view of the interested crowd waiting to go into the Town Hall for that evening's concert while Steve put his arms round her and held her so close that she could feel the hammering of his heart.

They drove out to the Lickeys and walked back and forth on Beacon Hill talking, but it was the kind of talk that went round in circles and relieved nothing. He told her he loved her and always would but that Cathy might need him and he couldn't just reject her. She told him that her thoughts about this evening had been fantasy and that of course Harry was the person who really mattered. She was glad that nothing had happened. Glad that they could be friends. So, exhausted and miserable, they drove home.

Instead of Steve, she took a bottle of wine to bed with her and resolutely drank it until she was unconscious.

All day on Saturday, her head thumping, Anna worked in the garden. The brief storm had not cleared the air and a sweaty blanket of pollution pressed down on her. Perspiration ran down her back and soaked her shorts and every now and then she stopped and wiped her dripping face with a dirty hand. Harry lay on the lounger contemplating the gloomy sky and even Bobble, depressed by the sweltering heat, had collapsed against the brick kitchen wall and was staring glumly at his paws. She had finished clearing one long border of brambles and nettles when George came out with a tray of lemonade glasses, the ice chinking. She stood up and arched her back.

'Bonfire?' he said, nodding at the shoulder-high heap on the grass.

'Better not, Dad. You know we're not allowed. I'll take it down the end in a minute and let it rot down and then maybe when I've done the rest I'll borrow Rani's pick-up and take it to the dump.'

'We can all pitch in.'

'Yes, thanks.'

She took a glass from the tray and gulped at it. Harry was ignoring his which George had left by his side so she picked it up and put it on the garden table to be safe from Bobble. She walked into the house and filled Bobble's bowl and took it out to him. He lapped politely and sank back into torpor. She finished her own drink and picked up the big fork again.

'Annie?'

'I don't want to talk about it, Dad.'

'I'm sorry if I pushed you into it against your wishes.'

'You didn't.'

George stood helplessly watching her dig, his face purple with heat and distress. 'So how was the film?' She bent down and wrenched out a bramble root and then swore as it tore a ragged line in her arm. 'Ok, stop now. Anna you need to stop. Sit down with me for a minute, please.'

They sat on the bench next to each other and Bobble came and leaned his hot body against Anna's bare legs. She groaned and tilted her head back. 'Cathy's talking about coming back. Steve's ex-wife.'

'But they're divorced?'

'I know, but he's so bloody decent he feels an obligation to her to see if she needs help.' She leaned forward and picked up Harry's drink, fishing an ice cube out with her dirty fingers and soothing the scratch with it. 'It couldn't have worked. With us, I mean.'

'I don't see why not. He was like a man possessed when you got taken that time. I thought he was going to kill someone. He thinks the world of you, Anna.' Harry moaned and turned on his side. They both looked at him.

'Just leave it, please, Dad.'

Faye and Tasha appeared shadowed by Alice. They slumped on to the grass, but after a moment Faye sat up and crossed her legs. 'Mum.' When Anna cocked her head to indicate listening, Faye went on. 'Wouldn't it be great to have a party here? Everybody else has proper gardens but this would be really good – nothing to trash. Tash and me will organise everything, you don't have to do a thing. Everyone's going away soon and we'll never see each other again and it's like a major milestone in my life, Mum.'

'We've got loads of Christmas lights we can put round,' Tasha pleaded. 'Everyone will bring chairs and we can have plastic glasses and we'll clean everything up afterwards.'

'Maybe some fireworks?' Faye pushed into the silence from the bench.

'Boz and his mates are starting a group,' added Tasha hopefully.

Anna stood up. 'No outside music, no fireworks, ok?' They threw themselves at her whooping. 'And no alcohol! I mean it!' She looked at George and grimaced. He shrugged.

'You're the best mum in the whole world!' This was seriously worrying. What had she missed off the list of forbidden items?

'And I'll be staying in.' There was a lull in the screaming. 'I'll stay out of your way but I'm not leaving the house, ok?' Rapid whispers were exchanged.

'Fine,' said Faye airily, 'we'll make lists. Come on Tash and you, Lisha, you can start making decorations.' She grabbed the little girl's hand. 'Oh, there's a message from Steve.' Anna looked at her. 'He says do you all want to go up to the Roaches next weekend? The club's going and he said you and dad could go.'

'And me go,' said Alice.

'Yeah. If you go, she can go. I've got a shift that day.'

'I'll call him,' Anna said, picking up the fork. 'I'll just do another half hour, Dad.' He put the glasses on the tray and turned towards the house.

So Steve had found a way to normalise things – to go back to where they had been - or almost there. She appreciated his thoughtfulness. Sending Faye with the message took the tension out of a visit or a call. It would be good to be away from the city and out in the Staffordshire hills walking the rocky ridge and feeling the breeze lift her hair and, with a bit of luck, her spirits. Harry loved the Roaches and so did she. He wouldn't be able to walk far but neither could Alice so the three of them could just take it slowly while the climbers did their thing. It was a happy place for all of them. Harry and she had camped there for their honeymoon and they had often taken the children there. As for Cathy, that could be something or nothing and in any case there was no point in dwelling on it.

'Mum!' It was Ellis shouting at her from the back door. 'Just taking Bobble for a walk, ok?'

'Good.'

'Can Mike stay for tea?'

'Ask Pops.'

'Ok.'

She stood, fork in hand, staring back at the house. She was so lucky to have her dad and her children, and even Len. What on earth had she been getting herself into a lather about? And Harry, of course, she was lucky to have Harry. She took the fork to put away in the tool shed and latched the door. She knelt on the grass beside her husband and tickled his neck. 'Fancy a rub-down with an oily rag?' He opened his eyes and crinkled them at her and then rolled to one side and let her help him stand up. She slipped her arm round his waist and they tottered towards the house together as the first grumble of thunder came from behind them.

'Maxon Blake!' Ted announced like a ring-master introducing an act. An elongated young man unfolded himself from Ted's special flatter-the-client chair which seemed far too wide for him and put out his hand.

'Anna Ames.' Anna enjoyed the small courtesy. We should shake hands more, she thought, and wondered if she had offered her hand to Kenneth Dawkins. Almost certainly not. 'How are you?'

'Real excited. I mean about finding out about my English family?'

Anna sat down on a hard office chair ignoring Ted's eye-swivel indicating that he wanted his space back as soon as possible. 'How much information do you already have?'

She guessed that Maxon Blake was in his mid-twenties but seemed younger because of his manner. He folded in on himself around a concave chest and his unfashionably long hair hung like a curtain over his face as though he was a shy actor peeping out to sense the mood of the audience. It was almost as dark as Anna's but unlike hers lay flat to his head. Unconsciously, as he spoke, he rubbed his hands together as if sloughing off something sticky. His features were regular and he could have been good-looking if his body would straighten, his shoulders go back and his eyes smile. The worried frown between his brows didn't help, either. 'I don't have too many early documents because not long after my great great-grandmother, Grace Thwaite, came to the States they were lost in a fire. Jane, that's my great grandmother, did write down what her mom told her about living in England and the family here but nothing official.' His voice was soft and deep but it seemed to catch in his throat sometimes and then he would cough and swallow. He was not what Anna had expected.

'So when did Grace Thwaite emigrate?'

'In the 1890's, but Jane had already been born by then - she was just a baby. Grace had been widowed here but there were some family connections, not relations, I mean business acquaintances of her husband over there and that's why she moved to Philadelphia.' Maxon spoke carefully, seemingly wanting to get it right for Anna.

'Hard for her. A brave thing to do.'

Ted coughed and shuffled and was ignored.

'Yes. I guess she was pretty amazing. She remarried not long after she arrived to a property developer called Albert Maxon. From Connecticut, I think.' He shrugged his shoulders apologetically. 'So, you know, the name. It was when there were thousands of immigrants coming from Europe and heading for the eastern seaboard cities and, well, they all needed places to live so it was a good business. My grandmother called my dad Maxon as a first name to keep the connection with the guy who was the founder.'

'And now you're the torch-bearer,' Anna said lightly, 'I see.'

Maxon, far from rallying at her pleasantry, seemed to sink even deeper into himself and his voice dropped. 'My family has been successful in property for, like, generations. My great-grandfather, Sidney Chadfield, set up an education foundation for the inner city kids in Philly during the depression and my mom sponsors charity concerts and stuff. They're very, um, well, everyone knows them.' The expression in his voice was an intriguing mixture of pride and desperation. Even Ted picked up on it and glanced at Anna.

'So I thought I would give them a real nice surprise gift. It's my mom and dad's pearl wedding anniversary this fall and it would be so great if I could kind of fill in the blanks of those early years of the family in England? Make a kind of scrapbook for them. I think they would really enjoy that.'

'Great idea,' said Ted, losing interest. 'I'll leave you and Anna to set up some meetings but if you don't mind I need to make a call.' They both rose and left.

Visitors were not allowed in the big open office so Anna took Maxon down the green glass stairs and into their vaulted lobby with its views across Birmingham city centre. They sat down on a banquette and Anna opened her phone. 'When would you like to meet next? We could make it for lunch if you'd like, if you're not wanting to get away from food!'

'Oh no, I'd really like that. I don't have classes during the day on Wednesday. Would that work for you?' He looked at her anxiously as though he expected to be yelled at.

Not a spoiled brat, then, Anna noted, far from it. She also noticed that Maxon did not consult a diary as though he knew he had no other engagements. 'Great. There's an Italian place on New Street you might like.' As they made the arrangements the young man relaxed and even smiled. It was good to see and Anna found herself becoming intrigued by this diffident youth, whom she must remember was a fully-grown man, not a kid, and wanted to make him smile more. They stood up and again Maxon politely offered his hand to shake. 'Are you ok finding your way back from here?' she asked.

'Oh yes. I've walked the city a lot in the few weeks I've been here. It's so fascinating, the history, and you just keep stumbling on one interesting thing after another. I look things up when I get home from walks and I'm keeping a journal.' Anna was pleased that this visitor was not prejudiced against Birmingham as so many British people were but she also noted that this sounded like a lonely life. How easy had this rather self-effacing American found it to make friends here?

As Maxon walked down the outside steps and on to the canal towpath to turn towards the city centre Anna watched him. He was wearing beige chinos and a chambray button-down shirt with the cuffs to the wrist. It was not odd or unusual but there was something of the middle-aged school–boy about his look. There were no markers of wealth about him but Ted would not have taken him on if he had not received an advance or had good reason to believe that he could afford this open-ended commission, so it was unlikely that he was lying about his family's wealth. It could all be very easily checked and Ted would be the man to do it. Maxon seemed more distressed by it than anything. Anna wondered if he was adopted and had been made to feel inadequate sitting on the edge of this eminent family's gene pool.

5

'A monkey?' Ellis's mouth gaped. 'Honestly?'

George waved his phone at him. 'So Diane says.'

Anna snapped off the television news. 'What did she say?'

'They've had a monkey brought into Safe 'n' Sound today. The RSPCA brought it. They'd picked it up from somewhere around Cofton Common – a dog walker had seen it and reported it.'

'Is it ok?'

'Starving, Diane says, only young. Must have escaped from somewhere or been dumped by someone and trying to fend for itself, I suppose.'

Faye materialised with that unerring instinct she had for anything dramatic happening. 'What? Pops – what's going on?' He told her and within seconds she and Ellis were texting. 'Can we go and see it, can Tasha come and Lisha?' She nodded bossily at her grandfather. 'Ask her!'

'And Mike,' Ellis said. 'We could go this evening – we could go now! Please Pops.' Within minutes they realised that they would have to take two cars because Steve wanted to see it and Harry must come, of course. Steve would pick up Tasha and bring all three girls.

It was still a slight surprise for Anna to see Diane and her dad kiss when they met. He had never had a girlfriend all the years he had been bringing her up as far as she knew, but now her infuriating mother was dead he had found Diane. It was Anna who had unwittingly brought them together, she remembered, over the Briony Clark case. Diane led them round the side of the animal sanctuary into the barn. She strode along with her bottom stuck out and her elbows working with George scurrying beside her chatting eagerly. Despite Diane's efforts to tidy George up, she rarely bothered about herself, but Anna liked her rough hands and even the broken blood vessels in her cheeks. She was, and had been for years, a woman on a mission. Safe 'n' Sound was a private animal refuge charity and had a small legion of dedicated volunteers, the place itself maintained by their shop and devotees' donations. It was an old farm which had lost its land to housing estates but which looked out on to open country with its own paddock and fenced-in areas for rescued animals to get some air.

The dogs, as always, were madly throwing themselves at the chain-link fence and Bobble was prancing around on the end of his lead, desperate to sniff bottoms and touch noses with every one of them. Ellis was having a hard time restraining him. He really was horribly badly behaved. They must get him to classes.

Diane glanced round. 'Ellis, you'd better tie Bobble up to the picnic table. He's remembering his puppyhood!' She looked more intently at the dog. 'I had no idea he'd grow so large when you chose him from here. Who knows who his parents are, eh? He'd frighten Charles, so make sure he's secure, ok?'

'He's very obstreperous,' said Ellis showing off a new word and earning a curled lip from his sister.

'Charles?' Steve asked.

George winked at him. 'Darwin.'

'Oh, ok, the monkey.'

Poor little thing, it was cowering in its cage and searching their faces for signs of threat. They all protectively stood back a little. Diane unlocked the door and reached inside. In seconds Charles was velcroed to her T shirt. His little hands pinched Diane's generous bust in a firm grip as he looked round.

Diane smiled down at him over her chins, stroking his hairy back. 'He's a Capuchin aren't you, sweetheart? It was monkeys like these that organ-grinders used in Victorian times. They'd attract the punters and collect the money. They're extremely intelligent.' She pursed her lips in pride. 'From Brazil.' She turned to look round the fascinated group. 'Does anyone want to give him a banana, he's due a snack?' Everyone wanted to give him a banana. George dashed off having been given his instructions and came back minutes later with a chopped up banana on a tin plate.

Alice, pop-eyed with excitement, was not quite ready to be first so Ellis had that honour and the little monkey did not snatch the food but took it soberly before cramming it in its mouth. Then there was a barrage of questions and jostling for who would be next. Steve stepped back a little from the group and without thinking Anna joined him.

'Still all right for next Sunday?' He smiled and touched her shoulder making it tingle. Since she had agreed to go up to the Roaches with Harry he had relaxed and they could be easy with each other. Like brother and sister. Or not.

'I'm looking forward to it. I'll bring some stuff for Alice to do and a rug so after Harry and Alice and I have had a bit of a walk we can picnic and play until you toughies are ready to go home.'

He laughed, tilting up his chin and flushing. She always teased him about the high-tech gear they used to climb the rock wall of the Roaches when Ellis and Faye had swarmed up it in their trainers when they were kids, but she knew it was a good place for the climbing club to take new members to practise safely and he knew she knew. It felt good to share an in-joke.

'Steve!' Alice called, 'Help me!'

'Coming, love.'

Anna watched him crouch and lift the little girl into his arms and then teach her how to feed the monkey. Her fingers were trembling with excitement and her lips parted in amazement.

Alice had been so ill after the accident. The first time Anna had seen the infant lying on her hospital bed she thought she had never seen anything so fragile. Alice's skin was still very pale and her silver hair stood out in a dandelion clock halo but she was the most determined, self-willed person Anna had met with the sole exception of Faye. The challenge with Alice was not that she needed protecting but that she needed disciplining, a far more difficult task for Steve. Anna noticed the contrast between them, the ruddiness of his flesh, the size of his hands, the crest of rich brown hair that refused to lie flat, and the child he held, ethereal, almost monochrome white gold. His hands had held a stethoscope to the tiny labouring chest every hour to check she was well when he had first brought her home; they had changed nappies, offered tiny scoops of food he had prepared himself, and now his arms held her almost every night while he read a story, sang a song, chattered nonsense with her. Anna clenched her belly as a visceral surge of feeling for him flooded her. She refused to name it to herself.

Harry was in the group around the monkey, too, but he was looking tired. Anna went to his side and slid her arm through his. 'Shall we go and untie Bobble? We can take him for a little walk round his old home and say hello to the dogs.' She turned to Diane. 'Does it matter if they make a noise?' Diane shook her head, concentrating now on feeding Charles with a bottle and watched by three open-mouthed girls.

Harry stumbled a little as they stepped over some rubble by the side of the barn and she tightened her hold on his arm. Bobble,

shocked and offended at having his movements restrained in this palace of delights, greeted them with rapture. Harry did not wait for him to be untied but walked over to the fence and grinned at the dogs leaping up and down. 'Woof!' he said, 'Woof, woof!' Then they all went mad including Bobble and after a minute or so Anna could stand it no longer and strolled off towing Bobble across the paddock. He seemed relieved to go which was hardly surprising given the wall of canine uproar he had faced. At the far side of the paddock she found a patch of grass almost thistle free and sat down, pulling the dog down beside her. He looked alertly back at the pack serenading Harry and then abruptly slobbered on her face. She cleaned him off herself with the hem of her T shirt and rubbed him behind his ears.
'Ok, dog,' she whispered, holding up one huge flap, 'you can tell me. Who's the Daddy?' He grinned and panted rank breath at her.

Then they all came out of the barn and waved their arms at her and it was time to go home and put Harry to bed and later curl up alone with her thoughts. She pushed the obvious worries away and thought instead of her upcoming birthday celebrations. It had been years since she'd done anything special - the years, in fact, since Harry's illness was diagnosed when their world had changed.

Kimi had informed her earlier that day that she had phoned everyone and everyone was coming. The tickets and restaurant were booked and all Anna had to do was turn up 'trying not to look your age' as Faye had instructed when told about the event. She had not asked to come, Anna noticed without surprise.

Even Briony had agreed to come despite knowing no-one else but Anna. Anna thought of the woman's incisive mind and elegantly-groomed appearance and wondered what she and Kimi, equally a force of nature but much less tidy, would make of each other. Both friendships had come from cases Anna had worked on and she and Briony still emailed back and forth about the progress of her dissertation being written in collaboration with the police and her professor of criminology on black websites set up to exploit women. The case involving Kimi had been the most dangerous and frightening Anna had ever confronted. Both women were financially secure and without men. Briony had no child but Kimi had a daughter, Rhea, a troubled girl now getting the help she needed, it seemed, although progress was slow and agonising to Kimi herself, who rarely spoke of her daughter's psychiatric illness.

Then there would be the funny and glamorous Suzy from work, Anna's reliable source of light relief and fashion advice, unsolicited but often sorely needed. Relentlessly sociable as she was, even she might find Kimi and Briony rather hard work especially if they were on their soapboxes. Then there would be Michelle, Faye's friend Tasha's mum and a psychiatric social worker, who had one time in a pub bored Suzy to flight with her refugee horror stories. Anna groaned. But, the whole evening could be redeemed by her choice of entertainment.

As Kimi and she had scrolled through theatre and club websites, listening to the storm crack and flash outside, they had come upon The Best Medicine club. It was fast becoming a popular venue for stand-ups, newcomers and established comics wanting to try new material. Sometimes they did improv. Kimi was doubtful, immediately imagining the worst – sexism and racism passed off as irony – but Anna had recognised the name of a featured comedian. Sara Pascoe. Perfect. She would be clever and funny and wise – Kimi and Briony would love the feminist slant and Suzy would enjoy the jokes about dating and boyfriends. Michelle, she hoped, would enjoy it all, she knew she would.

So, the Roaches on Sunday and a night out the following week. George and Diane were planning a birthday barbeque if the weather held and a tea if it didn't to which Len and Joan, her mother of choice, had been invited. The thought of Joan always made her smile. They were the same size, had the same sense of humour and she would have been so much better as Anna's mother than that nasty Lena. Don't think about it. She rolled over in bed and stretched.

For a second, as her mind began to dim with sleep, Anna mused about Maxon. Should she invite him to the barbeque? He seemed so alone. And, of course, Rosa. They must invite the magnificent Rosa.

Maxon was early but had managed to get a table in the window and the air-conditioning was a relief. It was too hot and sticky to sit outside in the noise and dust of the main drag. Today he had a satchel with him, a large canvas and leather affair which intensified his air of being a gawky tourist. He greeted Anna politely but watchfully like one of Kimi's horses.

'Let's order,' Anna said, 'and then you can show me what you have already.'

It seemed that the family in Shropshire had been minor landed gentry and the house they had lived in for two generations, The Mount, was described by Jane, quoting Grace, in great detail. Clearly, her mother had loved her home and probably was missing it in her new country.

'Why would she have left?' Anna wondered out loud. 'She had a family to support her – she could have had a comfortable life in England.'

'I wondered that,' said Maxon. 'Maybe she just didn't fit in. They may have wanted to put her in a role she didn't want.' Anna considered this, thinking it an unusual explanation and wondering whether he was projecting.

'Mm. Still, it's a significant move with an infant.'

Maxon rolled the ice round in his glass of black tea. 'Maybe she'd met this American business person on a trip to England and liked him?'

'You're a romantic, aren't you?' Anna laughed. To her dismay the young man dropped his head and looked upset. 'I'm sorry, I was just joking.' She couldn't seem to get the tone right. Each time she had made what was meant to be a gentle tease, it had upset him.

'That's what they think. My family. That I'm a dreamer.'

'But you run your own business, don't you?' Anna was puzzled by his sensitivity.

'It's a sandwich and coffee bar full of art students on South Street in Philly.'

'Sounds great.'

'Not to them. It's ok.' Maxon raised his head and stared out of the window. 'So what's the next step?'

Anna took the hint. 'Since you want to be involved in each piece of research, I think we should go to Shrewsbury Records Office, the Shropshire Archives, and really dig.' She glanced at Maxon. 'It's much easier if the family is prominent because there will be articles in contemporary newspapers and so on and the name Thwaite is a little bit unusual which makes it easier, too. Also, a house as substantial as The Mount is likely to be still standing, unless it was in the path of a major road or industrial development. Westbury village is only eight miles from Shrewsbury so we could see what we can find there on the same day if you like.' She looked round at the other tables. 'Next Wednesday? We could take the whole day. Now, I want you to make a big decision.'

Maxon looked so alarmed that Anna put her hand on the young man's arm for a second. 'I'm being silly. Do you want to share one of their chocolate hazelnut cheesecakes with me? Next table but one at two o'clock just about to go in for the kill - have a look. Fancy it?'

His shoulders straightened and he laughed for the first time. It transformed his face and Anna decided she would enjoy getting to know him over the weeks of research. It might turn out that he was of more interest than his up-market ancestors. 'Got to,' he said, 'research for my new and improved café menu.'

'Of course it is,' said Anna, raising her hand to the waiter.

She arrived home earlier than usual and saw that Rosa and Harry were in the garden sitting in the shade of the sycamore tree they shared with their neighbour. Anna got a glass of water and watched them from the kitchen window. Rosa had pulled the stained table across out of the sun and they appeared to be playing Connect Four which Rosa must have found in the stack of games by the piano. Harry was slumped and needing constant encouragement to take part. Bobble was prone at his feet. Suddenly, he made a deliberately rough movement and scattered the counters. Anna sipped thoughtfully, watching. Rosa picked them up and put them back in their case. She seemed to ask Harry a question to which he replied with a brusque shake of his head. Rosa sat back a little and looked down the garden as if wondering what to do. Anna went to the fridge and filled three glasses.

'Hi, how's it going Rosa? Hello, darling.' She kissed Harry who took no notice and pulled another chair into the shade.

'You're home early,' Rosa said, 'we were just thinking about a stroll.'

'It's a bit hot, maybe. He seems tired.'

'Yes.' Both women looked at Harry who had put his head down on the table in the cradle of his arms. 'I'll get the lounger into the shade and see if that appeals.'

'Thanks.'

Harry almost fell on to the old canvas and remained still, his head turned away from them.

Anna smiled at Rosa. 'Did anything special happen today?'

'No. He helped me with a bit of pastry making this morning, he usually likes cutting out shapes, but he got fed up. Yesterday was great, we was sloshing about out here in a bucket of soapy water cleaning the garden tools and he even splashed me - you know, playing.' Rosa's brow was puckered with concern and Anna reached out and took her hand.

'You're doing brilliantly. Honestly, Rosa, before you came he never did anything more exciting than shop-lifting.' Rosa laughed. 'You can get off early if you like. It must be fun to relax on a canal boat on a sunny afternoon.'

'It is when the midges aren't biting.' But Rosa stayed where she was at the table. 'Anna, can I ask you something?' Anna nodded. 'You find people, don't you, like re-unite families?'

'If we can. Usually someone's died first, though, so the re-union may be a bit too late.'

'Does it cost a lot?'

Anna was intrigued. 'Who do you want to trace?'

'My brother.' Rosa was turning her glass round and round in her hand in an unusual display of nervousness.

Anna glanced at Harry and could see that he was now asleep. 'Tell me the story.'

Rosa put the glass to one side and placed both hands palms down on the table as if to steady herself. She looked seriously at Anna. 'I haven't seen him since he was ten. My mum died two years before that when he was eight and I was eleven. She got drunk and drowned on the way back from the pub.' Anna was about to express her shock at this but Rosa went on as though she had said nothing of note. 'Dad tried to look after us for a bit but it got him down. He was a big bloke, I take after him, but Dean was like mum, a bit runty for a boy. It wasn't his fault but it seemed to rile dad and he went for him sometimes. One day he really lost it and Dean got taken to the Children's. After that they took him away and put him in a Home.' She explained herself. 'Dean, I mean, not dad.'

She put her hands together and laced the fingers tightly as though, she, too, might lash out. 'Dad wasn't allowed to see him and there was no way I could go on my own, they wouldn't let me. I sent letters and cards and things but I never got anything from him except once he sent me this.' Rosa took a small wooden box from her bag and opened it. Inside was a cheap gold-coloured chain with the letter R on it. It was nestling in toilet paper and there was a small post-it note stuck to the lid which read 'Dean xx' written inside a pink heart drawn in crayon. 'Someone must have posted it for him. When I was sixteen it was the first thing I did, go and try to see Dean, but he'd been moved and when I finally managed to find his last Home he'd been sent to Young Offenders. I couldn't get out there, it was miles away.' She sighed so deeply that there was a sob escaping too. 'I wrote but I don't know if he got my letters. He's not there now. No-one knows where he is.'

Bobble dragged himself to his feet and bumped Anna. She pulled his ears. 'In a minute. Rosa, what happened to your dad?'

'He's living with Moira the Mattress over in Smethwick. They've got a council flat.' She grunted without amusement. 'We don't see much of each other.'

Anna thought for a moment. 'Rosa, I'm happy to try to find your brother and there will be no cost. You have been the best thing that's happened to Harry for a long time and we're all more grateful than we can say. But, there is one warning I should give you.'

Rosa's head had jerked up at Anna's words. 'Thank you, thank you so much.'

'You may not like what I find out. Your brother may not be alive or he may be in serious trouble. Once you know, you can't not know. Do you see what I mean?'

Rosa looked at her intently, her eyes shining and her broad cheeks flushed. 'I'll deal with it. Anything. This not knowing has been doing my head in for so long.'

'Fine. I don't know how long it will take but I'll keep at it, ok? Just like you do with Harry.' They stood up and Anna was treated to Rosa's warm, herby embrace.

After Rosa had let herself out Anna took her library book into the garden. It had been a mistake – she found the writing turgid and the characters unbelievable - but it was perfect for helping her fall asleep. She tugged the deck-chair out of the shed and lowered herself carefully into it, noting that a few more millimetres of canvas had torn across the seat. Harry was now snoring gently and Bobble, happily outside his one meal of the day, was doing much the same under the tree. She settled back, took a deep breath and opened the book.

'Mum?' A shadow fell over her.

She shaded her eyes. 'Ell? I thought you were at the club?'

'Nah. They're doing something toxic to the grass so we're not allowed.'

'Ok, well.' She struggled with her overwhelming desire to nap and Ellis' uncharacteristically demanding stance. 'Was there something you wanted?'

'I need to talk to you about my future.'

She sat up hoping the groan had not been audible. They went to the table and sat opposite each other where she and Rosa had been in the same positions moments before. 'Go on, then. What's on your mind?'

'You know Mr Chessington?' Anna's memory scanned Parents' Evening and stopped at a bulky male person.

She nodded. 'Biology?'

'Yup. He showed me this tooth today. Well, he showed all of us but I had a good look after the others had gone to break.'

'Right.' Anna glanced back to the deck-chair and the book.

'It was from a dinosaur – an ichthyosaur. '

'Was it? Like the fossils Mary Anning found at Lyme Regis?'

'Probably. He said it was *at least* 66 million years old because that's when dinosaurs died out. Isn't that a kick in the head?' Ellis propped his chin on his hand and stared unseeing at the shed.

'Mm. Have you been watching Pops' Classic American Movies?'

'So I asked him how old the first human skeletons that had ever been found were and he said he thought that the homo sapiens ones may be over a hundred and fifty thousand years old – they've found fossils in the Rift Valley in Africa. But then he told me what scientists had found out from bones like when hunter gatherers became, um, farmers.'

'Pastoralists.'

'Yes. People got tuberculosis because they lived with their cows and things and their diet was mostly grain so they got shorter and much less healthy than when they'd been hunting. They can tell loads from bones – how they died and all that. Really interesting, Mum.'

'I know. I saw a documentary the other day with your dad that was about a civilisation in South America, well, meso-America, hundreds of years old, and they had a proper democratic system of organisation. We think the Greeks invented -'

Ellis interrupted this digression. 'So I thought I'd be an archaeologist. Not for buildings but for bones.'

Anna considered the idea. Harry had been a geography teacher, but more than that he had been endlessly fascinated by the way the landscape and the people on it interacted and influenced each other. She loved research and had inherited her dad's interest in quirky, esoteric facts and behaviours. 'I think you'd be brilliant at it,' she said. There was a pause while the weight of Ellis' ambition soaked into the afternoon.

'There's a school trip to the Natural History Museum in London.'

'Great. Go. Bring me something to sign.'

Another pause.

'Mum? Can we afford it? I don't mean the trip. I mean for me to go to university. It might take years before I finish. I'd need to go on to get a Ph.D. I talked to Mr Chessington about it.' Hard to remember sometimes that he was only eleven.

'Now listen to me, Ell.' She took his grubby hot hands in hers. 'Of course we can afford it. You will go to the best university that offers you a place, ok? I don't need to tell you to work hard because you always do. I do need to tell you not to worry because you always do that, too. There's a lot of misplaced concern about university fees and you often get funded for post-grad work like a doctorate - you might even go to America for it where they really appreciate UK graduates. It's complicated but totally do-able.' She pumped his hands a little. 'Do you hear me?'

He grinned. 'Thanks Mum'

Faye appeared. 'What's he getting? What's he thanking you for?'

Anna stood up. 'I told him he can go on the school trip to London.'

Faye beamed at Anna. Although her skin was fair it took an even milky-tea tan and she was looking so fresh and young, with no makeup and messy hair, that Anna's heart clenched with love for her. 'So then you'll give me the same for snacks and drinks for the party? It's only fair, Mum, you know it is.' She suddenly dropped her head forward and tore off her scrunchie, scratching at her scalp. 'Something's... Mum, has Bobble got fleas? Ellis, has he?'

'Covered in them,' Ellis told her, 'and ticks and lice and scrofula…' Faye leaped at him but he had gone.

'Let me see your list, Faye, and I'll see what we can contribute but it won't be a lot.'

As Anna sat and waited for her daughter to return she thought sadly about Ellis's question. Can we afford it? By the time Ellis was at university his father would be dead. The concern over how much a nursing home would cost, if needed, would be over. The worry over providing the short-term care in his own home had been offset, even if temporarily, by Kimi's father's generous gift which meant that they could pay Rosa, but the specialist had been gently firm that Harry would be unlikely to see Ellis start university. He was deteriorating more rapidly now. She let her eyes rest on his turned back, on the familiar line of his peaking shoulder and the bony ridge of his hip. He lay so still. She remembered the scene when she arrived home and wondered, not for the first time, if Rosa's efforts were over-stimulating him. He seemed irritable more often than before when he had been with George during the day. But George was re-invigorated with his release from constant care and the friendship, or romance, between him and Diane. He deserved it. She couldn't ask him to take on the whole responsibility of Harry's care again and, in any case, Harry's moodiness might simply be a symptom of this stage of his illness.

Faye bounced down on to the other seat. 'If you'll get the cheese and chicken strips for the skewers and things like that Tash and I can pay for the rest!'

'In other words, I should pay for the expensive stuff and you'll pay for the cheap rubbish?'

'Got it in one, Mum.' Before Anna could protest she had spirited herself away and would then claim that all had been agreed. Well, Kimi had insisted that 'the girls' would pay for Anna's birthday treat so she could run to this. Anna glanced at her watch. It was time to wake Harry or he might have a hard time sleeping tonight.

She knelt beside him on the grass where she could see his face. He hated being woken suddenly. 'Harry? Darling? Can you wake up now, it's time to go in.'

He opened his eyes without moving any other part of his body. The leaves rustling above him shifted mottled sunlight and shade across his stretched out limbs. As she smiled into his face a shaft of sunlight hit one iris and turned it to translucent amber. 'I've been on this train a long time,' he said thoughtfully.

'We're all on the train with you, Harry.'

'Love you, Anna.'

Instantly tears pricked Anna's eyes. When had she last heard that? 'I love you, too.' He contemplated her for a moment and then puckered his lips and she gladly leaned forward to meet them with hers. It had been so long since they had kissed like this, in the old habitual way, that it almost undid her and she had to pull back and breathe deeply to forestall the storm of tears. She could smell the scent of his body, that familiar warm, sweet musk.

They continued to regard each other. During every long second of that shared look her heart stopped beating. 'You are the sunshine of my life,' Harry whispered, barely making a sound. It was their song, their honeymoon song. How had that fragment remained? How had Harry's ravaged mind retrieved that long-ago phrase? Now she couldn't stop the tears. She was almost lying in the grass by his side so that she could stroke his face, his brows and cheeks and soft curve of his lips. She could only murmur his name over and over. He closed his eyes again and she pulled back and sat up, drying her wet face on her arm; she was stunned, overwhelmed.

She heard her father calling from the kitchen that dinner was ready and she touched Harry's bare arm. 'Darling, George is calling us in for dinner.' Harry groaned and rolled slightly away from her. 'Shall we go and see what it is?' She waited. 'Time to go in, Sweetheart.'

He rolled on to his side and looked vacantly at her. She stood up and moved back a little as he stumbled to his feet and began to walk towards the house. Their glorious moment was over. In the confetti whirl of Harry's disintegrating neurons, this bright speck had been captured and gifted to her.

After dinner was over and the others had wandered off, Anna asked George if they could talk about Harry. He made coffee and they sat together at the kitchen table with the remains of the cheese and crackers between them.

'What's worrying you, Annie?'

'He's been so moody lately, Dad. Rosa is great but do you think it could be a bit much for him, all this stimulation?'

'No, I don't really.' George put his warm hairy hand over hers. 'He's been moody for a while, love. I think it's what happens.'

'And I didn't notice?'

'You're bound to be more vigilant when it's not family looking after him.' He squeezed her hand. 'You know I'm not getting at you, don't you?'

'I know. You're right.' They sipped their coffees. 'Ellis told me this afternoon he wants to be an archaeologist.' George raised his eyebrows and nodded. 'Well, I'll get this sorted out.' She started to rise but George cleared his throat so she sat down again. 'What?'

'Diane's asked me to move in with her.' He flushed and mopped up crumbs of cheese with his finger not looking at her.

'What? At the farm?

'Mm.' He scrabbled in his beard. 'What do you think? I'd come here all the time because of you and Harry, of course.'

'And you'd need to be here for the mags - or are you going to take all your stuff?' Anna realised that she was more horrified by the idea of his shed being cleared than she was by the thought of him spending his nights with Diane. It felt as though the shed was his real home and she couldn't bear for him to leave it.

He looked equally alarmed. 'Oh, no, no. I would do all that here.'

Anna smiled at his embarrassed face. 'Just nights of passion then?'

He grunted. 'Hardly. But I've been alone a long time.'

'I know, Dad, I think it's lovely.' They sat in silence not knowing what to say next, both disquieted by the conversation for different reasons.

'Did you know that Capuchin monkeys can use money?' George said, brightening. 'They even engage in prostitution to get it!'

'I'm not going to even attempt to track that train of thought,' Anna said, laughing at him and picking up the mugs.

George stood up, too. 'Yes, and in the mosquito season they crush millipedes and smear their backs with the paste because that's a natural insect repellent! Aren't they clever?' He looked round at the messy kitchen. 'Do you want me to - ?'

'No, Dad, I'll do this. You get off to your shed.' She smiled at his back as he almost skipped out. She cleared up the kitchen and went into the living room to curl up in the armchair and mull over her memory of the honey-sweet moment in the garden. Harry must have been playing with the remote because he was watching Sun, Sex and Suspicious Parents with the sound off.

6

Saturday was cooler with a fresh breeze fluttering the bunting and rattling the sides of the tents. Safe 'n' Sound had organised the refreshment tent themselves since this would almost certainly bring in the most money. She dropped off her disappointing chocolate cake smothered in icing and moved on to the ring marked out with plastic ribbon where there would be judging of the owners most like their pets. A few pairs had already assembled and were looking each other up and down. She thought of Bobble who was somewhere towing Ellis around and wondered if Len could be persuaded to enter with him. Unkind. The fundraiser had not engaged Faye's interest but George and Harry had come to support them.

Joan appeared by Anna's elbow. 'Get me one of those daft masks, will you, dear? I've got to dash to the loo before we start.'

When Harry had had to stop work, Anna had left her job as a university librarian and gone to work for Harts. She needed the increase in salary because she was now the only breadwinner. In those turbulent months she lost touch with her previous work friends and hadn't the time or energy to make new ones. She realised now that work had also been a life-saver in the way of bringing new people to her – some of whom would become very close. Joan was one of them. Again, they had met over the Briony case because Joan lived next door to the young woman, then the object of her first solo search, and Joan had been there to comfort Anna over the nightmare of Lena.

She made her way reluctantly to the steward's table where a keen-faced man presided. 'Two please.'

'Bitch or dog?'

'Excuse me?'

He fussed at her. 'I can see *you're* a bitch but is the other one for a bitch or a dog?'

Anna had to look somewhere else. 'Another bitch.'

'Here you are, then. I'll give you Mandy and Froufrou. You're a mongrel and she's a poodle.' He handed over the cardboard masks with the animal residents of Safe 'n' Sound's photos printed on them. Had no-one at the shop thought this idea through, Anna wondered, as she looked round for Joan.

At the starter's call they began to jog off on their circuit but Anna and Joan had already agreed not to flog themselves. Neither of them had remembered to ask anyone for sponsorship money and they knew how much they would give out of their own pockets so it was immaterial. It would be the chance for a chat, however breathless.

'Whose brilliant idea was this?' Joan demanded, turning her poodle face to Anna.

'It is quite funny, though. The kids like it.' Gaggles of children were laughing and pointing but Anna was very pleased she could not hear the witticisms they were attracting from a gang of youths.

'I would have preferred a cat,' Joan panted.

'Or Charles.'

'No, not Charles. A bit too near what's underneath, that.'

'Nonsense, I'd have said an especially cute hamster.'

Diane had wisely decided not to put Charles on show but to walk round holding him. That way the maximum number of people could see him (and put their hands in their pockets to fill her bucket) but she could take time out whenever she felt it was all getting a bit too much for him. As far as anyone could tell, given his inevitably grim expression, he didn't seem to mind all the attention.

After a couple more circuits they peeled off to sit on the grass and have a break. Both swigged at water bottles and poured water over their heads after taking off the masks. Joan squinted into the crowd. 'Isn't that Steve? Who's that he's with?' She pointed.

'I don't know.'

Before she could stop her, Joan had stood up and was waving vigorously. 'Hey, Steve, over here!' Alice ran towards them. She was wearing a Boston Red Sox baseball cap. Anna got up slowly looking at the woman. She was almost as tall as Steve and her long sand-coloured hair blew out about her head in decorative pre-Raphaelite strands. She was wearing narrow jeans and a strappy top that revealed her tan. Crap, Anna thought.

'Look at my hat,' Alice shouted, 'And I've got candy! Candy!' It was a new word for a very nice thing but it didn't make Anna feel any better. She ran her fingers through her hair trying to tidy it and remembered that she had just poured half a bottle of water over it. Where her T shirt wasn't wet from sweat, it was wet from that. Brilliant.

'This is Cathy,' Steve said quietly. 'She wanted to come.'

'The more the merrier,' Joan laughed, 'we take everyone's money!' She put her mask back on. 'Look at this Steve, look what they've made us do!'

Alice picked up the Mandy mask and thrust it at Anna. 'Put on, Anna. Put on!'

Anna did her best to smile. 'Hello, how are you?'

Cathy laughed. 'Jet-lagged mostly but I couldn't miss this – a chance to see the famous Charles.' She looked around. 'I think I met your son? Ellis? He quizzed me about American universities. He's very advanced isn't he?'

Anna flooded with irrational rage. 'He's just thinking about what he'll study. It's top of his mind at the moment.' They stood for a moment looking around. 'So is tomorrow on or off, Steve?'

'Oh, definitely on. I'll pick you and Harry and the dog up around 9.00? Is that too early for Harry?' He was uncomfortable, too. Had Cathy just turned up with no notice?

'No, it's fine, but will you still have room in the car?'

'What? Oh, yes. Cathy's staying with friends – she's got plans.' Anna was grateful for that information and his knowing that it would be awkward for her to ask.

'Well, we'll let you enjoy the show,' Joan said cheerily, 'we've got five more laps to do. Come on, you mongrel, let's go.'

They joined the others and jogged slowly round. After a few moments the poodle face turned to Anna and asked, 'What's going on? Who is she?'

'Steve's ex-wife.'

'Oh.'

'Wondering if she made a mistake and may want to come back.'

'I thought you and him were, you know, not like that, but, um, cared about each other?' Being empathised with by a poodle was disconcerting. Anna jogged on. 'He seems very fond of you.'

'Mm,' said Mandy's fixed doggy grin.

Joan let this go. They rounded the turn and saw George and Harry in the refreshment tent. 'Only a bit more to go,' Joan gasped. 'I had an affair once, you know.'

'Did you?' Anna was startled. All she knew about Joan's previous relationships was the tragic accident when her husband and son had been lost at sea.

'Yes.' Joan lifted her mask and wiped her face and then replaced it. 'It was pure lust, of course.'

'How long ago?'

'I was about twenty-eight. The boys were only little. Walter was working with the Forestry Commission.'

Anna glanced sideways at the white-haired pensioner with little age-bulges over her elbows. 'I have to say that's a surprise. You always seem so straight. I don't mean straight-laced, I mean open and honest.' They stopped and bent over, breathing hard.

Joan pushed back her mask which was beginning to shred. 'Is anyone immune from passion? It wasn't that I didn't love Walter, I did. I loved all of them.'

'So what happened?'

'You know I went back to college when the boys went to school? That's where I started with computers – that IT course, only they didn't call it that then. Let's sit for a minute. We've only got one more lap that we promised ourselves we'd do.' They sprawled under a tree away from the crowd. 'He was one of the teachers. They called themselves lecturers.'

'I'm listening.'

'I used to go back to the village on the bus from town. One day he pulled up at the bus stop and offered me a lift.'

'Classic move.'

'Mm. He was a perfectly ordinary man. That's what I don't understand to this day. He wasn't very good-looking and a bit on the fat side, long side-burns – probably he thought he looked like Elvis or that Humperdinck singer.' She paused. 'Anyway, and you're not to tell anyone this, ok?' Anna nodded. 'He drove off the road into a little wood and told me he'd always fancied me and kissed me.'

'That's awful, Joan. He was abusing his authority.'

Joan glanced sideways at her. 'I know. I know that. And it wasn't that I was impressed by him or flattered. I thought nothing of him until that kiss. But sometimes your body seems to have a mind of its own. How can I explain? My whole body just fired up. I'd never felt anything like it before – I was consumed.'

'Really?'

Joan looked Anna full in the face. 'I was like a heap of hay that someone's put a match to. I could no more stop him or myself than stop a hurricane.' She looked worried. 'I'm mixing my metaphors.'

Anna smiled at her. 'That's ok. I'll let you off now I know you're a scarlet woman.'

Joan didn't laugh. 'No, it was awful. I couldn't get enough of him. I lied to Walter, I made up excuses to be late home, away on a Saturday, everything. I even bought new underwear when we could barely afford meat three times a week.'

'So how long did it last?'

'Five and a half weeks.' Joan hugged her knees. 'Then one day, again for no reason I can see except that he told an off-colour joke, I looked at him and saw him the way he was. Just a middle-aged man, not very nice, quite sleazy really, and I dropped him.' Anna considered this. 'I've never told anyone before.'

'How did he take it?'

'Oh, ok. He wasn't in love with me or anything. He just moved on to the next girl. Sexual attraction is a strange thing, isn't it? Usually it comes with friendship and love but not always.' She bent and rubbed her calves. 'Ever since then I've realised that I don't know myself, not really. I don't know what I'm capable of. Do any of us? It's a weird feeling. Like steering a car on the motorway with your elbows.'

'Have you ever *done* that?'

'No. Of course not.'

As they jogged on for the last lap Anna wondered why Joan had told her this. Joan had just admitted that she had observed how fond of each other Anna and Steve were. Had her dad said anything? But what would be the point of this confession now? Was she hinting that Anna should kill any feelings of that kind for Steve before things got out of control? Maybe she just felt like telling her and there was no covert message.

The breeze had dropped and the day was heating up. At the refreshment tent George was looking around for them and Anna decided to call it a day and go home so she could shower and change. Joan felt the same. They had done their bit. She felt churned up and depressed by meeting Cathy but she could see from Steve's expression that he had not been particularly cheerful either. Maybe tomorrow there would be an opportunity to talk or, at any rate, to listen.

They didn't chat much on the journey to Staffordshire on Sunday morning. The traffic was light and the fields and woods that sped past north of Uttoxeter soothed them. Every now and then Anna glanced back at Harry. He was staring out of the window, too, but she noticed that his eyes were not flickering as they would if he was actively watching the scenes flash by. His glazed look brought back her unsettling nightmare. In the driving seat Steve was singing along with Alice to *Girls Just Want to Have Fun* which she was playing on his tablet. Steve could see his niece in the rear-view mirror and Anna noted how frequently his eyes sought her for just a fraction of a second, constantly checking that she was safe and happy. Lucky little girl. In a weird way it was as though they were the parents of the child and the man in the back. She pushed that thought away but then the dream came back.

She was in some kind of druggy underworld scene where it was dark and too hot. There were other figures but she was on top of Steve. He was lying completely still on his back with his eyes fixed on nothing. She was doing something to him, something sexual and predatory. It reminded her of a television documentary she had seen. In the dream she was like the spider that lays its eggs in the paralysed tarantula; there was no love or tenderness in her, she was scheming, calculating, completely self-indulgent as she pulled at Steve's inert body. Then he was gone, as happens in dreams, and one of the maggot figures reared up. It was wearing an old-fashioned canvas straight jacket with the long sleeves chained behind and its face was swathed in bandages like a mummy or a screen zombie. It was staggering towards her and the bandages were coming undone and she knew that she could not bear the horror of seeing what lay beneath or feeling the touch of the creature. She struggled through the bodies and the darkness to find the way out, screaming to wake herself up.

When she did, her heart was pounding and she was slick with sweat. She lay for a moment summoning her left brain to calm and explain. She must have been thinking about Steve before she went to sleep (when wasn't she?) and the spider thing could have come from that wretched wildlife documentary. She found the habits of animals often unnecessarily cruel. '*Tyger, tyger burning bright in the forests of the night, what immortal hand or eye framed thy fearful symmetry?*' What indeed. Why do people think that children will like nature programmes and why do they? They're terrifying.

She shook her head trying to rid herself of the feeling that had gone with that nightmare, the horror of being in a feral dark place and herself the eager source of evil. Why didn't Harry come to her in her dreams as he had been that afternoon, sentient and loving? Maybe Kimi was right, dreams are just random firings of brain cells – there is no deeper significance.

'All right?' Steve was smiling at her. The sun was lighting up the side of his head so that one eye blazed crystal blue against the dim interior. She took a breath and nodded, smiling back. It was probably all the fault of George's four-cheese pizza and one too many glasses of red yesterday evening. She checked on Harry and saw Bobble's head pop up from behind the back seat where he was restrained. She laughed at his comical expression and Steve glanced in his rear-view mirror and laughed too. 'He keeps doing that. It's like he's checking that the pack's all here and not gone off without him.'

'He hates being left behind.'

'Don't we all.'

They parked in The Roaches Tearooms' car park and within minutes the climbing club minibus drew in. With toilet visits and getting water for Bobble and loading up with equipment there was no time to talk and eventually they all made their way across the lane and began to climb up the path.

Steve found Anna and pointed to his left. 'We're peeling off here and going over to that outcrop, can you see it? Straight up from the hut?'

'Yes.'

'Are you going to be ok with Alice?'

'Yes, I'll just go as far as they want to, probably a little way along the ridge towards you, and then we'll come down and I'll make a picnic in the field by the car park. Is that ok?'

'You're sure you don't want me to take Bobble? He's a bit of a handful.'

'No, it's fine.'

'Great.' He squinted at his watch. 'We should be done with the first session in about two hours and I'll join you.' He patted her upper arm. 'Phone me if you need anything.' Harry with Bobble on his lead and Alice were strolling ahead, Alice trying to match Harry's long stride, and the climbers had moved off. 'We need to talk, Anna. Let's try to find some time this afternoon.'

'Yes.' She let herself take his hand for a moment. 'Let's do that.'

Bobble was being unusually bashful in this new environment and not pulling at his lead so it was easy for Harry to control him. Anna watched him as she walked up behind them. The dog's body language reminded her of Faye at her first children's party – desperate to join in but scared to. He had never been in a wild place before and was overcome with all the smells and new sights. Anna caught them up and rubbed his ears. 'It's ok, kid, you're safe with us,' she said. He immediately dropped his ears and grinned at her.

'Is Bobble scared?' asked Alice.

'Just getting used to the new place,' Anna said, 'but I think he likes it.'

They walked slowly on up the trail, pausing to look at sheep's wool caught in the gorse or to pull Bobble away from a sheep turd that looked like a juicy clump of blackcurrants. The sheep themselves were moving off as they approached. It was all new to Alice, too. As the climb began to steepen and Harry stumbled a little, Anna stopped them and they turned to gaze at how far they had come.

They could look down on the roof of the Tearooms now and the car park with the minibus and Steve's Yeti. A few other cars had arrived. Beyond that the land dropped away like a rumpled emerald carpet down to the brilliance of Tittesworth Reservoir far beneath them. Instinctively, Anna looked up to see what the sky was doing and was pleased that there were wisps of cloud high above. Alice followed her gaze. 'Look,' Anna said, 'mares' tails.'

Alice contradicted her. 'Not mess tells,' she said, not knowing the words, 'that's silly.'

'Ok, then, what do you think they are?'

'Angels' feathers, of course,' Alice replied immediately.

Anna craned her neck back studying them and then smiled at the little girl whose silver hair was waving in the breeze like the very finest cirrus uncinus. 'Of course,' she agreed.

They went on and reached the top of the ridge where the path went right to rise steeply towards Hen Cloud or left along the almost flat trail towards the climbers. The novices were now roped up Anna saw, looking at the tiny figures in the distance, and they would soon begin to climb, their legs shaking with effort and excitement. She'd tried it herself once but hated the feeling of being at the mercy of tackle and her own inexperience. She should really try again.

'Ok Harry?' He nodded and they picked their way between the boulders to emerge on to the easy path. Anna took Alice's hand. Now the shining of the reservoir was edged by woods and they were high enough for a light thermal to lift their hair. She wondered if Harry would remember. They had stood here on the first evening of their honeymoon, their old Landrover sitting half a mile along the lane, and they had looked into the sunset. That's when Harry had sung to her in full voice, his face lit with gold, his copper hair in flames, what he had mouthed yesterday. 'You are the sunshine of my life.' But no, he was absorbed in picking his way along the path and she noticed that he was walking stiffly as though his legs were hurting. Just a few more steps to a flat rock she could see ahead where they could sit for a while and then they would go back down.

The climbers were invisible on the rock face from this position but she thought of Steve down there and pondered what he might want to say to her. Even if Cathy did want him back, would he want her? And what would that mean if he didn't – if he chose Anna instead? Her wild words at the restaurant could not be unsaid and he would not have forgotten.

Anna had read once that when serious accidents happen it is usually not because one large thing has gone wrong but because several small events have coincided. And so it happened.

She noticed that the laces on one of her walking boots had come undone. She let go of Alice's hand and knelt to do them up. At that moment a rabbit started from the hummock of bilberries beside the path and Bobble jerked his lead free from Harry's hand and dashed after it over the side of the rock escarpment. Alice screamed 'Bobble!' and ran fast towards the edge. Harry saw the little girl rushing forward after the dog and stumbled and flailed the few feet along the rock to try to stop her before she could fall, crying 'Stop! Stop!' Anna leaped up and yelled Alice's name but Alice had already halted. Harry had gone. There had been no sound. He had just gone.

Anna grabbed Alice and dropped to the ground with her, elbowing forward with the protesting child until she could lie flat and peer over the edge of the rock. Far below she could see one bent leg showing from behind a boulder. It was not moving. Bobble re-appeared from a crevice a few feet below panting and slobbering and joined them.

'Oh God,' Anna murmured, 'Harry.' Alice was oblivious, wriggling in her arms, trying to smack Bobble and scolding him for running away. Anna pushed back from the edge holding Alice tight until they were on the safe side of the path. She must not frighten the child. She must not show fear or distress. Alice had simply not noticed that Harry had gone. Her fingers shaking she pulled off her backpack, struggled with the zip, and called the dog to them.

'How about a biscuit, darling?' she asked, trying to keep her voice steady and quiet.

'And for Bobble?'

'He shouldn't have one but just this once.' Anna had an idea to divert Alice. 'Will you break it up into tiny pieces for him and give it him slowly so he doesn't get sick?' Alice nodded eagerly. Anna sat on the grass with the child between her legs and the dog's lead wrapped round her wrist and gave her two biscuits. Then she took out her phone and turned her head away from the girl praying as she had never prayed before that there would be a signal. There were two bars. It rang six times before Steve answered.

'Steve, something has happened,' she said as evenly as she could. 'We were walking along the top towards you. Alice is safe with me. She is right here with me having a biscuit with Bobble. Harry is not here. Harry is a long way down.' She paused. 'Do you understand, Steve? Do you understand me?'

There was a moment's silence. 'Yes. Where are you on the path?'

'We're by the rock that's shaped like a bear crouching, about fifteen metres from where the path up from the road joins the top trail.' Anna was running out of breath. 'Do you know where I mean? Steve?'

'We're going there now.' His voice was wavering, he must be running over the rocks. 'We'll find him Anna. Will you stay on the phone?'

'Yes. Hurry. Please.' She sat back, the phone pressed to her ear.

Alice raised a scheming face to her. 'Bobble says he wants another biscuit.' Anna fought to keep control of herself. 'Bobble says I've been good, too.' She took the packet out of her pack, fumbling with the wrapping her fingers were shaking so much, squeezing the phone into her neck while never letting go of Alice's waist.

'This is a special treat just for today. Ok?' She handed over the open packet and Alice grabbed it.

The paper rustled and Alice concentrated on breaking the biscuits. Anna could hear the small sounds of the snap of each one and Bobble's panting breath and feel the damp heat of Alice's body pressed against her own. The wind rising up the scarp face buffeted the side of her head. The grass was cool and scratchy beneath her bare thighs. Seconds went by and then minutes. Finally she could stand it no longer.

'Steve. Where are you?' There was a scraping noise. The phone must have been put down on a rock.

'I'm here, we've found him,' he said quietly. Then she knew. 'The paramedics are on their way.' She could hear voices but they were not urgent, they were subdued. 'I'm so sorry, Anna.' She let her head fall back and stared up at the sky keeping a tight hold on Alice. A skylark was piping like a bell tolling a long way away. 'I'm coming up to you. Don't move, I'll find you. I'll bring Alice down to the cafe by the other track. You'll want to be with Harry.'

'Yes.'

'Does she know what's happened?'

'No.'

'Thank you. I'm so sorry.'

Anna put the phone away and sat holding the child and the dog. She was empty. When Steve came she stood up and after he had taken Alice on his shoulders and the dog by his lead she hurried as fast as she could back down the path and then ran between the boulders until she came to her husband's body. The climbers were standing around and fell back as she approached. Someone had put a waterproof over Harry's head. She knelt down beside his body and peeled it back from his face with shaking fingers. One of the men said something but she ignored him.

Harry looked peaceful. His eyes were closed but he was very pale. She pulled the waterproof further away and saw that his throat had been cut on one side. The carotid artery was severed. Then she saw the dark stain spread around his head and neck like a lopsided halo. She looked up at the men and one of them raised a baked bean tin in his hand to show her, its jagged lid piercing the sky.

They wandered away as she stared at Harry. Had one of them closed his eyes? She lifted her body and leaned forward to kiss his forehead, the apples of his cheeks and then his full soft mouth –

still warm. She noticed a small patch of unshaven bristle just by his right jawbone glinting in the sun and chided herself for a sloppy job. She would do better tomorrow. She felt it with the index finger of her right hand. She sat back on her haunches and then, obeying an instinct older than custom or reason, stretched herself out on Harry's body. If only she was strong enough to lift him and carry him away home. Off the battlefield, away from strangers, to be safe with her. She grasped the limp, heavy arms, pulling them to her, gasping with the effort. One hand she trapped beneath her breasts and the other she dragged to her lips. The breeze lifted a torn flap on Harry's shirt and somewhere far away a startled sheep was bleating. 'Don't go, don't go, don't go,' she whispered continually with her mouth to his ear.

Then she lay still on his body scoured of thought or feeling. Remembering this later she couldn't have said how much time had passed before there was a light touch on her shoulder and a soft voice spoke her name.

So they took him away and she followed the stretcher down the slope. As she climbed into the ambulance she looked back up at the escarpment. This was the place that marked the birth and death of their marriage. She would come back and build a cairn, she would mark his passing in some way in this place.

That night Anna, Faye and Ellis slept in the big bed in 'Harry's room'. She had found Ellis there, his face discoloured with weeping, and had lain down beside him and then Faye had come and wordlessly crept to her mother's side. Anna lay on her back with an arm round each as they fell asleep, staring at the fissure in the ceiling that had needed fixing for twenty-eight years.

For hours she waited for Harry to come. He couldn't just be gone. People get visited by those they love. They don't just disappear, surely. A shadow by the bed, a presence in the kitchen, a few words clearly audible. There was nothing. Just a cosmic emptiness. As the night began to turn to dawn, her lips formed words. 'Where are you?' He had been such a kind husband, why didn't he come to comfort her? She felt furious and impotent. He had ceased to exist in a second and she had not been ready. It had been too soon. How could he be so thoughtless?

She remembered his body, bled out and waxen as she had last seen it at the mortuary. She felt impatient with the memory. What was the point of knowing where his body was? Where was he?

7

Over the next few weeks people came, brought food, said things. Arrangements were made, decisions taken and then the funeral happened.

Someone, maybe the minister, read St. Simeon's words:
I know the Immovable comes down:
I know the Invisible appears to me;
I know that he who is far outside creation
Takes me within himself and hides me in his arms

Anna found it incomprehensible. As she left she noticed Andrew Dunster at the back. He stepped forward and took her hand and she wondered why she had not thought to ask him to take the service – at least he knew Harry.

Cards arrived, some of Harry's colleagues appeared and then went away. Scabs began to form like burrs on a tree over Anna's wounds so that she could talk and even smile politely and make tea and hand out biscuits. She could walk to the park with Bobble. She could do washing and shopping and pay bills. Three days after the funeral she suggested to Faye and Ellis that they might want to go back to school and finish the last weeks of term. They were hesitant but relieved and went.

During this time George moved around her quietly and when she came out of the trances that overcame her, standing at the living room window or sitting on the top stair, she would notice that a mug of tea had been wordlessly placed by her side. The summer was merciless. Day after day of hot sunshine and flowers and trees showing off their juicy life, uncaring, unaware.

She got down all the photo albums, the boxes and envelopes of unmounted prints, negatives and slides and spread them out on the living room floor pulling out any with Harry in them. Then she went through all their digital files and made prints of every one that was of him. She instructed Faye and Ellis to search all their downloads and files and Facebook albums. She cried bitterly when she realised that they could have kept the answer-machine tapes from when Harry was first diagnosed before he had stopped leaving messages because he could no longer use a phone. Where was his voice? She scrabbled among old cassettes and found some mix-tapes from their dating years with messages to her at the beginning and even, if she was lucky, between the tracks. She kept copious notes and labelled everything, often pinning things to the bedroom wall.

One night she woke from a doze to the thrilling thought that there would still be hairs on his clothes. She turned on all the lights, ran to the wardrobe, and fed each centimetre of his jackets and sweaters through her fingers searching for copper threads. She found three and carried two of them to a velvet ring box, discarding the jewellery to a shelf, and stuck the third on the wall with sticky tape. She wondered briefly if she might be going mad.

Next she found his files from teaching, never sorted or thrown away, and anything in his handwriting, no matter if it was notes on a field trip's geology find or jottings for parents' evening comments, she kept, smoothing each sheet and stacking them tenderly in a large cardboard document box.

It was exhausting but she couldn't stop. She couldn't believe how profligate they had been while he was alive. Why had they not filmed every moment, knowing they were going to lose him? She could have had video of him playing the piano, throwing sticks for Bobble, anything, everything. What had she been thinking of?

One wall in the bedroom they had shared was already covered with photographs and scraps of paper and the work gave her temporary release. She dragged the stepladders out of the garden tool shed and up the stairs so she could reach the top bits. It was so hot that she stripped to a cotton nightie and knickers so she didn't need to change from night to day. She ate voraciously and snacked between meals washing the food down with wine or tea or gin – whatever came to hand.

When it was all done and she could find no more Harry anywhere, Steve came again. She had vague memories of him being here before but she had been too busy to bother with him. Now she was not busy. Now she was as stagnant as blocked drain water. She was in the kitchen leaning against the sink, looking out at the indifferent azure sky and found she hadn't the energy to turn and greet him. He came near her.

'Do you blame me, Anna? You wouldn't have been there if I hadn't suggested it.' He sounded utterly miserable.

She didn't look at him. 'No. I don't blame anyone. It just happened.' She didn't want to look at him. The thought of touching him made her flesh crawl.

'Is there anything I can do?'

People kept asking that. It was natural, she would have asked the same thing of others in her situation, but the question made no sense. What could anyone possibly do? There was only one thing and no-one was willing to do it. She wanted to talk about Harry. She wanted to re-live every moment, every joke, every argument they had had. She wanted to tell everyone about how he was, what he was like, but no-one would let her. Michelle had come and even she had tried to divert Anna, to take her mind off her loss when all she wanted to do was to hang on to him. People dropped their eyes, suggested activities or bereavement counselling or having a break, whatever that meant, but the one thing she wanted them to do, to listen while she talked about Harry for hour upon hour, they would not do.

'No,' she said. Steve turned to go. 'Thank you,' she managed to add with a great effort of will. When he had gone she climbed the stairs and went to lie again on the big bed, closing the door behind her. Tears came easily and frequently. They meant nothing and they neither helped nor made things worse. On the window ledge was a glossy dark green carrier bag and inside it in a plastic container was Harry. She had put it there thinking he might like to see out. She was suffused with shame.

A month after the funeral Len came. He had been fairly often she remembered and was surprisingly comforting, sitting wordlessly by her side, sometimes playing his flute in the garden when she was lying on the bed upstairs so that the melody came sweetly and faintly to her ears and she could doze. But today she wanted to be alone. He poured out two glasses of coke and sat at the kitchen table pushing one towards her. 'Want to ask you something.'

'What?' She tried to concentrate on him.

'Serious. You know Rosa?' She nodded and pushed the glass of Coke around. Was she the only person in the world who hated the sweet, fizzy drink? How long would she need to be polite to Len? Get it over with.

'Mm.'

'I like her, Sis, I really do. But it's like she just doesn't even see me.' Anna's dull thoughts swerved.

'You and Rosa?'

'Well, no, that's what I'm saying. There is no me and Rosa. What does a bloke do to get a woman to like him?'

'That's what you want to ask me? *Now*?'

Len drew up his huge bulk and looked at her sternly. His skin gleamed with grease and his hair hung in rats' tails on to his forehead and down his neck. 'I'm going to say something now that's for your own good, Sis. Everyone else is thinking it. You're mooning around when the truth is this is the best thing could have happened.'

'*What*?' Anna leaped to her feet shaking with rage and shock.

Len waved his hands about helplessly. 'What would have happened to him? If not this, what?' He stood up and scuttled round the table to her wrapping his arms around her neck in an ungainly hug. 'This is best, Anna, this is what he would have wanted. Out in the fresh air, with people, with you, saving Alice's life. Think about it.' If he had not been holding her she would have slumped to the ground.

At last she pulled away from him feeling spent but they sat down again, Len looking shaky after the emotion of the scene. He slurped his coke and then Anna's which she pushed towards him. She took a deep breath. She wanted him gone. 'Len, you want to know what to do to attract Rosa or at least not repel her?'

'Yeah.'

'Ok. What I'm going to tell you is harsh but it's non-negotiable. Wash every day and clean your teeth at least twice a day. Wash only half as many clothes in the machine as you usually do so that they actually *get* clean and don't put them away until they're completely dry.' He was watching her in bewilderment but with close attention as though she were revealing the secret of the Sphinx. 'Use deodorant every day. I mean it, Len. There is nothing so disgusting to a woman like Rosa, in fact all women, than the smell of stale sweat, bad breath and rank clothes.'

'Ok.' He looked as though he wasn't sure whether to be offended or grateful. 'I smell?'

'Yes. And get that coat cleaned and don't wear it in the summer.'

'Oh. I didn't know.' He looked hurt and puzzled.

'And Len, keep listening. You are a kind, loyal and talented man. Show her that.'

'You mean play my flute?'

'If appropriate.'

'Ok.' He got up to leave but at the door turned to face her. 'Thanks, Sis.'

After he had gone Anna picked up the phone and called Ted. Was she sure, was she ready? She could take more time if necessary. No, she would come in. She wanted to work. 'Give me Maxon Blake,' she said, 'unless you've given him to someone else, and when I'm not working with him, Ted, I want to be busy. Please.'

I want new, I want different, I want to be away from this house as much as possible she thought, but didn't say. Len's words had jolted her into action, had shattered the carapace of numbed shock from Harry's death, but Len did not know what fresh hell his rousing of her from her coma would catapult her into and from which she must now run as fast as she could.

As Anna walked into the open office silence fell as she knew it would. Some people turned pitying faces to her and some pretended they had not seen her, all of which she expected and understood – it would wear off.

She went to her desk to find a challenging stack of mail. Good, just what she needed. She was leafing through when she became aware of Suzy making towards her like a seagull in a headwind, dodging between desks until she had reached Anna and folded her in her arms without a word. When Anna began to pull away from the fragrant tumble of Suzy's hair, she whispered into her ear, 'One day at a time.' Anna nodded and Suzy was off calling remarks to left and right to break the nervous silence. Anna was grateful and sat down to see what she could find to do.

Jane Thwaite's birth certificate had arrived. Anna slit the envelope and drew the document out. She raised her eyebrows at what she saw. Jane Thwaite's father was listed, not as Robert Theophilus Thwaite as was on her death certificate, but as William Henry Thwaite. William Henry was described as a solicitor. Anna stared at it for a while, checked dates and then put it carefully away to show Maxon when they would go to Shrewsbury on Wednesday. Before she began to speculate about this anomaly she would check the census but she would wait to do that with Maxon since he wanted to be involved in every stage of the process. Odd, though. She was aware of an almost pleasant skating feeling. To think about this and not about that was to slide about on the safe, brittle surface of things.

As she was placing her opened mail in 'to do' order on her desk, Steve appeared. She did not look up but she was painfully aware of his smell, a mix of leather and hot cotton with a sweet overtone of after-shave. 'Anna?' She made herself glance up at him. 'I'm glad you're back. Fancy a coffee?'

'Snowed under,' she muttered, indicating the small pile of mail needing her attention.

There was a moment's hesitation, a pause during which she could not take a breath, and he moved away.

An hour later Ted came to find her, obviously feeling that a phone call to summon her was a little cold under the circumstances, and she followed him back to his office. He indicated the large and comfortable client chair so she sat in it for the first time. He stood and regarded her kindly for a moment and then she remembered to thank him for coming to Harry's funeral service. He waved his hand dismissively and perched on the edge of his desk.

'Are you really all right to come back?'

'I need to, Ted, I need to be occupied. In fact, this project with Maxon Blake is not going to take up all my time by any means – have you got some other jobs you can give me?'

'I want you to make him your priority, Anna. He's like a lost lamb, isn't he?'

'I know what you mean,' Anna said, understanding that it wasn't just because of Maxon's lack of self-confidence that Ted wanted her to support the man. 'He seems over-awed by his family.'

'Mm. Not easy to have a dynasty to live up to – earn your place in, I mean. I happened to look them up and they're top drawer. His dad's cousin is a senator.'

'So, I am making him my priority but it's not enough. Is there something else?' Anna could feel a rising tide of panic and it was taking all her strength not to show it in her voice.

Ted slid off the desk and went round to the chair side to rummage through a pile of scrap paper. It was an eccentricity that he had never overcome for all his comfortable income that he insisted on writing notes to himself and others on re-used scrap paper. It was always worth turning a note of Ted's over to see what was on the back. The office competed for the best indiscretions. Suzy had once had a note written on the back of an appointment for an obesity counsellor. Anna had had one on the back of a shopping list, presumably in his wife's handwriting, which among other things listed 'your haemorrhoid cream' and a well-known hair-dye for men but she'd thought that was a bit too embarrassing to share with the others. He found what he was looking for and held it up triumphantly.

'That Kenneth Dawkins you found?'

'Yes.' Anna was surprised. That case was finished. 'What about him?'

'He wants you to do something for him. He was insistent it was you even after I'd explained about why you were off – said he'd wait.'

'I don't know, Ted, I can't think of anything he could want me to do, there are no other relatives alive, I know that.' Then she realised who it was that Kenneth may want her to find and her heart sank.

Ted put his glasses further down his nose and held the scrap away from his face as though it was on fire. 'No, it's his ex-sister-in-law apparently. Someone called Janet?'

'He won't have any money to pay you, Ted, he was living on a state pension when I found him and he won't get the money from the house sale for ages.'

Ted beamed. 'Ah, that's where you're wrong. The bank that was acting as executors for his brother, can't remember the name, sent him an interim payment from a savings account.'

Anna resigned herself to taking this on and held out her hand. 'How much detail has he given you? '

'Enough - maiden name, date of birth. Give it a go, eh?'

In the two seconds it took Anna to stand up she saw as if it were happening now, Ken Dawkins seizing her arm in the car, his pale eyes piercing hers, ordering her to seize what she wanted, to squeeze the orange, and then what she had said in the Moroccan restaurant with Steve and his horrified reaction. She stumbled and almost fell. Ted was beside her immediately holding her elbow. 'Are you sure you're up to this?'

'Foot went to sleep,' she threw back at him as she left faking a limp.

Maxon was waiting in reception now wearing black chinos and a grey shirt and tie. His canvas bag was slung across his chest and a beige raincoat was hooked over his arm. When he saw Anna running down the glass staircase he moved quickly towards her, his brow creased in sympathy. Anna swore inwardly. 'Hi Maxon!' she said brightly and tugged her keys out of her bag to avoid the moment.

'Anna, I'm so, so sorry. I just can't imagine -' He looked as if he might burst into tears himself.

'Thank you,' Anna returned briskly. 'We'd better get off if we're going to drive round by Westbury – are you ready?'

On the journey Anna told Maxon about the unexpected name on his great-grandmother's birth certificate and asked if it meant anything to him but it didn't. He seemed happy to talk about the family, though, which was a relief. He knew every name back through the generations to when Grace had immigrated to the US and had little stories to tell about most of them. He described the substantial house which Albert Maxon had built in the early years of the 20th century in Ardmore, the fashionable mainline district north of Philadelphia where he himself had grown up, and listed various paintings, pieces of furniture and even kitchenware which had been acquired by relations. It was unusual for most people to know much beyond their own grand-parents and often not even that, but perhaps it was different if the family was wealthy and proud of itself. She imagined Maxon as a child, it wasn't hard, tiptoeing around the spacious rooms, running a small finger over carving and inlay, touching reverently the silver-topped walking stick which had belonged to Albert Maxon and still stood in its oak umbrella and coat stand by the wide front door. It seemed his father had often spoken to him, as a child, about the portraits which dominated the hall and drawing room, his father's favourite being his namesake, the founder of the family business.

Anna, wondering if they had time to stop for a coffee and deciding not, was happy to keep him talking. 'What did he look like?'

Maxon seemed to almost wilt in his seat. 'The portrait's practically life-size. It's a bit over-whelming to be honest. So, most of it is black tails, then a white waistcoat, there's a gold fob watch and chain and then right up high is his face. Whiskers, you know, like they had - I think they called them mutton chops,' he laughed, 'and a very determined expression. Not someone you'd mess with, I don't think. He was real impressive. All the family were in awe of him.'

'Since Jane wrote down her mother's account of the early days, did she write anything about him, about her step-father?'

'A little. She remembered the house being built – I suppose that would be exciting for a child – and that her mother promised her a pony when they moved in. She didn't say whether she got it. She'd been told to call Albert 'Father' and I do remember reading one time that Father was mad with her for playing with one of the cook's children. He liked to keep the family apart from the servants but I expect they all did then. She stopped writing stuff about the family when she married so there isn't much.'

'What do you know about his family?'

'Almost nothing. I get the impression, and of course he died in the thirties so this is old stuff, that he was a very private person and didn't like to talk about himself. I believe he was originally from Connecticut, not a Philadelphian. I think Jane was a bit scared of him even when she was a grown woman – I know he found a husband for her – one of his associates, Sidney Chadfield, and she seemed to accept that.'

'So Jane didn't have a son? Did she have any step-brothers or sisters?'

'No.   And she only had one daughter, Sarah, my grandmother. It seemed like the family could make money but not sons. My dad was the first son for three generations. I guess they'd been waiting a while to call someone Maxon.' He grunted. They were clear of the city now and Anna hoped Maxon was enjoying the patchwork of greens edging the road and the sight of a kestrel hovering over a hedge. She thought about pointing it out but he seemed absorbed in his own thoughts.

'So you got it, too. What about your generation? Do you have siblings?'

'Oh, I sure do. Sorry, I did.' He turned his head to look out of the side window and Anna waited, glancing at him only once. 'I had a sister older than me. They called her Grace with Thwaite for a middle name because, you know, they're so proud of their English roots.'

It was such a relief not to be in her own thoughts that Anna pushed him further than was sensitive. 'What happened?'

'Oh, just, you know.' Maxon sighed deeply.

'What?'

'Harvard, Wall Street, all that. She was working up to be an investment banker.'

'Very clever, then?' He had answered a question she hadn't asked and not answered the question she had asked, she noticed.

'Oh, you don't have to be so clever to get into Harvard or any of those Ivy League schools if you've got as much money and influence as my family has, but Grace *was* real smart.' Maxon pulled himself upright. 'If you've made lots of money, what do you do next? You get into politics, don't you? That's what Albert did way back, made Mayor of Philly for a while, and then each generation just got a little bit more into it, you know? It happens in America.'

'I think it happens everywhere. So what became of her, your sister?' Anna found she couldn't let it go despite his deflection of her first query and she was guiltily aware that she was beginning to bully this diffident young man for her own distraction.

'Died in a ski-ing accident. Are we about there, yet?'

Anna was ashamed. In any case, the satnav said they were approaching Westbury where The Mount was and the brief shower was over. Anna drove slowly down the deep country lanes through villages and past farms and Maxon craned his neck and took photos out of the window. Eventually they came to the crossroads at Westbury with a pub on their left and a sign to a school on the right so Anna turned that way since there was no church in sight. A few yards along a lych gate appeared with a graveyard beyond it but no church. 'There it is!' Maxon said. On the other side of the road was a modest sandstone building with a square tower and a gravel path up to the door. Anna turned the car round looking for somewhere to park and spotted the village shop at what seemed to be the centre of the village. She parked the car and they got out and gazed around. The houses they could see were a pleasant mixture of old and new and chatter and laughter came from behind the pretty iron gates to the little school.

'I can't believe it.' Maxon sounded almost awed. 'I'm standing where my great great-grandmother stood. She must have gone to that church, walked along this road. Hey, would the post-office have been there then?'

Anna looked at the long low cottage which contained the shop. It looked cosy and inviting and promised that shoes could be repaired, dry-cleaning taken, and if everything got a little bit too much, there was a defibrillator on the wall. Outside the door was a rack of newspapers, each one neatly folded.

'This run of cottages certainly was here but it could have changed its use. Let's ask inside.'

The post-master was friendly but couldn't help. 'I've only been here five years,' he said, 'but I've never heard of The Mount. That doesn't mean anything – a new owner could have changed the name.' Maxon's shoulders drooped. 'There's Mount View,' he remembered. 'I don't know what it looks like, I just remember the address. Our postman would know but he's out on his rounds.'

'Is it far? Can you direct us?'

It took only seven minutes to find Mount View and fewer seconds to know that it was not the ancestral home. It was a large modern building on a green-field site. 'Can we just drive round a bit?' Maxon asked, 'and see what we come across?'

Anna glanced at her watch. 'I'm sorry, we haven't got time. The appointment with Shropshire Archives is 11.00.' She saw how crestfallen he was and she worried that he had created a golden fantasy which he would document and bring home to present like a jewel to his parents. 'We can come back and maybe talk to the vicar or a churchwarden who could show us your family's names in the parish records.' Maxon's face lit up. 'They might even have records of The Mount.' Anna had to keep reminding herself that this man was in his late twenties. He was not a child.

As they crossed the Severn at English Bridge and began to drive on the one-way system up through Wyle Cop and the High Street, Maxon almost screwed his head off in delight and excitement. Shrewsbury's charms were certainly not lost on him – every few yards there was a building of interest and every side-street was worth a glance. It was like taking a child to a fun-fair and just as pleasing.

'I'm coming back here!' Maxon declared. 'This weekend – I have to – I have to explore this place properly. Are those buildings really as old as they look? Is that black and white building really Tudor? I can't believe this!'

'There's a good train service from New Street station, you wouldn't need to hire a car,' Anna said. 'You can come direct.'

'I can't believe this is real, it's like something out of a story book!'

Anna was puzzled. 'But you must have come to Europe before, on holiday with your family or on your own, and there are many towns and cities as old and beautiful as this.'

The line of cars had halted temporarily by the Old Market Hall which Maxon was frantically photographing out of the window.

'No, we never did. Grace came with her girl-friends a few times but the family never did.' He turned quickly to look back down the street. 'Anna, there's a sea-food restaurant that looks real good.'

'Ok, ok.' The traffic moved again and before long they were parking in a short-stay lot. She pulled her bag off the back seat and they got out. As they began to walk down Pride Hill and on to Castle Street towards the imposing stone edifice of the Library, she picked up the thread again. 'So where did you go for vacations?'

'Um, the same round each year, I guess. You know, Hawaii for two weeks in the summer and then we had the beach house on the Jersey Shore, so when we were kids we spent the summer there, although dad went back to Philly during the week. That was fun. Then in the fall we'd go up to the Poconos for a weekend, or up to New Hampshire maybe, and then skiing in the Cascades in the winter – usually there, sometimes Aspen. Oh, and the Kentucky Derby, that sort of thing. It was the same most years. Is that the castle?'

'No, the castle is on the other side, you can't see it from the road, but it's worth a visit when you come. That's the library – used to be a school.'

'Is that where we're going?'

'No, the archives used to be there but now they have their own building next door.' Anna persisted, 'So, what else did you all do?'

'The round, you know. Opera and concerts in Philly and New York over the winter, gallery openings, major baseball games, all that, mostly with the same bunch of people. Can we just stop for a second so I can get water?'

When he came out of the shop, Anna asked, 'No travel abroad, then?'

'Dad is kind of super-scared of foreign stuff – food, water, rest-rooms. I don't know why – I just always accepted it. I didn't know what abroad was in any real sense – just what I'd seen in movies. India was a total revelation when I went there, but this,' he waved his arm around almost knocking down an elderly man on a walker, 'this is where I come from. It's gorgeous but what makes it so extra thrilling is it's where I kind of belong!'

'Well, we're here,' Anna said. 'Let's see what Pandora's box will let fly at us,' and they turned off the road and walked through the archway to the Shropshire Archives.

'I don't mean to be rude,' Maxon said, as they glanced appreciatively at the pebbled roundel of Shropshire set in the pavement, 'but sometimes I don't know what on earth you're talking about.'

8

Anna signed them in and they stood for a moment looking round. She had been here before and was happy to come back. The modern building had been simply but elegantly designed to make optimal use of the space, and the chestnut surfaces of the long tables and cabinets glowed invitingly. Because he asked, Anna showed Maxon the microfiche system which had photographed the census records and the reading machines that looked like early computers, but she had switched to the internet to conduct the census search itself. He sat beside her, notebook and ballpoint in hand.

On the 1891 census Grace Thwaite was quickly found and her husband, the head of house, was listed as William Henry, solicitor. Jane was not born yet. Anna made a note of the address. Maxon was craning towards the computer screen, that little worried frown between his eyes. She entered Robert Theophilus Thwaite and found that he was married to Emily and had two children aged four and six months. He was described as an assistant bank manager. Again, Anna wrote down his address. She had pointed out the ages of all parties and they worked out their years of birth. Robert was the older brother but both men, William Henry and Robert, were in their late twenties. Maxon asked Anna to order all relevant birth, marriage and death certificates for his dossier. He was completely engrossed in the process, she observed, and even forgot at times to observe the considerable dimensions of his personal space. She didn't mind him crowding her since he was oblivious to what he was doing, in fact, it was comforting in the same way that Bobble leaning against her leg was when she sat down at her own kitchen table.

'It was definitely Robert Theophilus as the father on Jane's death certificate,' Maxon said, his face lit softly by the screen, 'I can't understand it.'

'It can't be that Grace and Robert were married previously because Jane is too young. It is a mystery but we just need to keep digging. It's amazing what stories come out of ancestral records but you have to piece things together. Let's just keep going?'

'Ok. What next?'

'I'm interested in these addresses. Maybe we could go and take a look at where William Henry and Robert lived? They're in substantial middle-class professions so their houses may still be there.'

'That would be great. I could take photos.' Again, Maxon reminded her a little of Bobble, flapping about in sudden excitement. She was surprised not to feel irritated but rather amused.

The archivist was happy to help and to show them maps but found that Chirk Street, William Henry's domicile with Grace, was no longer standing. The whole area had been bull-dozed for an industrial park in the 1960's. 'If you leave it with me I'll see if I can find some photographs or drawings of the street and have them ready for your next visit to the area. I'll email you, Mrs Ames.' He gave them a photocopied modern street map of Shrewsbury and circled the street where Robert Thwaite's house stood. 'That would be a very desirable residence,' he said, 'you'd have to be better paid than an assistant bank manager to afford that now.'

It was almost one o'clock and Anna was desperate for something to eat but she could see from the zeal in Maxon's eyes that they would have to visit Robert's house first. Mount Airy was on a rise over-looking the river and was lined on either side with attractive double-fronted stone built villas. Anna drove slowly while Maxon read out numbers. It wasn't easy, most houses had names and the numbers had to be guessed, but finally they drew up outside Mulberry House with the correct number and saw that the tree it was named for, or a more recent planting, still shaded the extensive front lawn. Maxon was ecstatic. They got out of the car and crossed the road to get a better photograph of the large detached house.

'Can we go look round?'

Anna smiled at his enthusiasm. 'We can try.' They walked up the drive to the front porch, which reminded her of a church vestibule, and rang the bell. The door was opened by a middle-aged Asian woman wearing black trousers and a flowing patterned top.

'Yes?'

'Please excuse us for bothering you,' Anna said, 'but we think this may be one of this young man's family homes from the nineteenth century. He's come from America to look up his ancestors.'

The woman smiled at Maxon. 'Yes, it's quite old. We've looked at the deeds and it was built, as all this street was, in 1882.' There was an awkward pause. 'I'm sorry I can't invite you in to look round but we have guests.'

'No, of course, we understand.' Anna pulled out her Harts card and gave it to the woman. 'I'm a probate researcher with Harts in Birmingham. Would it be possible to just photograph the house from the back? This is Maxon Blake and he's putting together a dossier for his parents' pearl wedding anniversary as a surprise.'

'Of course. I'll walk round with you.'

They went through a wrought iron gate next to what must have been a carriage house and was now a four-car garage and into a garden so large it could have been a park. Everything was clipped and mown and looking impressive. The house rose in four storeys of grey stone with a terrace accessed by French windows from what must be a drawing room. Anna glanced up at the small top-storey windows and decided that Robert's family would have been sufficiently well-off to have several live-in servants.

'Of course, the conservatory is new. The old one had to be pulled down but I think we kept the character.'

'Yes, it's beautiful,' Anna said politely.

'It just blows my mind.' Maxon finally spoke. 'To think my family lived here. My great great-grandmother probably took tea on this lawn with her brother-in-law and his wife and kids.'

The woman smiled and glanced at her watch. Anna thanked her, shook her hand, as did Maxon, and they left.

'Lunch?'

She re-parked and they walked back to the seafood restaurant that he'd spotted on their way up the hill. While they waited for their food she wondered what his thoughts and impressions were. He had been quiet since leaving Mount Airy. When their food came, grilled salmon for her, super-food salad and coujons of sole for him, she quizzed him gently.

'I don't know what to think,' he said, staring out of the window. 'The house has kind of made it real for me. Going there was amazing. But I just don't get the name-switch thing.'

'No.' Anna didn't say it, but she also didn't get how an assistant bank manager of a minor district bank could afford to live in such a house as they had just seen at such a young age. She decided to dig a little further back. For Robert to have a house like this (and perhaps William Henry's had been no less grand) there must have been family money. Grace had said as much to Jane. Anna would have to get one of the brother's birth certificates to discover their father's name and see if there was a Will which would shed some light on the source of the family's wealth. For all she knew Grace's family might also have been wealthy but her maiden name had been temporarily lost.

They wanted to get back to Birmingham in time for a late afternoon class that Maxon had, so after they had eaten they set off. They drove in silence for a while but finally Anna could not resist the distraction of conversation. She was only too aware that an empty house was waiting.

'So, what about you?' she smiled at her passenger. 'Did you take the Harvard route, too?

'Not really.' His buoyant mood evaporated.

'I'm sorry, I was being nosy. Just ignore the question.'

'No, it's ok. It's not like I ever forget it.' He twisted his eyebrows comically at her as Ellis might do and for a second she saw a different side to him. 'You know every family has a screw-up? Well, I'm it.'

'I find that hard to believe.'

'Oh, no, really, believe it. Here's the sorry tale. I hated grade school and goofed off as much as I could so dad took me out of regular school and put me in a military academy.' He rummaged in his bag and brought out two sticks of gum, offering her one. She shook her head.

'A military academy? What? How old were you?' Anna was shocked.

'It's what they do with the kids that disappoint. I must have been, say twelve, when I went. You don't have military academies here?' He popped the gum in his mouth.

'Not for kids!'

'So then I was the smallest fish in a pond stocked with big scary delinquents, druggies and drop-outs. All from rich families, of course. All boys. Military discipline, you can imagine. To make it worse I found that even if I tried hard I was a dope.'

'Oh come on. That's harsh.'

'No, it's the simple truth. Someone has to be bottom of the class and that was me.'

'How long were you there?' Anna glanced at his skinny frame. 'How did you cope?'

He pushed back against the seat and grunted. 'I heard a comic say on tv the other day that he got through his miserable school by making the bullies laugh. I didn't make them, they just did it anyway. I'm not proud of this, Anna, but I bought them off.'

'How do you mean?'

'All the usual ways you can get by weren't available – I wasn't especially good at sport, I was useless at lessons so no-one wanted to copy my work, I suppose I had no social skills, so I used the only thing I had. Money.' He scoffed at himself. 'Dad was tough on me but never stinted on my allowance. Most of the other kids had real strict parents who kept them short – probably thought they'd buy drugs, which they would've. I wasn't so stupid as to just hand it out but I kind of rationed it to kids who were half way decent to me or at least didn't try to flush my head down the john. It got to be routine. As I got older I was the one who could get the baseball tickets, sub the kids who'd gone through their own cash too fast, and then dad got me a car before anyone else had one and I told myself that it was my company they wanted but I knew all along I was just the chauffeur. Got me through.'

They were turning on to the M6 south now and the traffic had slowed. 'What did you do after you left there? Did you go to college?' She was beginning to warm to Maxon. He had clearly had a difficult time and it explained his anxious, self-effacing persona, but he was not self-pitying. There was a kind of wry humour in his account which she admired.

'At the academy the only subject I'd been half-way good at was art. I loved it – the peace of the room, the smell of the materials, and the teacher was, like, part-human. So I persuaded dad to let me go to art school. He was disappointed but he had an aunt who was an artist, a well-known one, and she put a bit of pressure on him. I guess he thought that I might be successful in that way, which kind of worked with the family ethos because they like to have a finger in the cultural pie.' He sighed. 'But the real reason he let me do it was because by this time Grace was flying so high. She had finished at Harvard in the top percentile of her class and an investment banker on Wall Street was just waiting for her to drop off that bough into his hands. I think dad knew him, too. So, you know, she was keeping the family honour going so I could be allowed to be a bit alternative. I think mom even thought it gave the family a bit of soul, you know, if Maxon is an artist we're obviously not bringing up our kids to be vulgar money-grabbers, so aren't we fine.' His tone had become bitter.

Anna was intrigued. There was nothing about Maxon that said 'art student'. She chided herself for her stereotypical thinking. At junction 9 the traffic came to a complete halt. 'So how did that go? Art college, I mean.'

'It was ok. But what had helped me at private school, the money, the name, became a liability. Those art college kids were mostly anti-establishment, anti-capitalist, and so I got flack for that. So, it was a little lonely although I did make a couple of friends who were oddballs, too.'

Anna thought about Ken Dawkins and his thwarted artistic development. 'Did you find you had talent?' The traffic now began to move fairly briskly and she felt relieved that they should get back to Birmingham in time.

'Ha!' His laugh was a bark. 'That was the thing. At the end of the junior year dad and mum came to the College to talk to my teachers. I'd shown them my work, of course, but they didn't even expect to know what to think. Who does about art? They saw one after the other, it was like Parent Teacher evening at school, and I went with them to each interview. The instructors tried to fudge, tried to be kind, but mom and dad kept getting the same message – tries hard but no talent. I wasn't surprised, I knew it myself, I could see what some of the others were doing and I was just not in their league. So they stopped paying the tuition and I dropped out.'

'But surely, they could have let you finish? There are lots of jobs you could have gone for with an art and design degree? Website design, commercial art from computer graphics – well, I don't know, but I would have thought so.' Anna realised that she was becoming ridiculously indignant and told herself to cool it – Maxon didn't need her mumsy protection.

'No, you're right. But something else had happened. That was a month after Grace died. They were crazy with grief and disappointment. And it hit me hard, too. She was always good to me, Grace. She never put me down. So the family kind of fell apart and I got a job at a café in Philly as a bus boy and we just didn't see each other for years.'

They were turning into the inner city now and Anna asked if he wanted to be dropped off near Summer Row. He picked up his bag from the floor and thanked her politely for the day's outing asking if they could go again next Wednesday. They made the arrangement and she drew to a halt by the curb. He was about to get out when she leaned across and touched his arm. Her conscience was bothering her. 'I hope it didn't upset you to talk like that to me?'

His rare smile broke out as he turned to her. 'No. As a matter of fact, it felt good.'

'You had a tough time.'

'I know, I feel sorry for me, too!' he laughed and manoeuvred his long body out. 'See you!'

There was no point in going back to Harts so she turned for home, her heart sinking. To pick up her spirits she thought about making a shopping list, maybe she could go and see Joan, maybe her dad would still be in the shed working on his latest magazine.

But the house was empty and silent. Ellis must have taken Bobble out with him. A ripple of panic zig-zagged through her as she texted her son. Where was he? Was he ok? When was he coming home? She got a cold beer out of the fridge while she waited for his response. The phone beeped and she read that he was at the club. He had taken Bobble round to Mike's and would pick him up later on his way home. He had eaten. Not to worry. She phoned Faye. She had gone with Tash and a couple of others into the city centre. Didn't know when she'd be home. She phoned her father. Diane answered saying he was napping. Did Anna want to hear the new noise that Charles was making? Not really, but she listened anyway and said something. She finished the beer and wondered about food for herself but she wasn't hungry and it was too much trouble.

She pulled her laptop towards her and ordered William Henry Thwaite's birth certificate. Then she made some expense claim notes, checked her emails, none of which she could be bothered replying to, and it was still only six o'clock.

Joan must have had her phone switched off but Kimi answered. She sounded as fed up as Anna. 'Why don't you come out here?' she said. 'I'd come over to you but I've got a mare foaling, you remember Beauty – Beautiful Dreamer? I can't leave her.'

It had been dry for so long apart from sprinkles of rain that evaporated almost before they touched the ground that the hedges had lost their sparkle and the field grass was beginning to fade to a tawny yellow in patches. Kimi was sitting on the wooden fence that divided the stables from the farmyard. She had a bottle of wine in her hand. She was wearing her home clothes of grubby jeans and a pulled-out-of-shape T shirt but her arms were tanned and muscled. Anna climbed up beside her and took the proffered bottle, swigging from it. Dust motes circled in the air and mosquitoes were beginning to pay attention to the fresh flesh. A muck-heap was steaming in a corner of the stable-yard and the mosquitoes were not the only insects having a great time. Kimi was, as ever, oblivious.

'How are you doing?' Kimi was the most unsentimental person Anna knew so there was no pity behind the query.

'Crap. I've got a new client though.' She thought about Maxon. 'Buckling under the weight of his mega-successful family.'

Kimi took the bottle back and had a long drink. 'Well, as you know I can identify with that. Bound to be a skeleton in the closet like you found in ours.'

'A crypt full of them.'

'Yes!' Kimi laughed. 'They're still at it, locking horns and mad as hell that no-one has overall control as it turns out.' She looked at Anna seriously. 'You were so great. I'll never forget what you did for dad and me.'

Anna thought of Gerald Draycott, shrinking inside his expensive suit but brave to the last. 'I was very fond of him.' Anna took the bottle away from Kimi. 'I'm even getting used to you, bossy as you are.' Kimi chuckled. 'Oh, I've never asked, what happened about my birthday thing. I hope you didn't cancel?'

'No, we went. Michelle brought a friend to take your ticket. Obviously we were a bit subdued over the meal with what had happened but Sara Pascoe was great. Good choice.'

'I'm glad. How did you get on with the others?'

Kimi jumped down from the fence and wedged the empty bottle carefully where she could retrieve it later. 'Let's go and check on Beautiful Dreamer currently experiencing a bit of a nightmare.' Anna joined her and they walked through to a large loosebox and peered over the door. 'They like to be alone when they're foaling because they're prey animals and it feels safer,' Kimi whispered. The bay horse was gleaming with sweat and grunting. 'She looks like she'll be a little while yet.' She pulled out into the yard a couple of folding chairs.

'I did worry a bit about how you'd all get on.'

Kimi laughed. 'Well, Suzy is an airhead and Michelle is a bit worthy but Briony and I got on ok.'

'Did you?'

'Yeah. We went for a drink afterwards, just the two of us, and she told me about what had happened to her in Chicago. I know you know.' Anna was surprised – Briony hated to talk about herself. 'So we've met up a few times since. She's been out here.'

'Does she want to learn to ride?'

'I haven't persuaded her so far but I wouldn't discount it. At least she'd have long enough legs.'

'That's hardly my fault.'

Kimi stood up. 'I'll get another bottle.'

'No,' Anna said, 'I've got to go. Ell will be home soon and I'm already a bit misty.' They walked back to the house where Anna's car was parked. 'How's Rhea?'

'She's up and down. Last time I saw her she hardly spoke but the time before we had a game of scrabble and she seemed fine.'

They hugged briefly and Anna drove home more slowly than usual, aware of a slight drag in her brain from the alcohol. As she drove, she mulled over Kimi's expression when she had talked about Briony – it had been soft, almost tender. Since Briony herself was a very tough cookie indeed, it was intriguing. Anna had only been home for half an hour when Ellis appeared with Bobble. She had been ready to make a snack for him, maybe beans on toast or a sausage sandwich but he had gone straight up to his room saying he had something he wanted to do. Bobble was outside on the patio gnawing a bone. She pulled a bottle of Malbec from the wine rack and uncorked it.

It was cooler now in the garden and darkness was sliding across the sky like hangar doors closing. Bats were wheeling around the edges of the house and she found that the routine of raising the glass to her lips, sipping, re-filling, sipping was making her feel better. The sharp-clawed beast in her gut relaxed its grip and in the pause between peace and the unconsciousness which would come, she picked up the empty bottle and glass and called Bobble to go with her. The lock was fiddly on the back door but she managed it and walking very carefully she climbed the stairs, pulled off her clothes and fell into bed.

The next morning her throat felt scorched and she was late getting downstairs. Ellis had gone to school but the neat stack of his dishes by the sink meant he had had breakfast. Anna groaned and sank into a chair then groaned again and stood up to make coffee.

The front door crashed shut and Faye appeared. She had half-moons of smudged mascara under her eyes and her hair was dishevelled. As she swept past Anna to the fridge she smelled something like seaweed. Anna's eyes were gritty and her gorge rose as Faye peeled off three slices of bacon and slapped them in a pan. She had not greeted her mother.

'Faye? Have you been out all night?' Anna's nerves were already on edge and the sight of her daughter looking like a street-walker was not helping.

'No, I've got a milk round.'

'Don't be rude to me. Where have you been?'

Faye lifted the bread out of its wrapper and sawed off two slices which she put over the bacon in the pan to soak up the fat. Anna almost gagged. 'I'm nearly nineteen. Just don't start.'

'I don't care how old you are – you should have told me!'

'Like you care.'

Anna was furious. 'What? When have I done anything but care? What is the matter with you?'

Faye whipped round from the stove and faced her, spatula in hand. 'What's the matter with *you*?' she demanded. 'We all miss him, you know, he was our father. You act like you're such a tragedy queen -'

'I do not!' Anna yelled, interrupting her. 'I am going to work, I'm shopping, cooking, cleaning - with no bloody help from you I might say!'

'So where were you when Ellis won his match last week? Did you even remember about it? Where were you when Pops moved out? You're in your own world, you don't know what's going on. And now this!' Faye strode over to the recycling bin and picked up three empty wine bottles waving them at her. 'Very bloody mature, mother.'

'How dare you!' Anna's head throbbed and she was choking on her words she was so angry. 'I'm not the only one in this house that drinks wine! Don't think you can get out of how you behaved like a slut staying out all night by trying to lay guilt on me!' She had gone too far and she knew it. The words had tumbled out before she could stop them.

'So I'm a slut now, am I?' Faye said quietly. 'Ok. You might as well know this then. I'm going to Edinburgh this weekend with Boz.'

'What? You don't even like him! Who else is going?'

'No-one. *We* are going.'

'Why?'

'To have fun, Mum. You know, that thing that *you* only read about in books?'

'You can't afford it.'

'Boz can.' Faye put the sandwich together and stuck it on a plate to take up to her room. 'And if you ever call me a slut again that'll be the last time you see me. Get a grip, Mum.'

Anna sat at the table shaking. What Faye said made no sense. She was not behaving like a tragedy queen, she was always texting them and checking on them. No, it was unfair, horrible. Faye was often challenging, but this? The ugly row had gone from nothing to catastrophic in minutes. The front door opened quietly and closed quietly. George came into the kitchen.

'Hello, love, I thought you'd have gone to work. Shall I make you a cup of tea?' When she didn't answer he sat down at the table. 'What's the matter?'

'Faye just called me a tragedy queen and said that I've been neglecting everyone and I called her a slut because she stayed out all night and she's going to Edinburgh with Boz and she said if I ever call her that again she'll walk out.'

George rubbed his beard and then his whole head. 'Oh dear.'

'I'm trying so hard to hold it together, Dad.'

'I know, love.'

'I'm all right at work, I'm all right out of this house. I just can't bear to be here.' She looked round wildly. 'It's when I get home. It's so empty – I can't bear it. Ellis is out most of the time, Faye is out all the time, you're not here, oh, sorry, I'm not trying to make you feel guilty - '

George took her hand and stroked it. 'I had no idea you felt like this, Anna. Don't worry too much about what Faye said – she's never pulled her punches.'

'What can I do if she's never here?' she wailed.

George made her a cup of tea anyway and put it by her. 'Would it help if I moved back in?'

'I couldn't expect you to do that.' She looked at her father's face and saw that far from regretful he looked relieved.

'To be honest, Annie, it would be a blessing for me. Diane is a wonderful woman, of course, but we're both used to being on our own and it's becoming a bit of a strain. Little things like I want to sit up in bed reading for a while to get to sleep and she says she can't sleep with the light on so then, if I can't read, I can't sleep. Then she does watch some rubbish on television. I was very surprised to be honest. All the soaps. I wouldn't mind but there's nowhere for me to go. I've got nothing to do at her place. I can't even write because I haven't got my stuff around me, my shed. Peace.'

'Won't she mind?'

'I think she'll be as relieved as me. She snapped at me the other day when I was doing my Mindfulness meditation in the living room when she wanted to watch Corrie. It's too small a space for us. I feel trapped and she feels invaded.'

'I would love it if you would come back, Dad, we all would.' Anna gripped his hands gratefully.

'I'll move back today. I'll tell Diane you need me. She'll be pleased.'

As Anna drove to work she told herself that this would be where things would begin to get better. Having George at home would be almost like going back to normal for Faye and Ellis, too, and they could start to mend their family. But underneath that thought she was sickeningly aware of another, much darker one. If George was at home taking care of things she wouldn't have to be. If she needed to go to bed early with a bottle, she could. But only, of course, on the nights that she felt the claws of that troll in her belly.

9

She spent the morning working on finding Janet Dawkins, aka Brown, and, as it turned out, Cooper. She was still alive and living in Great Yarmouth. Anna checked Google Earth and saw that she lived in a tower block half a mile from the station so if Ken wanted to see her he could go by train. She phoned Ken but couldn't get hold of him so left a voice-mail asking him to contact her on her work number when he could.

As she was walking past Steve's office, on her way out for lunch, he appeared at his doorway. 'Anna.' She halted, glanced at him briefly, and then looked away. 'I'm sorry but we have to talk. Please. Let's go somewhere and get a sandwich.'

'I haven't got long,' Anna lied.

'Ok. We can go to that little café on the wharf.'

After the dimness and air-conditioning of the office the sun hit her face hard and she was glad to put on her sunglasses. They walked side by side maintaining at least an arm's length between them. She was far too aware of him, his height, his long legs trying to keep pace with her short ones, his long brown toes poking out from his sandal straps and flexing with each step. She made her brain be empty of him, focussing only on the scene around them. The little café was crowded so they took their orders outside and sat on metal chairs against the red-brick wall and watched the narrowboats moored in the basin.

He didn't seem to be hungry and neither was she. 'How are you?' he asked.

'Oh, you know.' She felt that implied that she wanted to talk so she added. 'Busy.'

'Ted says you've got a rich American client.' He was trying to make small talk.

'Yep.' She had to say something. 'You? Is Alice ok?'

'Faye's round at our house a lot so she likes that. We did pop round to yours a couple of times but there was no-one there.'

'My dad's moving back in. He and Diane are getting on each other's nerves.'

'Oh, good – I mean, good that he's - um.'

She took a bite of her sandwich and found it became a ball of clay in her mouth. She couldn't spit it out and she couldn't swallow it.

'I want to tell you about what's been going on with Cathy.'

'You don't have to,' she said, so quickly that the clag in her mouth made her choke and she spat it out into a napkin.

'I want to. She does want to move back here for career reasons but she also has been talking about the two of us, well three with Alice, getting back together.' He sighed and dropped his head. 'She says that she feels bad about leaving the way she did. Got her priorities wrong.'

Anna stood up. 'You know what, Steve, I hope you'll be very happy. I have to go now. I told you I didn't have much time.'

'No, Anna, I haven't finished.'

'Well, I have.'

She picked up her bag and walked quickly away, pushing rudely past a group of German tourists and almost running along the towpath until she could turn into Harts, up the stairs and into the women's toilets. She stood, shaking, at the wash basin and then splashed her face with cold water. She knew Steve would assume she had run off because she felt rejected, jealous, abandoned. There was no way he could guess the truth and no way she would tell him. If he and Cathy got back together they might move away with Alice and then he might get another job and then she would never have to look at him again. Maybe then life would be bearable.

It was so good to come home at the end of the day to the sight of George scuttling round the kitchen humming and the background noise of a cricket commentary on Radio 5 Sports Extra. 'I'm making a salmon terrine,' he announced, 'I found the recipe in a ladies' magazine at the dentist last week.' He paused at the cupboard and felt among the rarely used crockery at the back. 'I like the sound of it.'

Anna poured herself a beer. 'It's so good to have you here, Dad.' He patted the top of her head with a plastic pack of salmon as he zoomed past. 'Do you know what the kids are doing?' She had changed the question at the last second. Being in the kitchen with her father making a meal was so familiar that she had almost asked the routine question, 'Where's Harry?'

'Ellis will be back from the club about 7.00 so he'll be here, but Faye has other plans.' He scrabbled in the utensil drawer and pulled out a potato masher and a grater. Anna's heart sank but she was still smarting from Faye's words so it was perhaps a good thing to have a cooling-off period. He started chopping things. 'Tomorrow night Rani is coming with Ashok to start up the poetry nights again so is there any chance you could join us?'

Getting back to normal. 'Of course I'll be there, Dad.'

He stopped chopping and looked at her. 'It might be hard.'

'Just don't give me anything emotional to read. A poem about alien life on a galaxy far away would probably be about right.' She finished the beer and looked at the fridge.

He grunted. 'I can do you a werewolf in hedge fund manager clothing, I'm sorry to say. The things young people write. I printed it off from an e-magazine in case Ellis comes.'

'Anything.' He had his back to her. She got up and moved to the fridge to get another beer. 'Is it ok if I go out into the garden and chill for a bit?' He waved his knife in assent.

After dinner Ellis took Bobble out to meet Mike and go to the park and George disappeared into the shed. Anna cleared up the kitchen and placed her laptop on the table. She had done nothing about Rosa's request to find her brother so looking for him should help pass an hour or two.

She started by simply keying in his name and date of birth on the website for electoral registers. He was not there which could mean several things, one of which was that he was not entitled to vote. That could mean, given what Rosa had said, that he was in jail. He had not died. It would be hard to track him if he was incarcerated as she knew prisons did not give out inmate lists and prisoners were frequently moved. She sat and puzzled over it. Steve could have found him. With his Home Office databases it would be no problem but she would never ask. Perhaps Dean had been reported in the local paper for a crime, but then, what local paper, he could be anywhere.

Idly, to do something, she Googled him. There were various people by the name of Dean Kelly – an Irish magician, a footballer in the minor leagues (wrong age) - but to pass the time she went through each page, the references getting more and more obscure. On the fourth page a Youtube reference was cited. It was probably not her Dean Kelly but she exited Google and went into Youtube to see what might be there. As soon as she had keyed in his name a video came up. It was grainy mobile phone footage of two men in hoods and masks holding up a corner shop. The shakiness of the video and the partial vision indicated that a customer was hiding and filming. As she watched, something blocked the view of the person holding the phone and then she clearly saw one of the hooded men being hit very hard with what looked like a metal bar. He crumpled and the other one dashed past the phone-camera and, presumably, away. She looked at the tag. 'Phillip Jones and Dean Kelly attempting to rob the Victoria Street corner shop in Bilston. Behind you, losers!' The date was January 18th of this year. Even if it was Rosa's brother she was no nearer to finding him. She didn't even know whether he was the one who'd been hit or the one who got away. She would have to find out which court would hold the hearings for that district and then go through the records but it was a long shot and very time-consuming.

She got up and walked to the wine rack trying to decide what to do. She had not seen Rosa since Harry's funeral and Rosa had tactfully not bothered her about her brother. She looked out of the window with the bottle in her hand. It was only nine o'clock.

Rosa answered her phone immediately. Yes, she was on the boat and would be glad to see Anna. 'Shall I come over to you?' she asked, but Anna needed to be out and the idea of seeing Rosa's home piqued her interest.

It only took a few minutes to find a parking place where Rosa had suggested and then a few minutes more to walk the couple of hundred yards to the third boat at the moorings. Knowing Rosa it was no surprise to see that it was traditionally painted with roses and castles and on the roof was a small garden of herbs and pelargoniums. At the porthole windows Rosa had stretched white cotton doilies and pretty lace nets at the others. On the bank she had even planted some columbine and sweet peas which had threaded themselves through the hawthorn hedge. She was sitting in the stern with a book and a cup of tea but put them down when Anna appeared. The summer solstice had passed weeks ago and Anna noticed that the light was beginning to fade. The summer, this cruel summer, was turning. She climbed carefully on to the deck taking Rosa's hand and sat in the other chair. Rosa disappeared into the cabin and then re-appeared with a can of insect repellent in her hand. She passed it to Anna with a wry smile.

It was so good to see her. She had changed her hair dye because it was now an emerald green and Anna commented approvingly. 'I use whatever's on offer,' Rosa said. 'I like this one, though.' They watched and waved as a hire boat chugged by. 'How have you been?'

'It helps to keep busy.' Anna paused. 'I've looked for your brother as you asked. I'm afraid it isn't brilliant news.'

Rosa sucked breath in rapidly and put a hand on her heart. 'Is he dead?'

'No, not at all. But I think he may be in prison.'

'That's not a surprise. I don't suppose you know what for?'

'Yes, possibly.' She told Rosa about the video, which she would almost certainly not have seen since she didn't own a computer, and the date. Rosa jumped up so quickly that the boat rocked on its moorings and Anna put out a hand to steady herself.

'So he could be in the area – I mean in the Black Country or in Birmingham!'

'He could still be on remand or even on bail but it's hard to find that stuff out.'

'No, not for me.'

'What do you mean?'

'I have a friend who – well, I won't tell you what the friend does in the courts but she could find out, I know she could, now I've got a crime and a date.' Rosa's smile faded. 'I just don't know if he'll see me.'

'Well, you won't know till you try.'

'Anna? I know it's a lot to ask. Will you come with me?' Anna remembered another prison visit years before; it had been one of the most distressing experiences of her life. But this was Rosa, Harry's last companion.

'If they'll let me, of course I will.'

Rosa smiled and got up to hug her and it felt so good to be folded into the warm arms that she almost whispered, 'Don't stop.' What a lovely mother Rosa would make and yet there had never been any mention of a man. As though on cue, she heard Len's voice from the towpath. Rosa released her and sat down. She looked neither pleased nor irritated to see him.

'Hiya Sis, why're you here?'

'Just visiting Rosa.'

He stood on the bank with his legs planted wide apart as though he was in danger of falling into the water. Anna noted that he looked considerably fresher than the last time she'd seen him. He was wearing a black T shirt with a spaceship printed on the front and jeans which still had their original colour. But it was his hair that caught her attention. She hadn't realised that it was so thick and wavy - every time she'd seen him it had been plastered to his head with grease. Maybe he'd even had it cut. It was not a totally successful make-over as he was also wearing plastic sandals and his toes were crossed, no doubt from their mother neglecting to buy him shoes that fitted as he grew, and were edged with horny yellow nails. But, he was trying. 'You look nice,' she said.

He looked thoughtful. 'You can't get three of us on the back.'

For a moment Anna didn't understand what he meant but then realised he wanted her to go so he could sit where she was. It was true that Rosa and Len were much bigger than average and the three of them in a small space would not work. She glanced at Rosa to see what she wanted. Rosa stood up.

'Just a minute Len, I'll walk Anna down to her car.' It was a tactful compromise. As Len put out his hand for Anna to jump off the boat she was almost knocked back by the acrid stench of cheap deodorant. Far, far too much of a good thing. Did he carry an emergency top-up can in his pocket?

They strolled back down the towpath. 'Is he being a nuisance?' she asked, feeling disloyal but also responsible.

'No, he's all right,' said Rosa. 'He just hangs around a bit, plays his flute, pushes off.' She glanced back at him. 'The other boat people like it. Little bit of free music. He's not a bad player.'

'You know he fancies you?'

'I've no time for that sort of thing,' said Rosa neutrally. She stopped at Anna's car. 'I'll tell you when I find Dean, ok?'

There was no-one in the kitchen so Anna picked up her laptop and the bottle of Merlot from the fridge and climbed the stairs. Poor old Len, did he know he hadn't got a chance? She thought about George and Diane, such good companions and such poor housemates. She got ready for bed and propped up the pillows to do one last check of her emails. If there was nothing of interest she could scan the sports news. Reading wasn't enough anymore to take the edge off and in any case reading fiction was unpredictable. You never knew what little incendiary might be waiting to blow up your chance of sleep. Sports stories were just engaging enough to distract but not exciting enough to keep her awake. Currently she was trying to become familiar with the tennis world for Ellis. It wasn't working well. Facts learned yesterday had evaporated by today. Her mind seemed to be acting like Bobble and dashing about without control or retention.

But there was an email of interest. The librarian from Shrewsbury Record Office had found a photograph of Chirk Street before it had been demolished and had attached it. It was in grayscale and showed a row of terraced houses of the poorest sort, their front doors opening directly on to a narrow pavement and a cobbled street. Anna stared at it. Perhaps this was one end and the better houses were at the other end? She turned her laptop to the bedside lamp and enlarged the photo. Very faintly she could make out a number 32. Grace and William Henry's house had been number 30. She was looking at it. Grace had certainly not told her daughter about this.

Anna shut down her computer and put it on the floor by the bed. She turned the lamp off and picked up the last slug of wine which she had been saving. The curtains were open and as she lay back on the heaped pillows she let her eyes rest on the silhouette of the ivy trembling in the cooler air and beyond it the roofline of the houses opposite, lit faintly yellow by the street lights. Above was a navy sky. She sipped. What was the truth about the Thwaite family? There were now two mysteries. Why was Robert's name on Jane's death certificate when her mother was married to William Henry? Why was Robert living in such affluence at the same time as his brother was, apparently, in penury? If there was family money, as she might soon discover when the will came, why would one brother be favoured over the other?

She put the bottle down on the bedside table, gratefully aware of a creeping numbness fogging her brain. She slipped one pillow over the side of the bed and sank down into the other. Maybe William Henry had died when Grace was pregnant and Robert, the successful banker, had become a guardian of his sister-in-law's child? Had she checked when William Henry had died? She couldn't remember. She closed her eyes and let the mist overwhelm her.

After her riding lesson on Friday Anna was sore, irritable and hot. Kimi had made her ride bareback to learn a sitting trot and it had not been fun. All she wanted when she got home was a long cool shower and an even longer collapse in the garden. Ted had been difficult at work, possibly his haemorrhoids playing up, and it had been impossible to avoid seeing Steve in the staff meeting that had taken place at 2.00. He had not attempted to speak to her which was a relief but it was difficult to ignore his presence. She would go straight upstairs to wash the day away.

But when she walked into the kitchen Rani was sitting at the table while George put together a cold spread. She had forgotten that Rani would be coming since she so rarely did. Anna had known her almost all her life and was fond of her but she was not the most tactful of women. Thank goodness Joan would be coming to the poetry evening, too.

'Hi Rani, nice to see you, is Ashok here?' Rani smiled and pulled out the chair next to her for Anna to sit down.

'He's putting the selection in order,' George said.

'Are Ellis and Faye coming?' George shook his head, trying to soften his disappointment with a smile.

Anna felt sad, too. After Harry's diagnosis, when everything had changed, she had taken what she thought was the central role in the family. George was there to help but she felt that for the last few years she had been the one holding everything together. Now, since Harry's death, she understood how he had been far more at the centre of the children's lives that she in some ways. He was almost always at home, he was always available for easy, sometimes silent, company. He would happily watch whatever they wanted to watch on television. He wouldn't ask them about their day, criticise their behaviour, keep track of where they were. He was not the same as he had been but he was still their dad and memories of affection and fun clung around him. He would even make them laugh sometimes.

And there was another way he glued them all together. Looking out for him had made them feel needed as working parts of the family machine. Now each person seemed disconnected from the others. Neither Faye nor Ellis was really interested in poetry but they had come to the sessions, she now saw, not for their grandfather's sake, but because it was where the family was – mum and dad. Now there was just her she wasn't enough. The house felt empty to them, too. They wanted to be somewhere else away from Harry's absence. It would help that George was back but it was too soon for them to make the transition.

She was desperate to shower but Rani's hand patting the chair beside her was insistent. 'I need to get changed,' she said meekly, but sat down.

Rani took one of her hands and chafed it, gazing into her eyes. 'Tell me how you are, darling,' she said. 'I mean how you really are.' Anna could hear her father clearing his throat in warning but Rani was impervious. 'You can talk to me.'

Anna struggled to keep her composure. 'I'm ok,' she managed to croak, 'keeping busy.'

'But you must not bottle up your feelings, my dear. You must let them out.'

'Food will be ready soon,' George said, 'maybe you should get changed now, Anna.'

Rani refused to let go of her hand. 'Such a lovely man,' she went on, 'you must miss him so much.' Anna was vaguely aware that Ashok had come in from the shed. 'But he could not have had a better wife than you were to look after him through his tragic illness.' She leaned towards Anna, her warm brown eyes welling up.

Anna leaped to her feet wrenching her hand free. 'I'm sorry Rani but please just stop this! I know you want to be kind but this is torture for me!'

Rani stood, too. 'That's right!' she said, her eyes shining, 'let it all out.'

Anna stood, rudderless, desperate. 'Dad?' George was with her in a second and had his arm round her shepherding her out of the kitchen while she wailed. She stood sobbing in his arms in the hall half-hearing the sound of Ashok's firm voice over-riding his wife's.

'I'm sorry, love,' he said when she quietened. 'I had a horrible feeling she'd come to, you know, help.'

'That's all right, Dad, I know she means well but I just can't deal with it.'

'You won't have to. When Joan comes I'll call you down if you feel up to it. I think she'll probably have taken herself off by then – poetry's not really her thing.' He patted her shoulder. 'You just go and have a nice shower and sort yourself out. You smell terrible, Annie, so goodness knows what the horse smells like.'

She kissed him on his whiskery cheek.

10

Faye slipped out early on Saturday morning so Anna had no chance to speak to her but George had seen her go and made sure she had money of her own to get back in case of a disruption of any kind.

'You'll never see that again,' Anna yawned, slouched at the kitchen table and blearily aware of another day of brilliant sunshine.

'I don't want her to be put in a compromised position,' George said, making toast. 'She needs to have her own fare home. Everyone does.'

'I wish she hadn't gone. I thought she'd back off at the last minute. What's going on, Dad? Do you think she's been sleeping with him?' Anna drank her coffee and pushed her toast around her plate.

'She's not a child any more, but I don't like it either. If they were in love it would be different but I don't think she is – it's more like she wants to be outrageous.'

'You mean rebellious. Against me.'

Bobble pushed hard against Anna's leg and she absent-mindedly gave him the crust of her toast. She glanced at her dad and saw his eyebrows raised. 'Sorry, wasn't thinking.' The dog crunched once, swallowed and smiled gloopily at her and she realised with a slight start that his face was now above the level of the table when he was sitting on the floor.

'Speaking of bad behaviour, we must get Ellis to take this animal to obedience classes.' Bobble rested his chin on the table and adored her. His brown eyes rolled round the table and then back to her, the whites showing at the edge. 'No more – I mean it, that was just a weak moment.' Bobble wafted his tail happily and she felt the breeze on her bare feet. 'What on earth are you, dog? St Bernard and Shetland pony cross?'

George stood up and took his dishes to the sink. 'Try not to be too hard on Faye when she comes home,' he said. 'Everyone's a bit fragile at the moment.'

But late on Sunday evening Anna was waiting for her daughter in the living room, having checked George's phone left on the kitchen table when she heard that he had a text, so she knew what time Faye would get back. She had been going over Faye's recent behaviour in her mind and becoming more and more indignant. When she heard a key in the door she leaped up - it was clear from the quiet closing of the door that Faye hoped to get up to her room without encountering her mother.

'Just a minute,' Anna said. 'I want a word.'

Faye looked exhausted. 'I can't do this, Mum. Our train was cancelled and the next one was packed so I had to stand in that cruddy bit by the loo for two hours. I'm shattered.'

'It's not a request. Come in here. I'll get you some supper when we're done.'

Faye looked as though she might start shouting but then meekly followed Anna into the living room and sat down, dropping her back-pack on the floor. For a moment Anna felt a pulse of compassion for the girl, pale with weariness as she was, but she hardened her heart.

'Is this going to be a regular thing now?' Faye was silent. 'Having sex with people you hardly even care about? Or is that what you've been doing all summer?' Anna had not planned to speak to Faye like this but now she had started she couldn't stop. 'Maybe for years for all I know. Is this what you get up to on your so-called girly sleep-overs?'

'Mum…'

'I thought you were different. I thought you had some self-respect, Faye.' To Anna's astonishment Faye began to cry. The tears were not noisy, dramatic ones but just a quiet seeping of water from her eyes.

'I didn't do anything with Boz.'

Anna stared at her trying to make sense of this – her depressed pose, her tears, her denial. Was she really that deceitful that she would try to act her way out of this? 'You expect me to believe that when you've been away with him all weekend?'

Faye's demeanour changed in a flash and she erupted, jumping out of her chair. 'Believe what you like! You don't care about me so don't pretend you do!'

'I care about you very much. That's why I can't bear to see you demeaning yourself like this!'

Faye pushed back her hair and almost spat at her mother, '*Demeaning* myself, what sort of word is that? Tell it to Ellis, I'm the thick one, remember? You know what word I understand, don't you, because you think I'm a *slut*! My own mother!'

They were both standing now, Faye a head taller than Anna. Anna tried desperately to control her rage, to pull back from this hideous confrontation. 'If you tell me you didn't sleep with Boz, I believe you,' she said, her voice trembling. 'I want to believe you.'

Faye was silent but the look of contempt in her eyes pierced Anna's heart. 'Well, for your information, I did not have sex with Boz for two reasons. Are you taking notes? One is that he is a pillock. Two, I'm planning on having sex with Jason and Boz didn't like that, not that I care. Ok?' She was shouting now and pushing herself forward so that she was centimetres from Anna, her face crimson with anger. 'Shall I tell you if Jason's going to wear a condom? Would you like to know whether it will be missionary position or a knee trembler? Are you up to speed on whether I wax or not – shall I rate my orgasm for you?'

Anna slapped her daughter's face.

Faye stood stock still for long enough for Anna to see the red marks appear that her fingers had left, then she turned, picked up her backpack and walked up the stairs. Anna collapsed on the floor.

She had never struck either of her children in their whole lives. What was happening to her? Where had that hurricane of rage come from? Yes, Faye had been provocative but Anna was the adult, the mother, the carer. What had come over her? She sat shivering on the floor, incredulous about what had just happened. She tried to re-capture the steps that had led to Faye's outburst and her violence. Had she been so wrong to question the girl? Did other mothers just let this sort of thing go with an indulgent smile? What were the rules? But she knew in her gut that this had been different, not because Faye had taken off for the weekend, but because she herself was different. She had lost control because for a moment she had allowed that sick and savage beast that gnawed at her heart to leap out and speak.

By Wednesday the weather had turned fresher and Maxon was wearing a light sweater over his button-down shirt. They had two appointments, one with the churchwarden at Westbury and one at the Records Office in Shrewsbury.

'How are you?' he asked cheerily as he got in the passenger side of her car.

She wondered how long it would be before the headache pills kicked in. 'Fine,' she said, 'ready to get some more stuff for your dossier?'

'Yes, indeed. I was thinking it would be so cool to find some graves with the family names on in the churchyard.' Anna was grateful for this merry and bright Maxon but she needed to gear up to it.

She turned out of Harts' car park and on to the inner ring-road. 'And we should ask if any of the church furniture, you know the pulpit or a pew or something, was donated by your family. It often happened in late Victorian times that a well-off local family would give something like that to the church in memory of someone who'd died. Sometimes it was even as grand as a new stained-glass window.'

Anna's head felt packed with vacuum cleaner dust. She had to get Maxon talking. 'So did you go back to Shrewsbury for a look round?'

'Oh yes. It was brilliant. You know that Old Market Hall in the square we saw? Well, it's really old but now they use the upstairs for screening films – I mean modern movies. How cool is that?'

'Very cool,' said Anna reflexively, wishing he would just talk and not ask her to respond.

'And then I went into a place that said Music Hall to visit the Tourist Information but it turned out to be a real neat museum with Roman stuff ...' Anna saw again Faye's incredulous, horrified face and felt her own body fill with a silent scream. What was happening to her, what craziness was taking her over? She forced herself to listen to Maxon. '... a four-poster bed from, like, hundreds of years ago with these fantastic curtains and bedspread and, guess what, they'd been made by women around here in the last fifteen years! Beautiful work, so skilled, it just took my breath away.'

They drove in silence for a while and then Maxon laughed. 'I almost told mom and dad that I was doing this. They Skyped me last night. But I really want it to be a surprise.'

Anna thought of the anomalies discovered so far and was glad he had not. 'Let's wait for the whole picture, shall we? Or, as much of it as we can piece together.' She glanced at his smiling profile. He seemed to be in a chatty mood so if she could get him talking she could work on feeling normal. 'So, you and your parents aren't estranged now?'

'No. We didn't speak for a few years but then mom had a health scare and she made dad come and find me. It was awkward for a while but, you know, time passes.' Anna thought again about Sunday night's appalling row with Faye and wondered how much time was going to have to pass to get over that. They had avoided each other since but it was constantly on Anna's mind.

'So do you live in the family home now?'

'Oh, no. That would be a step too far for all of us. Dad would hate having to keep introducing me as his dead-beat son and I would hate being beholden. No, I have a studio apartment in Philly near the cafe. Mom wanted to put me on an allowance but that would have just been a humiliation too far - I make enough from my little business to get by. I enjoy it, to be honest.'

'What aspect of it?' Keep him talking.

'Everything, really. The guys have been with me for years now and it's like they're my family. You don't need to be super-smart to run a café but you do need to work hard and, like, keep up with the trends. I'm not too good at that but they are and it turns out I can put food together in a way people like, and we have little gimmicks like a special coffee every week and stuff in the evenings like gigs and poetry slams, you know. It's low-key but that's what I like.'

'I think it sounds really fun,' Anna said. She smiled at him. 'Do they know who your family are? Your staff I mean.' Look at me, she thought wearily, this is nice Anna.

Maxon drummed his fingers on his knee. 'Yeah, they do. At first they were pretty wary of me but that was years ago and now I think they've forgotten. They know I pull my weight and don't put myself over them – heaven forbid, why would I?' He shifted in his seat, grabbed his camera and photographed a pony and trap going by. They were now on lanes rather than A roads. 'I'm learning a lot here, though. Most of the stuff is too high-end for my place but I can simplify some recipes and develop others and there's some great tips on running a restaurant from the business angle.'

'Are you making friends?' And I went off at Rani for being intrusive, she chided herself.

'It's getting easier – I'm not such a novelty any more. There's a girl - ' His voice tailed off.

'And here we are again.' Anna drew the car into a small space by the helpful village shop and they got out, stretching. It was so quiet. Anna checked with the shopkeeper that it was all right to leave her car there and they strolled the few yards along the empty road and through the metal gate, crunching up the gravel path to the church.

She turned the heavy iron circle and pulled back the door. Maxon's eyes were wide as they stepped into the church and she imagined that he was struggling between good manners and taking photos of everything. It was pleasantly gloomy inside, the colours from the stained glass casting blushes of soft colour on the stone. They were a little early for their appointment so they prowled round separately, reading wall plaques, gazing up at the wood-beamed arch of the nave, noting the cross-stitched hassocks scattered about in the pews. There was no Thwaite name that they could find. Maxon was just crouching down to read a brass marker when the door creaked open and the churchwarden came in.

She was a smart blonde woman, probably in her mid-thirties. She greeted them warmly, apologised that the vicar could not be present since this was one of five parishes he had responsibility for and he was run off his feet, and invited them into the vestry. They found that she had efficiently prepared for their visit and the relevant baptismal, marriage and funeral records were spread out on a table. Next to those tomes was a plan of the churchyard over the road which recorded the location of graves. Anna introduced Maxon.

'Not every birth is in the baptismal record, of course,' Gillian said, 'as dissenters would have their own arrangements or a baby might die before it had been baptised.'

'I'm afraid we only have one date of birth,' Anna said, ' and we're not sure she was baptised here but we think it's likely because the family home was in this village, we believe. But there may be weddings recorded, and deaths, of course.'

'We were wondering if we could look for any mention of the family name if that wouldn't take too long?' Maxon said.

Gillian checked the dates on the leather-bound books. 'These pretty much cover the second half of the nineteenth century,' she said. 'This was one of the coal-mining parishes but it was never densely populated. It shouldn't take too long to go through them. I would start near the back with the 1890's since that's your main interest, you said, and then work back from what you find.' She turned to the graveyard records. 'I did look for Thwaite on our graves list but I couldn't find any. Is there another name, maybe?' Maxon shook his head, disappointed.

'Ok. Well, I have to go to the shop and then I'd like to visit a lady who has just come out of hospital so I'll leave you to it and be back in about an hour?' They nodded and she left.

'Shame about the graves,' Anna said. 'What do you want to do, births, marriages or deaths?'

Maxon thought for a moment. 'Marriages, I guess, because it would be so neat to find Grace's marriage to William Henry.'

'Ok, I'll start on the births and see if Jane is here.'

In all three books there was not one mention of the name Thwaite. They sat down on a bench and Maxon fished an envelope folder out of his canvas satchel. He pulled out a photocopy of Jane Maxon's record of her mother's memories of home. He scanned the pages, frowning, and then turned to Anna, his finger placed half way down one sheet. 'Look, she clearly writes Westbury for where the family came from. Is there another one near Shrewsbury?' Anna shook her head. When Gillian returned they had to tell her they had looked through all of the three books and found nothing. Gillian suggested they could also look in the Parish Packs in the Archives since they were headed there.

As they were leaving the church and Gillian was closing the big door, Anna asked if she knew of a large house nearby called The Mount. 'I'm sorry to disappoint you again,' the woman said, 'but no, I don't. John at the post office said you were looking for that and we talked to the postman but he's never heard of it.' She looked questioningly at Anna. 'You don't mean The Mount House, do you?'

'We might. Where's that?'

'No problem finding that, it's very famous. It's where Charles Darwin grew up in Shrewsbury.'

'You're kidding,' Maxon said, his eyes popping.

Anna put her hand on his arm. 'Um, I don't think so. Unless Grace's last name was Darwin, which would be amazing. We can certainly check it out.'

As they drove into Shrewsbury Anna could sense Maxon's bewilderment and decided they should have a coffee first and she could show him the photo of where his great-grandmother had really been born in September, 1896. She had checked the address against

Jane's birth certificate and it was the same house in which Grace and William Henry had lived, in 1891. She had hoped that Westbury would be a source of data, a key to unlock the mysteries, but now she was beginning to put a question mark over more than one aspect of Grace's recollections. She was beginning to wonder about Grace herself, who had been married to one man and conceived a child by his brother, it appeared.

She parked and they walked towards Shrewsbury town centre. It wasn't long before a cosy coffee shop appeared and they slipped inside. Anna found a quiet table at the back and while they waited for the waitress she asked Maxon if he was forming any theories about his family.

He had been studying the chalkboard menu, presumably with a professional interest, but now he turned to her with that familiar complex crease between his eyebrows. 'I'm wondering if Grace had a poor memory, to be honest. Jane was probably about twelve when she wrote down her mother's account of her life in England and it may be that Grace had just forgotten some stuff or got confused. Jane may have misheard what her mom said. But it's definitely Westbury in the original account in Jane's own writing.'

Their coffees arrived and Anna noticed Maxon sipped speculatively and then lost interest. Probably not up to his usual standard. 'That is a possibility,' she said, 'but I do have some more information. I'm afraid it makes things more mysterious rather than less. The librarian emailed a photo to me of Chirk Street.'

'I remember – where Grace and William Henry lived and probably where Jane was born.'

'Yes. Yes, she was born there.'

'Oh, cool. Let me see it.'

Anna drew the print out of its plastic sleeve and passed it to him without comment.

He was having a hard time understanding what he was seeing. 'So this is all one house, right?'

'No. It's not a great photo but if you look closely you'll see a row of front doors.'

'Townhouses. A little like the old Trinity houses in Philly.'

He laughed. 'They're tiny but so fashionable now.'

Anna had to spell it out. 'These are not fashionable houses, Maxon. They were probably among the poorest housing in Shrewsbury at the time.'

'But – we saw Robert's house?'

'I know. That's why I say this has added another mystery. I've sent for William Henry's birth certificate because then I can get his father's name and see if there's a Will available and then get that. It may help to explain where any family money came from, what property they owned and so on.'

He looked even more closely at the photo and then at her. 'But William Henry was a solicitor? Why would he be living like this?'

'I don't know. Let's hope today's search will shed a little light.'

At the Shropshire Archives Anna showed Maxon the website of the British Newspaper Archives and entered the names of the two brothers, the geographical area, and a time frame of 1890-1895. Several references to Robert Theophilus Thwaite came up in The Salopian Journal but none to William Henry. Anna didn't want to scroll through microfilm unless she had to, so asked the Librarian if they could see the original papers. He said that wouldn't be possible but they were digitised and she could search online. He put out his hand. 'I'm Hwyl Griffith,' he said. 'What name is it you're looking for? I might have a look myself when things are slack and see what I can find.'

She gave him the names of the two brothers but also said that anything with a Thwaite name from that period would be of interest. 'Thank you so much Mr Griffith,' Anna said, 'that would be a huge help. We're kind of feeling around in the dark a little.'

'That's genealogy,' he smiled.

They hunkered down over a computer terminal. 'What does Salopian mean?' Maxon asked. 'I keep coming across that word.' Anna explained it was an adjectival form of the old name for Shropshire. There were four small articles about Robert and one large one. The small articles were the earlier ones from 1890 to 1892 and merely mentioned his presence together with others at various civic events. He did not warrant a photograph. But in 1894 there was an article on the second page which took up eight column inches under a photograph of a man in a top hat, smiling and shaking someone's hand. It was Robert T. Thwaite. He had been appointed manager of the District Bank and the article described how he had become a prominent citizen of Shrewsbury, a member of the Rotary Club and on the board of trustees of the local hospital.

Maxon stared at the photograph for some time. 'I wish we could see his face more clearly, but I must get a copy of this.' He glanced away for a second at Anna. 'Can I print this off?' They went back to the desk to check.

'Could we copy this page, please, Mr Griffith?' Anna asked.

'Of course. Call me Hywl,' he said, 'I think I may have found something else for you.'

'That was fast!'

'I just widened your search to go from 1885 – 1899 and two items have come up about William Henry Thwaite. Then there's one wedding announcement for a James Thwaite but I don't know if that will be your family even though it is the same name. I've jotted down the references.' They hurried back to their computer terminal like excited kids.

The first reference was in the births, marriages and deaths section which stated that the wedding was announced of James Thwaite, widower, of Glebe Farm to Eliza Pound, spinster, of The Mount. Maxon leaped out of his chair. 'Look! The Mount! How about that?'

'But notice the date,' Anna said quietly, 'James got married in 1888. Grace must have been an adult by then and it isn't Thwaite property, it belonged to Eliza Pound. Shall we go on?'

'Yes, yes. This is just fascinating.'

In a March, 1889, copy there was a small article about the Shropshire Rifles, giving a list of newly commissioned officers. William Henry Thwaite was one of them. 'But he's a solicitor?' Maxon queried, 'why would he join the military?'

'Commissions were usually bought in those days,' Anna explained. 'The main Boer War was later, 1899 I think, but there were lots of skirmishes and battles before that and possibly he wanted to go and do his bit. And of course Britain still had an empire where military careers could be made.'

'So he may have died in South Africa? That may be why Grace was widowed?'

'It's possible, but it doesn't explain why he was living on Chirk Street in 1891.'

Anna typed in the next reference. It was later the same year, October, 1889. She found she was at the centre spread. Court Reports. There was William Henry Thwaite arrested for discharging his weapon and wounding a fellow officer of the Shropshire Rifles in

119

a card game which he had lost. The court report described him as coming from a respectable farming family but having accrued debts and become an inveterate gambler.

'Blimey,' Anna said, 'these court reports would be actionable today but they do make lively reading!'

'I thought shootouts over gambling only happened in the Wild West!' Maxon laughed.

'Does it give the sentence?' Anna and Maxon were racing each other as they read.

'No, look here,' Maxon said, 'the judge let him off with a caution since it was a first offence and he came from a good family but look, he lost his commission.' Maxon stared into Anna's face. 'Would he get his money back?'

'No, he would not. And commissions weren't cheap. His family must have already paid for his legal training, no grants then, so this must have been a second blow if the money came from them and it usually was from the family coffers.' Maxon grimaced. 'While older brother Robert was doing very well at the bank,' murmured Anna. Fortunately, Maxon did not join up the dots in the way she had.

'So, money was very tight and that explains the house on Chirk Street. But still, he had his profession – lawyers generally aren't poor?'

Anna pressed the print button again. 'Maybe he wasn't very good at it?'

They went to sign out and Hwyl Griffith was free and asked how they were getting on. They told him what they had discovered. 'We're looking for a house called The Mount,' Anna said, 'Where could we find that?'

'You don't mean Darwin's house?'

'No. It's definitely The Mount and outside the town.'

'Just a minute.' Hwyl consulted his screen and jotted down a few directions and there it was, within their reach, the fabled Mount. Anna could hardly believe it, she was beginning to think Grace had made the whole thing up. What was more, Hwyl told them that Glebe Farm was only a quarter of a mile away from it on the same lane.

They emerged into sunshine and made their way into town for lunch and a breathing space to mull over what had been discovered. 'I suppose James Thwaite could be a cousin,' Anna speculated, looking forward to the small glass of house red she would allow herself. 'It's not that usual a name round here – more so in Yorkshire.' They ducked into a café-bar and ordered.

Maxon bit into a turkey club sandwich and then put it down and peeled back the layers. 'Why isn't the bacon crispy?' he said. Anna shrugged. 'What do you make of William Henry?' he asked, pulling the flaccid bacon out with a fork.

'It's not good, is it? But however he died, it wouldn't have been easy for Grace to live in the same town as Robert's family on a shoestring.' Anna pulled out her folder. 'Let's just run through the timeline, shall we?' She had finished her salad and pushed her plate to one side, studied her notes and drew a line on a blank page. 'Taking everything into account, there's the marriage of James and Eliza in 1888, which may have nothing to do with our search, followed by WH buying a commission and then losing it in 1889. We know he and Grace were already married in 1891 living on Chirk Street but we don't know for how long or why.'

Maxon interrupted. 'Grace told Jane that she had been married for five years before she got pregnant.'

'That would make the wedding taking place in 1889. She may have hoped for better things than she got, of course, since his family is described as respectable. She could have married him after he'd bought the commission but before he got sacked. Being an officer's wife would be seen as quite glamorous, I imagine. Then, Jane is born in 1894 and a year later in '95 Grace emigrated with her to Philadelphia. So what happened to WH between getting Grace pregnant and her emigrating? There is no death certificate for him. Meanwhile Robert is becoming one of the local great and good.' Privately, Anna was wondering if Grace had decided she had thrown her hat at the wrong brother.

'Of course, they could have simply been renting for a time when they were on Chirk Street?' Maxon asked.

'Absolutely. In theory, they could have been between mansions!'

Maxon laughed and put the rest of his club sandwich to one side. 'I quite like having a rogue in the family,' he said, 'makes me feel better about being such a loser.'

'You're hardly a loser,' Anna said, 'let's go and find The Mount before we have to drive back.'

They came to Glebe Farm first on the lane out of Shrewsbury and stopped to look at it. It would have been like thousands of farms built in the nineteenth century of red brick with a yard and outbuildings for storage of farm equipment and animals. There would have been a muck-heap down one end with hens strutting about warbling and a couple of heavy horses to do the field work.

Now the land had been sold from around it and the house and barn and stables had been expensively converted to luxury residences. Instead of a dirt or concrete yard there were cobbles, immaculately clean, edged with troughs of bright annuals and decorative grasses. Under cream sunshades each apartment had its table and chairs, discreetly screened from the neighbours by rustic trellis. In the car park which circled the outer side of the condos were a Nissan Juke and a Range Rover. Anna had to talk Maxon through this. To him, country living was what hicks did. It was inconceivable for a financially comfortable person to choose to live remotely among fields and woods. Only the super-rich, for reasons of privacy, and eccentrics would do that by choice in the US - anyone who was anyone lived in a city in his view. Why would you not want to live near theatres, opera houses, concert halls, good restaurants, other rich people? He risked a few photos so as not to have to come back if James did turn out to be of interest, but the character of the old farm was almost completely obliterated.

They drove on the short distance to The Mount and Anna stopped the car as they gazed at it, open-mouthed. This was a very different proposition. It was a large Georgian house set back from the lane behind substantial stone posts accessed by an elliptical sweep of gravel. The freshly painted wrought-iron gate was hospitably open. Anna searched for a sign. This was just the sort of house that lent itself to being converted to an expensive nursing home for the elderly, or even a private school. She backed the car up on to the lane they had just left. In tasteful maroon and gold she saw a sign reading, 'The Mount Hotel, Banqueting and Functions Exclusively Catered for Your Special Day.'

'So is this it, do you think?' Anna asked Maxon who was rapidly turning the pages of Grace's dictated memoir.

He found the page and read, 'Where I grew up, The Mount in Westbury, was a splendid house built of stone, the finest in the neighbourhood. Carriages would sweep through the gates to the front door, one after the other, when Mama and Papa were giving their parties. I will never forget the candles in every window and the butler greeting each new arrival. At the right time, at a signal from Mama, wearing my most exquisite gown, I would walk slowly down the sweeping staircase into the grand entrance hall. I felt like a princess.'

'Let's go look,' Anna said. They parked to one side and crunched up to the double bevelled-glass doors. Maxon pulled one open and ushered Anna in and immediately they saw it ahead of them across the marble foyer; a sweeping staircase, the mahogany newels deeply carved, the broad stairs now carpeted in crimson and set off with brass rods across every step.

A glossy young woman appeared soundlessly at their side. 'May I help?'

Maxon was too excited to hold back. 'I think this is my great great-grandmother's home, where she grew up. She told her daughter about it!'

'Did you want to book a function here?' The woman had a slight accent. 'I can discuss the tariff and dates with you, if you wish?'

'We'd just like to look round a little if you don't mind,' Anna said, 'but if there is someone who knows the history of the hotel, I mean before it was a hotel, when it was a private home, it would be great if we could have a word with them?'

The woman flicked an eye over Anna and Maxon. Anna never dressed to impress unless Ted ordered her to and no-one looking at Maxon's nondescript clothing would take him for the son of a billionaire. The hotel was silent. 'I'm afraid we're very busy,' the lipsticked mouth said, 'and we know nothing of the hotel's history so -' She paused pointedly.

'Could we just wander round a little?' Maxon pleaded. 'We won't touch anything.'

'We have a function, I'm afraid that would be impossible.' She moved towards the door.

Maxon hissed to Anna that he wanted at least to photograph the outside but she knew that to ask would be to be denied and then they couldn't do it. If they didn't ask, they could do it and risk the consequences. 'Hush,' she told him.

At the car she got out her large map-book and ostentatiously studied it with her silent phone clapped to an ear while he slipped round the side of the house with his camera. He was gone for ten minutes but when he came back he was jubilant. 'This is it, Anna! There's a walled garden off to one side that she described as the kitchen garden. It's full of ornamental stuff now and benches, but that would be it. She said that they grew peaches up the south facing wall. Wow. It's fantastic! I can't wait to tell mom and dad about this.'

Anna smiled at his enthusiasm. 'I should wait a little. Remember this was Eliza Pound's house.'

'Maybe Grace's maiden name was Pound? Maybe something happened to her parents and Eliza inherited it after she had married William Henry?'

'It's a possibility. I'll do some sleuthing as soon as I get a chance. But we need to go back now or you'll be late for your class.'

Maxon clapped his hand to his head. 'Oh, yes, the joys of digitising stock – like I'll use it ever.' They drove out through the gates and turned on to the lane and within ten minutes they were back on the A5 to Birmingham.

For a while they were absorbed by their own thoughts but Anna was finding more questions than answers as she pondered the day's discoveries. Maxon probably thought the mystery was solved. Grace had grown up in The Mount, now a hotel, and then giddily married, perhaps in a state of grief over her parents' deaths, the dashing soldier from 'a respectable family.' Her husband had let her down and rather than live in straitened circumstances when he died she decided to take Jane to Philadelphia where a contact of either Robert or her well-connected family would look after her. It was more or less the story she had told Jane.

There were several problems with this. Grace had placed The Mount in a village eight miles to the south-west of Shrewsbury, Westbury. If her memory served her well enough to recall the candles in the windows of The Mount on party nights, she would hardly get the name of the village wrong. In fact, The Mount was very near to Shrewsbury. Why would she lie?

Second, why was there no death recorded for William Henry? He must have died in a very narrow window of time if he had, indeed, passed away.

Third, if Grace did come from the Pound family, how would they let her languish in poverty? Such a family must have been well-known in Shropshire society and it would reflect very badly on them even if she had made a hasty marriage. Normally such a family would have a proper Will and have settled money on their daughter. But then Anna remembered the Married Women's Property Acts and struggled to clarify her memory of what they had meant. In 1870 an Act was passed that allowed married women to keep their own earnings, and then in 1882 another Act meant they could also keep property brought with them into the marriage. It was 1893 when women got full autonomy over goods and earnings acquired both before and after marriage. Grace married in 1889. If Grace had had money settled on her before her marriage, she would have been able to keep it legally so the young couple should not have been so poor. There were two possibilities as far as Anna could see: no money had been settled on Grace, or William Henry, who seemed dodgier by the minute, had conned her out of it and wasted it. Nevertheless, she should not have been left to live in an almost destitute state. Come to that, why had Grace not told Jane what her maiden name was? The certificates had been lost in a fire, it was believed, and her mother's name when she was single would be the sort of detail that a twelve year old girl would never think to ask, but why would Grace not make sure that it was recorded if she was indeed a member of the prestigious Pound family?

Then there was the original mystery of Jane's death certificate with Robert named as her father. They were no nearer to unravelling that. Well, they had some new names and she would find out what she could. William Henry's birth certificate should be arriving soon so she could try to get a copy of his father's will. She would search for Eliza Pound, Grace's maiden name and a few other names when she got home and would order more documents.

Home. At the thought her spirits sank. She had to try to see Faye and do something about the bitter row they had had – she would try to track her down. But George should be there and Ellis would probably be in for dinner so it was ok.

11

There was no sound in the house when she got back but she saw her father's shopping bag leaning against the cupboard so she would go through to the shed in a moment. There was no need to change, she had not dressed up for the trip to Shrewsbury, she would just take a few minutes to relax. The bottle in the fridge door was Chardonnay, not one of her favourites, but she couldn't be bothered to open a new one so she took a large glass into the living room and sank into an armchair.

What could she think about? What would engage her thoughts for five minutes? Ken Dawkins had not got back to her but it was a case that didn't hold her interest much and she would give him a little longer. She wondered if Rosa's contact had come up with anything on Dean and, if so, what the next step would be. If she did find out where he was, if indeed he was in prison at all, she would have to write to him to ask him to send a Visiting Order. Would he be willing to do that? She hoped so, she was fond of Rosa and she seemed very committed to finding her brother. She stood up. The glass was empty so she carried it back into the kitchen and went out through the utility room and down the short path to the shed.

The door was open so she stepped inside ready to be amused and diverted by the sight of her father sorting through heaps of books or writing so furiously that his ball-point pen pierced the paper, or wrestling with the old photocopier. But he was not doing any of those things. He was there, he was seated behind the desk, but sitting completely still. His hands were folded in front of him resting on the bare wood. He had been staring ahead so Anna saw, in the second it took for him to register her presence, that his expression was one of almost desperate sadness. She felt shocked, as though she had intruded into a very private moment and witnessed a side of her father which she had almost never seen.

'Anna.'

'Sorry, Dad, I didn't mean to barge in. I was just seeing where you were.'

'Sit down, please.'

Her thoughts took off like a flock of magpies. Was he ill? Had something else terrible happened? She felt her heart thudding up against her diaphragm making it hard to breathe. She sat on the ancient car seat. 'What's the matter?'

'I try not to interfere, Anna, but I'm very concerned about Faye.'

She relaxed. 'I know, she's behaving very badly. I've tried to talk to her.'

Her father looked at her steadily without smiling, his hands immobile on the table. He was hardly ever like this – no fussing with his beard, no scuttling about, no eyebrow twitching or little grunts or sighs – just still. It was unnerving.

'We had a talk this morning,' he said quietly, 'Faye and I.'

'Oh, good. I'm sure that helped her.'

'She said you struck her, Anna.'

Anna dropped her head. Without really thinking about it she had hoped that her father would never know what had happened; his unconditional love for her was the firmest ground to stand on that she had just now. She could hardly believe what she had done herself and the last thing she wanted was to dwell on it. She shifted in her chair. 'I shouldn't have done that, I know. I just lost it.'

'*Lost it*?' he repeated in a voice so cold that it chilled her blood. 'Are you a feckless teenager from an American sitcom, Anna? You're an intelligent, educated woman. You'll have to do better than that.' His voice softened. 'Please tell me – this was so unlike you – what was going through your mind?'

'I was so ashamed.'

'Of what?'

'Her. How she was behaving, how I had let Harry down by not being enough for her, not being able to control her.' She turned and looked into the garden.

'Anna, she needs to be loved, not controlled.' She said nothing. 'She's outspoken and can be provocative, I know, but she's going through a hard time, too.'

Anna felt a desperate need to justify herself. 'Is she? Or is she just running wild, throwing herself at anyone?' A little of the rage that had consumed her that night leaped up like a gas flame. 'She wouldn't have been behaving so badly if her dad had been here!'

'But he isn't.' George looked down at his hands for a moment and then back at her. 'She's very hurt and shocked.'

'I'll talk to her.'

'How can you, Anna, when you don't really understand yourself why you did it? Any apology would be empty and I don't sense that you're ready to make one sincerely, are you?' Anna pursed her lips. 'She's gone to stay with Tasha for a while. I think it's for the best.'

Anna was numb. How could her dad be so unforgiving? As a child and even as an adult, when she had made mistakes, been rude or thoughtless, lazy or wilful, one word of apology from her would result in instant forgiveness from him. Now she had cobbled together some sort of reason for the way she had behaved with Faye, she had said she was sorry and he was still serious and sad. She stood up.

'I'll go and make dinner. I'll check with Ellis and see if Mike wants to come over.'

'Good idea.'

At dinner Bobble provided a welcome distraction from the tension between herself and her father. Ellis and Mike had taught him a new trick. So far his repertoire included fetching things which did not need fetching and substituting towing whoever was on his lead for walking to heel. But this trick was so amusing to watch that the boys kept making him do it. They had tied a short rope with a knot in its end to the knob of the door leading to the hall. The latch hadn't worked for years but the door closed well enough by friction so no-one had bothered to fix it. When Ellis said 'Door!' to Bobble he raced for the knot on the rope, grabbed it in his mouth and pulled backwards showing the whites of his eyes so that the door swung open. Ellis would then run to it and shut it again so it could be repeated. This was cute but the really amusing thing was that after every successful grab Bobble would do a victory dash round the kitchen barking his head off with joy. His voice was now as deep as a Great Dane's but he looked more like a black rag rug on springs. When they had tired of the game and she was getting up to clear the table, Anna noticed that her father had disappeared.

Ellis politely offered to help with the dishes but she wanted to be alone and thanked him rather more profusely than he was used to, trying to be a nice mum instead of a nasty one. She moved slowly between table and sink and dish-washer, feeling sore and hollow about her father. What could she do? He had advised her to leave Faye alone for a while and his instinct was usually flawless in these matters. To be truthful, she didn't want another run-in with Faye and he was right, she wasn't ready to apologise. Part of her thought Faye should be the one doing the apologising.

She was wiping down the counter tops when the door-bell rang. Hoping it was Joan or Kimi, she hurried down the hall and opened the door. Standing on the front step was Cathy. Anna glanced to left and right but there was no sign of Steve.

'I know you're not expecting me,' Cathy said, 'but can I come in?' Anna stood back to let her pass and showed her into the living room. Looking with Cathy's eyes she could see that it had received scant attention for some time – newspapers strewn about, cushions flattened, a brown banana skin perched on the mantelpiece. Oh well. Cathy was wearing a pretty voile dress with a batik design and her feet were bare and tanned in strappy gold sandals. As she brushed past, Anna breathed a warm sandalwood fragrance. She had always foolishly imagined Cathy wearing a white lab coat and thick glasses. This floaty creature was a surprise.

'Please, sit down.' Cathy sat in Anna's armchair.

'How are you doing?' she asked, flicking her hair back, 'Is it getting any easier?' If Michelle or Kimi had said this Anna would have been fine with it but from Cathy whom she had met only once, the question was too intimate.

'I'm ok,' she said. There was an uneasy pause. 'How are your plans?'

'That's sort of what I'm here to talk to you about.' Cathy seemed almost relieved to be given her cue. 'I've been weighing up my options, thinking about the future.'

'Well, I'm sure you'll come to a good decision,' Anna said so formally that she sounded rude.

Cathy looked at her and cleared her throat. 'I know what I want now,' she said, 'but I think it may depend on you whether it can happen.'

'I don't see how.' Anna thought she might see exactly how and could feel her anger rising. 'Would you like a glass of wine?'

'Um, no. Thank you.'

'Perhaps you should just say whatever it is you want to say. I don't have a poisonous bite as far as I know.' The woman's tentative approach was making her want to snarl.

'Look, I made a mistake when I left Steve. I was so focussed on my career and we had never even considered the possibility of children so when Alice, you know, when her parents died and he decided to look after her…'

'When she was born they had asked him to be her guardian if anything happened to them and he had agreed.' Anna interrupted. 'It was not a choice, it was a legally binding commitment.'

Cathy looked startled but brushed this aside. 'Yes, well, no-one expected anything to happen, did they? She had grandparents, she still has.' Anna struggled to keep control of her feelings. 'Anyway, I thought he made the wrong decision. He was such a brilliant physicist – I don't know if you can understand – he could have been really important.'

'I expect Alice thinks he *is* really important,' Anna could not stop herself saying.

'Of course.' Cathy was becoming agitated and Anna was spitefully pleased at her loss of composure. 'Anyway, I was saying that I made a mistake. I've had a few relationships over the years but they've just made me realise how special Steve is!' She went for a girlish moue to go with this statement and Anna found her emotions becoming dangerously unstable.

'The thing is, you see, I think we could make a go of it. All three of us, I mean.' For a mad moment Anna thought she was included in the trio but of course Cathy meant Alice.

She stood up. 'If you'll excuse me, I had poured a glass of wine out before you came and I'd like to go and get it. I'll just be a minute. Are you sure you won't have one?' Cathy shook her head and Anna walked calmly to the kitchen, closed the door and went to the sink to splash her face with cold water and to shock herself into control. She drank a long glass of water and then poured out the wine. By the time she'd had a couple of swallows and topped up the glass she was feeling steadier.

When she went back into the living room Cathy was examining a framed photograph of Harry from just before he had been diagnosed. He and Ellis were on the top of a sand dune, their identical coppery hair blown upright by the wind off the sea. Both were grinning and waving at whoever had taken the photo. It had been her. She almost snatched it out of Cathy's hand.

'Is this your husband and your son?' Cathy asked. 'Steve told me about the tragic accident – it must have been awful.'

Anna carefully placed the photo back where it had been. 'I'm sorry, Cathy, but I don't see what your situation has to do with me. Surely it's between you and Steve.'

'But that's the thing.' Cathy almost touched Anna's arm since they were now standing close to each other, but on second thoughts drew her hand back. 'He refuses to see it the way I do.'

Anna picked up her wine and sat down in her own chair leaving Cathy to perch on the sofa. 'Well, I can only repeat, surely that's between you and Steve.'

'But it isn't, is it? You must know he has feelings for you.'

Anna sipped steadily. There was nothing she was able to say. 'If you told him there was no hope then I think he'd be able to get back with me.' She looked at Anna apprehensively. 'I don't want to be callous, Anna, but you and he have hardly seen each other since I've been back however close you were before. That's hardly a coincidence is it, you must see that?' Pointless to tell Cathy that it was Anna who was avoiding Steve and the reason for that had nothing to do with her; she would never believe it and it would raise questions Anna didn't want to answer even to herself. If Cathy believed that Steve was avoiding Anna that was fine.

Anna drained her glass and stood up. 'Do you know what, Cathy? My husband only died two months and eleven days ago. There is no me and Steve – there never was in the way you imply and quite frankly under the circumstances I think your request is not only crass but offensive to both of us. He has been a good friend to the family and to Harry especially and he is a valued work colleague. I think you need to look closer to home if things aren't working out the way you'd hoped. I can't help you.'

Cathy's face dropped, the smile vanished. 'Well, if you can't be honest – then there's no more to be said.'

'Good. I'll see you to the door.'

That night Anna lay in bed for hours unable to sleep. She had stared at the wall of photos and letters, an abstract monochrome in the moonlight, played three games of patience on her laptop, listened to the world service on Radio 4 (more bad news), tried to remember the countries round the coast of Africa and recall rivers from A-Z. She was still wide awake. At 2.30 she got up and went downstairs to the kitchen and the wine rack.

She was late in to work but found she didn't care. Suzy came over with a large glass of iced water. Anna sipped it and raised her eyebrows at its refreshing coolness. 'I brought it in my thermos,' Suzy said, perching on the desk, 'I'm hoping it will re-hydrate you to full size. You've been a shrimp long enough.' Anna couldn't help but smile despite her thumping head. 'That's better. I knew it wouldn't crack your face.'

'Things not too good just now.'

'Do you want to talk?'

'No – thanks. I can't. Work helps.' Suzy touched her on the shoulder, slid off the desk and moved away. Anna clicked on to her emails and began to scroll down but stopped almost immediately. There was one from Hywl Griffith which contained an attachment.

Opened up a wider date window on the Thwaite family and found this from June 1903 in the Western Daily Press archives. I thought it might be of interest.

Anna clicked on the attachment and an announcement from the obituary column of the paper sprang on to her screen. William Henry Thwaite had died in Sydney, New South Wales, Australia, on June 5, 1903. He left a wife, Emma, to whom he had been married for seven years but from whom he was estranged. So, as well as everything else, William Henry had been a bigamist. When he married Emma, Grace and Jane were in Philadelphia, very much alive. Anna wondered how much of a scandal that small announcement had made in Shrewsbury when people did their sums. So when had he left England? When, for that matter, had Grace married the American, Albert Maxon?

Anna scrolled back and forth among her notes and her timeline and saw that Grace had emigrated in the summer of 1895, according to Jane's account, and married Albert Maxon in 1897. So, William Henry must have left Chirk Street after Jane's birth in November 1894, or at least after her conception, and before Grace emigrated in 1895. Did Grace know that she, too, was marrying bigamously? Australia would have been connected by telegraph to the rest of the world by that time (wasn't that line laid in the 1870's?) and messages could be sent in minutes as well as there being a regular mail service which was virtually global. People corresponded regularly by post throughout the world. But, did she know he was in Australia or had he just disappeared one day without telling her where he was going leaving her alone, deserted? Did her husband *want* to communicate with her or vice versa? Probably not. Did Grace know William Henry had married? Did she know he had died? Anna could access the Sydney press of the time since this was, helpfully, all on the Trove database and she was itching to do it but it would have to wait.

She continued to scroll down her emails deleting everything she could and making brief replies to those which couldn't be ignored. Her internal phone rang – it was Josie, the receptionist, with two messages for her. One was from Ken Dawkins asking her to phone him on his new number, his old phone had been stolen, and one was from Rosa. She called Rosa.

Dean was in prison as had been assumed. Rosa's contact in the court system had tracked him down quite quickly and it turned out he did want to see her and had sent her a Visiting Order to come to Stafford prison tomorrow at 14.00 hours. Rosa's voice was trembling with anticipation. She had written to him already and he had made a brief phone call from the prisoner call-box to her. She couldn't wait to see him - please would Anna come? Anna checked her diary and agreed. The great thing about having an unusual client such as Maxon Blake was that she was building up quite a lot of extra hours and she would take them for this visit. She had a feeling that Rosa's mood on the return trip might not be as joyful as the outgoing one.

Anna gulped the remainder of the now tepid water while she searched for Stafford Prison. Her throat felt raw and rough. Stafford didn't look too bad. Dean must be category C. Anna read from the screen that Stafford had training programmes, education, a library, but also that it was an old Victorian building where most prisoners ate in their cells and usually shared them with another inmate. She quickly checked visiting rules remembering her horrific experience at Chicago's Cook County Jail but this seemed much more relaxed and humane. The implication was that she might be allowed to go in with Rosa. She closed the site and started to work on the pile of mundane jobs she had foolishly begged Ted for. At one point Steve passed through the office to speak to someone and she instinctively guarded her face with her hand while she wrote. Her message was clear - keep away - don't speak to me.

At the end of the day Anna found she didn't want to go home. George would make something for Ellis if he was in and she hadn't seen Faye now for days. The strain between herself and her father was a new and terrible ordeal to live with and although they had both tried to chat and pretend that things were back to normal, they were not. Whenever Anna thought about it she wanted to both weep and scream with rage. She wanted to shout and stamp her feet like a four-year old and have her father pick her up and comfort her and say he was sorry. He was supposed to be on *her* side. She texted him that she was going to see Kimi and would he please see to dinner? He texted back politely. It was awful. If Faye had not behaved so badly none of this would have happened.

12

When she arrived at the farm Kimi was in the kitchen peeling lids off containers. 'Potato salad, superfood salad, green salad,' she intoned, slapping the containers down on the table, 'with smoked salmon or mackerel, ok?' Anna sat down and nodded. 'Linda makes all this stuff up for me after she's done the house – it's great.'

'Cooking not your thing?'

'Not really. I suppose I could learn if I had to but by the end of the kind of day I've had at Drakes this is fine by me.' She jerked her head towards a box of wine on the far counter. 'Get us a couple of glasses of the Merlot would you? I think there's a fresh loaf in the bin – I'll just put it out.'

But they had barely begun to eat when the doorbell rang. It was Briony who greeted Anna in her usual cool manner and joined them at the table. Kimi seemed unfazed, as though this was a regular thing, and got another plate and glass and before long they were comparing their days. Anna was surprised to find that Briony was a good raconteur and soon they were all laughing at her mischievous account of a faculty meeting she had attended as student representative. 'Talk about blood on the dance-floor,' she said, 'by the end all the long-serving lecturers had knives sticking out of their backs. It reminded me of that old movie, the vision of hell as a bunch of people who hate each other stuck in the same room for eternity!'

'You should come to a board meeting at Drakes,' Kimi said, re-filling everyone's glasses, 'it's getting to the point where we should have a canapé taster to check for ground glass!' She looked in the fridge. 'While I'm up does anyone want chocolate mud pie?'

At some stage in the evening they moved to the sitting room which Anna had never seen before and collapsed on to large chesterfields. 'It's too buggy outside,' Briony had said and Kimi agreed.

Anna was feeling deliciously numb and slipped her shoes off and lay down without asking, propping her head on a musty-smelling cushion. It was ok, everything was ok. She let Kimi and Briony take the conversation so she didn't have to bother. It was like having the radio on in the distance. From where she was she could see out of the deep windows across a gentle slope of lawn down to trees. The branches had turned black against the flame of the dipping sun and every now and then flocks of birds wheeled past squawking and glittering like chopped gold foil thrown into the air. Anna studied the way the branches of the trees forked and forked again until they were filigree scratches on the peach sky. She listened to her own heart and imagined the blood coursing through smaller and smaller veins. She examined her finger tips to see if she could see the minute capillaries. Then there were river deltas, weren't there? Branching and forking and dividing until the fresh water and the sea water invisibly mingled. 'Fractals,' she murmured and then, savouring the word, repeated it. 'The world is made of fractals.'

Kimi laughed. 'It spoke!' She appeared in Anna's vision as an upside down face fringed with what looked like unravelling ropes backlit from the lamps which had now been switched on. It was a disconcerting sight, Anna thought, and pondered Medea or was it Medusa? 'I think we'd better get you to bed.'

'Got to go home,' Anna muttered, feeling for something to pull herself up on.

'No way you're driving like that,' Briony's voice said. 'Give me your phone, I'll text your dad – George, isn't it? You're incapable.'

'Nonsense,' Anna lisped, 'tell him I'm still at work.' She heard both women laugh and move away and then she was lifted and somehow her feet did seem to move and she was bumped and pulled a little and then she was horizontal and it was cool and soft and heavenly.

Anna had never seen Rosa like this. 'You clean up well,' she said admiringly, and then hoped that wasn't insulting.

Rosa laughed. 'Just this one thing! You can't keep stuff you don't use on a boat.' She looked down and stroked the embroidered silk kaftan. 'I found this in a charity shop in Harborne – had to have it.'

'Well, it suits you – you look magnificent.' Rosa's hair was now a deep vermilion.

'Not too much?'

'I imagine prisons as being a lot of grey so seeing you in that gorgeous thing will light up the place, let alone make Dean proud.' She glanced at Rosa's alert profile. 'How long has it been since you saw him? You told me but I've forgotten.'

'He was ten - I was thirteen, so it's been over ten years.'

'Do you think you'll recognise him?' Anna turned on to the M6 north and settled down to an hour's drive to Stafford.

'I've been worrying about that. He'll know me because I put a photo in the letter but I'll feel bad if I don't recognise him.' Anna smiled at her and they drove on in silence. After a few miles Rosa said, as though she were continuing a conversation they had been having, 'So how did you and Harry meet?'

Anna was startled and gripped the steering wheel hard. Recovering, she said lightly, 'Oh, it was very romantic – I was behind him in the canteen queue in the university union. I think he was by the tray of steak and kidney pud and I was by the parsnip and swede mush. He turned round and looked at me and I was gone. Those eyes, you know.'

'Mm. Love at first sight.'

'Yes, it really was. I had caught a glimpse of him another day but only from the street when he was playing his trumpet. I saw him through the window of his bed-sit.'

'So you stalked him?' Rosa grinned.

Anna laughed. 'I would have done if I'd known how, but then we just bumped into each other over a hotplate. The funny thing was that all the clichés came true immediately. Annoying, really – you feel as though you should be able to have a unique experience when you fall in love because it feels unique, you know, as though it has never happened to anyone else like this, but the world does suddenly change into techni-colour, you do hear the birds sing, you are on fire, the songs are all about you.'

Now she had started she couldn't stop. Something deep inside her was bubbling with the sudden release like when a cap is taken off a shaken fizzy drink. She dreaded Rosa interrupting, changing the subject, reverting to talking about her brother. She felt that if that happened she would explode. But Rosa didn't do any of those things, in fact, every time Anna stopped talking she asked another question. It was bliss to talk about Harry and Rosa was a good listener, chuckling at funny memories, quiet when Anna was serious. The hour went by in what felt like five minutes. As they drew up in the prison visitor car park Anna touched Rosa's arm. 'Thank you,' she said.

They were searched, of course, and the drawing books and felt tips Rosa had brought for Dean were scrutinised but passed.

They were told the rules about touching and so on and then, together with the other visitors, they were shown into a room full of tables and chairs and they sat down to wait. Anna glanced round. There were toddlers and babies with their mothers and a corner of the room had toys and games. There was no barrier between the prisoner and his visitor. She had a flash-back to the filthy plastic screen and the yelling voices of Cook County Jail in Chicago and the stench of sweat and fear and bodily fluids that had made her gag.

Rosa was sitting very still as though if she even took a breath he wouldn't come. Five men came in and went to their tables and then a thin man with a shaved head and owlish eyes picked them out, hesitated, and loped towards them. Rosa erupted from her chair like a dolphin from the waves and folded him in her arms. For one second he paused and then he had his arms round her and they hugged. A prison guard moved towards them so they separated and sat down but their hands were joined across the table, Dean's skinny grey knuckles threaded between Rosa's plump pink ones. Dean glanced at Anna once but she only smiled and was quiet.

'Look,' Rosa said, leaning forward slightly, 'I'm wearing the pendant you sent.' Dean's eyes shadowed as though that time was so far back in his life as to be lost. 'I want you to come and live with me on the boat when you get out.'

'Our dad's boat?'

'No, it's mine. I bought it from him.' Rosa massaged his hands slightly. 'It looks different now, you wouldn't know it.' He was silent and seemed to be puzzled by the thought. 'I know you had bad times with dad on it but he never comes. I wouldn't let him.'

'Still alive, then.' Dean loosed one hand and rubbed his nose. 'I hoped the old bastard had croaked.'

'I never see him,' Rosa said. 'Please come, Dean. No one would bother you and I earn enough for us both.'

'Well, Miss La-didah!' Dean laughed but it wasn't unkind. 'No fella then?'

'Not interested,' Rosa said. 'How much longer have you got?'

'It depends. I could be out in four.'

'Weeks?' Rosa looked thrilled.

'Months.'

Anna stood up. She wanted to leave the two to talk now that the first moments were over. She didn't offer to shake Dean's hand

and neither did he expect it so she smiled and left to sit outside and wait for Rosa.

As she went through the outer door and into the car park her smile faded. Rosa was so happy, ecstatic even, to have her brother back in her life that she probably had not noticed what Anna had noticed. Dean's pupils were dilated and the whites slightly bloodshot. He frequently pulled one hand away from Rosa's to rub his nose so the hit must have been recent, maybe just before he had come down for visiting. But then she realised that it wouldn't make any difference to Rosa anyway. Even if Dean were a rapist or a predatory paedophile or a murderer Rosa would try to love him back to health. What would a drug habit matter to her now she had her brother back?

The rush hour was only beginning when they got back to Birmingham and Rosa asked to be dropped off near the city centre so she could try to find a card for Dean with a narrow boat on it. She was neither exhilarated nor depressed Anna saw – she was determined. Perhaps she had observed as closely as Anna and knew exactly what the struggle ahead may entail but was almost visibly mustering her considerable qualities of courage, resolve and creativity. Anna felt herself shrink by comparison. She wouldn't go home yet, she would go into Harts and see if there was anything there she could do.

When she got to her desk most of the others were leaving and she was relieved to find that they were back to teasing her again. 'What was it today, polo or a champagne lunch?' She even managed a joke back, 'No, we popped over to Paris on his private jet. Sorry there wasn't room for you plebs.'

The note with Ken's number on it was there, centre front, so she picked up the phone and called him. He answered on the second ring and sounded pleased to hear from her. 'I wondered what had happened when you didn't respond to my message,' Anna said, 'but if you had lost your phone -'

'Stolen more like,' Ken replied. 'You have to watch your stuff every minute here, don't you?'

'Mm.' She was glancing through her emails. There was a pause.

'So, why did you phone me? Do you have any news?'

'Oh, sorry.' She pulled her eyes away from the screen. 'I just wanted to let you know that I've found Janet.'

There was a sharp intake of breath in her ear. 'No. Does she remember me?'

'I haven't talked to her, I thought you would want to do that, but I know where she lives. She's Janet Cooper now. She's in Great Yarmouth.'

'So she's living with whatsit Cooper, her husband?' He sounded almost breathless, like a teenager.

'No, she's widowed and living alone.' She let this sink in. 'I can give you the address and phone number.'

'No, no. I mean, yes, ok, but Mrs Ames, Anna, I can't go on my own.'

Anna misunderstood, thinking that Ken had been out of the country for a long time and had no car. 'You could go on the train, but of course you'd have to check she'd see you first. Maybe ask her for a place in the town centre to meet?'

His voice had risen almost to a squeak when he replied. 'No, I mean I daren't go on my own. You know how it was – she was the one. I'm too nervous, I'll make a fool of myself, please come with me.'

Anna rolled her eyes to the ceiling and tried not to sigh. This was not what she was paid for and she had already taken her time in lieu to be with Rosa which she didn't resent at all. Ken was a very different matter. 'This isn't really what I can do, Ken, I'm sorry.'

'I'll pay your train fare, Anna, and I'll buy you a meal, anything. We could go on a Saturday when you're not at work. I just can't face it on my own.'

Anna was just about to refuse when she realised that this would mean she would not have to be at home all day putting up with George's infuriating concern and reproachful glances. She didn't want to go to Great Yarmouth and she certainly didn't want to meet Janet but Ken was all right and maybe she could get him to talk about Trinidad and distract her.

'Ok, I'll do it. But you must talk to her first, Ken. I don't want to go over there on a wild goose chase. She's got to be willing to see you.'

'I see that. I will. Thank you.' He thought for a moment. 'If she's agreeable I'll get the tickets for this Saturday and I'll phone you and tell you the time. Ok?'

Anna hung up feeling like a guilty truant, resentful of her father for making her feel that she was not comfortable in her own home. There was nothing of particular interest in her emails and she was able to delete most of them so she turned to the small pile of mail placed on the side of her desk. Among the papers was a long envelope from the General Register Office. She slit it open and pulled out William Henry Thwaite's birth certificate. A connection was immediately obvious. James Thwaite, the widower who married Eliza Pound, was his father. William Henry had been born at Glebe Farm in 1862. It seemed that James Thwaite owned Glebe Farm, he was not a tenant, so he would have belonged to the fairly comfortable yeoman class in the hierarchy of agricultural workers.

Anna immediately searched for a Will for James Thwaite on Ancestry.com, 1858-1960, and copied down the details. She would pay the fee and get a hard copy for Maxon and herself to read. It may tell them nothing to help with their questions but it seemed logical that James would have sold Glebe Farm when he married Eliza, since neither of his sons would seem to want to follow him. Did he make loans or gifts to his sons at that time? He was, after all, marrying a wealthy spinster. Perhaps this would explain how Robert could put a deposit on a grand house and William Henry could buy an officer's commission? Wills were almost always of interest, especially from the 18th and 19th centuries. People did not tend to hold back on their feelings about their family members and often power plays were clearly in evidence.

She sat for a while and mused on how much to tell Maxon with whom she was making her third visit to Shrewsbury on Wednesday. The only proof she had of William Henry's escape to Australia was the small announcement in the Births, Marriages, Deaths section of the Western Daily Press. She wanted to find out more before she told him anything, but why? Partly, she wanted to put off the revelation that both his great great-grandmother and his great great-grandfather were bigamists because she couldn't foresee how he would react. He might be amused, of course, but he might not. For all that he talked about the burden of his family's great fortune and high status, he was proud of them, too. Proud that he was part of such a prestigious dynasty whose self-concept (and success in finance and politics) depended on legitimacy.

But, Grace may genuinely not have known that William Henry was still alive when she married, he may have got someone to write to her and tell her he had died on foreign shores or anything, and he had been guilty of desertion. On the other hand, she may well have seen the advantage of lying if a wealthy bachelor asked for her hand in Philadelphia. She had already had intimate knowledge of two men, it seemed, in rather a short time, so a third may not trouble her conscience at all. She seemed flirtatious and dangerously headstrong, like someone else Anna knew. She decided to tell Maxon about James but not, at this point, about the Australian adventure of his wayward son.

She glanced at the clock. It was 6.30 and she should go home, but this would be an ideal opportunity to research the Sydney papers for anything on William Henry. The office was silent apart from the distant hum of vacuum cleaners and it was peaceful. She leaned back in her chair and took a deep breath. She didn't need to phone her dad, he would assume she was either working late or with Rosa. She texted Ellis to say she hoped he had had a good day and did the same for Faye and then turned with relief to the internet and entered Trove in the search box. It took very little time to find the Sydney Herald from 1894 – 1904. She typed in William Henry's name and sat back feeling that thrill of anticipation that makes such research addictive.

Her phone beeped. It was Ellis asking if there was any chance she could come to the tennis club that evening? She texted back, 'Sorry, busy, ask Pops.' There were, excitingly, three entries for the name. She clicked on the first one and saw it was a marriage announcement for September, 1896. William Henry was described as an eminent barrister from Manchester who was setting up a practice in Sydney for 'the most select and discriminating clients'. He had decided to make the expanding colony his home as an altruistic gesture of faith in the remarkable opportunities available in the Antipodes. Emma Noakes, his fiancée, was seventeen years old and from a prominent local family who did not, Anna noticed, express much delight at the match as was the usual phrasing. William Henry would have been thirty-five at the time. The wedding was an extremely low-key affair even for those times and Anna could find no engagement announcement relating to the pair. Reading between the lines it seemed as though Emma might have either been persuaded to elope with William Henry or been so dazzled as to become pregnant by him and a very hasty marriage had then been arranged by her family to attempt to mitigate the disgrace.

She could have subsequently lost the baby. There were other possibilities.

The second article was from the front page of October 12, 1897, just over a year later and took up half the page. 'Pommie Fraudster Exposed,' ran the banner headline. It had not taken the resourceful Noakes family long to do a bit of detective work among contacts in England. The telegraph wires, which ran thousands of miles across the vast heart of Australia and connected with Asia and Europe, must have been humming. A photograph of William Henry looking dignified illustrated the article and Anna leaned in close to examine the face of this feckless man about whom she now knew more than his own family in all probability. He was handsome, no doubt about that. His thick dark hair and neatly trimmed whiskers framed a face of regular features and his posture was upright and commanding. 'You're a very naughty boy,' Anna whispered to the screen and then giggled at herself. She glanced around automatically to see if there was anyone she could share this with but, of course, there was not. Maybe she would call in on Joan on the way home and tell her the tale. It would be nice to unwind in her garden with a glass of wine.

The melodramatic language pulled no punches – no political correctness and concern about litigation here: 'bounder seduces innocent young girl,' 'charlatan attorney countersues for slander and libel but Australian justice promises no hope of success,' 'mortified family,' 'ruined heiress,' and the more witty 'failed solicitor forced to beg,' and so on. But, Anna noted, no mention of bigamy. William Henry must have presented himself as a bachelor, not a widower, as the latter condition would most certainly have been investigated by the family in the hopes of annulling the unfortunate marriage. More of a bounder than they knew as it turned out.

She printed off the articles and closed down the site thinking longingly of Joan's pleasant little garden and a large glass of red.

13

It was nine o'clock when she walked into her own hallway and she paused for a moment to listen. There seemed to be no-one home so she climbed the stairs to the big bedroom, had a word with Harry on the windowsill, smiled at her favourite photo on the wall and changed into cotton pyjamas. Slipping a loose robe over them and pushing her toes into flip-flops, she went back downstairs and into the kitchen. She had told Joan she had already eaten since she knew the pensioner liked to eat early but now she was home she found she wasn't hungry anyway. She took a bottle out of the rack but couldn't find a clean glass, they must all be in the dishwasher, so she unscrewed the top and slapped her way down the path to the recliner. No-one had bothered to put it away and it was littered with leaves and twigs from the tree and, Anna saw with distaste, a white bird dropping was splashed on the raised end. She picked up a stick from the grass and poked the worst of it off and sat down.

The grass needed cutting. She peered at the garden. Why could no-one else ever do anything? Why was it always her? She drank deeply from the bottle and let its cool comfort rest between her breasts. If she put it down on the ground it may fall over and spill. By the third draught of wine her abdomen relaxed, her head went back and her eyes closed. What should she think about? William Henry had been an excellent diversion but his escapades raised problems that she couldn't quite focus on at this moment. It had been a long day and although Rosa had done brilliantly, Dean's release was going to be a bit of a strain. Not her problem. Nothing was her problem. She dozed lightly for a moment but then heard George's car turn into their drive. She leaped to her feet and dashed into the house and up the stairs clutching the bottle to her and just clicked her bedroom door shut before she heard him in the hall. He and Ellis were talking but she couldn't make out the words. She leaned against the door, her heart banging with adrenalin, and then, as no-one called her, she relaxed and lay down on the bed. They would know she was home because of her car in the drive and just assume that she needed an early night.

She folded her arms beneath her head and looked at the green carrier bag containing Harry's ashes. They were surprisingly heavy and at some point she would have to do something with them. She wondered where he would like to go. He had wanted to go to

Australia, like William Henry, but it would have been the Great Barrier Reef for him. Could she take him there? Full fathom five.

A few more swallows and she would enter the numbness and not have to worry. She congratulated herself that she could now calibrate precisely how much alcohol she needed to drink to put the malevolent beast that was poised to claw at her to sleep. She was functioning fine at work and soon she probably wouldn't need this medication to help her and she could stop. She had never been much of a drinker – it was just to get through this difficult time while she must keep an exhaustingly tight grip on her mind. Everything fades, she told herself, laying the empty bottle on the carpet, it's just a matter of time.

Maxon was looking better. He was straighter and had allowed himself to have a more fashionable short back and sides haircut which emphasised the clean lines of his jaw. He was even wearing a fitted shirt in two patterns and close-fitting navy jeans. Peculiar that when he had worn the smart-casual, middle-aged American uniform of chinos and button-down shirts he had looked much younger and more gawky than he did now. Now he looked his age and it suited him. As he got into her car he was carrying a paper bag and two paper cups.

'Croissants and coffee,' he said, 'Made by my own hands. It's time you learned to drive US style sucking on caffeine and messing your outfit with food.' Anna laughed.

As they drove she told him about James Thwaite and what her theory was about the money. He wanted to know more about Grace, convinced that she must have been part of the Pound family since her account of the house had been so accurate, and Anna could tell that he was beginning to build a character from their bare data.

'I reckon she must have been a real looker. Grace. I've seen photographs of her in middle age and she was stately then but you could see that she must have been a beauty in her earlier years. But she was unlucky – how could she have known that her husband, the officer and gentleman as he appeared, would turn out to be such a dead-beat? And then, when he died somehow, she didn't sit round feeling sorry for herself, she got her and Jane over to Philadelphia and started a whole new life with someone who was worthy of her. It took guts.'

'Mm.' Anna was non-committal. He might be right about Grace, it made no difference to his view that William Henry had not died. She may not have known that. It was only July but some of the trees were turning, she noticed. It had been such a dry summer that the few hours of rain had not been enough and farmers were having to expensively irrigate their crops. The grass was losing its fresh green and the exposed fields were turning a dull ochre colour. She was suddenly sick of it all and wished she could fast-forward out of this year, out of the constant threat of melt-down. Maxon's croissants would have been delicious probably if she had eaten them on another day but the pastry had stuck in her parched throat and the chocolate had tasted sickly. She seemed to be developing a delicate stomach. She took a gulp of cool coffee and realised too late that the sour liquid only made her feel worse.

This may be their last visit to Shrewsbury, Anna thought, since its purpose was mainly for Maxon to take photographs of the steep town streets and buildings that would have been part of his ancestors' lives – the river, the ornate Library, the old Music Hall. They would pop in to the Archives Office because they both wanted to see if there were any newspaper articles on Eliza Pound which would flesh out her character. If there was time, Anna thought, she might look in the Kelly's Directory for Chirk Street which might give her an idea of the occupations of the inhabitants in the 1890's although she could be pretty sure what she would find.

Maxon turned out to be a gifted photographer. Instead of simply snapping the sights as she would have done he took time to frame a shot and had a knack of taking telling close-ups of pleasing arrangements of colourful baskets and tubs set against ancient mullioned windows and so forth. But after an hour she had had enough. She could have murdered a good long drink and knew it was hours away.

During lunch Maxon told her about his sister. Anna ate her food and listened quietly, knowing from recent experience that it was a relief to talk about loved ones who were lost when that tumble of memories was unforced and unjudged. After a while he said, 'She was like a big tree in a way. I could, like, hide under her branches and get by because everyone was so focused on her.'

'Were you jealous?'

'Oh no. Quite the reverse. I don't know why it is, but I just don't have an ambitious bone in my body and it was great that she was doing all the success stuff and I could just be left alone. To be honest, even though my dad tries hard now not to say mean things to me, I know he feels disappointed. Sometimes he looks at me in a certain way and looks away and I just feel as though I've been disembowelled. He would chivvy me along when I was little and I'm sure they hoped I would step up after Grace died and fill her shoes but the truth is I not only can't, I don't want to. They're having a tough time coming to terms with that. He keeps saying, "We do it all for you," and what can I say to that? I didn't want you to, I didn't ask you to? That would be so ungrateful, unkind.'

'But things are better now between you?'

'He tries. My mom doesn't care so much as long as she can see me – have some semblance of family life. She misses my sister so much.' He stirred his green tea and fiddled with the string on the bag. 'Actually, something else has come up. We had a long talk yesterday, my dad and me, well, he talked to me, and I don't know what to do.' Anna sipped her spritzer and covertly checked her watch for their appointment with the Archives. They were all right for half an hour. She nodded to Maxon to show she was listening.

He sighed. 'I should have thought of this before but, you know,' he smacked his head, 'dumb and dumber.' Anna shook her head and smiled in denial. 'He's thinking about his legacy. He had a health check not long ago and he's fine but it got him thinking what would happen to his money when he died. Obviously, mom would be well-provided for and all that, but what would he do with the rest?'

'Leave it you, I suppose.'

'His failure son?' Maxon did not seem bitter, more anxious, as though he had put himself in his father's shoes and was looking at the problem from his point of view. 'I'm not just talking a couple of million here, Anna.' Anna counted to five and said nothing. 'He's talking about setting up some kind of trust so, you know, I could be involved but have no responsibility. He'd put managers in for that and tie it up tight with his attorneys.'

'What about the rest of the family? Wouldn't they expect to inherit some?'

Maxon gargled his tea and almost choked. 'I don't think so. Dad would never go for that and why should he? They're all doing just fine and they're not saddled with a useless kid. My cousins are all right out of the approved mould.'

Anna was annoyed with him. 'Stop saying you're useless, Maxon, it's almost self-indulgent. You are perfectly fine but just not interested in money-making. It doesn't make you a failure. This may come as a surprise to you but there are other people in this big world who don't care about making huge amounts of money either!' Nevertheless, she thought about how Grace had been pretty quick to grab the main chance when she could.

'Wow. Where did that come from?'

'I'm sorry, it just seems sometimes as though people like your family live in a bubble and they've lost touch with the rest of the world. What was it Carnegie said? You should be ashamed to die rich. Of course, he only said that after he'd been ruthless in acquiring his own wealth.'

Maxon stood up. 'I guess I'll pay for lunch then?' They both laughed and Anna's moment of irritation passed. As they walked out he told her about an inscription he'd seen in India. It was in the Deccan region where the Ajanta caves are, the oldest discovered Buddhist cave paintings, still glorious in their colour and detail. One of the wealthy merchants who had sponsored the decoration of a cave, thinking of his own legacy, had written: *Paradise is enjoyed for as long as a man's memory is green in the world.*

'Perhaps you should mention that to your father?'

Anna had a quiet word with Hwyl at the Archives asking him not to mention William Henry's death in Australia to Maxon. 'Thanks,' she whispered, 'but I'm trying to get the whole story before I tell him.' He nodded. Maxon was studying a map of Victorian Shrewsbury on which he found Glebe Farm and The Mount, only a mile out of town, and came over to ask permission to photograph it.

Once again, the digitised newspapers were full of interest. Eliza Pound's name came up five times in just the decade from 1888 to 1898 when she had died. Two of the items concerned the marriage to James Thwaite which they had already seen and an obituary notice. Apart from those her presence was noted at the County Shows awarding prizes for dairy cattle, and there was a wonderful photograph of her bowling along a lane in a dog cart with a smiling man by her side who may well have been James since the date was May, 1889. She is looking regal with the reins in her hand and a large dog, which could have been an Irish wolf-hound, peering over her shoulder. Anna wondered about whether Bobble had a bit of that in him. The caption read, 'Mrs James Thwaite, nee Eliza Pound, enjoying the spring sunshine in her new trap.' Anna thought she looked splendid and turned eagerly to her obituary to find out more.

She and Maxon read the item together. Eliza had been the only surviving child of her family so that when her parents died The Mount and the whole estate had come to her. She had managed it well and enlarged it so that at the time of her death it included five tenant farms, two rows of houses in Shrewsbury, neither of them on Chirk Street or Mount Airy, Anna noticed, and a former small workhouse which she had paid to have re-developed as a cottage hospital funded by a charitable trust she had organised. No filling her time with flower arranging and teas with the vicar, it seemed. As well as this there was, of course, The Mount, but she had not been selfish with this property either. As was the old country custom, she had a dinner and dance for everyone on her estate once a year at Christmas but also she made it available for her tenants' families' wedding breakfasts. After a church service everyone would congregate at The Mount and Miss Pound, later Mrs Thwaite, would provide food and drink for the party.

'Oh, look,' Anna pointed to a paragraph near the end. It told how the estate families had followed the coffin behind James, now widowed for the second time, from the house to the church and filled both it and the graveyard to overflowing. She had no family left of her own when she died but she had the affection of all who knew her. Not a bad life. Maxon watched while the printer got busy. The scrapbook was thickening.

Maxon was subdued, Anna noticed, and thought that it was quite a coincidence that this obituary notice had come to their attention so recently after the conversation about his father's anxiety over his legacy. But Mr Blake senior and his wife seemed philanthropic in their own way, as Maxon had told her. She led him over to the shelf of Kelly's Directories and explained their purpose. Getting down the one for 1894 when William Henry and Grace lived on Chirk Street, Anna sat down at a table and opened it up to the correct page. There were few surprises. Mr and Mrs W H Thwaite had neighbours who were tradespeople and comprised a drayman, two laundresses, a carpenter, a clock repairer and similar poorly paid occupations. Coming so soon after Eliza's obituary it was rather depressing to see how low William Henry's fortunes had sunk for all the money that had been spent on 'improving' him. It was also surprising. After all, it was only a few years since his father had married well in addition to, Anna assumed, the proceeds from his own farm. Had something else gone wrong?

Maxon got up to look at the large framed photographs of Shrewsbury in Victorian times that made an attractive frieze above the cabinets and tables while Anna idly turned the page of the directory to see what trades there might be further up Chirk Street. It had been a long street and she was about to stop reading when the name of a pie-maker, Susannah, caught her eye. She made a note to investigate further another time, she was suspicious of coincidence from years of experience, and gathered her things to join Maxon and remind him of the time.

On the way home, excited by what they had discovered about Eliza and James and The Mount, Maxon decided that it would be a great culmination of his project to book his parents and himself into the hotel with as many of the extended family who wanted to come to celebrate the pearl wedding anniversary in the old house. It was now a location for functions after all. He chattered away about the idea nearly all the way back to Birmingham which was a relief for Anna and made the journey pass quickly.

But as he got out of the car she did feel the need to suggest gently that he did not do anything just yet. There may be more information to come.

She was very tired and her head was thumping so she went straight home after dropping Maxon off for his class. As she turned into the drive she noticed that a piece of guttering had come loose over the front door and would need to be fixed quickly before it brought the whole run down. She groaned. Money was not as much of a worry as it had been now that Faye was enrolled in an apprenticeship rather than a university course, but it was still true that four people depended on her wage and her father's pension.

She opened the front door and was instantly mobbed by Bobble, barking wildly, now taller than her when standing on his hind legs by at least five inches. As she pushed him to make him get down he couldn't let the opportunity slip to slobber on her face. It was disgusting - some of it had got in her mouth. She dropped her stuff in the hall and ran for the kitchen sink but as she pushed open the kitchen door three faces looked up at her. Faye, Tash and Alice were painting at the kitchen table. She brushed past them and splashed cold water on her face straight from the tap. 'That bloody dog,' she spat between handfuls.

'Hi, Mrs Ames,' Tash said brightly. Anna picked up a towel and rubbed at her face and hairline. Faye had ignored her and Alice was absorbed in her task. Really, it was a charming sight to see the young women and the child so enjoying making pictures, she told herself, but she couldn't feel it. She could try.

'Hi Tash, Alice – hi Faye. What are you painting?'

Tash turned hers round for Anna to see. 'Queens and princesses,' she said, 'all very un-pc but that's what her highness here ordered!' Faye said nothing.

'I'm the princess!' Alice shouted, dabbing violently at her paper, 'and I'm the queen!'

'You're the princess *and* the queen?' Anna asked, trying to enter the mood.

'Yes!' Alice shouted again and then jabbed her paintbrush at Anna. 'You're the witch!'

'I don't want to be the witch,' Anna said, feeling her smile becoming more forced.

'You *are* the witch! Witch! Witch!' Alice was now standing on her chair and yelling.

In a cool place at the top of her head Anna knew, of course she did, that Alice meant nothing, that the word was fun to shout, but something tight and hot inside her was stirring. Then she saw that Faye was smirking and the dark, hot thing leaped up. 'Faye, could I have a word with you outside?'

'Busy,' Faye said automatically.

'Now,' Anna snapped, and walked out.

They faced each other by the table under the tree. Faye was lolling, her arms folded and her head down avoiding Anna's eyes. Anna was so angry she could taste the bile in the back of her throat. 'Have a look round, Faye, what do you see?'

Faye looked up for a second and then dropped her eyes again. 'What?' She sounded irritated, annoyed, put upon. Anna knew she was losing control but she couldn't stop herself.

'I'll tell you, then, shall I? I'll tell you what I see. The grass needs cutting, the house needs cleaning, the pile of clothes you dropped by the washer needs washing, drying, ironing. Maybe you've been too busy shopping, cooking, seeing what you can do to help Pops? Is that it?' Her voice was now rising and had an embarrassing tremor in it. 'You do nothing, Faye! You get up late, go to bed late, run around enjoying yourself from dawn to dusk and who knows what you're getting up to with your friends! I'm sick of your selfishness – sick of having to be the only one doing anything round here!'

Faye was beginning to look scared but this only spurred Anna on. 'And you can be thinking about how much you're going to give me from your wages when you start work at Mecklins. You needn't think you're going to live here and pay nothing – you can bloody well start pulling your weight!' It was the speech Anna had promised herself she would never make.

'My wages?' Faye said.

'Yes – room, board, the lot. How much are you going to contribute?'

Faye was now staring at her in disbelief. 'You said I could get a car to get to work.'

'That was before. This is now. Get the train and walk!'

Faye straightened and glared at her mother. 'All right then, I'll move out! Why would I stay here anyway? Alice is right – you have turned into a fucking witch!' Both women were shaking.

'No one is going anywhere,' said a quiet voice. 'Faye, please apologise for swearing at your mother. Anna, come into the shed.' Faye was on the brink of tears, Anna saw, and she was feeling wretched herself, but the girl muttered, 'Sorry,' and walked off quickly.

The shed smelled of sun-scoured wood and printing ink. It was a smell as familiar to Anna as baked beans on toast. She dropped into the beaten-up car seat. Instead of going behind his desk George sat down by her side in the garden chair. He took her hand and stroked it gently. After a few moments she pulled it away. She dreaded what he was going to say but was ready to defend herself. Nothing she had said to Faye was unjust. Nothing.

'Diane and I are thinking of having a barbeque,' he said unexpectedly. 'Out at Safe 'n' Sound, of course. We thought we'd do it before the weather breaks so probably next Sunday if that's all right for you?' She said nothing. 'We could invite all your friends, you know, Kimi and is it Suzy from work? Joan, of course, and Len, and, well, everyone. Ellis likes the idea.'

'Why?'

'Just to get together. It's not been a good summer. It helps to spend time with the people we're closest to.'

'The gutter needs fixing, Dad. We can't afford this sort of thing.'

'Of course we can,' he patted her shoulder, 'it'll be pot-luck. Just make sure you ask your rich friends and then we might get some good stuff. Diane and I will provide the meat and sausages – we might even do some kebabs – but other people can bring the rest. If you give us the go-ahead Diane will phone round and make sure everyone doesn't bring a quiche. Ok?'

She felt exhausted. The anger and resentment had sunk down like a wave through sand. He had done it deliberately, of course. He knew her so well and even though he'd never seen her like this with Faye, he knew that she had got herself beyond reason and needed distraction like an over-tired toddler. She said, 'I'm working with a young man who's worrying about what to do with the billions his father will leave him.'

'Good! Ask him to bring the drinks,' George said.

14

It wasn't until she sat down at her desk on Friday morning that Anna remembered there had been three items mentioning William Henry Thwaite in the Sydney Herald newspaper. The office was humming pleasantly with the voices of the researchers and Suzy had placed an iced Danish pastry on Anna's desk next to a small bottle of orange juice. She waved at her across the desks but Suzy was on the phone so she left it at that. She switched on her computer and brought up the site again entering the details as before.

The third item was an obituary. Anna paused for a moment before she went on. So much death lately – good deaths, bad deaths, worry about dying. Harry. Had he been able to hear the kind and true things his friends and family had said about him at the funeral? It was a whimsical but seductive thought. There was no printed obituary for him like Eliza had had – he wasn't famous or rich - but his life had been of huge significance to the people who knew him. Where would future researchers find out about him – the kind of man he had been, the respect and affection he had earned? She remembered the moment that she had looked back at the Roaches and thought she would build a cairn for their marriage. It seemed a hollow gesture now. She shook her head and clicked on the article.

There were only a few column inches and no photograph. William Henry Thwaite had died at the age of forty-one as a result of a head injury incurred during a fight in a bar over a poker game. He had been living in a men's hostel. In an oilskin bag he had a life insurance policy for £50 on which the latest three annual premiums had not been paid. All he had, apart from the clothes he died in, was a lace-edged handkerchief, a photograph of Emma and a few coins. He had been buried in a mass paupers' grave.

Anna thought about his life and wondered how it was that an apparently good and steady man like his father could have raised such a son. But the beliefs of our age were not those of the Victorians, she knew. To them each person was responsible for his or her own moral character. Now, parents take the blame for their children's faults and vices and even their unhappiness. She thought of Faye and the bad scene in the garden last night. The girl had been so pale, so astonished at her mother's angry and bitter words. But Faye *had* behaved badly. Was Anna to blame for her selfishness and, she tried to bite back the word but couldn't, her promiscuity?

Was Harry? Had they been too kind, too indulgent, too willing to give her autonomy? Perhaps James Thwaite had spoiled William Henry and bitterly regretted it?

With a shock she realised that Steve was standing by her desk. 'I don't know how you can let that just sit there,' he said, smiling and indicating the untouched Danish pastry. 'I'd have wolfed it in two seconds.'

'Have it,' Anna managed to say, sensing the blood draining from her extremities to flood her heart.

'No, I couldn't do that to you.' Silence. 'I do need to talk to you, though, well, I need us to talk. It's been weeks, Anna, nearly three months and you've barely spoken to me.' She sat staring at her mouse pad, noticing that the altocumulus design printed on the plastic was scuffed in the middle creating a black hole where one couldn't exist. 'Anna.'

'I know.'

'It's a beautiful day outside. Come with me to the reservoir and we'll walk a little. We don't need to talk if you don't want to.' He waited. 'Please.'

Without thinking or planning, her body got up and followed him out. He drove wordlessly to the reservoir in Edgbaston, the canal feed from the old system. On one side it was wooded and the path that edged the trees curved through grass and shrubs down to the water where mallards and moorhens bobbed about in the reeds. On the dam end a cobalt sky reared up dizzyingly until it was scrawled across in a wide arc, high above, by a crayon contrail. Alice could have done it. On the water, appearing and disappearing in dazzling dots and dashes of light was a flat boat with some men working. They stood and watched.

'Can you look at me?' Steve asked. It was not a command, it was a genuine question. Could she look at him?

She lifted her head and met his eyes. She was standing with her back to the sun so that it shone directly into his face and again there was that familiar start, jolt, at the crystal blueness of his eyes. His hair was short – the crest that leaped up rebelliously had gone and in its place was an animal pelt. 'You've had your hair cut,' she said stupidly.

He laughed and the sound of it made her sad. Looking at him caused an ache under her ribs to rise up into the base of her throat. 'I had to. Alice cut a chunk off while I was asleep on the sofa. The thought of her with scissors near me still makes me tremble with fear! I got off lightly.'

'She called me a witch yesterday.'

He laughed again but then stopped abruptly seeing that Anna was not smiling. 'It's her favourite word at the moment. She doesn't mean anything by it. She called Bobble a witch the other day.' He was being gentle with her and she was ashamed.

'I know.'

They began to stroll along the path. 'How's Kimi? And Rhea, of course.'

She wondered if he was asking to remind her of that time just a few months ago, the most terrifying experience of her life, and afterwards when she was in hospital and he had been waiting there for her to wake up so that he could greet her with tenderness and kisses. The nurse had thought he was her husband but, of course, he was not. Harry was still alive. 'Fine,' she said. 'Well, Kimi is.'

'I want you to know something, Anna.' Steve glanced at her and then when she was silent, went on. 'Cathy has gone. She wanted something I couldn't give her.'

'You don't have to tell me that.'

'Yes, I do. Of course I do.' Steve sounded exasperated and when she glanced sideways at him he was running his fingers over his head in the old manner but now he had no crest to lift. 'Is that why you've been so distant, Anna? Did you think I wanted Cathy?'

An elderly couple were walking towards them, heads bent together as they chatted. The woman had a stick and one arm threaded tightly through the man's and he carried a cloth bag which drooped, pear-shaped, with a few purchases. Anna watched them come with envy and despair. 'No,' she said. The couple passed.

They were strolling into patches of shade and sun now and Steve moved a few inches closer to her. 'I told her that even if you didn't want me I would never go back to her. It can only ever be you, Anna, you and me.'

She stopped and faced him. 'No, Steve, you're wrong.'

His face had flushed and she noticed a pulse leaping in his neck. 'I'm not wrong. We've known for years how it is between us, Anna. It has always been me and you, only me and you.'

'No, it has not,' Anna said quietly. 'It has been me and you and Harry and now he's gone.'

Steve's forehead creased and then relaxed. He gently took one of her hands and, for a moment, she let him. 'So this is grief. You're mourning him, of course you are.'

'Oh, grief!' she flung out immediately. 'You think this is about missing Harry? It's not grief! It's not about Harry!' The words had fallen out of her before she could stop them. They hung in the air like a message on an auto-prompt screen. She stared at them, appalled. She felt her mind stumble backwards, try to scramble back up the wall it had fallen off. 'No, no. Of course it's grief, of course it's about Harry.' She pulled her hand free.

Steve regarded her attentively, waiting for something else. When there was nothing he said, 'I am trying to understand.' He seemed deflated, thwarted by her. 'But please remember that I'll love you in whatever way that is of use to you, Anna. Please don't cut me out.'

'You should have taken Cathy's offer,' Anna said sadly, 'I'm of no use to you and I don't think I ever will be. I'm not right, Steve, and I can't cope with this – with your feelings. I can't manage my own. Maybe Harry kept me sane, I don't know. I'm like the kids you see in the playground whirling around until they fall down but they're doing it for fun. It's not fun and I don't want it to happen but I can't stop it. And the worst thing is that I'm hurting other people. I don't mean to – I'm just – I've got no brakes and no steering wheel when I'm round people I love. I'm hazardous.'

'Won't you let me help?' Steve began to reach out to her and then folded his arms sensing that she could not stand his touch. 'We've been through so much together, Anna. Alice's illness, Harry, the things those men put you through, and I know how brave and resourceful you are. I know it, I've seen it. We were a team. We were partners. Now you're going through something worse because it's making you doubt yourself, torture yourself. I can see it on your face, in your eyes. I don't know what it is but I want to be by your side in this, too. I love you, Anna, I'll do anything for you, anything.'

A tide of pain rose up in Anna and a red fog obscured her vision. 'Then leave me alone,' she said desperately. 'I mean it.' She turned and began to stride back towards the car and Steve had no option but to follow.

At work the post had been delivered and a couple of long envelopes from the General Register Office had been placed on Anna's desk. On top of them was a pink post-it note from Josie. Ken Dawkins wanted her to know that they were on for Saturday and he had bought tickets for the train leaving New Street Station at 9.22. He would meet her by the ticket office at 9.00. She sighed and made a mental note to find out the trains back. She hoped he'd bought open tickets.

She and Steve had talked on the way back from the reservoir but only about the barbeque, what he should bring, what time they should get there. Anna didn't know and suggested he call Diane. They had parted without speaking at Steve's office door. He had shut it behind him.

She pulled the first envelope towards her and slit it open. It was William Henry and Grace's marriage certificate showing that they had wed in August, 1889. He was listed as a solicitor living at the barracks of the Shropshire Rifles. So far this was known information for the most part. Grace's details were of greater interest to Anna and she quickly saw that Maxon would have to give up his wishful notion of Grace being part of the Pound family. Her maiden name was Smith and an occupation was listed for her as seamstress. Ironically, her address was number 14b, Chirk Street. The 'b' mattered. Before her marriage Grace would have been so poor as to live in only part of one of the meanest houses on that street. Her father was listed as being at the same address which made it even worse. There could have been a whole family there – it would be easy enough to check.

Anna brought up the census for 1881, eight years before Grace married. The Smith family comprised head of household Edwin, general labourer, his wife Hannah, seamstress, and four children, the oldest of which was Grace at nine years of age. She was listed as 'servant' so she must have been hired out to skivvy each day for a few pennies in someone else's house until she was old enough to follow her mother into a sewing job although she must have also been at school since universal education had come in by then. William Henry must have appeared like a knight in shining armour to whisk her away from all that squalor and drudgery into the leisured glory of the middle classes. And yet, two years after the wedding, if not before, she was back on that same dreary street, and a few years after that became a deserted and probably penniless mother of a baby girl - Jane. Perhaps she had gone back to Chirk Street to be near her family for support. Nevertheless, she had gone on to marry well in America and found a glittering dynasty so maybe not such a poor girl after all. Perhaps, having failed to be lifted socially by her first husband, she'd been more canny with her second. Maxon had been right – she might have had courage and must have had tenacity or at least a well-developed instinct for self-preservation. Perhaps he had also been right that she had been very pretty. William Henry had no other reason to fall for her, after all. Anna wondered where the two had met but it could have been anywhere – Shrewsbury was not a large town and working women like Grace would have moved about freely in the course of their employment.

She shuffled through the rest of the mail but there was nothing else pertinent to this case so she sat back and thought about it. What a relief it was to have this interesting and curious family to investigate. She had already pushed away the distressing talk with Steve until she could barely glimpse it from the corner of her brain. She wondered how many unhappy marriages were resolved by emigration in the last decades of the nineteenth century? How easy to assume a new status as widower, widow, bachelor, spinster. Who would know? For the British, the far-flung countries of the Empire would have been like a magnet drawing the discontented and wayward as well as the idealistic and entrepreneurial. For Grace it had been America that beckoned.

But, wait a minute, Anna thought. Maxon believed that Grace had gone there, specifically to Philadelphia, because of useful family connections. Had she been part of the Pound family then that was credible but now that it was established that she was not from that background, in fact, came from a desperately poor family, what would draw her there? How did she get the passage money for herself and the child and how did William Henry pay for his long voyage to Australia? James Thwaite did not die until after his son so the money did not come from an inheritance as far as she could tell. Did everything come from the sale of Glebe Farm? Did William Henry's legal training, his commission, Robert's financial security all come from that source and then did a very generous (or despairing) father also pay for William Henry, Grace and Jane to disappear? If so, why? She sensed a scandal.

But it could be as simple as family antipathy and social stigma. James married up the social scale, perhaps he was angry with his younger son for marrying down. It was a common cause of fracture in families in the days when social class and income were of huge importance. Anna had been thinking of James as a kindly father and an affectionate husband but perhaps he wasn't. Perhaps it was he whose example William Henry was following but with less skill and acuity when he rushed Emma into marrying him in Sydney. Perhaps he had been looking for a wealthy woman like his new step-mother but a young one. James must certainly have been relieved to see the back of his son, surely, especially since he was now moving in elevated social circles. She could only wait for James' Will and see if that yielded anything of interest. Besides that there were a few loose ends she could follow up but she and Maxon may have to reconcile themselves at some point to an unsolvable mystery.

It was poetry night. George had made a cold spread for everyone and Anna felt it would be mean-spirited to miss another Friday evening since it meant so much to her father. He had not gone on about her last run-in with Faye so she owed him it to him. She trailed out to the shed with her plate and glass thinking that at least Faye never came to these events since Harry's death. Again she had the sense that the family had lost its real heart when Harry had died for all George's bustling efforts to keep things going. As she walked down the short path she smelled the sweet green fragrance of mown grass and was pleased to see the lawn had had a haircut. Was it Faye? A gesture like that would make such a difference to how Anna felt about her daughter.

Ashok was there but without Rani, and so was Joan, who was looking through her own folder. Good. Joan was a thoughtful and sensitive writer and would have the sense to monitor what she would read. Diane had come along and was frowning at a marked page in a collection that George had put into her hands. 'What's this word?' she asked him.

George peered down his glasses, which had slipped to the end of his nose, letting his mouth hang open. 'Crepuscular,' he said, 'shadowy.'

'Well why couldn't this chap,' Diane glanced crossly at the poet's name on the cover, 'have said that?'

'Scansion?' suggested Ashok, smiling at her.

'Oh, don't start that filthy talk,' snorted Diane, 'and don't say you've forgotten our vitamins!' Ashok laughed and reached into his bag to get out the traditional chocolate orange. No-one pointed out that Ellis had always been the one to tap it smartly and hand it round. He was growing up, he had his own passions to tend.

Now Ashok handed it to Joan saying, as always, 'One of your five a day!' and Joan passed it to Anna. It was soft and gluey. They took it in turns to read the poems George had selected for them except for Joan who read her own. Ashok read a couple of George's choices but then said he would share something he had just finished. Anna settled back and took another sip of wine to wash away the chocolate clinging to her teeth. When he had done, she would go back to the kitchen and get a refill. She glanced over to where her father was sitting with his legs crossed in his desk chair, now pulled round to the front. There were grass cuttings stuck to his hairy shins. Not Faye then. A stab of bitterness passed through her.

Usually Ashok's work was intricate, almost Byzantine, full of rich flourishes and purple passages but this was different. It was a poem about his father and specifically about a game of football they had played together when he was a boy in Uganda. They played on sandy soil in bare feet, not from poverty, they were shop-keepers, but from custom. His father would pass to him and he would try to take the ball around the man and score a goal. He remembered his father both shouting encouragement and trying to stop him score – being coach and opposition. The shouts became the refrain of the poem: 'Run faster! Try harder! Use your noddle, boy!' but the verses described how that mantra had not saved the father from the sad events of his life: exile, dislocation, a vertiginous fall through the strata of society when he came to England after being ousted by Idi Amin, and then the final defeat by cancer in his gut. Point and counterpoint – try hard, do your best, but never forget that life is made up of random events outside your control and that your own personal efforts, no matter how courageous, sometimes come to the same end as a sparrow caught in a hurricane.

The poem silenced them all and Anna felt a chill whisper over her skin. Was moral courage an irrelevance as Ashok's poem seemed to say, and if so, would that be a comfort for her rather than a cause for lament? She got up and went out to get a couple of bottles to bring back to the shed. When she re-joined them Joan and Ashok were talking about whether anyone ever feels entirely at home in their own lives and Diane was yawning and looking at her watch. They shook their heads to her offer of another glass and stood up. 'I'm sorry you have to run me home, dear,' Diane said to George, 'I should have thought about it earlier.'

'My pleasure,' George said gallantly. 'A moment with you is as an eternity in heaven.'

Diane rolled her eyes. 'You see what I have to put up with,' she said to Joan.

After they had gone, Anna extended her leg and kicked open the shed door to let in the evening air. The numbness was one and a half glasses away. What she had to calculate was whether to let it arrive here, where she was comfortable and cool, which meant she would have to climb the stairs, brush her teeth and all that malarkey, or should she just take a bottle up with her? She got to her feet and pulled the sticky T shirt away from her skin. She couldn't risk George finding her here, asleep, with an empty bottle.

As she climbed the stairs she remembered something George had told her about Mindfulness meditation. One part of the point of it, it seemed, was to stay in the present moment, neither consumed by the past nor fretting about the future. She was all for that – no memories, nothing clutching at you spitefully with bloody talons, no dull fear of tomorrow - but it was so much easier to just have another drink and achieve the same result much faster. She snorted. If she cut out the bathroom routine she could be numb in about three minutes and then the day would release her.

15

Why on earth had she agreed to this? Anna waited wearily on the granite concourse outside New Street Station's ticket office - with a bit of luck he wouldn't come and she could go home. But no, here he was looking eager and fresh with a bunch of gerbera in his hand. By the end of the journey they would be wilted, of course. He saw her looking at them. 'I thought of roses, but, maybe too soon?'

'They're pretty,' Anna said. 'Can I have my tickets, please?'

As they chatted on the platform Anna observed that he, too, had had his hair cut and was wearing a new shirt which still had the packing creases in it. His jeans were at least an inch too long so they rucked up around his ankles but were also new. He was flushed with excitement and more talkative than she had seen him before.

She got her Kindle out of her bag. 'I've brought this to read on the journey,' she said firmly.

'I won't be able to read anything,' he said. 'I still can't believe this is happening. She sounded the same on the phone, well, almost the same, and she wants to see me! I can't believe it.'

'Did you mention that Bill died?' Anna asked.

'Oh yes, I told her right away about that and that I'd inherited the house and the savings.' Anna's heart sank. 'I didn't want there to be any more secrets or misunderstandings between us. I want a fresh start and I think she does too.' Of course she does, Anna thought, another woman down on her luck looking for her meal ticket.

Just before they reached Great Yarmouth Kenneth took an A4 white envelope out of his bag and handed it to Anna shyly. 'I've always kept this with me. I brought it to show her.' It was a pencil drawing executed with considerable talent so that it was not merely a description of an object but had liveliness and warmth, a real sense of a personality. The eyes were turned to the sketcher and the face lit softly from below as though the sitter had a book or newspaper on her lap or a white skirt which reflected the light up. The hair was a tumble of curls which framed the face and softened the shoulder line. It was a tender study. Either a pastel or a very soft pencil must have been used as there were no hard lines and the lips were rendered so skilfully in this medium as to look like crumpled petals – almost tactile. The look in the eyes was fond, intimate, slightly playful. She didn't need to ask. He had written 'Janet.'

'This is beautifully done,' Anna said. 'It shows how much you cared for her.'

'It shows how pretty she was,' he corrected.

Anna gave it back to him and he returned it to its envelope. 'That was a long time ago,' she said gently.

He laughed. 'Oh, I know she won't look like that now, well, not exactly like that,' he said. 'But I don't, do I? I'm no oil painting.' He looked at Anna shyly. 'Do you mind if I ask you something?

'What?'

'Are you, er, Italian? Or maybe some Spanish or even Indian blood?'

'Oh, no. Nothing so exotic. A bit of gypsy on my mother's side, I think.' Again, Lena's face appeared in her mind's eye. She realised that she had never, that she could remember, seen her mother in any other context than a hospital bed. The dark head with its badger stripe of undyed parting, the hooded bitter chocolate eyes, the sallow skin. She pushed the image away.

There was a fine mist of rain over the Suffolk coast with a cool breeze coming from the sea which made them shiver after the long, hot journey. Anna got out her phone and studied the route to the Sea-Front Hotel where they would be meeting Janet in half an hour. 'Let's walk along the prom a bit,' she said, 'I haven't been to the seaside for ages.' Clutching his now listless flowers, Ken followed her. The sea and sky resembled a continuous sheet of wet tarmac so that only the dark smudge of a container ship far out in the Channel marked the horizon. On the beach were a few families, their waterproofs whipping and rippling in the on-shore wind, so much stronger on the front. On the promenade people hurried about their business past buildings that seemed as forlorn as the holiday-makers' hopes of a sunny day.

'I think we should go now,' Ken said, 'I wouldn't want to start off by keeping her waiting.'

The hotel lobby was packed with a wedding party noisily waiting to get into their function room for a reception. Girls checked their straps and hair-do's and the men unbuttoned their tight collars. They were all excited, nervous, wearing their smart clothes and ready for a riotous afternoon so their voices were loud and provocative. Ken seemed to shrink from them. Anna went to the receptionist's desk and asked for directions to the Embassy Lounge.

It was down a narrow corridor, up a short flight of stairs and then through double-doors. Ken was almost fainting with nerves and Anna decided she would order a stiff drink for herself – something more fortifying than wine was called for and, after all, she wasn't driving.

They walked through the doors and halted to look round. Anna looked for the bar which was reassuringly at hand and not busy, and Ken looked for Janet. 'She's not here,' he said, 'she must be running a bit late.' There were only a few people in the bar, two couples, all elderly, a man and a woman and two women, and a young man in a black suit tapping at his laptop.

'Ok, let's get a drink,' Anna said, 'and that table by the window. Are you sure you don't want me to leave you to it? I can be over in the corner?'

'No!' Ken almost shouted, 'Just stay around for a bit, ok? You can push off when we've got talking.' He remembered that Anna was here as a favour to him. 'What would you like to drink?'

They sat and sipped and waited. After ten minutes Ken got out his phone and wondered aloud whether to call her. 'Give it a little longer,' Anna said, but he texted Janet anyway. The ring tone he had put on this new phone was the mournful trill of Bob Marley's 'No Woman No Cry.' He answered it immediately. 'She's here,' he said, screwing his neck round. The two old women got to their feet and made their way across the carpet. Anna stood up and pulled two more chairs to the table to give Ken a chance to collect himself.

One of the women was using a three-wheel shopping walker and having a hard time with it on the plush carpet. She was grey and beige all over and gasping. The other woman was wearing a candy pink suit and sling-back black shoes with a shiny plastic bag to match. Her tufts of hair had been dyed a rusty shade and revealed a pink scalp. The flesh on her face was rumpled but lines of black and red were drawn on it to mark out the features. She peered at Anna and Ken while her companion sank gratefully into a chair. 'Are you Ken, then?' she asked.

Ken was so shocked he could only stare. 'Yes,' Anna said, 'this is Ken Dawkins. Are you Janet Cooper?'

The woman's black-lined eyes swivelled to look at Anna. 'Who are you, then? His daughter?' Anna explained and they all sat down. Ken was still silent so Anna suggested she buy drinks and the business of that took a few minutes. She was relieved to be able to leave the group. It wasn't a surprise that Janet had neither aged well nor adjusted to the fact that she had not, but it was still a disappointment. Anna fought with herself not to descend into an even deeper prejudice against the woman. What did she want her to be like, anyway? At home in her skin, at peace with herself, sociable and pleasant, dressed in something simple and elegant with stylishly cut grey hair? Was that the mark of value of a person? Had Anna really turned into such a snob? Janet might still be kind or at least, good fun to be with, interesting to chat to.

She returned to the table with a small tray. Janet was in full flow while her friend seemed glad of the opportunity to rest. 'I was telling Ken that I came here with Mr Cooper, Les, when he got a job in Tesco as under-manager. A very good job. We used to go to the golf club dinners and I danced with everyone - I danced with the mayor once!' She settled back in her chair and raised her glass of gin and tonic. 'It was awful when he died and left me alone, I was still a young woman. Well, you can see I like to dress nicely and make something of myself.' The silence from Ken was now becoming difficult to bear and Janet was feeling the strain. 'You've aged,' she snapped. 'You have to make an effort, you know. A tie wouldn't have come amiss.'

'Sorry,' Ken said, startled.

'Are those for me?' Janet demanded, looking down her nose at the wilting bouquet lying on the table. Ken froze like a rabbit in a searchlight. 'Well, give them me then!'

'What line of work were you in?' Anna asked, desperate for something to lift the conversation.

'Work? Do I look like a woman who has to go out to work?' Janet said, barely glancing at Anna. She stared at Ken. 'I thought you had a bit more about you than that wet tea-bag of a brother I married but I'm beginning to wonder. I think a man should be a bit lively, hold up his end of the conversation, don't you? Never mind, I expect you're overcome – it has been a while.' Her eyes narrowed. 'Still, I do think you'll agree a man should know how to provide for a girl. You have got the house, haven't you?'

Ken looked horrified. 'I just thought we could meet and say hello,' he stuttered.

Janet leaned forward exposing a deeply crumpled cleavage and chucked him under the chin. 'Oh come on, lover,' she said, 'You didn't come all this way for a half of lager. I know what men want!' She sat back licking her lips. 'I always knew what you wanted, didn't I?'

Ken leaped up so suddenly that his chair tipped over backwards. He faced Janet with his fists clenched. 'My brother said you were a bitch to live with and I didn't believe him,' he gasped, 'but I do now. This was a mistake, I wish I'd never come.'

Anna had to run to catch him up as he strode out of the hotel and down the promenade to the sea-wall. When she got to his side he was sobbing into the wind. She put her arm round his waist and leaned her head on his slumped shoulder and said nothing.

'You must think me such a fool,' Ken said after a while.

'Not at all,' Anna said sincerely. 'You're capable of love and loyalty and she isn't, it seems.'

'Bill told me in the letter, didn't he, but it was just so far off what I believed about her. I'd kept hold of her as she was for so long – I didn't want to believe any different.'

They stood side by side watching the sea come in and go out, shushing itself on the sand. The rain had stopped and the breeze was quieter. The water had a yellowish tinge to it like putty made with linseed oil and the sky had become mottled with hints of blue between the flocked greys.

'What a waste of my life,' Ken said. 'I knew some women in Trinidad, well, one woman. She was called Phyllis. She waited for me for years and then married the man who ran the computer store, Norris. She was good-hearted, kind. What a fool I was.' He shook his head in disbelief. 'It was like Janet was the gold standard – no-one could come up to her.'

'The girl you drew.'

'Mm. Was she like this then do you think or has she got that way? Maybe she had a hard life and got hard herself?' Anna said nothing. 'No. I can't go on lying to myself. She screwed me over for Bill and screwed him over when she got a better offer. Who knows how many others.' He roused himself and looked around. 'Shall we go back?'

Anna glanced at her timetable. 'Let's get fish and chips and eat them out of the paper on the train!' She grinned up at him.

'Well, at least you're easily pleased,' Ken said, trying for a smile, and suddenly she was glad that she had come and been able to be here to keep him company as the one great illusion of his life was shattered. At least she had done the right thing for this man whom she hardly knew.

Sunday was a perfect day for the barbeque. George set off early to help Diane and Joan get things ready and Anna spent a couple of hours in the kitchen making a lemon drizzle tray cake and a pile of filled rolls. Faye was nowhere to be seen and Anna found herself rehearsing mean things to say to the girl and then chided herself for it. Had Faye always been so loose and selfish, Anna wondered, trying to remember. Images of a furious red face came to mind from the times Faye had been thwarted as a child, but other images came too, of Faye making them all laugh with some dry comment or doing a 'show' with Tash which mainly involved miming to the latest pop video. But she always had to be the centre of attention, Anna thought grimly. She was finding it very hard to take. Ellis and Mike had been co-opted to set up trestle tables and run back and forth with supplies so at least they were helping. By the time everything was packed up to take she wished it wasn't happening. She had worked herself up into a bitter mood.

As she drew up in the Safe 'n' Sound compound she saw Kimi's car was there and one she didn't recognise. It was still early. From the barn came hoots of laughter so Anna took her offerings into the kitchen and then went out to investigate. Diane had Charles on her shoulder and Kimi and Briony were feeding him with pieces of dried apricot.

'He'll be squitting all over the place later,' Diane said fondly.

'He's adorable!' Kimi said. 'Oh, hi, Anna.'

'No Rhea?'

'No, I asked her to come but, you know, too many people, not her thing.'

'I've brought Bob,' Briony said, looking down at the old black lab collapsed at her feet. 'He's a bit worried I'm going to leave him here, I think. He didn't like it much before, did he?' Tact had never been her forte, Anna recalled, but Diane didn't easily take offence.

'Only because it was cold,' Anna said, bending to stroke the coarse fur on Bob's back. Bob regarded her indulgently with rheumy, red-rimmed eyes. She wondered if he remembered her. She crouched down beside him and rubbed round his ear and he had the good manners to thump his tail on the dusty floor.

'Ellis has tied Bobble up by the house until we get things sorted out,' Diane said to Anna, 'he's very naughty isn't he?'

'Not compared to Faye!' Anna instantly retorted. They all stared at her.

'I mean the dog,' Diane said, 'not Ellis.'

Charles had lost interest in the group now that no more treats were forthcoming and had hopped off to see what he could find. Diane seemed unconcerned so this must be a regular thing now he'd settled in.

Joan appeared, a miasma of accelerant wafting around her. 'Can someone help? George and I can't seem to get this thing going properly.' Kimi and Briony went out with her and Diane and Anna made their way to the kitchen. Bob groaned and stretched out on the warm concrete to mull things over in his own time.

An hour later Len turned up having begged a lift from Rosa, and Faye, Tasha and Michelle arrived with Tasha's younger sister Nicola. Then Suzy and Rob swept up in his Mini Cooper and by that time good smells as well as smoke were coming from the barbeque. Mike had positioned himself behind a cloth-covered card table by the fragrant meat and sausages and was filling buns with aplomb, his home-made chef's hat wobbling cheerily. His mum and dad were coming later. Every now and then he would lean over and advise George, now looking like a raspberry ripple on the melt, on a culinary point. The trestle tables covered with plastic gingham were stacked with food, plates and napkins and under each one was a cool box with wine and soft drinks sitting on a cushion of ice. People had been asked to bring folding chairs so now an assortment of them were scattered under the trees or near the house depending on whether people wanted to sun-bathe or be cool.

Joan came over to Anna as she was filling her beaker. 'It's all going really well, isn't it?' she beamed. 'I'm so glad the weather held. Oh, look!'

Steve's Yeti had turned into the access drive and was coming up to the farm slowly raising a cloud of dust. Anna looked away and put an egg and mayonnaise roll on to her plate. She picked up her wine and made her way to where Michelle was sitting looking a little lost. She dragged a chair across to join her.

'I've been meaning to say,' she said, 'thanks for letting Faye spend so much time at your house.'

Michelle chewed her burger thoughtfully. 'It's no problem.' She looked at Anna. 'She's a lovely girl.' Anna took a bite of her roll wondering if Faye had been bad-mouthing her. 'She's done so well to get that apprenticeship at Mecklins – I hear that they're like gold. I know someone whose daughter is predicted to get straight A's but they didn't take her. She was hoping for a two-year placement before she went to uni but Faye is very creative and they spotted it.' Anna bit back the comment she wanted to make that Faye was very creative about getting her own way and doing exactly as she pleased.

'Has that boy been over? Jason? He's one of the apprentices.'

'I don't think so. But she is almost nineteen isn't she? They go out a lot – they want to have fun while they're young, don't they?' she added. Anna sipped her wine feeling, not for the first time, that Michelle was far too permissive with the girls.

Mike's mum and dad arrived and then Ashok and Rani and the party was complete. Anna glanced round and saw that wherever Rosa was, Len was not far away. He wasn't talking to her, he was just hovering at a distance. Rosa was being how she always was, helpful if needed, quiet and content if not. Anna envied her self-possession, her calm. Ellis let Bobble off his rope now that all the cars had arrived and he couldn't bite their wheels while they were in motion as he liked to do. He dashed to the chain-link fence and yelled greetings at the assembled dogs behind it which had only just stopped barking at all the goings-on themselves. They yipped and bayed back. Behind them the compound with the cats was, as usual, calm and disdainful of the ruckus.

Suzy was drifting about elegantly in white linen trousers and a silk top talking with everyone in her sociable, easy way. Rob had drifted over to Faye but Anna, watching out of the corner of her eye, saw someone point at her and he glanced over, recoiled and withdrew. Faye's top was far too revealing and she was wearing the cut-off shorts that Anna had especially asked her to burn. A fold of buttock was clearly visible beneath each ragged cuff. Tasha was in her usual T shirt and pedal-pushers looking like a girl who respected herself should look. Anna was glad she could wander about filling her beaker every now and then without attracting comment to keep the rising tide of irritation at bay.

Alice had a new game. She had found that she could crawl under a folding chair from behind without being seen by the occupant and then pop up at the front shouting 'Boo!' This inevitably had the pay-off of causing a startled reaction and then earning her a smile and even a cuddle. She had done it to Anna several times, once causing Anna to spill her drink, and the joke was wearing thin as children's jokes often do. But for the most part the afternoon ambled along pleasantly as Anna moved from group to group, avoiding Steve as skilfully as he was avoiding her. She was beginning to feel more mellow. She half-wished she had invited Maxon as George suggested but it was too late now.

Everyone had now had enough to eat and George swabbed his face with his apron and came out from behind the barbeque. His hair looked as though he'd been wiping his fingers on it. He beckoned Diane and she joined him. 'Er,' George said, 'Can we have a word?' He flapped his hands around.

Diane stepped forward. 'Oi! Can we have a bit of hush? Ellis, will you get that dog out of the rubbish?' Ellis jumped up and grabbed Bobble who was up to his armpits in a black bin bag. 'George has something he wants to say.' Everyone cheered and laughed.

George made damping down movements with his hands. 'No, it's not a speech. I just want to say a couple of things.' Anna leaned back in her chair and felt charitable towards him. This gathering had been a good idea and he had softened towards her lately so maybe there were almost back to their old closeness. There were bound to be ups and downs in families. George drew his eyebrows together and looked round. 'It's been a difficult year for our family, for all of us, and I thought we needed to remember our friends and how much they mean to us.' There was some soft applause and murmurs of assent. 'But,' he raised his head, 'there have been some very good things and we must not forget those. Where are you Faye?'

Anna was surprised and sat up, looking round for her daughter. She was being pushed forward by Michelle.

George pulled her gently to him and put his arm round her shoulder. Her thick chestnut hair was lit to Viking gold by the sun and her long limbs had tanned to the colour of honey. Anna felt a stab of longing for how she used to love looking at her daughter, how beautiful the girl was, how spirited and funny. She was blushing slightly and grinning at her grandfather. 'Pops, so embarrassing!'

'This young lady,' went on George, 'as you all know, has won an apprenticeship with the most prestigious toy maker in the country!'

'Hey!' Faye interrupted, 'in the *world,* please!' People laughed.

'In the world,' George amended, 'and I just want to say how very proud I am to be her grandfather! Well done, Faye!' People clapped and Tash and Nicola whooped. Anna felt ice cold. Why had she not been included? Why had George said that he was proud and not that they, the family, were proud? She felt it as a deep slight and it was all she could do to clap and smile. But George had not finished.

'And another member of the family has distinguished himself, hasn't he?' What? What was her father talking about? Had Len got some kind of music award he hadn't told her about or what? 'Come forward, Ellis!'

Mike made a pantomime of dragging Ellis up to where George stood and most people laughed and looked at each other not knowing what was going to be said, although John and Maggie Bryant were smiling and nodding. Bobble barked and ran forward to join the game.

'This young man,' George put an arm around Ellis' shoulders and shook him a little so he grinned, 'has only been playing club tennis for a few months but he's practised so hard and he's so talented that last week he won the under twelve tournament trophy! Congratulations, son, I was so proud to see you lift that cup!' This time there was a cheer and shouts of, 'Well done!' and, 'Good for you, Ell!'

Anna got up unsteadily. What was going on? 'Just a minute,' she called out, 'why did no-one tell me about this?' There was instantly silence. 'Why didn't you tell me that you were playing for the cup, Ellis?' She was dimly aware that she was making a scene but she didn't care. She was hurt and it wasn't fair.

Ellis flushed with embarrassment and looked down. 'I did try to,' he mumbled. 'You were very busy that day.' Anna was furious. How dare he and her father make her look so bad in front of their friends?

She stepped nearer to them. 'Why didn't *you* tell me?' she demanded of her father. George looked miserable and at a loss. 'Am I not part of this family anymore? Am I just the one who goes out to work every day to pay the bills?' Now George was moving towards her, hands reaching for her. Her pulse was pounding and she was on the brink of tears. She wanted to run. She turned blindly and tripped. Alice had been right behind her.

'Boo!' yelled Alice.

'Oh for crying out loud, stop it!' Anna shouted at the little girl. 'Get out of my way!'

George had reached her and was trying to embrace her but she shook herself free from him. 'Why can't you just stop bloody interfering in my life, Dad?' she cried, 'Stop telling me what to do!' Even in her gale of emotion, she knew that she was making no sense. She was furious with him.

Alice was now wailing and Faye had rushed over to pick her up. 'What is the matter with you? What's Pops ever done to you, Mum?' She rocked Alice and petted her head to calm her but her expression towards Anna was so hostile it made Anna quail. 'Why are you being so horrible?'

Anna stared at her, unable to say a word, and in the silence Rani could be heard explaining that anger was a stage of the grieving process. Anna rounded on her. 'That's rubbish Rani! There are no stages to the grieving process, as you call it, so why don't you just put a sock in it and keep your half-baked theories to yourself? The last thing I need is a bloody grief troll!' Now even Alice had stopped crying and there was complete silence.

Ashok said quietly, 'Anna.' Rani looked as though she might burst into tears.

Was this really happening? Had she really said those things? Anna could see Joan making her way towards her and grabbed her bag and ran to her car. Steve got there before her. 'Don't drive,' he said. 'If you want to go home I'll take you.'

She wrenched open her car door. 'Fuck off, Steve!' she shouted, and burst into tears. The car was scorchingly hot from where it had been parked in full sun and the steering wheel burned her hands as she grabbed it and buried her face. She heard the small jingle of keys as Steve removed them from the ignition. He got in to the passenger seat and sat silently waiting.

After a while she sat up and rubbed her face with her arm. Steve handed her a handkerchief and she used it. They sat quietly for several minutes until Suzy appeared with a cup of tea. She gave it to Anna. 'Milk, no sugar,' she said softly and left.

'Why didn't they tell me about the tournament? I could have gone. I would have gone.'

'You've been pushing yourself hard at work. Maybe it slipped your mind.'

'Because I'm such a bad mother.'

'Because grieving is hard work and takes a lot of thinking time. I know, I lost my sister, remember?'

Anna felt spent, exhausted by the storm of anger and tears. 'I've ruined dad's day. He was trying to do something nice for us.' She looked out of the car window at the groups standing about quietly. Even Bobble was subdued. She got out of the car and walked back towards them with Steve a few steps behind her.

As she approached everyone turned and looked at her, some with encouraging smiles, others with incomprehension and hurt. She stopped by her father who was messing about around the charred barbeque and wrapped her arms round him. 'I'm so sorry, Dad,' she said, 'I don't know what came over me. I didn't mean what I said.' He patted her back. She searched the group. 'Faye? Ellis?'

'They're playing with the monkey in the barn,' someone said.

Anna looked round. 'Rani, I'm so sorry. You've never been anything but kind and supportive to me and the way I spoke to you was unforgiveable.' Rani opened her arms and nodded her head as though to say she understood. 'Please forgive me everyone, I'm so sorry to have spoiled such a lovely day.'

She walked to the barn concentrating on not weaving or staggering, conscious of the eyes on her back. The teenagers and Mike, Ellis and Alice were all there throwing a little ball for Charles to catch. They stopped abruptly as she appeared. 'I've apologised to the others,' she said, 'but I want to say sorry to you, too. I over-reacted badly.' The boys looked down and Ellis mumbled something, Alice stared at her with knotted brows as though she was a monster, and the older girls looked sullen and defiant, their arms crossed.

Nothing she could say would make any difference now. She went home.

16

Anna was early in to work on Monday morning. She walked over to Suzy's desk and laid a posy of tea-roses on it which she had taken from the garden that morning. Some of them still had beads of dew trapped in their petals. Against them she propped a little card. Later she would write a note to Rani and Ashok and apologise again. George had been quiet when he came home but they had got through the evening civilly. Ellis was playing Mindcraft at Mike's and, of course, Faye did not appear. Anna wanted to ask whether she had helped to clear up, but how could she, she hadn't helped herself.

There were plenty of emails to occupy her and it was a couple of hours before she sat back and rubbed her eyes. Josie rang. Would Anna sign for a package? She ran down the glass stairs to reception and saw a bulky brown envelope on the counter. She signed quickly, thanked the postman and ran upstairs with it. It was a copy of James Thwaite's Will dated February 15th, 1889.

She spread the photocopies out on her desk and smoothed them. The copperplate writing was not hard to read except on some of the folds. She scanned the pages, phrases jumping out at her, 'my beloved wife, Eliza,' 'indenture of settlement,' 'hereditaments,' and, of the disposal of Glebe Farm, 'thereinbefore declared,' and a strict warning that William Henry could not 'intermeddle therewith.' She raised her eyebrows at this.

Anna went back and read it properly and then read it again. The meaning of it was very clear. Knowing Eliza to be a wealthy woman in her own right and having discussed his decision with her, James had left all he had to his son, Robert, and his grandchildren by him and his wife. Eliza would dispose of her assets to her own beneficiaries. He had not sold the farm, it seemed, he had rented it out to a tenant so that Robert could choose, when James died, to either continue receiving the rental income or sell it and release a lump sum.

Near the end of the Will was a very pertinent section which Anna highlighted in soft pencil.

'Be it noted that my son, William Henry, is not to inherit from my estate on my death since he begged his inheritance in 1888, which I signed to him on the nineteenth day of November. He had thought that he might have expectations from my marriage to Eliza but I

made known to him that his share would be solely from my own worth as it would be with Robert. I gave him half the value of Glebe Farm, which amounted to the sale of all assets and stock, excepting the farmhouse itself and the land. I was in some distress that he hoped to profit from my marriage which was unjust, it being the marriage of my heart and my dear Eliza's, and she not being related to him. But I met his request in hopes that he will prosper as a soldier more than he did in the practice of the law.'

The Will was signed, dated and witnessed. Anna sat back and considered what had been revealed. It was more or less as she suspected that William Henry, having blown his commission, had nothing more to expect from his family and decided to try his luck elsewhere. Poor James – just a few months after this Will was written his son would marry a penniless girl and then disgrace himself and his regiment, in the process wasting the generous premature inheritance from his father. Meanwhile, Robert was climbing the promotion ladder at the bank as though jet-propelled and it seemed that the funds for the house on Mount Airy had not come from James since he would get nothing from him until his death in 1917. Perhaps he, too, had married money.

Anna was about to put the papers back into their envelope for Maxon to read when she saw that the backing piece of paper, which she had thought to be blank, had a few lines of writing on it. It was a codicil dated December, 1896.

'It grieves my heart,' James had written, *'that I was not kinder to my daughter-in-law, Grace, and my grand-daughter, Jane, when it was my Christian duty to be so. My wrath over William Henry's dishonourable behaviour, and subsequent flight from those who should have been dear to him, and who depended on him utterly, made me blind to their plight. I turned them away from our door despite the entreaties of my dear wife, Eliza, and I now daily bear the burden of that act made from anger and hardness of heart towards my son, even though they were the innocent and wronged parties. I pray that no harm has come to them wherever they may be, and that I may, before I die, have the opportunity to redeem myself for what I have done.'* He then made a small bequest, *'if they ever be found.'*

'The roses are just lovely, thank you,' Suzy said, smiling Anna back to the present. 'It's lunch-time. Come out with me and we'll get something fresh and healthy followed immediately by something squishy and wicked!'

Anna sighed and felt humbled. 'How can you be so nice to me, Suzy, when I was such a hysteric yesterday?'

'I expect you had your reasons. Now, come on, look lively – I'm starving.' So it was easy to sweep past Steve's office and out of the building into a pale gauzy day where the sun made hardly any shadows at all.

At home Anna found Ellis in the kitchen at the stove. He glanced at her and said, 'Making Pops a boiled egg, do you want one? This one's only just gone in.'

'Doesn't he want any dinner? I was just about to start on some salmon steaks.'

'Feeling a bit off. Says it was probably a dodgy burger.'

'Ok, put another couple in will you, Ell, and let them hard boil. I can stick them in the salad.' She hovered, half wanting to apologise again and half hoping he had forgotten her outburst.

'Mum?' Ellis was at the fridge getting more eggs and only caught her eye for a second as he returned to the pan.

'Mm.'

'Are you ok?'

She flushed, her heart suddenly pounding again. It was sore – she was getting sore at heart as a physical pain, not a metaphor. 'I'm not sure, Ell. Thanks for asking.'

He eased the eggs carefully into the pan. 'Do you want to see what Mike and me have done on Mindcraft? It's totally amazing.'

'Later, yes. I'd like to see the trophy as well.' She moved towards him wanting to hug him but knowing it wasn't the right moment. 'I'm so proud of you.'

He turned a serious, foxy face to her and again there was that surreal moment where she saw glimpses of Harry, the adult man, flickering among Ellis's gold-green eyes and turbulent auburn hair. 'Sorry I didn't tell you about the tournament properly, Mum.' She wrapped her arms round him and held him close.

George was on the sofa in the living room with his feet up and a jumper over his legs. 'What's up, Dad? What's this lady of leisure routine?' But because things were not right between them it sounded like an accusation when she had only meant a gentle tease.

He coughed and turned off the television. 'Just a tickle in my throat. I think it was the fumes from the barbeque got stuck.'

Anna sat down. 'You don't need to turn the tv off. What were you watching?'

'Oh, what Diane calls my rubbish. A series I recorded on the great poets. I'm on Rumi at the moment. Astonishingly prolific, and easily as famous in the Muslim world as Shakespeare is here.' Anna sat in her usual chair. Bridges needed to be built and what better subject than this. 'I remember you reading him to me when I was a teenager. Wasn't he a Sufi, Dad? I can't remember his dates but I think he was before Chaucer, wasn't he?'

'Yes, born in 1207 in Persia and moved to what's now Turkey to get away from Genghis Khan's invading army.'

'As you would.'

George managed a polite chuckle which turned into a cough. 'Have you eaten?'

'I'm going to do something for me and Ell soon. Do you want your egg in here?'

'No, I'll come in when it's ready. No fun eating a boiled egg on your knee.'

'Have you seen Faye?'

'She popped in for five minutes with that new lad. Seems ok.'

'Right.' Anna got up not knowing what else she could say. She walked out of the room and up the stairs to the bedroom. There isn't a word, she thought, for the pain of polite conversation with someone you love and have hurt.

Harry's ashes reproached her but she turned away from them and stood for several minutes in front of the wall of photographs and messages. What was happening to her? She seemed to be living on different floors of the same building, sometimes simultaneously. When she was at work, as long as she ignored Steve, she was on the top floor with a balcony and fresh air and could breathe. When she was at home she seemed to be stuck on the stairs between kitchen and basement, at any moment to be knocked down into the darkness and fear. Sometimes she seemed to be neither inside nor outside herself but whirling loose. There was no safe place except out of here, out of her real house, and even then she could be ambushed and winded. She felt like a sub-atomic particle or wave, holding both states in herself simultaneously. She needed to be numb – she needed a break. It was too early to start seriously drinking. Besides, the effectiveness was wearing off and more was needed and that extra quantity must be taken faster. As she stared at the collage on the wall she had an idea of how to get through the evening. It was only six o'clock. She could make dinner, look at Ellis' game and trophy and then she could go out without feeling guilty. She pulled out her phone and dialled Maxon's number.

Maxon had rented an apartment in one of the elegant cream-washed Georgian houses on Hagley Road so she arranged to meet him in the Old Orleans nearby. She found an outside table and ordered a large glass of wine. All around were couples and groups talking and laughing, smoking and drinking. The hubbub was soothing and she almost regretted the sight of Maxon apologising his way through the tables to her. He was still painfully thin. His linen slacks hung on his hip-bones like canvas on tent poles. She waved to him to try to make him smile but when he sat down the triple crease was back between his eyebrows.

'You don't look very happy,' she said, finishing her wine and waving to the waiter. 'What's up?'

'Failed my fish,' he said gloomily.

'What, you didn't praise it enough and it left home?' The second she had said this she regretted it – would he think she was mocking him? She hadn't meant to, it was just that the speech-guard had gone off duty. Fortunately, he just looked confused.

'Seems like I can't even cook.'

'Nonsense, everyone has bad days. What are you drinking?'

She told him about the Will and the codicil and they talked about it for a while. He was upset that Grace had taken Jane up to The Mount to plead for help and been turned away – how desperate she must have been at that point. Things had happened so quickly after Jane was born. William Henry, her putative father, had disappeared and Grace had been left destitute. Within months she had taken passage to America to start a new life.

'What a jerk he must have been.' No longer was he amused by his feckless ancestor, she noticed. Real emotion was beginning to take hold as the years between the generations were starting to concertina closer together and these names were becoming living, feeling people.

'Who? William Henry?'

'Mm.' Maxon's frown deepened. 'You don't think I take after him, do you?' My goodness, thought Anna, his family did a job on him.

'Do you cheat, manipulate, abandon and generally leave up shit creek those who love you?' she asked, pretending to be serious. He managed a half grimace. 'No, didn't think so. You're nothing like him, Maxon.' She thought for a minute but the wine had relaxed her and she wanted to talk. 'Actually, I can tell you more about him if you want to know.'

He sat up straighter and the frown disappeared. 'Really?'

'It's not good.'

'No, I want to know. But I want to know how you know, too.' He took out of his bag his small notebook and ballpoint. Despite what he said of himself he seemed to her to be a natural student – maybe he just wasn't interested in some of the things he had been expected to learn.

So, as the strings of lights around the patio got brighter and the sky darker, she talked him through most of what she had learned. Like all his other opportunities William Henry had blown his chances in Australia by lying and gambling and, perhaps most of all, by not being good at his profession. She did not mention the marriage. Maxon was chewing the end of the plastic tube between his front teeth and thinking hard. 'You know, I may not be related to him at all, anyway.'

'How do you mean?'

'Well, I've been thinking. They were married for five years before Jane came along. Maybe someone else was Jane's dad, I mean, someone we don't know. Maybe that's why William Henry left. Maybe Grace told Jane Robert was her dad because, well, he was respectable. She would never think that Grace would meet Robert or any of the family over here. Maybe she wanted to wipe William Henry off the record since he turned out to be such a loser.'

Anna nodded. 'Yes, that's a possibility.'

Maxon's mouth suddenly dropped open. 'Just a minute,' he said, 'when did he die? I mean when did William Henry die?'

Anna took a deep draught of wine. '1903.'

'No!' Maxon stared at her. 'So she married Albert Maxon bigamously!'

'So it would seem.'

'Damn!' Anna wasn't sure whether Maxon was admiring or shocked. It turned out he was both. 'She couldn't have told him – Albert, I mean - she must have said she was a widow. But you can't blame her, can you? She had this great second chance. Wow, she must have been a looker to catch him even though she had a little kid in tow.'

Anna pondered this statement but decided to let it go. 'She may not have known that William Henry was alive, or where he was,' she said. 'Anything could have happened. He could have got someone to send a letter saying he'd died somewhere. We only know fragments.'

Maxon was writing furiously in his tiny script. Anna considered her plan. The numbness was sort of up to her belly button, she mused whimsically, but she still had to drive home so maybe she would finish this glass and go.

He looked up at her empty glass. 'Can I get you another?'

'I shouldn't. I'm driving.'

'Why don't you park in my space outside my building over the road? I'll get a taxi home for you. I'm kind of wound up, Anna, and I'd really appreciate unpacking this stuff, do you mind?' So she strolled out to her car, re-parked it, returned and found a large glass of wine on the table and a plate of nachos to share.

As she sat and sipped he read through his notes, sighed, and finally looked up at her. 'So this is it, right? This is all you know so far? No more bombshells?'

'Um. There might be a tiny one.'

'Go on.'

'William Henry married a seventeen-year old heiress in Sydney, a girl called Emma Noakes. I don't know how he managed that as he was old enough to be her father but he did, not long after he arrived boasting about how important he was.'

'Good God.' Maxon shook his head in disbelief. 'There was no way *he* wouldn't have known he was committing bigamy.'

'That's right.'

'What a bastard. Were there any kids?'

'Not that I could find. You may be right that he wasn't able to father children for some reason but he wasn't with her for long.'

'How come?'

'It was her family that tracked him through contacts back in England and exposed him and took Emma away.' Anna ran her finger round her glass. 'I imagine that she'd gone off him fairly quickly, anyway, and was only too happy to be taken back into the bosom of her family.'

Maxon was quiet for a while, eating the nachos without seeming to taste them. 'All this is a bit of a shocker for me.' Anna nodded. 'All my life I've been told how great and noble we all are – like pillars of the American establishment rooted in good old English soil. I've heard so often what a 'good' family we come from, you know, what 'good' stock we are. Like moral fibre is in our DNA. I wouldn't have been surprised to find a minor aristocrat or two once I started looking.' He grinned at Anna in self-mockery.

'You think aristocrats were any better behaved?' Anna scoffed. 'Seriously, though, has this changed how you see them?' What she meant, she realised, was has it changed how he saw himself.

He chewed his lip for a while. 'Not really. I feel sorry for Grace and if she could make a good marriage when she got the chance I admire her for it. She'd done nothing wrong, had she? It wasn't her fault that her husband turned out rotten and you're right, she might have believed he'd died.'

Anna wasn't sure whether Grace had done anything wrong or not but Maxon clearly wanted to think the best of her despite the huge question marks over her behaviour that Anna could see. There was an inch of wine left and the numbness was almost to her lips. She got out her phone to call a taxi. 'I have to go. We can talk more another time. Let's meet and I'll give you all the photocopies I've got.'

Maxon stood up and pulled out his wallet, passing her a £20 note. 'Thanks for talking me through this.' He laughed suddenly. 'I just don't know how much of this is going into the pearl wedding anniversary dossier! I'll get the check and wait with you.'

It was pleasant to be wafted home without effort and she found she was smiling and even humming some tune that had been on the taxi radio as she cautiously climbed the short flight of steps to her front door and let herself in.

17

Anna woke at 4.35 by the red numbers on her clock-radio in a lather of sweat. Her heart was pounding and she was shaking as she put her legs out of bed. What the hell was that all about?

In her dream she had been in a dim pool somewhere feeling relaxed and almost decadent in the warm soupy water. She was talking to someone, no-one she knew, just a vague presence. There were other people about in the distance but something weird was happening in the water. A sort of ball of some kind, like an old-fashioned leather case-ball, kept bobbing up by her side. It was annoying and she kept pushing it down while she chatted. Finally she took both hands and held it down under the dark water but it slipped from between her fingers and sprang back up to the surface and it was only then that she saw it was a head. It was Ellis's head. She had drowned him.

She banged the side of her own head with the heel of her hand to get rid of the horror of the image and couldn't stop herself crying out with small stifled screams. She stumbled down the stairs into the kitchen and switched on every light she could. She made tea and sat at the table cradling the mug in her hands, her eyes staring. It was hideous, terrifying. Why would she have such a nightmare?

'Mum?' It was Faye. 'What's the matter? What's happened?'

Anna tried to speak and couldn't get the words out because her teeth were chattering. In fact, her whole body was trembling violently. She set the mug down and laid her fingers on the smooth oak of the old table. Faye hesitated and then sat down beside her and took her hand. Anna stared at the two hands interlocked; Faye's was tea-coloured and glossily tipped with rose and had longer, slimmer fingers. But there was something strange about her hand that Anna couldn't make sense of. It had fantastical faces traced in darker brown on the tanned skin like gargoyles, like devils. Everything was unreal. The slipperiness of her emotion was making her head reel.

'Your hand,' Anna said. 'What's the matter with it?' She looked at Faye properly and saw that her daughter was not in night-clothes but in a black vest top and those denim shorts that she hated. Her hair was hanging down in a tangled mess. She reached out and touched it and found that it was wet and cold like Ellis' head in the dream and it made her shudder. 'Have you just got home? Why are you wet?' She stood up, shaking off Faye's hand.

'Oh, Mum, don't stress. Don't start all that.'

'Where have you been? Who have you been with?' The terror of her dream seemed to fizz into a tight ball in Anna like a drop of water in hot fat – she felt scalded.

Faye stood up, too, looking frightened. 'Just a bunch of us – we went to Jason's house in Solihull. He's got a pool in his garden. We just floated around and looked at the stars.' Anna tried to make sense of this. She had dreamed of drowning Ellis and now Faye was here soaking wet and telling her that she had been the one in the water. Anna fought to clear her brain but it was still muddled with wine and crowded with bad images. 'Mum?'

'Your hand. What's on your hand?'

'Oh, I know. It looks spooky, doesn't it?' Faye held up her hand and smiled at it. 'Parminder's sister's getting married so they've got buckets of henna at the house so she pinched some and we all drew on each other with it.'

'Anywhere else?'

'What?'

'You must have been naked in the pool,' Anna heard herself say, 'have you been graffitied anywhere else?'

Faye stopped smiling and pushed back her hair. There was a moment of utter silence and then she let fly. 'Oh, do you mean the target sign on my boobs or the arrow to my pubes?' She was pale with fury. 'I'm going to bed. I don't know what's happening to you and I don't fucking care.'

It was Friday and the office was festive. It was Nigel's thirtieth birthday and the place was festooned with balloons. At twelve o'clock everyone stopped work and crowded round him with gifts of a walking stick, denture cream, hair loss treatment and so on. It was all very good-natured and Nigel had bought boxes of cream cakes to pass round. Anna felt so tired she could barely keep her spine vertical. She glanced longingly at the grey hessian carpet and wished she could just stretch out on it for ten minutes and close her eyes.

There were a few loose ends from the Maxon Blake project, one of which was the bequest in James Thwaite's Will. It was a painting of 'little monetary value but of sentimental interest' and she pondered what could have happened to it. Almost anything. James' solicitors, even if the firm had continued for the next hundred and twenty years, would not have stored such a thing themselves. To whom might James have entrusted it if his daughter-in-law and grand-daughter had not been found by the time he died?

She brought up the Shrewsbury town website and worked through all the pages hoping for inspiration. She saw that the Museum and Art Gallery included artworks of local interest but in the 1890's it had been a music-hall. Was it the Music Hall which now housed a museum? It was worth a try and she couldn't bring herself to tackle any of the other jobs she had to do so she picked up the office phone and rang them. It took a while for her to be connected with the curator but when he understood her query he turned out to be interested and helpful.

'Do you have any idea of the subject matter of the painting?' he asked.

'No, I'm afraid not – Mr Thwaite said it was of sentimental interest which could mean anything.'

'I'm just checking our inventory, Mrs Ames. Can you give me an idea of when the painting might have come to us?'

'It was 1917 that Mr Thwaite died, but I suppose a family member could have held on to it for a while after that. I imagine the Music Hall and Assembly Rooms were used for their original purpose still at that time.'

'Ah, but there was a museum and art gallery in existence when Mr Thwaite was alive – in fact there has been one since 1835 – it just wasn't in this building for much of the time. The museum would have been at the Vaughan Mansion, where it has now returned, for part of the time. It's a wonderful 13th century building behind the Music Hall and now we use it again for that purpose, but the Art Gallery has had many homes over the decades and sometimes things have to be let go.'

'Of course.' Anna could hear the man humming quietly as he scanned his screen and wished she could be wandering round the serene rooms she imagined outside his office inhaling the peace and otherness. To escape from her own skin would be bliss. Someone called her name and she glanced up. The researchers were going to continue the celebrations at the pub and were waving her to join them. She smiled and mouthed 'later' having no intention of going.

She had slipped out of the house early this morning to catch the bus into town and pick up her car. She didn't want to see anyone or answer any questions. The thought of going home after work made her feel sick. The nightmare of Ellis and the nightmare with Faye kept swimming round her brain. She seemed to be losing control of her tongue as well as everything else and being around them all for two days could only make things worse. The sensation of skidding, sliding, not being in control was blistering up under the thin layer of her coping workaday self.

'Sorry to keep you.'

'No, it's fine. Thanks for looking.' Anna was about to ask whether he had any other ideas for tracking down the painting.

'I've found it, I think.'

'Really?'

'I need to just check some things with you if you don't mind, just for security?'

'Of course.'

'Where was Mr Thwaite living when he made the bequest?'

'Well, he still owned his farm, Glebe Farm, but he was living at The Mount after he married Eliza Pound in 1889.'

'Ok. And to whom did he leave the painting?'

'It was to his daughter-in-law, Grace, and his grand-daughter Jane, but they had disappeared. He felt very badly about what had happened with his son especially when he lost contact with them. In fact, they went to Philadelphia but he never knew that, I think.'

There was a pause as though the man was writing. 'And who is it now who wishes to claim the painting?' Anna explained who Maxon was but could hardly say he was claiming the painting. She assumed he would if he knew it still existed and worked on that basis. 'And can Maxon Blake prove his connection to James Thwaite?'

'Oh, that's no problem. We have birth, marriage and death certificates coming out of our ears!'

'Could I ask you to hold on just a little longer?' Anna agreed and she could hear a chair scraping and then a door hinge whine. After a few minutes he was back. 'I just wanted to have a word with one of the trustees who is in the building. We think this story may have some interest to people in the area and rather than just hand the painting over, given the appropriate proofs, we would like to have a little ceremony and maybe invite the local press. Do you think that would be acceptable to Mr Blake?'

'I think he would absolutely love it.'

'Shall I leave it to you to discuss dates with him and let me know?'

'Yes, I'll do that. I'm so pleased you have it.'

'Well, I'll look forward to meeting you and Mr Blake in due course.'

Anna almost hung up and then asked, 'Sorry, but could you tell me the subject or the title of the painting? We have no idea.'

'It's titled The Mount. It's a painting of a large house with a young woman and small child in the foreground.'

'Thank you.' Of course it was. James must have had it painted especially for them – to say how sorry he was for excluding them from all he had, from his good fortune. He couldn't put the real people into his house as Grace and Eliza had begged him, as he wished so vehemently he had done, but he could put them into a painting of the house. It might even function as an invitation to come home if they saw it – a statement that The Mount was where they belonged. So Grace did get to live in The Mount after all in a strange and sad way.

Anna came to a decision. She stood up and walked through the empty office to Ted's door and knocked on it. She told him that she needed to leave early – there was something she had to attend to urgently and he shrugged and nodded.

At home George was out so he must be feeling better and there was no sign of Faye. Ellis didn't break up for the summer until next week. She ran upstairs and threw a couple of T shirts and a spare pair of jeans into a bag together with her washing stuff and underwear. At the kitchen table she Googled St Ives Accommodation and within minutes had a single room not far from the harbour. She texted her father that she was going away for the weekend and gave him the number of the B&B. She left a message on Ellis' phone to say he should help Pops and she would be back on Sunday night. She added kisses. The text to Faye was harder. In the end she wrote: 'Sorry. Going away for a couple of days. See you Sunday night, I hope. Love you.' She picked up her laptop and phone and the bags and almost ran out of the door. She had been in the house for twenty-five minutes.

As she was putting on her seat-belt she loaded the first of her stack of Linda Ronstadt CDs and turned the volume up. Hours later she had left the motorway at Plymouth and turned on to the A38 with no worrying thought having had the mind-space to attack her. She stopped for a cold drink at a service station and thought she would cleanse her musical palate with a little Purcell – she had grabbed one at random from the stack. It was still fine and sunny; it had been an extraordinary summer of long hot days and sudden downpours and people were becoming irritated by it. She overheard a woman at the pay kiosk in the petrol station complaining that there was 'no air' and what a nuisance it was to have to keep watering the garden. The man next to her said longingly that a break in the weather must come soon.

She set off again and noted with a sinking heart that the traffic was building up for the long stretch down the spine of Cornwall to her turn to St. Ives. This CD of Purcell alternated jolly rumpety-tumpety triumphal tunes with mournful dirges. She always much preferred the latter and allowed herself to feel just a tickle of pain from them as if someone had laid a cold knife across her throat with a flat blade. The landscape was low undulations here and she was becoming tired after the long day but at least the open aspect meant that the sunlight slanting from the west didn't strobe her eyes. She pulled the sun visor out and twisted it sideways to cut out some of the glare. The traffic was fairly heavy on this stretch but moving well and she glanced at the dashboard clock, calculating that she should be at her B & B by nine if she could keep up this pace. She wondered what she would do about food; the Co-op would probably be closed by the time she got there, or would it? Maybe it had extended its opening hours. She certainly didn't want to sit in a restaurant or pub and wait for food. Perhaps she would stop at the next service station to buy a sandwich and, if possible, a bottle or two of wine. She drummed her fingers on the steering wheel, shifted a little in her seat to sit straighter and that's when it hit her.

She had forgotten that on this CD was Dido's Lament. She was in the fast lane of the road when it hit and quickly made the decision to stay where she was. 'When I am laid, am laid in earth,' came the plaintive voice. She could cope with it, if necessary she could just turn down the volume, but within seconds it had netted her. The long, agonised call came finally, 'Remember me, remember me, but, ah, forget my fate.' She couldn't see where she was going.

For a mad moment she considered switching on the windscreen wipers to clear the wetness blurring her eyes but then signalled, moved, signalled, moved and thankfully the cars were attentive and let her pull on to the hard shoulder. They were probably cursing her, thinking she had had a phone call on her mobile, or more charitably that she had detected a fault with the car.

It would not let her do anything but weep. She could not turn it down or off, she was captive. She bent her head and the surgical precision of the pain sliced into her heart. Each falling cadence, each note in a minor key dragged out excruciatingly, the agonised vocal refrain, every trick in the composer's book stabbed into her like a stiletto applied again and again and again, slower and deeper each time until she was completely undone. At last it finished and she tore the CD out of its slot and flung it on to the back seat. She rummaged desperately among the stack she had in a box on the passenger seat, found The Best of Abba and stuck it in. She dried her eyes, took a deep breath and pulled out into the slow lane behind a container truck, her hands trembling on the wheel.

Two hours later she noticed the lifting of the light, even in the evening, that announces the sea is nearby, the opposite of the dimming caused by an eclipse, she thought, but just as powerful in its effect. We feel it – the atavistic delight or dread, awe or relief that there are forces greater than ourselves which are indifferent to us. She turned down the road towards the tip of the coast and directly into the sun which was now slipping very low and was blinding her so that she had to shield her eyes with her hand as well as with the visor.

She stopped once more at a convenience shop in Carbis Bay and then, in minutes, she was negotiating the little lanes through the town and driving along a packed wharf to the public car park where she would have to leave the car, there being no parking near the cottage on Downlong. In her rear-view mirror she could see the oily black humps of rock heaping to the Arts Club and as she waited in the slow-moving file of cars she narrowed her eyes against the shortbread creaminess of the sand in the harbour to admire the racks of houses climbing up towards The Island in a mosaic of mustards, whites and tawny browns.

Her room was tiny but it had everything necessary and she couldn't resist half an hour out on the harbour in the cool red-gold light before a nightcap and bed.

18

There was a thick mist the next morning but she knew it would probably burn off and in any case she wanted to get going. She had a programme. She felt excited and almost light-hearted as they always did at the start of a fine day on holiday. The self-catering cottage they always booked was over the headland up from Porthminster beach and she may go and look at it later but this morning she would be striding out along the southern coastal path towards Zennor. How many times had they walked that path? Dozens. As the children got older they went further, not plodding doggedly on to clock up miles, but stopping, exclaiming, finding little treasures to take home, sitting on the scratchy turf and gazing out at any shipping passing, lying back and staring up into a huge bowl of blue or lumpy skeins of grey. She smiled as she walked quickly past Porthmeor beach and up on to the tarmacked path that led to the coastal trail. Harry, veteran of many field trips, had long ago found an insulated box which fitted exactly into his large back pack and he would have been up before breakfast slicing up salads, boiling eggs, hulling strawberries, wrapping the saved cold cooked sausages in greaseproof paper and stacking all the tubs neatly into the big cold box. The plastic cutlery would be wrapped in a tea-towel and stuck down the side. Later it could be used for wet feet and sticky hands and faces. As they passed down Fore Street they would pick up fresh cobs of bread from the deli and bottles of drink. Faye and Ellis were responsible for carrying their own drinks and tissues and Anna would grab the small knapsack always ready packed with plasters, antiseptic and anti-bite cream, sun-blocker, digital binoculars and a camera. The moment when, as now, the tarmac petered out and they felt the grit and sand beneath their feet was always the real start of the treat.

It was almost the school holidays and a few families were already ahead of her picking their way along but mostly it was pensioners making the most of having the trail to themselves for a little longer. She passed them, smiling and nodding, as they trundled along at a good pace slowed only by chatting and stopping to admire the view. By the time she reached the half-way point the mist had cleared and she could look back to the clenched fist of St Ives with its beaches tucked between each knuckle. She would drop down to Zennor and have lunch at The Tinners Arms as they always did and then make her way back across the fields. Her legs ached a little at the unusual exercise and she slowed her pace and then stopped and stood, as everyone must, to gaze out across the rippled expanse of the sea. Her landlady at the cottage had told her that her father's family had been farmers and miners. 'It was either that or fishing,' she said. 'We never bothered about being bought things when we were children, I mean, things to play with. We had the beaches and the harbour and The Island. Even now, it's the same with mine, it's all they want. They're out all day. The rain don't bother them – they've got wetsuits. It's only at night and in the worst of the winter they want games and telly. I'm happy for it.'

And she was fine, she really was. The pub was just as she remembered it, as dark inside and as pretty outside with its soft-coloured stone and bright tubs and baskets of flowers and she sat contentedly for half an hour sipping Clodgy and eating her salmon and salad with hunks of crusty bread as slowly as she could. Then a couple came out and sat at the next table and a little girl skipped up to join them having been to the loo, as she announced. Anna smiled at her and was met with a hard stare so she turned her smile on the parents instead. They glanced pleasantly at her and then went back to their conversation while the child wriggled on her seat and made slurping noises with the straw in her lemonade. Then, at something the man said, the woman laughed, her chin tipped up, her mouth open, her eyes shining into his as he leaned towards her, his expression teasing and delighted.

Anna stood up so rapidly that her chair almost fell over but she quickly pulled it upright and slung her pack over her shoulders deciding instantly not to go across the fields but to take the lanes back. She didn't want to walk those fields alone now, even cars would be some kind of company. Her legs felt heavy and her body was rebelling against the fierce pace she was attempting. Stupid. She had not only eaten too much, she had forgotten the power of the local cider. How much had she had? Probably a pint. Half way up the lane to the main road she gave in and climbed a gate into the field. The ground was tussocky and covered with prickly, itchy grasses but she lay down anyway in a patch of shade using her knobbly back-pack as a pillow. Within seconds she was asleep.

When she got back to the town she was exhausted and spent the afternoon lying on the harbour beach with her back against the wall. Whenever hard thoughts began to intrude she read. By the end of the day she was stunned with sun and stumbled back to the B&B almost blindly. She thought she would shower and change into tomorrow's clean clothes and maybe do a little work on her laptop before finding somewhere for dinner. There were messages on her phone from her dad and Ellis. George had texted: 'Go for it. Good idea. Take care.' Ellis had written, 'Wish I was there, school sucks.' She had been selfish to come away without them but there would be another time when they could all come, wouldn't there. No point in beating herself up over that, too. There was no message from Faye and the now familiar throb of guilt and resentment bit her gut.

She piled up her pillows, sat back into them with her laptop on her knee and opened the Maxon Blake folder pondering what to do with it. She put the B & B wifi code in so that she could do a bit more research. There wasn't much to do unless she went back further with the Thwaite family into preceding generations. Maybe another time, if Maxon wanted her to – he hadn't shown any interest in anyone beyond his great great-grandmother. What else? She scrolled down her notes and looked for the red highlighting that indicated more work might be useful. She hadn't yet told him about the painting she had tracked down and the planned ceremony but she didn't want to phone him now. She would rather talk to him about it on Monday.

It was frustrating not to have an answer to the mystery over Jane's paternity but the old possibilities still could be true. If William Henry had proved a disappointment and Robert had, as he clearly had, done very well for himself in a small town way, then Grace, who had already proved she was capable of fictionalising her past, may have decided he was a more fitting father for her daughter and lied to the girl. Certainly there were notable omissions from Grace's dictated memoir and she had sensibly caught her daughter at exactly that point of her childhood where she would have been interested enough to write it all down and keep it but not sufficiently worldly wise to ask awkward questions. By the time Jane would have been canny enough to ask them, her mother had died. It was also still possible that Grace and Robert had had an affair which William Henry might have found out about but James, his father, had never discovered so that his son's behaviour in abandoning his wife and daughters would have seemed both inexplicable and appalling. Grace may have miscalculated that Robert would ditch his wife for her. If one brother had bombed, the other might have made a tempting target.

Anna opened the document she kept on side-issues – little pieces of information that might or might not be relevant to this case. The first bullet point concerned a Herbert Pound whose name came up in an article about farm machinery but he had turned out to have lived in Hereford and was of little interest.

The next bullet point was a note about Susannah, the pie-maker from Chirk Street, who had lived twenty houses away from the Thwaite family. Anna looked her up on the 1891 census. Anna peered at it wondering if she would soon need reading glasses and then sat back in astonishment. Susannah Maxon was the wife of Albert Maxon, head of household. They had a daughter and a son, an infant and a baby. Anna made a note by hand on her pad adding that Albert's listed occupation was rent collector. He was twenty-three years old. Quickly she exited that page and brought up the 1901 census. He was not on it. She entered Susannah's name and there she was, living at the same address with her children, the older of the two now working as a pot-boy, presumably in the local pub. Albert Maxon had gone. Anna's heart was beating rapidly with excitement. That moment when facts, non-negotiable, documented facts, gave a sudden insight into lives long finished was the most exciting part of her work. She stared out at the small patch of rooftops and blue sky visible from the cottage window and thought hard.

The first step was obvious. She checked death records for Albert Maxon and found nothing. The next step was to load the website which held data for outgoing passenger lists on ships bound for the United States. She had found Grace and Jane on this site travelling steerage, so she tried the same year, 1895. There were no results. Ok, he may have gone out ahead of her to prepare the way so she worked her way back through 1894 and, to be systematic, through 1893, 1892 and even 1891. Nothing.

When she looked up again the sky was deep rose pink and a glance at her watch told her it was after nine o'clock but she was too wound up to eat just yet. She knew she could get fish and chips until late. She poured herself a glass of wine, drank that, and then poured another. She felt in her bones that she was within a whisker of finding out something momentous and she had to go on.

She decided to work the other way chronologically and brought up the passenger lists for 1896. She keyed in his name. There he was. 'There he is!' she cried out loud. He was on board a steam-ship bound for Philadelphia but there was a difference between his listing and Grace's from the previous year. Albert Maxon, late of Chirk Street and a lowly rent collector, was travelling second class, not steerage. This meant that Anna could track his luggage and it was the work of a few seconds to do so. He was literally loaded. Six tea chests, two cabin trunks and numerous smaller items of baggage were listed. He had no travelling companion. Anna exited the website, closed the laptop and jumped off the bed. She needed to walk, to think. Finishing the wine, she pulled out a sweater from her bag which she had barely bothered to unpack, tucked the room and house key into the zip-pocket of her trousers and ran down the narrow staircase and out into the street.

The sun had slipped down past the horizon some time ago and the sky was now a dark pearl, the water in the harbour slapping gently and rocking the boats at their moorings. She pulled on her sweater and queued with a line of others for fish and chips. The line mounted stairs on one side of the barrier and happy customers came running down the other side clutching hot parcels. This was the chippie they always went to – the food perfectly cooked, piping hot, crunchy and delicious. While she waited she thought about what she had discovered, forcing herself to be rigorous, to look at all possibilities, but really, Maxon on its own was a fairly unusual name and the combination of that with Albert and the destination of the vessel made an explanation of coincidence almost impossible. She mounted another step. Not almost impossible but completely impossible. She was at the top and standing in front of the glowing hot-plate and racks of delicious food.

She took her bundle and wooden fork out on to the harbour wall looking around for seagulls on the hunt. She couldn't see any but that didn't mean that one or even two might not swoop down on her from behind just as she was raising a golden chip to her lips. It had happened several times before. Then she spotted a woman with a large dog sitting further down and chatting into a phone. She moved to sit by her hoping the dog would be enough of a deterrent to the birds.

As she ate, huffing over the heat of the food but unable to resist wolfing it, she let the startling new information roll around her mind. The shadowy harbour with its dinghies and little fishing boats, the sea wall cluttered with people chatting, laughing or staring out across the water, the bright rope of lights behind her all disappeared and she was conscious in her mind's eye only of a young man standing on the deck of a trans-Atlantic ship in late July wearing a sharp suit, cut tight in the legs and body as was the style then (as it is now), probably wearing a boater set at a rakish angle, his tanned face lit by the excitement of his adventure. What had he done? He had stepped out of his humdrum predictable life, the life where he would be expected to die as poor and restricted as he had lived; the life where each day he came home from his rounds to crying children and a harassed and exhausted young wife asking him for money, perhaps. Anna felt no sympathy at all for him but she understood why he had done it. How many men or even women had done the same? William Henry had taken himself away from all that, too. Grace had. It must have been so easy and so tempting. Now, it would be hard for anyone to run and hide in quite that way what with passports and visas and border controls, but then?

The woman and the dog moved away. Anna was thirsty from the salt on her food and glanced behind her along the quay. Opposite the life-boat ramp was a pub and a knot of customers milling good-naturedly outside. She had never been in it. When they had come down here it was always a family holiday and the evenings were spent playing board games until it was time for the children, Ellis first and then Faye, to go to bed. Then she and Harry would chat a little about what to do the following day, read, and go to bed early, curled up close in the double bed that was too short for Harry's length and murmur to each other until sleep came. They never made love in that cottage, inhibited by the thin wall between themselves and the children.

Anna shook her head to clear it of such thoughts and stood up. She balled the fish and chip papers and pushed them into a full bin and then made her way around to the pub. It was called, appropriately enough, The Lifeboat Inn and she was halted for a moment by the pub sign. It showed lifeboatmen in a rowing boat at sea at a perilous angle up the side of a huge green wave of water. It wasn't clear whether they would make it or not, their figures were so small, the oars useless, the wave so huge. She shuddered.

There was some sort of football match commentary going on but it couldn't be heard above the din of chatter from the bar. She pushed her way through and ordered two large glasses of red wine. If it was like this now it would be impossible in half an hour and once she'd found a seat she didn't want to lose it. She backed out holding them and searched for a spot. Up against the wall there were two couples, a young one and an old one, clearly not together and she thought she could with a bit of assertiveness get herself into the space between them. Sure enough, they moved their hot thighs and she was in. She put one wine glass on the table to her left and one on the table to her right. It somehow looked better that way. A roar went up from the people near the screen and she saw that goals were being replayed. She stared at it for a direction to look in but it was only so that she could think and seem occupied.

The obvious, huge question was where had Maxon Blake got his money from? He was going to join Grace Thwaite in Philadelphia and he was not arriving empty handed. Had she really run away to America distraught and ashamed with no one to help her at home having been abandoned by her husband, as James, her father-in-law, believed? Or, had she and Albert Maxon had a plan and if so, when had it been conceived? And thinking about conception, whose daughter was Jane? Maybe it was only the truth when Grace told Jane to call Albert 'father.' Had William Henry known? Was that why he left?

As Anna finished her first glass of wine and replaced it with the second she allowed her thoughts, now slowing to a comfortable speed, to return to the money issue. She no longer bothered to pretend to be watching the screen. She gazed ahead and sipped. What were the possible explanations? Albert could have been left some money by a rich relation who had died. He could have been given the money by a living rich relation or friend. Yes, that was possible. He might even have had a big win at the races. But staring her in the face was that copperplate hand-writing on the 1891 census. Occupation: rent collector. Had Albert Maxon and Grace Thwaite planned that when she was safely in Philadelphia and had found lodgings he would do a moonlight flit when the best opportunity came? Do a runner with that month's rent owed to his employer? Or, had he been creaming off the collections for some time and had been keeping his fingers crossed that he would get away before his fraud was discovered? She could check the local newspaper for coverage of a theft but she doubted that the landowner would tell the police. If other rent collectors got the idea that they could do the same, it could be very dangerous.

The noise of the bar and the blur of the people were beginning to make Anna feel light-headed. She ought to make a move back to her room but she couldn't summon the energy to fight her way out. The bolted fish and chips were now lying heavily on her stomach and she was feeling queasy. Her lips were a little numb and the din was making her head ache. She looked at the bar in case the crowd was thinning and an easy route out could be seen but she couldn't really concentrate on the task. Then she saw Harry.

He had his back to her and he was wearing what she called his hare-and-hounds check shirt with his beige slacks. But it was not his height or his clothes that made her notice him, it was his hair, the rare rich shade somewhere between chestnut and auburn that curled around his ears and down his neck rimmed now with gold from the bar lights that made her recognise him. She lurched to her feet ignoring the protests of the people either side, and stumbled and pushed her way to the bar until she was inches away from him.

'Harry,' she breathed, hardly daring to say the name, 'Harry.' The man turned, feeling her hand on his elbow, and it was not Harry. Of course it wasn't. 'Please,' she said, beginning to well up with desperate tears, 'please can I touch your hair? Can I?' He stared at her, his young, stranger's face confused and alarmed.

'Um, I think you've got me mixed up with someone else.' He was flushing with embarrassment while his friends teased him.

'Oh Harry, let me touch you!' mimicked one, and then, 'You can touch my hair any time, lover! Or anything else that takes your fancy!' The roar of laughter crashed into her head.

Anna only just made it outside before she was sick, vomiting a revolting mix of food and wine down the side of the harbour wall. Then she felt a hand on her shoulder. 'Come on, we'll walk you home,' a man said. His girlfriend stood just behind him looking at Anna warily. It was the young couple she had been squashed up against in the pub.

'I'm all right,' she said automatically, feeling as though her body had been turned inside out.

'I know. But we'll just walk you home anyway, ok?' They went either side of her linking arms with her so that she could stay upright.

'Up there,' she nodded towards Downlong. 'Not far. Thank you.'

After a few steps the woman said, 'You thought you knew that man at the bar? Friend of yours?'

'I thought he was my husband,' Anna said, her eyes overflowing beyond her control.

'Was he meeting you here?'

'No.' There was no light now in the sky, no sign of moon or stars. The water of the harbour was a flat black. 'He died. He died three months ago.'

When they reached the B & B they helped her find her keys and open the door. She had sobered a little and they sensed that she was over the worst. 'Well, we'll wish you good night,' the man said and the woman leaned to her and hugged her.

'Thank you. Thank you so much.'

'Just sleep.'

She climbed the narrow staircase, hauling herself up on the rail, and managed to let herself into her own room. It was pitch black. She switched on the main light and fell on to the bed. It had been a mistake to come. Harry was everywhere here and nowhere. When she first arrived she had rejoiced in the memories but now all she could feel were the empty spaces where he should have been. She wanted to be with her family, she wanted her dad and Ellis and Faye and everyone. She even wanted Bobble. She had never felt more alone.

She picked up her phone to text them or maybe it wasn't too late to phone? There were four missed messages from Diane. She read each one in turn and buried her head in her hands, groaning. 'Yr dad worse. Been 2 dr – with me now. Come home.'

Drunk, exhausted, it was impossible for her to go now however much she wanted to. She set her alarm for 4.00 in the morning and fell on to the bed, the room reeling around her.

19

She arrived just after the morning rush hour in Birmingham and was able to drive quickly taking the road home first. She didn't bother to take her bag in, just ran upstairs to check what was happening. It was Sunday morning and Ellis' room was empty but when she moved to the window she could see him playing with Bobble and an old tennis ball in the garden. She knocked gently on Faye's door and opened it carefully. There she was in a twisted heap of duvet, her bright hair spilling across the pillow and one flushed cheek visible. She was snoring softly. Anna closed the door as carefully as she had opened it and dashed out into the garden.

'Hi Mum – I thought you weren't coming back till tonight? Are you ok?'

He shouldn't have to worry about his mother, Anna thought miserably, I should be the one worrying about him. 'Yes, I'm fine. Just missed you all and decided to come back early.' Had he been told about his grandfather?

'Look at what Bobble can do. I'm training him.'

Anna forced herself to slow down and smile. Her head was thumping and her throat burned sore and dry – she had driven straight through. 'Go on, then.'

Ellis told Bobble to sit and Bobble barked and wagged his tail. 'Wait, wait, he will do it.' Ellis moved to the dog and placed his hand firmly on his lower back. 'Sit!' Bobble, willing to indulge the boy who must have weighed much the same as he did, sat.

'That's brilliant, Ell.'

'I've been looking it up – how to be your dog's pack leader. He has to believe I'm in charge. I'm going to try doing stay today.'

'Good idea.' Bobble was now up and prancing around on his huge paws, every now and then bowing to the tennis ball. Anna made herself wait a moment and then said casually, 'Pops at Diane's?'

'Yup. She texted me yesterday and said he wanted to see a love-bird or something they've got in and then decided to stay the night.' Ellis stopped throwing the ball for a second and grinned at her. 'Love-bird!'

'Aargh,' Anna joked, 'let's not think about it, eh?' Ellis laughed. So they hadn't told him. 'Actually, Ell, I want to pop round there myself, will you be ok for a couple of hours?'

Ellis' pride was piqued – she had been thoughtless. 'I've been all right on my own for all of yesterday. I'm not a kid, Mum.' He hadn't meant it as a rebuke, or at least not for her negligence, quite the contrary, but she felt it keenly.

'Ok, back soon.'

As she drove to Safe 'n' Sound her anxiety mounted. They probably had told Faye so there would be an adult around for Ellis but not Ellis himself. In that case, it was not just a cold that her dad was suffering from – it must be considerably worse. She found it now incredible that she had taken off to Cornwall in the way she had. How selfish, how reckless she had been. She was the sensible one, the planner, the delayer of gratification, the one who figured out a three-month forecast budget so they could manage. Her dad had told her all her life to be less conscientious, more impulsive, and yet this one time she had been he had been put in jeopardy. She urged the car on driving slightly faster than the speed limit until the turning to the farm appeared. Thank goodness for Diane.

She had texted from home to say she would soon be there and Diane was outside waiting for her when she drew up. She jumped out of the car. 'Is he ok?'

But Diane was not smiling. She had her arms crossed and her face was grim. In a flash Anna realised that this was not sadness or concern, this was anger. 'No. He is not. What on earth were you thinking?'

'Diane?'

'Have you ever spared one moment to think about what he's been going through? Have you stopped feeling sorry for yourself long enough to even notice him?'

Anna could only stare at her in horror.

'Ever since Harry died you've been in your own world, Anna, and I thought that was understandable even though the kids were having a very hard time and you were paying them no attention.'

'What?' Anna felt as though the walls of her world were falling around her like scenery in a stage fiasco.

'So your dad stepped in, grieving for Harry as he was. Rosa has only been around for a few weeks – before that it was George that was with Harry all day, Monday to Friday for years. Bathed him, cheered him up, made him feel better about losing his moorings on life, watched the person who was a son to him slowly dying.

Every day while you were at work it was George that was with him, putting his own life on hold because he loved Harry, and all of you, so much. He was devastated when he died.'

'I know.' Was this really Diane speaking?

'Do you? I don't think you do. So then he had you to worry about, you going off the rails and all this drinking and the Faye business.'

'Just a minute, Diane.' At the mention of Faye felt something sharp and hot rise up in her gut.

'No, I'm speaking now. I don't often like this, but I am now.' Diane was looking her straight in the eyes and Anna felt the full force of her fury. 'When you slapped Faye and then wouldn't make it up to her it was George who took the strain, not you. He talked to her for hours trying to make her understand what you may be going through, telling her you *did* love her and all that, trying to help her through her own pain.' Diane was now red-faced with anger. 'She lost her father, Anna. She lost her dad and so did Ellis. You weren't the only one! And yet you've done nothing but pick on her and attack her and leave George to pick up the pieces.'

'I'm sorry -' Anna's legs were beginning to give way and she was afraid she would sink to the ground. Was the woman never going to stop this onslaught?

'No. I haven't finished. What you said to him at the barbeque was unforgiveable. I can only imagine you were drunk. He has spent his entire life putting you first – his entire life, Anna! You know that. He has been mother and father to you since you were a tiny tot. How dare you be so selfish, so unkind to him?' Horribly, Diane began to cry. She turned on her heel and stalked into the house. Anna stood frozen feeling something in her chest grab like a clenched fist and then went after her, numb with shock.

George was in bed. It was the first time that Anna had seen upstairs at the farm. The room was small and cramped by the old-fashioned double bed where George was propped on a heap of pillows, his skin grey and gleaming with sweat. He was dozing and she heard the breath labouring in his chest. She pushed round the door and sat on the edge of the mattress, taking his hand. 'Dad?'

He opened his eyes and smiled. 'Thought you were in Cornwall, love. Had a nice time?' His voice was hoarse. Anna bent her head in shame.

'Dad, I'm so sorry I went. I had no idea how ill you were.'

He patted her hand. 'I'm ok.' He coughed deeply and swallowed. 'Diane's been a wonderful nurse.' Anna turned to look at her standing in the doorway and then back to her father.

'You need to see someone, you sound awful.'

Diane frowned at George. 'They're on their way. The ambulance is coming for him. I thought this morning about seven that it had turned to pneumonia. The doctor said yesterday it might and to call him out.'

'He was very good,' George croaked. 'Came out to see me. I thought they didn't do that any more.' He coughed painfully again and Anna heard the squeak of the in-breath that followed. She felt his forehead and kissed it.

'I'll stay with you, Dad. We both will.'

'Can I have a word?' Diane had retreated on to the landing. Anna got up and followed her.

'Yes?' She was humbled and if this was another tirade she would take it without comment.

'I'll see him checked in and I'll make sure they do things right but you need to go home and see to the children. They'll have to be told, Anna. Later on, if he's settled and they say it's all right, you can bring them out to see him. I'll let you know.' Anna could do nothing but nod.

She watched him be carried into the ambulance and then got into her car and followed it down the drive. She couldn't process anything, not now. Now was the time to put the children first, not the tsunami of guilt and fear that was towering, waiting to overwhelm her.

By late afternoon George had been pumped full of antibiotics and was blearily dozy. Ellis, having never visited anyone in hospital before and being unsure of protocol, kept glancing around to see what was going on with the other beds. He had no idea what to do or what to say. He had never seen his grandfather ill but now he was lying in bed, frail and depleted, and it was almost too much for the boy. George had been placed in one of the large single rooms in the QE that look out on to the south of the city. It was an afternoon of hazy low stratiform cloud and the whole city seemed to be, like George, only semi-conscious.

'Can you see Frankley Beeches?' Anna asked, trying to sound bright. 'Look for a copse of trees high up on a hill. It's the landmark your dad used, do you remember?' Ellis looked down at his hands and seemed about to burst into tears. What a stupid, insensitive thing to say. The last thing he needed as his grandfather lay seriously ill was to be reminded that he had already lost his father. Anna looked at Faye to see if she could help lighten the moment but Faye only glanced at her coldly and then her attention went back to her grandfather.

'Can I get you both a drink?' she suggested desperately, 'Or a snack?' Faye didn't bother to reply and Ellis shook his head.

Diane came in looking cheerful and put her hand on Ellis' shoulder. 'Now you're not to worry because I've had a word with his nurse and they're very pleased with him. The antibiotics will kick in very soon and he'll be turning all this into one of his poems before you know it, probably a whole book full. Boring me silly.' Faye looked at her gratefully and smiled a little, standing up for a hug. 'Now we should all push off because he needs to sleep. It's the best thing for him.' She looked over at Anna sitting on her own by the window. 'Perhaps you could come back this evening for an hour since you'll be a work tomorrow and I'll pop in, in the morning.' Her words sounded natural and normal but Anna could see that there was still ice in her eyes. She nodded.

'Can I come in tomorrow, too?' Faye said. 'I don't have to work till late. What time will you come?' They spoke quietly and hugged again. Ellis went to Diane and put his arm round her bulky waist and she kissed him on the top of his head.

They all said their goodbyes to George and hurried down the corridor, Anna, unwanted, trailing in their wake. She drove the children home and Faye immediately disappeared to her room with a firm click of the door. Ellis and Anna went into the kitchen and she decided she would do something caring, something motherly, and bent down to lift out of the cupboard the heavy yellow and white mixing bowl. 'I think I'll make a cake,' she said as gaily as she could. 'Pops will want to have something nice when he comes home.'

Ellis was studying his phone. He turned an anxious face to Anna. 'Mike's going over to his cousins' and they've got a new trampoline. Can I go? I won't if you need me.'

'Of course you can, darling,' Anna said, glad to be able to please him even a little. 'Have a lovely time and there'll be chocolate cake for you to come home to.' Ellis gave her a worried look. This gushing was not her normal maternal tone and he was unnerved by it. She felt completely phoney herself but she had somehow lost her bearings on how she should be, what she should say. Diane, the no-nonsense newcomer to their lives, had given her children more comfort than she had been able to. She kept getting everything wrong.

As she creamed the softened butter and sugar her phone went. She saw it was Diane and she steeled herself against what new attack was coming, or maybe not, maybe it would be an apology. 'Are you alone?' Diane asked abruptly.

Oh no, much as she usually loved Diane, she had had enough of her for one day and didn't want her coming round, Anna thought mutinously. 'Um. Just doing a bit of baking. Ellis is out and Faye's up in her room.'

'Right - so now I'll tell you what the doctor really said.'

Anna slumped into a chair. As Diane talked she traced with her other hand the old-fashioned moulding on the chair Harry had always sat in. The chairs were a mis-matched collection and some were coming apart at the joints, especially the one Len favoured to rest his huge bulk. Len, she had forgotten to tell him about her dad. She would do it immediately after this. When the call ended she got up and turned on the oven. It was on the third cracked egg that she burst into tears and stood, head bent, dripping water into the bowl. She dried her eyes on a tea towel and finished the job carefully. When the mixture was in the tin she made the call.

'Len? It's Anna.'

'All right?' Len said.

'No, not really. It's George – he's come down with pneumonia and they've taken him into the QE.'

'Poor old bugger. Still, they'll soon have him fixed up. My mate Jacko, you know the one that plays keyboard?' As usual it wasn't a rhetorical question and he waited until Anna was able to murmur assent. 'Jacko got a really bad chest when was at that gig in Bradford and he was spitting green stuff and groaning and lying around like he was on his last legs but once they give him something he was back to normal in a couple of days.' He paused for effect. 'You know, spitting and groaning and lying around! Ha!'

'It may be a bit worse than that, Len. Diane says the doctor is really worried. The next twelve hours will be crucial, they said.'

She saw that the oven had come up to temperature and that the cake mixture was beginning to sweat.

'He's not going to croak is he?'

'Oh, Len, don't even say that.'

There was a pause. 'I'd come over Sis, but we've got a practice in about half an hour. Tell me where he is and I might go in to see him after.' Another pause. 'Er. Try not to worry.'

'Thanks Len.' At least he was trying to be kind which was more than anyone else had been.

When the cake was in the oven she looked round for Bobble. It had been such a disorientating, exhausting day that she had forgotten about him and so must Ellis have done since he had run out to the Bryant family car so quickly. She opened the back door and looked down the garden but there was no sign of him. Then she heard a whimper and the thump of a tail. He was in a strange position, half hanging by the side gate with his front paws in the air and when she went to him she saw that his collar had snagged on a thick wire hook and in trying to free himself he had made it tighten. He must have been jumping up at the back gate trying to get attention. 'Oh, poor boy,' she exclaimed, freeing him. 'Poor boy!' How long had he been like that? They had been out for hours. Immediately he was free he was licking her face and squeaking with gratitude and love. She ran to his bowl and filled it with fresh water which he gulped and then brought out his food.

It was too much. She walked numbly into the kitchen, picked up a bottle from the rack making sure it had a screw cap and returned to the lounger under the tree. She set the alarm on her watch for fifteen minutes and took the first long swallow from the bottle. It was four o'clock near enough. She would get the cake out to cool, have another glass of wine and then go upstairs for a nap until it was time to visit her dad. She didn't want to think, to feel, to remember. She had been awake since 4.00 in the morning, driven two hundred and seventy miles without a break, been torn apart by Diane and devastated by the sight of her dad and now had been told that he was critically ill. Faye had treated her with contempt and between them they had inadvertently tortured the dog. A mad part of her wanted to laugh. It had been nothing but misery all day and she could not allow herself to think about how much worse it could get.

Bobble clattered his now empty dish trying to find any speck he'd missed and then came to her, flopping by her side so that she could dig her fingers into his hot rough coat and stroke the wiry face and be, for a few moments, loved.

She made an early light meal of salad and hard-boiled eggs for herself and Faye, who had not re-appeared, and put one portion in the fridge under plastic film. She looked sadly round the kitchen, almost always empty these days, and remembered how only months ago the table would be crowded; Faye and Ellis would be picking at each other, George would be bustling and spouting little gems he'd read or heard that day, Harry would probably be arranging a line of peas in order of size on his plate or something equally touching and bizarre. Even knowing Harry's time was limited, although not as limited as it had turned out to be, she had unthinkingly assumed that was normal – that was the way it would carry on being, especially when Faye got the job at Mecklins and would not be going away to university. Instead it seemed as though they had come unstuck as a family. Some element of gravity which had drawn them together was now a centrifuge pushing them apart. She pressed a post-it note on the kitchen table for Faye, brought Bobble in and set off for the hospital. Ellis had sent a text that he would not be back until about nine o'clock.

George was more or less awake but finding it hard to talk. Anna had taken in a few of the newly arrived collections of poetry and the paper for the cricket results. It turned out he had no real appetite for either but he smiled when she started to read and slipped into sleep again. She looked at the chart at the end of his bed which stated that he had had a full meal of beef casserole and potatoes with steamed pudding and tea. Somehow she doubted it. But, he was clean and comfortable and it was reassuring that nurses regularly came in to check on him. He was linked to a heart monitor and an oxygen unit which was connected through his nose. Anna couldn't bear to look at the large purple bruise on his hand where the cannula was stuck into a vein and taped down for the antibiotic feed. It was distressing to see that squashed damson under his skin. The truth was he looked old and frail and she had never seen him look that way before.

The door opened and Faye crept in, her eyes huge. She moved softly to George's side and stared at the sleeping face sucking the knuckle of her thumb like she used to as a baby. Anna was sitting at the window but was hardly acknowledged. Faye's hair was hanging undressed down her back in a cascade of rich ochre colours, her face was bare of make-up and she was wearing old jeans and a T shirt. Anna got up to go to her and comfort her and, she admitted, herself, but as she approached Faye straightened up and turned to her with narrowed eyes. She looked down at her mother with not a vestige of warmth.

'Is he going to die?'

'Of course not, darling. Don't say that.'

'The nurse told me he might – I've just asked. I know Diane was lying yesterday.'

'Oh,' Anna breathed, at a loss. 'He's a very strong person, there's no reason -'

Faye pushed past her almost knocking her down. 'Well, if everyone is going to die on me I'm going to party. And I mean party. You'll see me when you see me, not that you care.'

She was gone. Anna looked at her dad's face to see if he had heard but the rhythm of his distressingly audible breathing had not altered. She pulled a chair to his side and took the hand that was not taped to the drip. 'Dad?' she whispered, 'Dad? You're needed. I need you. We all do. Just fight hard, will you?' She bowed her head to his arm noticing how thin and scrawny it had become. What was that famous poem of Thomas' written when his own father was dying: 'Do not go gentle into that good night'? She couldn't say that to her dad because Mr. Thomas had died anyway.

After a long time a nurse came in to take his temperature and she sat up. 'How is it?'

The nurse smiled, wrote something on the chart and left. She got up and read the note. It was one degree higher than the previous reading. An announcement came over the PA System that it was time for visitors to leave. She kissed his hot forehead, picked up the books and the untouched fruit salad she had made and walked slowly out. What would she do if he died? She knew better than anyone how badly she was coping as it was. It was unthinkable that she would have to go on alone with a double burden of guilt and grief.

She wanted to be home for Ellis but when she had filled the cake with buttercream icing and tidied the kitchen it was still only 8.45 and there was no sign of him. She phoned Kimi, Joan still being at her poetry retreat, and told her what was going on.

'Shall I come and see him with you?'

Anna had visited Gerald Draycott, Kimi's father, in hospital during his last days but she had got to know him well and they had built a friendship in the weeks of working on his case but Kimi had barely met George. 'No, but thanks. He wasn't really conscious today.'

'Sorry Anna. It sucks. I know.'

Anna wanted to shout at her, no, your dad was dying, mine isn't! But of course she couldn't. Instead she said, not meaning to, 'It's my fault. It's because of me.' So then she had to explain what she meant and then she couldn't really explain at all and the words tangled and she fell silent.

Kimi was stern. 'This isn't like you, Anna. Why don't you get that nice guy you know, Steve is it, to help? Maybe have a couple of drinks, let it out. Get snot all over your face, eat ice-cream, you know.' Anna mumbled something. 'Well, blaming yourself isn't going to achieve anything, is it? I didn't think self-pity was your line.' Anna was wishing she had not phoned.

'It's ok, Kimi, I'll be all right. I just needed to offload.'

'Oh any time,' Kimi said breezily as if to say, well, thank God that's over. 'That foal that Beauty had is a real corker. I reckon she's first class show material. You should come out and see her and have a ride on Maisie – do you more good than moping.'

'Good idea,' Anna lied. 'See you soon. Bye.' Had she really thought that Kimi was the one to go to with a torn and bleeding heart? But she was right, under different circumstances she would have gone to Steve and he would have comforted her, put it all in perspective, made her feelings the centre of his focus. Another loss. Another self-administered twist of the knife.

The front door closed and Ellis came into the kitchen. Bobble sprang from his mat and leaped up at him almost knocking the boy over. Anna tried for a light touch. 'Have you taught him 'down' yet? Might be an idea!'

Ellis rumpled the massive ears. 'Has he been for a walk?'

'Yes, I took him to the park earlier but we can take him out again if you like.'

'I'm a bit bushed, Mum. I got up to thirty-six jumps on the trampoline all in one go – they said it's a record.' The words sounded happy but she could see that he was struggling. He hid his face in Bobble's neck as the dog tried desperately to kiss him with its slobbery mouth.

'Ok. Do you want some cake?'

'Mm.' He came to the table. 'Have you been to see Pops?'

'Yes, I went in for a couple of hours. Took him the cricket results.'

'I thought we were supposed to try to cheer him up.' They smiled politely at each other, acknowledging the attempt at normal banter.

She cut two wedges of cake and put them on plates while Ellis went to the fridge for his lemonade and she put the kettle on for a cup of tea. 'Faye popped in, too.'

Immediately he looked devastated. 'I should have gone. I thought it was just you tonight so he wouldn't get tired.'

'No, you're right. She must have suddenly decided. She was only there for a couple of minutes and he was asleep.'

Ellis bit a large chunk of cake and she watched him, needing this solace of being able to comfort him even though it was only with food. He looked up at her thoughtfully as he chewed, his long freckled face serious. 'Have you and her had another fight?'

'Another? What do you mean?'

'Oh, never mind.' He got down from the chair and called the dog to him. 'Come on, dinosaurus bobbelus, let's find the Frisbee. Come on!'

Anna sat on in the kitchen sipping tea and watching the sky turn from aqua feathered with fluffy lines of pink altocumulus to dull pewter. She could hear Ellis calling and then he came in and went wordlessly upstairs with a waggle of his fingers to her. Bobble collapsed on his mat. Anna looked longingly at the wine rack but she would not allow herself to have a drink. Anything could happen in the night and this time she needed to be ready even if it meant that long hours would be spent reading and watching television until dawn because without the numbing effect of alcohol sleep might be impossible, and to lie awake and silent, open to a bat colony of black thoughts, was more than she could even contemplate.

20

On Monday morning she phoned the hospital, heard there was no change and went to work. She knew she should tell Steve about George. He was there, in his office, his back turned to the door, perched on his chair in front of a bank of screens but she couldn't bring herself to. In the second she allowed herself to glance through the window at him, she took in the crisp cotton shirt with the sleeves rolled up, the hair beginning to rise again now as it grew into its usual unruly crest and the muscled, tanned forearms resting on the edge of the keyboard as he stared at a screen. The pain in her solar plexus was so sudden and severe that she almost cried out.

Half an hour later Ted arrived at her desk and dropped a clutch of notes on it and then passed rapidly on to do the same to the others. Anna glanced round. Everyone was covertly turning the scraps of paper over to read the backs. Desperate for diversion she did the same. She had half a telephone number and a scrawled 'handicap???' on one piece, and on another a doodle of a hanging man with an arrow to it and the initial letter R. The rest was torn off. Nothing was of interest and she turned them over again to see what jobs Ted wanted her to do. But the minute he closed the office door Suzy stood up and waved silently, grinning. Everyone looked at her.

'"Darling,"' she read, '"I can't stop thinking about you and what happened last night..." Oh please, someone, you must have some more pieces!' There were hoots and hurried re-shuffling of the notes but nothing fitted. They groaned and went back to work. Anna dropped her head. In her opinion Suzy should not have done that but then, neither should Ted. She blocked the next thought and phoned Maxon.

'Can you talk? I mean, you're not in a class?'

'No, this is good. I'm on a break. Have you got more news?'

'Yes.' She made an effort to lighten her tone. 'It's really good, actually. You know the bequest that James made to Grace and Jane if they were found?'

'Yes, of course. Don't tell me you've traced it?'

She laughed. 'It only took one phone call as it happened. The Museum and Art Gallery in Shrewsbury has it – it's a painting. Quite a coincidence!'

'Me being a failed artist you mean,' Maxon said drily.

'You being interested in art,' Anna corrected him, too exasperated by his self-abasement to flatter him. 'But there's more.'

'Great! Give.'

'The curator, a very nice man called John Lansdowne, was interested in your story and so are the trustees so they want to do a little presentation to you of the painting with the local press there. Would you be up for it?'

'Are you kidding? Oh, but just a minute, I wouldn't want that stuff about bigamy and all that to get splashed over the media.'

'No, they don't know about that. I only said that you had been researching your family history and that the painting was left to your great great-grandmother in the 1890's but she had emigrated before James died and then could not be traced so it had gone to the museum.'

'Anna this is wonderful! I can ship it home with me and show mom and dad – they would be so pleased.' His voice quietened. 'I haven't decided yet how much of the other stuff to tell them.' Anna thought about the bombshell she would still have to drop and said nothing. 'How soon can we do it, though? I'm leaving next week – classes are almost over.'

'Ok. I'll phone them and make it as soon as possible.'

'I've written everything up and done timelines and so on but I would appreciate you looking them over, if you don't mind, to make sure I haven't screwed up.' Anna silently rolled her eyes. 'And I'd like to take you out to dinner to thank you for all you've done.'

'Maxon, there's no need, this is my job.'

'No, I want to. As well as your expertise, obviously, you've made this research so much more enjoyable for me. You've been a real friend.' The validation felt good. Nice Anna was still viable, it seemed, however phoney that felt.

'Ok. Thank you.' She would just see how things went with George and would cancel the dinner in a heartbeat if he was struggling.

Mr Lansdowne called her back within the hour saying that they could do the brief ceremony on Tuesday, the next day, as one of the trustees was free and the press were always ready for a story. She called Maxon back and made sure that he would bring all the necessary documents to prove his rightful ownership of the painting.

At twelve o'clock she left to visit George having put Ted in the picture. The weather was close and sticky and her car steering wheel slipped in her hands. She drove the few miles to the hospital, parked on the top of the multi-storey taking the last space, and made her way into the airport style atrium. How quickly routines are set up. They used to come here with Harry – turn left, along a corridor, greet the nurse, take a seat. Now she walked to the far end of the huge space and waited for the lift. She had phoned Diane that morning and received much the same report – that there was no change. She felt that her dad was floating, rocking dreamily in a little boat on a Stygian river going neither forward or back. She wanted to wake him, shake him, make him take charge and come back to them. She pushed open the door to his ward.

Steve was there. He was seated close to the bed and she saw that he was holding George's freckled skinny hand in his strong muscled one. This would have been what Harry would have done if he could: tenderness without embarrassment, the mark of a good man. He did not release it when he turned and saw her but only said, 'Faye told me.'

She went round the other side of the bed and kissed her father's forehead noticing that it was still very hot. 'I should have. I'm sorry.' He didn't contradict her but he didn't seem angry. He seemed sad. 'I phoned this morning early – has there been any change?'

'No, I don't think so. It took hold so fast the nurse said and attacked both lungs, so now the medication is having to fight hard.' They both sat looking at George as he lay, like a fallen gnome, his white beard bristling out from the raised pillow and his eyelids flickering as he slept. It was very quiet in the room and Anna realised sadly there was no-one she would rather have here than Steve despite everything.

Eventually he spoke. 'I wanted to tell you something, anyway. I've been thinking about the future and I'll need to be applying for school places soon for Alice. My parents aren't too well and I may sell up and go up to live near them, where I grew up. Get her into a school there.'

They did not look at each other. 'But I thought you liked the school Faye and Ellis went to,' Anna said bleakly.

'I do. But what's the point?'

'Your job, what about that?'

'There are others.' He looked directly into her eyes, his expression as serious as hers. 'This is too difficult for me, Anna. This, with you. If you don't want me then I have to be somewhere else. That's all there is to it.' He gently released George's hand and stood up. 'I need to get back.'

Anna sat by the bed for another half hour. George rallied once a little and opened his eyes to smile at her but then was gone again. She felt empty, drained, hopeless and alone and none of it was anyone else's fault.

Anna checked with the hospital before she left for work on Tuesday and Diane promised to call her at 11.00. The nurse had told her that he seemed brighter and the signs were good.

Maxon was waiting for her in Harts' car park and they set off immediately. She had told him that she would not be able to hang around in Shrewsbury as she needed to get back but he should stay if he wanted to as it would be his last visit for a while. She had explained that her dad wasn't too well without going into details. He had made an attempt to dress for the occasion in a well-cut cream jacket she had never seen before and dark blue slacks with matching shirt and a plain tan tie. 'You look nice,' she smiled at him, making the turn on to the inner ring road.

'My public awaits – what can I do?' he snarled in a Groucho Marx imitation. 'How's your dad?'

'Well, he seems to be picking up a bit, thank goodness.'

'I appreciate you coming with me – you must want to stay at the hospital.'

'Well, his partner is there and, as I say, the news is hopeful, and I'd like to be at this celebration too, and see the painting.'

'Yeah, I forgot to ask, what's it of?'

Anna smiled at him again. 'You'll see.' She drove for a few minutes in silence. 'I was wondering how you're feeling. You know, going home soon with all that you've discovered. Are you disappointed?' What a blessing it was to step outside her own head for a while.

'Um. Mixed feelings, I guess. In one way it's a huge relief that they weren't, like, paragons of virtue, that they were just as messy as other people's families. But in another way it's kind of unsettling. I come from two bigamists and a whole lot of lying, or, put politely like you said, fantasising. It makes me wonder what other skeletons in the closet there are, you know?' He paused and gazed out of the window at the summer fields in their gold and green livery. 'It's making me think about how they got so rich. I'm pretty sure my mom and dad are as straight as most folks but what about the generations before them, the ones that made so much money so fast? I'm not so naïve that I think people always get rich because they invented a better mousetrap. But that's unfair – I don't like to think that stuff.'

'But surely that doesn't affect you, does it? I mean, what your ancestors did?'

'I don't know. What I know now has kind of shifted the ground under me. Do you know what I mean?'

'Made you question the things you've been told all your life.'

'Yeah.' He grinned at her, shaking the hair out of his eyes. 'Maybe time for Bambi to grow up, hey?'

At the Music Hall where the Art Gallery and Museum was housed the curator had produced a little posse of interested parties and made the most of the small occasion by providing a spread of coffee and sundry pastries in the Museum café. An easel stood near the group with a draped painting on it. Anna was pleased that she had not told Maxon the subject now that there would be an unveiling. It would add to the drama, improve the story for him. Maxon was introduced to a pretty young woman from Radio Shropshire and a not so pretty octogenarian trustee whose head poked out of his loose collar like a tortoise. The curator's office staff were also there and the archivist. Maxon was drawn to one side by the trustee for his documents to be scrutinised while everyone grabbed another pastry and then the group re-assembled and John Lansdowne stepped forward smiling. Maxon himself looked nervous and excited. It must be unusual for him to be the centre of positive regard.

'I'm so pleased to be performing this very pleasant duty,' John said, beaming. 'Our job and our joy at the museum is to preserve things of beauty and interest from the past as well as the present. When, as now, we are able to fulfil the dying wish of a local man to pass on to his heirs something of great significance to the family, the day is a very special one. This painting has been cared for lovingly for over a hundred years and now it will go to its rightful owner. It may not be worth a fortune in money but to you,

Maxon Blake, I'm sure it is priceless.' Everyone clapped and Maxon nodded energetically.

The curator stepped forward and carefully uncovered the painting in its ornate gold frame. Anna was standing near Maxon and heard the intake of breath. 'It's The Mount!' he cried. He stepped forward to look closely at the image.

John Lansdowne waited and then said softly, 'You may want to turn it over.'

Maxon read the note on the back silently and then out loud. *'For my dear daughter, Grace, and my grand-daughter, Jane, if ever they be found. This is your home. The Mount, 1896.'* Maxon stood with his head bowed for a moment struggling to control his feelings. For him it was more poignant than most of the spectators could know. This had been the home that Grace had lied about and now, miraculously, through James' generosity of spirit that lie was resolved. The Gallery photographer flashed his camera.

He faced the group holding the painting. 'I'm sorry but I can't help being emotional. My great great-grandmother talked to her daughter about this house and I've heard the name most of my life. Thanks to Anna here, I've visited it, although not as thoroughly as I plan to when I'm a guest there!' People who knew the current usage of The Mount laughed. 'I think my great, great great-grandfather James had the artist paint Grace and Jane playing on the lawn to show how very much he loved them and missed them. I could not be more pleased and more touched and more grateful to you all for keeping it safe so my family could have this treasure.' Everyone clapped again smiling at him. There were even a few tears.

Then the radio reporter drew him off to one side and they sat down at a table so she could interview him. Anna thanked the curator and the trustee and made small talk for a few minutes until everyone drifted away. Maxon glanced at her, stood up and the reporter did too, although less willingly. Anna guessed the girl would have liked to have asked him to go for lunch. It was thoughtful of him not to keep her waiting, knowing she was anxious to get back.

They wrapped the painting carefully in a travel rug Anna always kept in the boot and then wedged it gently with a couple of wellingtons and a bag of dog food. 'She says she'll email me the photos and send me a link to the podcast of the story,' Maxon said, still glowing from the whole experience. 'She's going to get the local press to cover it, too, and she'll mail me the actual paper.'

'But aren't you off home soon?'

'Oh yes. She said, no problem, she'd send it to my apartment in Philly so I gave her that address.' Anna smiled. Smart girl – she'd got his email address and where he lived in a slick five minutes. Perhaps she had already researched the family and found the whole package of considerable interest. They got into the car.

'It's a great thing to have happened, Maxon. I couldn't be more pleased for you and you handled it all very well.'

Maxon raised his eyebrows at her ironically. 'Well, shucks, ma'am.'

She grimaced. 'Sorry, that was condescending, wasn't it?'

'No, I'm kidding. I've just got hyper-active radar.' He turned to her and touched her arm. 'Seriously, Anna, thank you for everything. To be honest it's been great to talk about stuff with you as well as all the research. You're so pulled together and well, sane, it's been totally cool.'

Anna drove without speaking. Pulled together. Sane. He was speaking about that other Anna, the one she had been before Harry died, the one she now struggled into and zipped up for work but which fell away in tatters when she was near the people she loved most.

'Maxon, can I ask a favour of you?'

'Sure.'

'There's something I need to tell you, something else I've discovered that you have a right to know, but I'm desperate to check on my dad. Would you mind if I drive straight to the hospital and see him and then maybe we can grab something to eat there and talk?' She glanced at him. 'Give you a chance to experience institutional food. It's pretty good at the QE, actually.'

He was intrigued. 'Can't you tell me now?'

'I'd rather not.'

'Ok. Fine by me. But you'll surely want to stay at the hospital for a while so I'll get a cab back to my apartment. I've got some stuff to sort out and I want to write up what happened today, too.'

Anna thought he would have quite a few pages to write after their conversation but said nothing. Could she just not tell him? That would be the easiest way out but she knew it would be dishonest. The job was not yet complete, she was still working for him and it was his right to know. He wouldn't be too thrilled, she guessed, but it was such an integral part of his family's story. He couldn't mind too much, it was all such a long time ago.

She left him in the coffee shop on the ground floor of the hospital and almost ran along the corridor to her father's room. It was only 1.15 and Diane was still there, sitting solidly in the visitor's chair and knitting. 'Hello dear,' she said in the old way and Anna felt the squeeze on her heart relax a little.

George seemed a little pinker, a little fuller in the face. 'He looks a bit better.'

'Yes, they say he's beginning to turn the corner but is not out of the woods,' Diane said wryly, making a joke.

'Quite active then,' Anna smiled back.

'I'll just finish this row and be off. A couple of volunteers from the shop are holding the fort at Safe 'n' Sound but I don't rate them. Well-meaning but clueless.'

Anna picked up George's hand and his eyelids fluttered. 'How's Charles?'

'Worse than a two-year old. He's found out how to pick the child-lock on the biscuit cupboard.' She stood up and looked around her for scattered belongings, poking the knitting roughly into her big bag. 'Ok. Leave you to it.'

'I'm just going to get some lunch and then I'll come back for a couple of hours.'

'Righty-ho.' Diane looked sharply at George. 'Tell me if there's any change. I'll pop back tonight, you get some rest.'

When she was gone Anna kissed her dad's whiskery cheek, felt his head, still too hot, and whispered. 'I'll only be a minute. Keep on rowing back to us.'

21

Anna and Maxon climbed the curving staircase to the next floor and went into the cafeteria. They didn't have to wait long despite it being the lunch-hour and she saw Maxon glancing around at the layout and procedure with professional interest. 'This may be my last chance to have fish and chips!' he laughed, 'I'm going to miss this!' She picked up a ready-made salad nicoise.

They found a table near the curved glass window and looked down on the people weaving in between each other across the atrium below like fish in a tank. 'When I used to come here with my husband to see his consultant,' Anna said, 'there were always men in uniform, I mean, army uniform. This is where they brought the casualties from the war in Afghanistan.'

Maxon stuffed his mouth. 'No kidding.'

'Yes. It was awful to see those young men without legs in wheelchairs and sometimes with their heads all misshapen.' She took a forkful of egg. 'You feel angry and sad at the same time. I think it was a huge miscalculation and such a waste of life on all sides.'

'Mm. My uncle's a Republican and he's very gung-ho about all that. I keep out of it. Just grateful I didn't have to go. I saw enough of military discipline at school – I just can't get my head round anyone volunteering for it.'

'Well, it's a job, isn't it? And to some it's an adventure, a cause even.'

'I guess.' Maxon swallowed. 'So what was it you wanted to tell me?'

Anna laid down her fork. 'It might be a bit tough for you to hear. It certainly took me by surprise but it does all check out.'

'Does it explain why Robert's name was on Jane's death certificate?'

'No. That will probably always be a mystery.' Anna paused. 'But it may explain something else.' Maxon had now stopped eating and was giving her his full attention. 'Ok, brace yourself.'

The cafeteria was emptying now as the lunch-hour came to an end and they were alone in their part of the dining area so she did not have to lower her voice. 'Your family believe that Albert Maxon was an American from New England, don't they?'

'Yeah. Well, from Connecticut they say.'

'And that Grace met him in Philadelphia after she had emigrated. Later they married, of course.'

'Yes. Don't tell me they didn't even get married, that we really are a bunch of bastards?'

'No.' Maxon's smile faded. 'But Albert Maxon was not from New England, he was not American at all.'

'What do you mean?'

'He lived on Chirk Street at the same time as Grace and William Henry.'

'I don't understand. You mean someone of the same name?'

'No. It was the same man. He emigrated to Philadelphia the summer after Grace and Jane went, in 1896. I have a copy of the passenger list for the ship he was on.' She waited for this to sink in. Maxon's face was blank. 'He travelled second class, not steerage like Grace, and he had a great deal of baggage with him.'

'But the people on that street, you showed me, they were poor. It was a real down- market place.'

'Yes.' He let that go for the moment.

'So you think they knew each other before Philadelphia?'

'I'm sure they did.'

'It was planned.' He drew back. 'You're saying it was planned?'

'William Henry had left to go to Australia a few months before Grace emigrated. I don't know how planned it was, I mean, I have no idea of when they decided to do what they did.'

'So he could have just gone out there and looked for her? Maybe wanted to help her out, felt sorry for her, wanted to have a fresh start himself?'

'Yes. He could.'

'Maybe he'd always been in love with her and followed her when she was free of William Henry?'

'Maybe.'

'But why would they pretend he was an American? Why not just say it like it was?'

Anna waited, unsure of whether to let him work things out himself or to tell him her conclusions. Maxon was staring ahead, his forehead creased with the effort of coming to terms with this extraordinary new information. He turned a puzzled face to her so she explained, 'He was a rent collector. That was his job – to collect rents for a local property owner with considerable holdings.'

The penny dropped. 'Fuck,' Maxon said. 'Hell.' His face drained of colour so rapidly that she thought he might faint. She glanced round to see where the water fountain was. 'He stole it, he stole the money! That's why they couldn't let on who he really was. He would have been wanted by the law in England!' Anna said nothing. Maxon was now rigid in his seat as his thoughts raced. Then he made the connection Anna had hoped he wouldn't. Clearly he was not the dullard his parents thought him. 'That's how they started the business – that was their start-up money! They must have bought their first development property with that hot cash!' He jumped up as though trying to escape his own thoughts. 'So did he run out on a family, too? You might as well tell me!'

'A wife and two children,' Anna admitted, beginning to be alarmed at Maxon's reaction.

Maxon whooped and clapped his hands. 'Terrific! The hat-trick in bigamy! Bastards!' People were beginning to look in their direction. A couple of young men in theatre scrubs took a step towards them as if Maxon might need restraining.

He was beyond worrying about who was watching or where he was. 'They were criminals! My so, so respectable family were bigamists, liars, thieves! For all I know they still are! All my life I've been in awe of them and they were nothing but a bunch of cheap crooks!'

Anna began to protest. 'Maxon, I think you're - '

'And you!' Maxon shouted hoarsely at her, 'You couldn't just have kept this to yourself, could you? You couldn't have just left me a shred of illusion to cover my ass? You had to dig and dig and get up all the dirt and dump it on me! Why? What the fuck do you get out of it? What good is it for me to know this crap?' He leaped forward and leaned into her face. 'I thought I was a poor useless dumb-ass from a great family. Not perfect, but I could live with it. Now, thanks to you, I'm a useless fuck from a family of cheats and charlatans!' He pushed the table away from him so hard it hit her in the stomach. 'Well, thank you, Ma'am, thank you so much!' He made a deep mock bow and reeled away pushing the men watching him to one side.

'Are you ok? Should we get security?' one said to Anna as she stood up shakily.

'No. No, I'm ok. He just had some bad news. He's not a bad guy.' The other one brought her water and though the glass chattered against her teeth, she drained it. They left, glancing back at her as she sat down again and dropped her head into her hands.

She had expected him to be disapproving at worst, intrigued at best, but this was awful. She had never heard him even raise his voice before. She had believed him when he said that his prominent family oppressed him and that he was a disappointment. She hadn't realised for a second how precious that narrative was to him. He had wanted to believe that they were admirable; he had been willing to accept a low-status role as long as he came from a high-status family. He had crafted a story to explain himself, as we all do, one in which he made much of his identity as an under-achiever because he was somehow balancing out the rest of the family. He was the counter-weight to their heft. If they were exposed as morally bankrupt what place was there for him? With her revelations his family had collapsed around him.

Had she been right to tell him? Why had she? She had told herself it was her professional responsibility to share all information with him but was that really it? Was there, deep down in the mad, radioactive core she now carried inside her, the desire to disillusion, to hurt, to sting, to make someone who had so much suffer?

She walked dully down the stairs and made her way to her father's room. She sat with him for two hours doing nothing but stare out of the window and hold his hand. Twice he opened his eyes but seemed not to recognise her. The nurse said he was doing all right and it took a little longer for older people to recover from such a bad bout of pneumonia. She had been on a twelve hour shift and he had been awake more in the night, she said. They had even had a chat about the use of maggots for infected wounds. 'He's a character, isn't he?' Anna hadn't been able to smile at this although it would be exactly the sort of thing her father would talk about so she didn't doubt it was true.

Eventually she got up, gathered her things and went home. Maxon's precious painting was still in her car boot. Would he still want it? Would she ever see or talk to him again? She couldn't raise the energy to think about that.

There was no-one at home. Defeated by the many domestic jobs that needed doing, Anna wandered to the far end of the garden and stared at the shrubs she had planted being choked by leaping blackberry brambles. The clearance in the early summer had made them tougher, battle-hardened, eager to capture more and more territory. She eyed the barbs on the brambles. A movement caught her eye and a rat ran from one clump to another. It was huge. Her phone went and she was told that she was owed funds from PPI. She didn't text Ellis or Faye. What for? She crossed her arms and returned slowly to the house. She had handled the revelations to Maxon very badly. Why had she assumed that the man would be pleased that his too-perfect family had flaws? For all Anna knew every generation since Grace and Albert could have been kind and philanthropic. It seemed that her sure touch had deserted her since Harry's death. She was blundering into people's feelings blindly, hurting them and herself in the process.

She kicked a pebble off the path to the back door, noting and dismissing the need for weeding between the cracks on the patio. Sod it. The kitchen was as blank and empty as when she had left it. She pulled open the fridge door and saw a space in the door rack with a dried red ring on the plastic where a bottle of Malbec should have been. The wine rack was empty. How could that have happened – she'd bought half a dozen bottles only days ago. She would have a word with Faye; all the teenagers were running wild now that school was nearly over. It seemed an age since she'd seen Faye now she thought about it. Not last night, maybe the night before? Ellis had been in bed by ten both nights, or at least in his room, neither of them spent much time in the living room any more, but it was summer and why would anyone want to be inside on long summer evenings? She didn't want to be in the house herself.

She walked down to the convenience store on the High Street. The sun was so low that long yellow wedges poked between the shops and she was partly blinded by the glare. Some boys drove past far too fast in a cheap little car, shouting and blasting the horn. She watched them go feeling a hot tide of yearning for that youthful joy and energy. She could taste it in the back of her throat.

'Mrs Ames, hi!' It was Nicola, Tash's sister. She was leaning on a gangly youth with hair down to his nose.

'Hi. Ok?'

'Yeah.' She stood a little straighter. 'Oh, sorry about – um.'

'Mm.' Anna wanted to move on.

'But we're still having the party at yours, right? Faye said just leave it a bit?'

'We'll see.' Anna pushed past them appalled at how close she had been to yelling, no, you self-centred spoiled brats, we are not having a party so you can all get off with each other in comfort in *my* house. Shaking slightly she pushed the door open and went in and down to the end where row upon row of gleaming bottles stood. She went back for a basket.

At the check-out an elderly man was fumbling for every coin to pay for his frozen dinner. Anna fumed and tapped her foot. She banged her basket down on the conveyor belt and laid each bottle down facing the cashier to hurry him up. The cashier lowered her glance and waited for the old man to finish paying. Anna knew she was being rude and unkind and didn't care. She imagined what it would be like to lift her foot and kick him in the back. Finally he was shuffling off and it was her turn. The girl took each bottle and scanned it and Anna packed them in the flimsy plastic bags because she had forgotten their canvas bags. She couldn't wait to leave, to get home, to force this mad maelstrom in her head to stop, to go away, to fade to black. Finally the girl met her eyes. 'Thirty-five pounds, eighty-two,' she said.

Anna had not picked up her purse before she left the house.

She stood for a moment and then found that she was howling right there in front of everyone, open-mouthed like Alice, utterly without restraint because restraint was no longer possible. The girl must have pressed a button to get help because there were two navy arms around her and garlic breath in her face. Words were being said to her but she couldn't comprehend them. She was being moved, turned, and she hit out at what was doing it and then kicked viciously at something bulky behind her. The screaming was going on and on and getting on her nerves.

'Anna. Look at me. Anna.' She gasped for breath and saw in front of her Andrew Dunster. She stopped still.

Behind her someone was saying, 'I don't get paid for this, crazy alky spitting at me.' Did he mean her? How could he? She wasn't crazy, she wasn't an alcoholic, she hadn't spat at him, surely? She scanned Andrew's face to make sense of what was happening.

He moved a little closer and held both her hands and it helped her to become steady. 'What's happening to me?' she said, or maybe only thought because he didn't answer. She took a deep, shuddering breath and glanced round at the shocked faces near her.

'I'm sorry, I'm so sorry. I don't know what just happened.' The girl on the checkout tightened her lips and looked away.

'Let's go, shall we? Let's just walk a bit?' Andrew let one of her hands go and led her out of the supermarket and then tucked the other hand under his arm. She went with him feeling as though she were in a dream where the volume on her hearing had been turned down and her feet seemed to float above the pavement. The bands of sun and shade hit her eyes like a strobe making her dizzy and disorientated. If one hand had not been firmly anchored beneath the crook of Andrew's arm she felt she could have fluttered away like a dead leaf.

Then they were in the kitchen of his vicarage and he was making tea. Eventually he sat down at the small table with her and pushed a mug towards her. Automatically, she picked it up and sipped but then she had to put the mug down because of the trembling. Brown liquid was splashed all over the worktop. Her mind was empty of everything. She felt as though she was a tiny speck in the middle of a wasteland, an apocalyptic desert of sand and rock. She saw Andrew get up, go to a cupboard, get things, come back and then a small tumbler of brandy was set down in front of her. It was a nostalgic, mesmerising colour, golden brown, amber lit by the sun. She put her head down on the table and wept.

At some point something soft and warm was placed round her shoulders. When the tears stopped the shuddering began and when that stopped she was finally able to breathe. Andrew waited for her to lift her mucus-smeared face and gently wiped it with tissues. She gulped once and was quiet.

'Come and sit down somewhere more comfortable.' They went into the living room and she was placed in a deep armchair and the brandy was put into her hand. 'Just try to sip a little. Rest, I'll be back soon.' She sipped the brandy and then put the glass down. Her whole being ached for oblivion and by the time she had leaned back into the cushions she was asleep.

22

When she woke there was still some light in the sky, a greenish glow behind the roof tops visible from the vicarage window. Lamps had been switched on. Andrew was sitting on a sofa near one, reading. Anna realised that she must not have moved at all while she was unconscious, her arms and legs and body were in exactly the same place as before. She lifted her hand to rub her face and it felt numb.

'How long have I been asleep?'

Andrew looked at the clock on the mantelpiece. 'About an hour. Not long.'

'I'm sorry, Andrew, I doubt this was what you had planned for your evening.'

'Do you want to talk?'

Anna's heart began to race as her body flooded with adrenalin. 'No. I can't. Sorry.'

'Ok.'

She glanced round the room. On the mantelpiece was a photograph of a young woman in cap and gown looking radiant. On a bookshelf was another photo of a younger Andrew and a different woman. 'Is this your family, Andrew?' She had never thought of him being married but then, their encounters in the past had been brief for all their drama; like the night that Ellis had gone missing when he had driven into town in torrential rain to take her to people who might help.

'Yes. My wife is a retreat director for the diocese, in fact, she's off checking on one tonight, and that person there,' he waved at the picture on the mantel, 'is our daughter, Elizabeth.'

Anna wanted to stay in this chair away from her own house so she needed to think of something to make him talk. 'So you always wanted to be a priest?'

'Far from it.' He turned and stared out of the window into the dusk. 'Do you remember, Anna, a few years ago when Harry was at the stage of wandering off and he came in to the church? I think it was the organ music that attracted him.'

'Yes,' Anna said quietly.

'You asked me then about why random stuff happens, bad things. I suppose you were trying to make sense of Harry's condition. He had never hurt anyone, he was living a good life and yet this hideous illness was robbing him of everything. And all his family, of course, especially you, were losing him day by day.'

'Yes. You said, we don't know why there is suffering, we just have to grit our teeth and believe in goodness.' But that had been then, Anna thought, when she was still innocent, it was different now. Harder to believe in goodness.

'It took a long time for me to get to the point that I could say that.' He shifted in his chair and turned to look at her. The lamplight hit his face sideways and deepened the grooves in his forehead and the fold from nose to mouth. 'You asked me if I had always wanted to be a priest. In fact, I would have scoffed at that idea when I was choosing my profession. I would have thought it was a cop-out, an easy, self-deluded option to avoid the real world.' He stood up and went to the window. She was grateful that he was letting her get out of her own head. It didn't really matter what he said.

'I was the only child of adoring parents, Anna. We were comfortably off and my childhood was as idyllic as a childhood could be. I excelled at everything, sport, academics, and then later, getting girls. I'm not boasting - it was how it was. My father was a doctor, a GP, so I found it easy to study medicine at Oxford and did so well that I was encouraged to specialise to become a consultant. My field was paediatrics. I chose that, I think, not because I liked children but because at that time it was an unfashionable area and I wanted to go where I could make a name for myself. My self-confidence had become arrogance, Anna, and any criticism must result from jealousy, I thought. I was one of the youngest consultants in the field and had a minor surgical procedure named after me. The hospital staff mostly took over from my parents in validating me – I was treated with huge respect and deference.'

Anna let the pause last for a few moments and then said, 'What happened?'

'I was treating a child with a rare form of anaemia. I read medical journals and I was vaguely aware that a new procedure was being tested in California with good results but I was automatically dismissive. What could Americans teach me? I had never treated this condition before but I felt sure I knew what to do. I was keeping notes so that I would be able to write the case up, perhaps publish something of my own. I would rather trust my own instincts than some unknown professor. There was a conscientious and intelligent nurse on the ward and she mentioned the US findings. I felt challenged, insulted, and wouldn't discuss it. I went ahead with my treatment and the boy sickened and then died.' Andrew dropped his head and Anna waited until he was ready to go on. Passive listening was not so easy now and her pulse quickened in an unwelcome way.

'The nurse would have liked to file a complaint but it was a grey area. I was defensive, all doctors lose patients for one reason or another and it was a rare condition. I did look up the article and realised that the boy would almost certainly have benefitted from the new treatment, but I put it out of my mind and went on as normal.' He seemed reluctant to continue. Something like a ripple of pain passed over his face, as though he had silently suffered an electric shock. 'The parents thanked me, Anna. They thanked me for all I had done for their boy.'

He looked again out of the window. 'I need to walk. Will you come with me?'

They left the house and turned down the hill towards the park. Now most of the evening light had gone and stars were coming and going between wisps of cloud like a parent playing peep-O with a child. As she walked Anna realised that it had been days since she'd checked on Ellis properly. They had passed each other on the stairs, she'd glimpsed him through his open bedroom door, but they hadn't talked. She had been too busy. She texted him. She should have been home hours ago but he replied immediately and said he and Mike were watching Spiderman 3. He added an X and she felt a throb of relief.

Once they were in the park Andrew slowed down and began to talk again. 'Months later I was just about to start my ward rounds and I fell apart. I literally fell down in the corridor. You can imagine all the tests and the hypotheses and my parents worrying but there was nothing wrong with me. I mean, nothing wrong with my body. But I had fallen off a precipice into a new world. It seemed to me as though everyone I encountered was suffering. I couldn't watch the news, I couldn't even walk down a street – I was in physical pain. Everywhere I saw distress, loneliness, horror, despair. The only thing that numbed it was alcohol and for days I was drunk most of the time.' Anna bowed her head and was silent. 'Let's sit here if it's not too chilly for you.' The metal rungs of the bench struck cold through Anna's thin trousers but she barely noticed – she was beginning to tremble.

'So I did the logical things. I went for therapy - but it was no use. They could give me descriptions of what I was going through, even attempt explanations neurological and psychological, but explanations in my case didn't take away the pain. Family and colleagues reasoned with me, told me I shouldn't blame myself, we all make mistakes, I had done what I thought was best, and so forth but that didn't help.' He folded his arms tightly across his chest.

'You see, Anna, I could have dealt with something from outside making me suffer. As bad as this is, I could have coped with becoming ill or the loss of someone I loved through a traffic accident or a tsunami or, I don't know what. Those random events we talked about. But I wasn't the victim, I was the perpetrator – the cause. What I did, I did for one simple reason – pride. People focus on immoral sex and misuse of wealth and other bad behaviours but all the great faiths say far more about pride than anything else. Thinking you know best – self-righteousness. Setting yourself up as a god in your own world. The oldest sin of all. I knew I had committed that sin and I had killed the boy in my care. I was not religious yet I knew it in the cells of my body and nothing anyone could say would change that.'

They sat quietly for a while and Anna felt the frantic anxiety that she had been trying to keep at bay at the edge of her consciousness since Harry's death vibrate dangerously like a wheel with loose bearings.

'So I did what people have done since time immemorial. I prayed to an unknown god for help. It worked. Instantly, I felt the presence of God, a connection with everything, an active powerful force of love. I was astonished. Grace was the last thing I thought would get me, but it did. I have peace now, well, most of the time. Perhaps if I lived in a Muslim country or a Hindu one, I would have become a priest in one of those faiths – I don't know. But what can I do but spend the rest of my life trying to get closer to that powerful love I experienced? Trying to make it available for others?' He took Anna's hand. 'To deny the reality of that experience would be like denying I love my family. So I have a different kind of work now. It's not for everyone but it's right for me.'

They watched a fox trot down the path looking to left and right and then lift its leg against a tree. It glanced at them and padded off on its own business. She took a deep breath and gripped his hand as the blood thundered in her ears.

'I have to say something I've been fighting not to admit even to myself for months. I did wrong, too, and I caused the death of the man I loved. It's been driving me mad with guilt and shame.' She started to shake. 'I am responsible for Harry's death, Andrew. It happened because I took a demented man who was not in control of his body and a wilful child and an untrained dog up on to a cliff edge. On to a precipice. Why did I do that? Because I was not paying attention – I wasn't even thinking about them. On the ridge I was not paying attention to the danger because I was imagining how it would feel to make love with another man – another man I love. At the very moment it happened I was thinking of having sex – I was completely unconscious of my responsibility. As I bent down to tie my shoelaces letting go of Alice's hand I was not there. I was with Steve. I let go of the love that has bound Harry and I together for twenty-five years. Harry fell because of my adulterous imagination, because of my failure of love for him.'

Andrew said nothing but kept hold of her hand. Her teeth were chattering now.

'Harry had told me only days before that he loved me. He even sang a few words from a song which was special to us. I was moved, of course, but later I let it slip my mind. It was as though he had been struggling through the muddle of his mind to call to me, to reach me, to pull me back to himself. But I was only half-aware, half listening - it faded from my mind because I was so obsessed with this other man, the man he called his brother.'

'Sometimes people sense that they are going to die. He could have been saying goodbye to you,' Andrew said softly.

'I've been in a fog of panic. I couldn't believe that I would be so careless, so venal – so disloyal. I couldn't believe I would be so sexually driven to blindness. The only thing that's helped has been work and booze. I've pushed people who love me away - people who are grieving for Harry, too, because I didn't want to face the truth of what I've just told you. I've been like a crazed dog with a fire-can tied to its tail desperately running and never being able to escape while all the time on the surface I've gone through the charade of being calm, competent, caring. It's exhausting. It's been a nightmare.'

'I can see that. I can see that you've run yourself into a wall.' He lifted his chin and thought for a moment. 'George Herbert said that the price of love is love.'

She looked at him intently. 'What do you mean?'

'Think about it.'

The image of her daughter rose before her. Faye frightened, in tears, hurt. What on earth had she been thinking to be so hard on her? And then it all fell into place like reversed film of an explosion. 'I've just realised why I've been so mean to Faye.' Anna groaned and buried her face in her hands. 'I couldn't bear my own behaviour so I dumped it on her and punished her for it. My own daughter, Andrew. How could I do that?'

'It's the oldest defence mechanism in the world - the Buddhists knew all about it – projection. You externalise the dark things about yourself you don't want to face and then attack them in others. Projection is responsible for quite a bit of domestic violence in my experience – as well as wars, of course.' He touched her arm with his forefinger. 'Don't be too hard on yourself, we all do it, and you have suffered a shocking loss.'

They were stiff and chilled when they finally stood up and moved off. Andrew walked her to her drive and then went back to his own home.

She let herself in and hearing no sound from the living room climbed the stairs to Ellis' room. The light was still on and she knocked and went in. Ellis was sitting up in bed reading. He looked at her warily, judging her mood and state. Her heart constricted. She sat down on the bed.

'Hey. What's the book?'

'Stone circles. The first built environment.' His golden-syrup eyes searched her face.

She bent forward and put her arms round his bony shoulders and kissed his sticky hair. 'Sorry I've been out of it lately, Ell. I'm back now.' She felt his body relax.

'Did you know that the Ring of Brodgar in the Orkney Isles is over four thousand years old?' he said into her hair. 'There are loads of circles up there. It was there before Stone Henge, even.'

She sat back and grinned at him. 'No shit, Sherlock.'

'Mum, that is so lame. No-one says that anymore.' He wagged his finger at her. 'If you're not careful you'll become an anachronism!'

She high-fived him. 'Wow! Good one, Ell.'

Ellis feigned a faint. 'I need a hot chocolate after that.'

She stood up. 'I fancy one myself. Is Faye around?' He shrugged and went back to his book.

Faye's bed was empty but unmade which could mean almost anything. Anna went down to the kitchen to put milk in the microwave and then text her daughter. There was no answer. She rang Michelle on her mobile who confirmed that Faye was there and the girls were watching DVD's in Tasha's room. She had asked to stay the night – was that all right?

'That's fine,' Anna said, 'just give her my love, will you?'

She tapped 'Dad' on her phone and hesitated. She put the phone down and went out to the shed. It was dark so she switched on the desk lamp and searched the shelves above. She knew that George's apparent chaos belied an esoteric filing system that rivalled the fabled Alexandrian libraries. Fortunately, it was easy to find being one of the thicker books and had the trademark red cover of Rumi's masterpiece. The pages fell open with the ease of a much consulted text and she found the lines she had been looking for. She returned it to the shelf, switched off the lamp, went back to the kitchen and texted: '"*We are all far from home/ language is our caravan bell.*" This is my chime – I love you and I'm sorry I hurt you.'

By that time the milk for their hot chocolates needed heating up again.

At six o'clock the next morning Anna was startled awake by her phone. It was the hospital telling her that George had vomited blood in the night. As she pulled on her clothes, not stopping to wash or brush her teeth, she frantically reviewed the options for Ellis. It would take time to find someone to look after him but neither could she simply leave a note and rush off. If she just left he might assume she had gone to work early but then he would be devastated not to have been told. She remembered how wounded he had been when she had not told him before about 'adult' crises and she made her decision.

She tried to wake him softly and at first there was little response but then he opened his eyes and within seconds of hearing the message he was out of bed and struggling into jeans and top.

They reached the front door together but Ellis stopped short. 'Just a minute, Mum, I'll let Bobble out into the garden – we may be gone hours.'

'Good thinking – make sure he's got water.'

The light was low and dazzling and Anna drove with one hand over her eyes as fast as she dared. Another heartless blue sky trapping them under its vast perfection. Only at its edges, its horizons, where humanity dirtied it, did it waver into grey and concede to lives being lived and lost.

At the hospital they got the lift straight away and ran down the empty corridors to the green push button on the double doors to George's suite. A startled nurse appeared and opened them. 'Are you Mr Walcott's daughter?' she asked Anna.

'Yes. You phoned me, I mean, someone phoned me.'

'His grand-daughter is here already – he's gone to the HDU. Do you know where that is?' The nurse was getting ready to make it all very clear and if necessary repeat herself.

'No, no, please,' Anna begged, not knowing what she was begging for except time.

'I know, Mum,' Ellis said, 'I saw it on the way in.' They didn't stay for instructions but set off again running. Ellis had got it right and within minutes they were in the waiting room. The only person there was Faye. She sat hunched on a chair, her fists pushed deep into her fleece pockets. She looked about four years old. Anna didn't hesitate - she went straight to the girl and took her in her arms. Faye gripped her hard in response.

'I had a dream,' she said when she pulled back from her mother's embrace. 'That's how I knew.' Her eyes were wide with awe. 'He was a long way away, like on the other side of a river and he was calling.' Anna hugged her again, inhaling the unwashed body and greasy hair and wishing she could hold all of it for ever. Ellis leaned against his sister on the other side and Anna could see from his thoughtful expression that he was wondering why Pops had come to her in a dream and not to him and was feeling slightly side-lined.

'Have they told you what's happening?'

'It's a bleed from an ulcer in his stomach. Something to do with the meds he was put on not suiting him.' Faye was badly frightened. 'They've taken him off those and now they're waiting to see if he has another. The longer he goes without another bleed the better. They'll come out in a minute and tell us. We can't go in.'

They sat in awed silence.

'What are they doing to him now?'

'I'm not sure, Ell. They've put a gastroprobe or something down his throat to look at his stomach and that's how they found the ulcer.' Faye noticed Ellis' shocked face and said gently, 'He'll be all right. Don't worry.' She took his hand and he let her.

Faye was too tall for her to put her arm around her shoulders so Anna stroked the girl's face and kissed her cheek. 'I'm sorry I've been so unkind to you lately, Faye. It was nothing to do with you, I was dumping on you because of my own demons. I don't blame you for being angry with me. Alice was right, I was a witch.'

Faye gazed into her face gravely. Mascara from the day before was smeared under her eyes and each inner corner held a tiny black bead. 'Why? What was going on with you? You were such a bitch, Mum. I've never seen you like that – it was scary.'

'You weren't horrible to me,' Ellis said loyally. 'You were just spooked.'

Anna looked at him in wonder. 'You are exactly right, Ellis. That is exactly the right word. I was spooked.'

'And poor old Pops took the brunt of it, Mum. He nearly chewed his beard off worrying about it all.' But Faye was not hostile now, just uncomprehending.

'I know.' Anna paused. 'I behaved very badly and I know it. But it's over now. I understand the pit I dug for myself and I've been helped out of it. I love you all very much, just so there's no doubt about that.' Tears stood in her eyes but she was determined not to give way in front of them, frightened as they were by this new crisis. 'Now the only thing that matters is that Pops gets better and that you both forgive me. It'll take a long time before I forgive myself.'

This unusually soppy mother was too much for Ellis. 'I saw a machine down the hallway,' he said. 'Can I get a hot chocolate? I'm starving.'

'Yes, love, get us all something would you? Maybe some granola bars?' Anna got out her purse and gave it to him. She stood up and went to see if there was anything visible through the double doors' porthole windows. They were covered. She turned back to Faye. The girl was so pale, so vulnerable. Anna went back and sat down beside her again, weaving her arm under Faye's so she could hold her hand.

They sat in silence for a few moments and then Faye spoke. 'Mum?'

'Yes.'

'You know those things you said. About me. About me being a slut.'

'Oh God, Faye, I was out of my mind, I'm so sorry. Of course you're not.'

'Mum.'

'Yes.'

Faye was looking humbly into Anna's face, her pallor accentuated by the harsh strip lights. 'I didn't sleep with Boz in Edinburgh or with Jason.'

'It's ok, you don't have to - '

'Mum,' her voice was almost a whisper. She dropped her eyes almost as though she was confessing to something bad. 'I haven't done it with anyone.'

Anna could no longer hold back the tears. When Ellis pushed open the door with his foot, balancing three paper cups and various packages between his hands, he was alarmed. 'What's happened?'

'Nothing,' Anna said wiping her eyes with her sleeve. 'Nothing's happened. It's all good.' She kissed Faye briskly and Ellis distributed the snacks.

The double doors opened and a man in mask and plastic apron came out. Anna sprang towards him asking about George. 'Oh, I'll call his nurse,' said the man and put his head back inside. 'He's just coming,' he said half-smiling, and then strode off.

They all stood up. A tired-looking man appeared and put out his hand. 'Good morning, I'm Nasim.' He looked round at the worried faces.

'How is he?'

'So far, so good. No more bleeding that we can see. He's much clearer in his chest, too, and his temperature is dropping.' Faye and Ellis whooped and high-fived but Anna heard in her memory what Diane had said wryly only yesterday about her dad turning the corner but not being out of the woods. She couldn't celebrate yet. 'We'll keep him here for a couple more hours and then we'll be moving him back to the wards if he's still doing fine, ok?'

They stood looking at each other after the nurse had gone back into the Unit. 'Mum?' Ellis said, 'Is he going to be ok?'

'Looks like it.' She squeezed his shoulders.

'Well, can I go? It's the Super-Quiz final at school and I'm my team's leader. Is it all right?'

'That's exactly what Pops would want you to do.' Anna looked at Faye and saw that the girl was exhausted. 'How did you get here?'

'Taxi.'

Anna pulled out a £20 note and gave it to her. 'Get one from outside and drop Ellis off at school and then get some rest.'

'Eugh! You can't let him go to school stinking like he does!'

'Better than looking like an endangered species,' Ellis instantly retorted.

Faye snatched Anna's bag and pulled out her small lipstick mirror, studying herself with horror. 'Mum! Why didn't you say!'

'She can't keep the change, can she, Mum? It'll only be a fiver, won't it?

'Turd. Loser.'

As the door closed behind them Anna leaned back in her chair and closed her eyes. Then she sat up abruptly. Diane. She glanced at the time and decided to phone, not text. Ten minutes later her phone rang and it was Len. She explained the situation again.

'I couldn't come in to see him,' Len said. 'Hospitals. You know, since mum.'

'No, I understand. Don't worry about it.'

'You ok?'

'Yes, I am.' Anna rested her head against the wall. 'I'm better than I've been for a while, thanks.'

'Thank Christ for that,' Len said. 'You've been weird.'

'I know.'

'Deranged.'

'All right, Len. Let's drop it shall we? How's Rosa?'

'I met the brother. He's no good.'

'I know. But she loves him. Don't go on about it to her.' Suddenly she had a brilliant idea. 'Look Len, I'm not sure at this moment how long it will take for dad to recover but when he feels better will you ask Rosa to come over for Sunday lunch at mine?' She remembered the empty kitchen and was determined to fill it.

'Ok.' She heard him breathing loudly and knew from experience that he had something else to say. 'Can I come too?'

She almost shouted at him. 'Of *course* you can – I meant to bring her *with* you!'

'Oh. Ok. Ta.'

By the time Diane arrived George had been moved on a trolley out of the HDU to his old room so she came there. They stood either side of the bed until George opened his eyes and wriggled his straggling brows. He looked from one anxious face to the other. 'If I wasn't so ill, I'd die of fright looking at you two,' he whispered. 'I'm not going to shuffle off, you know, so relax.' He moved his head to look sideways at his bedside cabinet. 'Where are the grapes and the chocolates, anyway?'

'If you don't watch it,' Anna said, 'I'll read you the cricket scores.'

George's look lingered on her. 'I read your text message,' he said gently. 'Thank you, Annie. I think we must have the same ring-tones on our caravan bells.'

'Well,' said Diane, 'it's nice to see that you're back to your old nonsense.'

'Dad, I have to go into work for a couple of hours but I'll be back this afternoon, ok?'

'You don't have to - '

'Yes, I do.' She kissed him, hugged and kissed Diane and left, almost skipping her way along the curved corridor filled with light from a beautiful day.

23

'How's your dad?' Ted asked as they almost collided in the corridor to his office.

'Ok, I think,' Anna said, 'but it was touch and go last night and it's not over yet.' She felt a little more was needed. 'Sorry I'm late in.' She had forgotten to phone him.

Ted was already on his way to his office. 'Just phone that Mr Blake, will you? He's been hassling Josie to speak to you. Settled his bill, I'm happy to say, so I won't have to cancel the milk this week.'

As she made her way to her desk she pondered how thoughtful it was of Maxon not to use her mobile number knowing that her father was ill and not wanting to intrude. Or he had lost it. But then the scene in the hospital came back to her. Maybe he just wanted to have another go at her, or more likely, in fact, certainly, he was trying to get hold of her because the precious painting of The Mount was still wedged between two rubber boots in the back of her car and he would be leaving very soon. She'd forgotten all about it. She picked up the office phone.

'Oh Anna, thank God. How's your father?'

'He's on the mend, thank you,' she replied formally not knowing what would come next. 'You'll need to pick up your picture.'

'Yes, I do, but I have to see you, too.' Anna looked out of the window for inspiration on how to avoid this. She was drained and more angst was not what she needed. 'I apologise profusely for how abusive I was to you when you told me what you'd discovered. I had no right to behave that way, especially when you were so worried.'

'Oh, that's ok, Maxon, it was a shock and maybe I was wrong to even tell you.' She began to sort through the mail on her desk. 'So, you're leaving tomorrow?'

'Yes, but Anna I have to see you. I have something to tell you and I can't do it on the phone. I know you're real pushed but if I come there, if I come to Harts, could I just have five minutes of your time? I can pick up the painting, too. Please, Anna.'

'Well, ok. Make it before noon because I want to get back to the hospital. Is that ok?' He was a nice man and he would want to thank her and say good-bye properly even though she half-wished he wouldn't. His case was over and she had stopped thinking about it. So much had happened in the last few days that the doings of the Thwaite family over a hundred years ago had faded from her mind. But, of course, he did have to get the painting and it would save her a journey.

Among the official mail and scrawled memos from Ted there was a large yellow envelope that looked like a greetings card. Inside was a picture of a palm tree on a tiny atoll of sand surrounded by a sea of turquoise and cobalt blue. It was simply but freshly done for such a hackneyed image and she turned it to the light to confirm that it was not a print, it was hand-painted. Inside, in a bold slanting script she read, *'Gone back to Trinidad, nothing for me here and I miss the company. Will use the dosh to buy a little bar and grill in my old stamping ground. I came back for Bill and the pension. Missed out on one but got the other. Thanks for holding my hand. Cheers, Ken.'*

Anna thought about Ken's sun-ravaged face and wiry arms. He would make his home in the bar (and probably sleep in a room behind it) spending his days with regulars playing dominoes and chess and gossiping and he would pay a pretty girl a pittance to serve the customers. He would love it. He might even start painting again just for the fun of hanging his own work on the walls. She mentally raised a glass to him to wish him luck. What an odd coincidence, she realised, that both Maxon who came from great wealth and Ken from poverty had found the same solution to their search for meaning and connection in their lives. To create places for people to be, to meet, to talk, to eat together; to be a part, however small, of other people's lives was not a bad way to pass your days. Both were oddballs in their own worlds, self-proclaimed failed artists, and yet both were honest, kind and unpretentious.

'Hi, Sweetie.' It was Suzy looking unusually crumpled as though she had been out all night. 'I'm on automatic – but it was so worth it.' She smiled dreamily and then her face changed abruptly. 'Oh, stupid me, sorry. How's your dad?' Anna laughed.

She ought to see Steve and tell him how George was but she felt shy about it. How could she face him after how she had been? She glanced towards his door which was shut. 'Much better, thanks, but still in hospital. Um, did you notice if Steve's in yet when you came past?'

Suzy rubbed both cheeks vigorously to wake herself up. 'Oh no, he's not in today. He's gone for a job interview Josie Know-all says. Poor us, eh?' She yawned and trudged off towards her desk.

Anna opened her laptop and pretended to read. He had been serious, then. She needed time to think, time to work out how on earth to explain to him why she had been so rejecting, so indifferent to him. What could she say? She remembered the humiliation of the scene in the Moroccan restaurant before Harry had died and flushed at the memory. But she couldn't just let him go. She couldn't let him go. She sat very still, blood pounding in her throat.

Her desk phone rang. 'Mr Blake is here,' Josie said. Anna took some deep breaths, stood up and walked down to meet him. He leaped up from the banquette and came towards her with his hands outstretched.

Despite it all England had done him good. He had been in the constant company of young people from diverse economic backgrounds and many countries who neither knew nor cared about his family. It had liberated him and given him space to grow like a border perennial transplanted away from the showy shrub that had spread over it and cut out its light. Perhaps it had helped for him to realise that his sense of himself had been shadowed by a family that was itself compromised. He was wearing slim-fitting dark jeans, fashionably pointed tan shoes and a dark shirt that emphasised his broad shoulders and slender body. He looked like a different man from the one she had met in baggy chinos and button down chambray shirt. Hadn't he said he'd met a girl? She wouldn't ask but wished him well. She took his hands.

'Thank you so much for seeing me. Can we just step outside? I saw a bench on the towpath so maybe we can talk there? I won't take up too much of your time.'

They sat down and gazed ahead as a narrowboat chugged slowly down the stretch of canal with a muscular little terrier sitting happily on its roof between trays of cherry tomatoes and an upturned bike. Maxon turned to Anna. 'You've changed my life,' he said vehemently. Anna felt this was rather effusive and hoped more would not follow. She smiled politely.

'Well, hardly that, but I'm pleased you're pleased.'

'No, you don't understand.' He dropped his head to stare at the path as if thinking about how to go on. 'Do you remember I told you that dad is worrying about what to do with his legacy being as my sister is gone and I'm hardly Warren Buffet?' Anna just nodded. 'Well what you told me in the hospital really fired me up. I could have coped with the fantasy tale and even the bigamous marriages because I know things were different and it wasn't easy to get out of a bad marriage then, but to find that our whole financial enterprise was based on a major theft was a kick in my stomach.'

'That was conjecture.'

'Technically. Anyway, I did some research of my own that night. I was so shocked, so furious that we had been lied to for generations but my one hope was that having done that crime Albert would have used the money for good. After all, I had always been told that they provided housing for new immigrants who couldn't afford much and were sort of benefactors, you know?'

Anna was interested now. She remembered how carefully Maxon had recorded not only the results of her research but also how she had gone about the process. 'Right, I can understand that you would want to do that. What did you find?'

Maxon turned blazing eyes to her. 'I went into the Philadelphia newspapers of the time and keyed in the name of the company, Blake Enterprises. There was plenty to read.' His tone was grim. 'Starting from as early as 1897 when Grace and Albert married, their buildings, boarding houses, were the subject of scandals. There were petitions from tenants who were being over-charged and crammed into insanitary rooms, sometimes fifteen in a room, Anna, and then thrown out on the street if they complained. Some of the local politicians tried to make a cause out of it but they were always discredited. Story after story of hardship, diseases from dirty conditions and lack of basic sanitation kept cropping up. A Presbyterian minister tried to rally the rich and powerful, you know, appeal to their consciences but it always got swept under the carpet. The establishment was so corrupt that I'm even surprised the newspaper printed the stories.'

'How awful. They were slum landlords, then? We certainly had our share here – still do, I'm afraid.'

'Yes. But then, in 1901 the worst thing happened. There was a fire that burned one of the tenements to the ground and because of the overcrowding hundreds of people died. As the fire crew pulled body after body out of the ruins no-one could avoid the count of men, women, children, babies and no-one could deny any more what had been going on. It was a massive scandal. Also there were photographs. A photographer in New York had invented a kind of early flash-bulb using magnesium powder and he had photographed conditions at night inside the slums in the Lower East Side – appalling conditions. The same thing must have been happening in all the Eastern Seaboard cities. Well, a young reporter in Philadelphia, Jonas Ride, took up the idea and had gone into a Blake building secretly two weeks before to photograph conditions. It was the one that caught fire. His editor wouldn't publish the pictures at first, too frightened of the paper's backers, but when the fire happened and there was a huge public outcry he published them all.'

'You must be devastated.'

'No, wait. There was talk of prosecuting Albert but he argued that if he had not provided housing where would these people have found shelter and that it was not his fault if the tenants he had agreements with brought in extra people without his knowledge – you know, you can imagine the rest. So, somehow, not only did he not get prosecuted, although the building manager went to jail as the scapegoat, he got himself on the board of a new housing scheme where purpose-built apartments would be provided by the City at a reasonable cost.' Maxon was staring at a cat strolling along the wall on the other side of the canal but Anna knew he was seeing nothing except the pictures in his mind.

'Well, at least that was a good outcome.'

'It was good for about five years but of course he nudged other board members off one by one, got his own people in, and in no time at all the rents had gone up and the maintenance had lapsed. So, he then got huge lucrative contracts from the city to maintain the places but pocketed most of the money. Then he got the city to let him buy out the buildings as a private concern at a knock down price and never looked back. The notorious Blake Enterprises was re-named MB Holdings and most people never made the connection. By the outbreak of World War One he had his fine house in Ardmore and a very profitable business and he always made sure to keep it just the right side of new housing regulations. Poor people were not only his bread and butter but his champagne cocktail too. As long as there were poor, desperate people, and when aren't there, he could make money.'

'Maxon, this is awful. How are you coping with it?'

'Oh, believe me, I'm coping very well indeed!' He sounded so fierce and strong that she was surprised.

'What do you mean?'

His face was flushed with energy and his eyes glittered with the intensity of his mood. 'I know what dad must do with the money we have.'

'But it was all so long ago. Surely your family's interests are legitimate now?'

'Oh, of course. Controls are much stricter and quite honestly I don't know if dad has any idea about all this. He's not the kind of guy to dig.'

'So?'

Maxon gripped his hands into fists. 'At the first opportunity when I get home I'll take him to one side – I mean like when mom isn't there. She's not 100% even now and I'm not going to be the one to stress her. Then I'm going to lay it on him. How the family business was built, where the money came from and the lies that have been told, to say nothing of Albert's criminally ruthless acquisitiveness. Then I'll tell him what I want him to do – to set up new-build or good re-con housing association properties in Philly and also out of town places where there are jobs, like out near the suburban malls where there is work but poor inner city people can't afford to travel for it. Rents would be fair and there would be an escrow account set up for each tenant so that a percentage of their rent would go into that towards a down payment on their own property along the line.' He paused. 'I want to do it right in exactly the same sector as Albert and Grace did it so wrong.

'Blimey, Maxon, when did you think all this up?

'I suppose I've thought about it for a while but not, you know, in a focussed way. Most of the guys who work for me can't afford to live in Philly and their travel costs eat up way too much of their pay. The same thing the other way with the out-of-town malls. I just never thought I could do anything about it. I haven't slept thinking this through. And then,' he was almost falling over his words now, 'I thought each block could have a proper crèche for the pre-school kids with well-trained staff, bi-lingual ones, too, so that their parents can work and the kids can get a decent start.'

Finally he stopped talking but one foot was tapping fast on the cobbles. Anna was impressed by the scale of his vision but there was the obvious flaw in his reasoning. 'What if your dad doesn't want to? What if he thinks it's a hare-brained scheme that won't make money?'

Maxon threw back his head and laughed. 'I've got everything. I've got all the certificates, the newspaper photocopies, the photographs, the names, the dates, all the gen. My famous dossier! I'll tell him that if he doesn't see it my way I'll write a book and put it all in, every last carbuncle. I've scanned it all on to my hard-drive but I've got a flashdrive with it saved to keep in the café safe, too.' Anna took a deep breath and let it out slowly. There was no doubt about it, Maxon had become his own man.

They were silent for a while mulling this over. 'Actually,' Maxon went on, 'I think in a way he'll be relieved to do it. He doesn't enjoy being so ridiculously wealthy – his tastes are simple and so are my mom's. This can be his legacy so that he will retire with a pat on the back and the knowledge that he's done something good with his life.'

'So you wouldn't manage the project?'

'I could. I'm not a money person but I could hire good people. But I'd like him to be the face of it if possible – I can be his second, take over after he's gone. Otherwise I'd feel as though I was cutting him out, making him look like the bad guy and I don't think he is. And to be honest I like having the coffee shop – I wouldn't like to give that up entirely. I'll put Kirsty in as manager.'

'I think it's a wonderful plan,' Anna said, standing up. 'And I know you'll see it through. I couldn't be more pleased that you've found a way to turn all this murky stuff we've uncovered into something so worthwhile.' She hugged him. 'Come and get your picture, the car's just back here.'

As they walked around the side of the building she touched his arm. 'I bet you've got a name already, haven't you? For the company I mean.'

He grinned at her. 'You know me too well. I did think of calling it the Robin Hood Foundation but, um, you know. A bit hokey. So instead I'm going to get dad to call it The Fresh Start Housing Trust. Easy to remember and it makes me feel good because this is a major fresh start for me, too.'

Anna opened the boot of her car and pushed the wellingtons to one side. Maxon lifted out the bubble-wrapped and reinforced picture and tucked it under one arm. She closed the boot and they stood smiling at each other. Maxon took her hand and kissed the back of it. She was touched. 'I have a gift for you,' he said.

'Oh no, please.'

'This is a gift you can't refuse. Well, you can, but I hope you won't. The first apartment block we open will be called the Anna Ames House. How do you like that?'

Anna stared up at him, open-mouthed. 'What?'

'I'll send you photos when it's done. Would you come and open it for us?'

'I don't know what to say.'

'Say yes.'

Anna nodded and Maxon bent down and kissed her on her cheek. Then, with a wave of his free hand, he was gone round the corner of the building and away.

She stood by her car for a while feeling the noon sun beat down on her shoulders. She thought about the awkward, odd boy that she had met only weeks ago and the confident man full of purpose that Maxon now was. Family. For good or bad they form you, they set you up or knock you down or both, but you form them, too. Maxon would now be the one to lead his family in a completely new direction. It felt good to know they would stay in touch.

Anna took out her phone and called Josie to tell her that she was leaving work for the day. She couldn't wait to see her dad, to talk to him, to hear his voice, to be by his side.

24

At the hospital it was better news than she'd feared. Under the new medication regime George had had no more bleeds and his pneumonia was well under control. He would be discharged in a few days if all continued to go well. Ashok was there and the two of them were taking it in turns to write a doggerel poem line by line about the hospital. Ashok was crouched over a yellow legal pad balanced on the bed; George was staring into middle distance clearly in the throes of the muse. Ashok read aloud to Anna.

'They fix you up, your doctors do -' George had written, paraphrasing Larkin's notorious line, and Ashok had added, 'If they don't, tell 'em you'll sue -' but they wouldn't show Anna any more after that, giggling like schoolboys. It was balm to her heart to see her father restored to good spirits like this, so she took a seat by the window smiling at them both like the indulgent parent in the playground.

Anna noted that George was still short of breath and a little hoarse and that he had lost quite a bit of weight. She would have to sort out his room so that he could be made comfortable for bed rest; it was clear that he wouldn't be back to normal for several weeks at best. As she sat back away from the bed listening to the two old friends chatting, she wondered how the family would cope. Faye could hardly be expected to look after her grandfather's nursing needs and neither could Ellis, but someone would have to be there for him when she was at work. Diane had her own work and in any case would be a rather brusque carer Anna thought. Rosa? She hesitated at the thought. Rosa was a trained dementia support worker but would she be willing to work with someone she knew so well in a different role – rather an intimate one? Would George want her to? Something would have to be in place for next week. She had already taken all her annual holiday leave when Harry died.

She gazed out of the window and saw that high up against the blue were balled tissues of clouds each in its own vast space, each slowly disintegrating in lonely arabesques. What could she say to Steve? What would not sound foolish or desperate? Obviously she could apologise for her behaviour but then what? He wouldn't allow her to leave it at that – he would want to know why and she could never tell him, never implicate him, uninvolved as he was, in that distracted, careless decision that had cost Harry's life. He had cautioned her not to go up there with the dog but she had been giddy with the touch of his hand. No, she would never tell him that. What then?

A nurse appeared at the door with a wheelchair. 'We're moving you again, Mr Walcott, this room isn't for malingerers like you – it's the big ward for you tonight.' She winked at Anna.

'Oh, not the brick wall of Sartre's hell,' Ashok muttered, getting up stiffly.

'So will there be No Exit?' George queried owlishly and Ashok snorted at the joke. 'Exterior décor still by Pigeon Droppings Inc. I assume?'

Anna had a leap of memory and was back in her mother's ward in this very hospital. Her bed had been by the window with its muddled vertical blinds and beyond it had been that brick wall stained with splashes of white and grey. George would be on a different floor with the same view. She shook her head free of the distressing image of the old woman lying there dying. She found she had clenched her fists.

'I have no idea what you're talking about and you're both very naughty, but yup,' said the nurse.

She moved to the bed and George flapped a hand at them. 'Go and get a cup of tea or something – I don't want an audience, thank you.'

Ashok consulted Anna outside the door. 'You go home,' he said. 'I'm happy to keep him company for another hour or so and then he'll be ready for a nap, anyway.'

'Are you sure?' In answer he kissed her on top of her head and gently pushed her down the corridor.

She made her way to the lift and started thinking about what to get for dinner and what extra supplies she should lay in for George coming home. As she stepped out into the huge atrium she was trying to decide whether to stop on the way home or go home, get changed, and then shop. But there was something different, something going on. The atmosphere was charged. She halted and scanned the crowd milling around her but she must be wrong, there was no incident. Then she realised that her eyes had seen and her body had reacted to what her brain was still processing.

Steve was walking towards her. He had not spotted her and had a troubled, tired expression on his face. Her heart banged against her throat and she glanced round to see if there was time to move away, but as she did so he saw her and immediately his face flashed recognition and delight almost immediately followed by a carefully neutral expression. It was like watching a door pulled open on to a well-lit room and then slammed shut. He was with her.

'Hi. You must have just seen him. How's he doing?' She kept her voice under careful control and told him briefly what had been happening and where George now was. 'I'm so sorry – how frightening for you,' he said. 'For you all, I mean.'

They stood in silence for a moment while the crowd surged round.

'Did you try to contact me?' he asked. 'I mean, to help?' There was something in his voice, some plea that she had to resist.

'Um. It was all so fast and very early in the morning. I was going to tell you,' she added lamely. Now his face was completely shut, the eyes half-hooded, the lips in a firm line.

'No problem. I'd better head up there. Faye has kindly picked up Alice from nursery but I'll need to get back soon.' He didn't wait for her reply. 'Bye.'

She walked out to the car park and drove home sadly. She was still trembling slightly from the unexpected encounter, the nearness of his body, the faint spicy fragrance of his hair, the intensity of his look before he had switched it off.

The end of term. Ellis and Mike had some friends round and the back garden was full of yelps both human and animal. Anna glanced out of the kitchen window as she put groceries away. The boys were playing Frisbee with Bobble who wanted to play tug of war instead. She stopped in her tracks as she was about to re-fill the tea caddy. Who would look after Ellis? It had never been a problem before because through the years of Harry's illness her dad had always been here. He would make sure Ellis and Faye had a snack when they got home from school, check what homework needed doing and have a bit of a chat about their day before everyone went about their business. Holidays were no problem – she hadn't even had to think about who would be here for the boy.

Could she ask Faye? She dismissed the idea immediately. She picked up her phone and called Rosa asking if she could visit tomorrow late afternoon. Rosa was pleased, saying she had news of Dean and had been planning to pop in on Anna but Len had told her how things were with George and she didn't want to intrude.

Anna started to make the salad for dinner calculating numbers in her head. There was still most of the money left from Gerald Draycott's handsome gift for Harry's care so some of that could be used to pay Rosa to be here while George got his full strength back. Maybe a month or six weeks? That would take care of the school holidays, too. She threw the chopped up celery and grapes into a bowl and got the bag of walnuts out of the cupboard. It would be very good to come home to Rosa, she realised. It would be more than practical help – she would be another adult working together with Anna to run the family until George could take her place. Was it fair on her to ask her to do this? Full time work for only six weeks could be worse than nothing if she had to give up other regular long-term paid commitments. Well, that would have to be her decision. All Anna could do was ask. She mixed in chopped cucumber, red pepper and a generous dollop of mayonnaise and got a frozen quiche out to put in the oven.

She texted Faye.

'Bn C Pops all gud. Getting piz w gals, CU l8r xxxx,' was the reply. Anna hoped 'piz' meant pizza.

'Mum!' Ellis was so hot that he was steaming from the top of his head. 'Can we go bowling tonight to celebrate? The other boys were pushing behind him with eager faces. He had been so undemanding, so brave, surely she could do this for him, but what about visiting George?

'Just let me check something, ok? Do you all want to stay to dinner first?' There was the usual chorus. 'Phone your parents then while I just do this.' She moved into the hall. Diane picked up and said of course she was going in to see George this evening, what did Anna think? 'Give him my love, then,' Anna said. 'I just need to do something nice for Ell. But, Diane, phone me if there's a problem, ok?'

So, after the quiche and hastily cooked oven chips were made short work of, chocolate ice-cream and wafers were wolfed down. They piled into Anna's car making the usual fart jokes and yodelling with laughter and she drove off for an evening of being bowled into humiliation by eleven year old boys. She didn't have time to think and the sore place under her ribs could be easily ignored.

Rosa's narrowboat was a cheerful sight snuggled up against the grass verge to the towpath. On the far side of the path in the shade from a hedge sown with convulvulous and sweet peas were placed two folding chairs and on them were sitting two large people. Rosa lifted her sewing and waved it at Anna like a scarlet starter's flag. Len carefully turned his torso to see who was coming. Odd to remember that scrawny little Dean was her brother and not Len.

'I was just saying,' Len greeted her, 'that I've got a gig in Droitwich.'

Rosa smiled at Anna. 'Cup of tea?' She stepped to the back of the boat and brought out a stool for her to sit on.

Anna lifted the bag she was carrying. 'I've brought strawberries and clotted cream and a bottle of rose. I've hulled the strawberries and there's some plastic dishes and so on – you don't need to do anything.' She took the items out and put them on the tiny picnic table they had between them.

Len eyed the bottle. 'You're not off on one again, are you?'

'No. What's the gig?'

'Green burial.'

'That's cheery, then. Didn't you do one of those for a friend last year? You must advertise yourself as a niche balladeer. What are you going to play?' Anna spooned out the fruit and cream and handed the dishes round. "Everything's coming up roses?"'

'I said he should play, "Nobody loves me, everybody hates me, going to go and eat worms,"' Rosa said, laughing sideways at him.

Len maintained a dignified smirk. 'They want "Where have all the flowers gone?"' Rosa and Anna groaned. 'They're like, old hippies.'

'As long as they're paying you.' They sat silently and worked their way through the fruit and cream while Anna wished she had added a packet of shortbread to go with it.

Rosa broke the silence. 'I popped in to see your dad yesterday.'

'That was kind of you.'

'Mm. He's much better isn't he? Quite jokey, but frail. It will take a while before he's back to his old self. Faye was there. She made him a fruit cake.'

'Really? I had no idea she could bake.'

'Makes a change for her to lift herself,' Len muttered.

'It was dad I wanted to talk to you about, Rosa. I know it's a big ask but I wondered if you might have some time free to look after him for the next month or so? I can't take any more leave.' She would pay Rosa above the going rate for the short notice. Rosa took her phone out of her pocket and tapped on it.

'Would you want me all day?'

'I wondered if you could fit round the jobs you have. I can get dad washed and ready for the day before I go to work. It's just I don't want to leave him for hours on his own.'

'If I can be away by four each day I can do it. I've got a chap whose day carer goes home then and I cover until his son gets back from work at 7.00. Would that be ok?' She put her phone away and picked up the sewing again.

'That would be great – I'll just tell Ted that I have to be home for four but I'll do some work from home to make up for it. He should be fine with that, it's only for a few weeks.' She hesitated. 'Ellis will be off school. Do you mind?'

Rosa brightened. 'Oh no. I've got a bit of time for him, he's ok. We can play Red-Handed with your dad when he feels like it.'

Len had put his meaty hands on his knees with the thumbs turned in and his elbows turned out. Anna noticed this sign of irritation. 'When am I going to see you, then?'

'When you get lucky,' Rosa replied pleasantly without missing a beat. Len scowled.

'So how's Dean? Any news on a release date?'

Rosa put down the embroidery and sighed. Her hair was showing signs of inattention unusual for this woman. The most recent application of Prussian blue was revealing an inch or so of natural colour. Anna was intrigued to see that Rosa was a blonde. 'He's got caught with some stuff and they've stopped his parole for six months.' Len looked carefully at a passing duck while registering no expression. Anna was impressed by his self-control and took it as a measure of his feelings for Rosa who shook out her work to find where she had left the needle. It was an odd-shaped piece of red velvet but now Anna could see that Rosa had embroidered a stave, a treble clef and notes in black silk. 'That's an interesting design, Rosa, it looks great. What's that for?' In answer Rosa flicked one of her elbows at Len.

'Really? So...'

'Waistcoat front. It's his birthday soon.' Of course it was. What with one thing and another Anna had totally forgotten. Getting as bad as their mother, she thought bitterly, remembering how Lena had almost never bothered to mark the birthday of her supposedly adored little Lenny. Too bloody self-centred. She surprised herself with the rush of bitter bile she felt.

'What's the tune?'

Len was looking soft and happy as he watched Rosa sew a gift for him. 'Dunno. Can't read music, can I?' He shifted anxiously. 'But I really like it, I really do.'

Anna gently took it from Rosa as she had to stop to re-thread her needle. She hummed a few notes in her head and then put it back, giving Rosa a fond look. What a fortunate day it had been when Rosa had come into their lives. For a moment she wondered if she should ask her advice about Steve but she shrank from that much disclosure.

'Well, I'd better get back.' She stood up from the stool that Rosa had given her. 'I'll be in touch. We don't know yet exactly when he'll be discharged.'

'No problem.'

Len squinted up at her, the early evening sun enriching the colour of his skin to a hot brick. 'Will you do me a party like last year?' Last year Harry had been there. This would be the first of many family occasions when his absence would be silently noticed and mourned.

'I'm very happy to, Len, but I know dad would want to be part of it so we may have to delay it a couple of weeks. Would you mind?'

'Sweet.'

'Have something here on the day, if you like,' Rosa said casually. 'I wouldn't mind.'

Anna picked up the plates and plastic glasses and packed them away in her bag but left the half-full bottle. 'See you, then.'

George was dozing. Anna quietly took her place in the chair by his side and started to read the newspaper she had bought at the shop in the lobby, but she couldn't concentrate and when she found she had read the same opening paragraph in an article about HS2 three times she gave up.

She slipped back deeper into the upholstered seat and thought about Steve. So many memories from the years they had known each other – so many times she had turned to him for support or him to her. But in a strange way they had been more free to admit their feelings, not less, when Harry had been alive. The bond they both had with Harry had been a fire-door, a moat, a no-man's land which neither could cross without violating each other and themselves, let alone Harry's trust. Now that there was no barrier she didn't know how to behave or what to say. In one way it was nonsense to let him go. She loved him. She admitted that to herself at least. Was she going to lose him through shame, embarrassment, shyness about telling the truth? Surely she was not so weak and proud.

The truth was that it had only been a few months since Harry's death and it felt too soon. He had quite literally slipped from her in a second and part of her still couldn't believe it. How could someone be alive one moment and dead the next? Sometimes she dreamed about it but in her dreams he didn't lie blood-soaked on the rocky turf, he spun and gambolled like a leaf in the wind until she woke, bewildered and sad. There was no reason not to move on, and surely she could find a way to explain to Steve why she had been so tormented, why she had needed to push him away but, she realised, reason had nothing to do with it. She was only now beginning to grieve for him. The fiery guilt that had twisted and burnt her had obscured the sorrow and now that guilt had been laid to rest the grief was revealed, heavy and inert like cooling lava, blocking any move towards Steve.

'I expect it will sort itself out,' her dad said. For a second she thought his voice was in her head but then turned to find him smiling at her.

'Hi Dad. How are you feeling?'

'Better. Annie, while we're alone I need to talk to you – I need to apologise.' She shook her head in bewilderment. 'No, I do. Just hear me out.' She moved close to the bed so he could speak without effort – his breathing was not right yet.

'Dad, there is absolutely nothing you need to be sorry for.'

'What you said at the barbeque...'

'Oh, don't.' Anna covered her face with her hands.

'No, you were right. You told me to stop interfering in your life. No-one else would have understood and of course Diane was incensed because she thinks I'm very hands-off and you were being wrong and unkind.'

'I was.'

'No. I knew what you meant – she didn't. You meant that I should not have suggested, however obliquely, that you start a relationship with Steve. You know I did and you know I meant a physical relationship.' Anna bowed her head. 'I wanted so much for you to have some happiness. Harry could have gone on for years and it was so unfair on you, and Steve.' George's eyes pleaded for understanding. 'I just wanted to give you permission, you know, to be happy. I should have known that you couldn't be happy that way. It was foolish and wrong of me, Anna.'

He lay back on the pillows and took some deep breaths. 'I knew that there was more to your pain than loss. I watched you slowly self-destruct – I heard you up all hours at night and I saw the shrine you made to Harry in your bedroom and then you started drinking and I didn't know what to do because I didn't know why you were doing it. Of course people can get crazy with grief but I just don't think you're that kind of person. So, if it wasn't grief entirely, what was it?' He took Anna's hand in his while she sat mute with shame. 'You had no reason to reproach yourself for anything that I could see, and yet you were showing all the signs of guilt and remorse because you seemed to be trying to block something out – drown it.'

'I was running from it.'

'Yes. But it wasn't until you started attacking Faye that I became seriously worried. You are not that person. I've often seen you exasperated and furious at Faye's provocative behaviour but I've never known you ever be vicious and cruel like that.'

'It just felt like something vile was pressing up inside me, something hot and dangerous but, I'm ashamed to say, exciting, too. Every time I lashed out at Faye I was appalled by myself but I felt powerful. Then it would all drain away and I would be left looking at the wreckage and just hate myself.'

He patted her hand. 'Just let me say my piece, Annie. I thought a lot about your reactions to her behaviour and it was almost always about her sexuality, wasn't it, that you saw as wanton, wicked, self-indulgent gratification? So then, it doesn't take a psychologist to guess what you were tormenting yourself with.'

Anna looked steadily into her father's worried face. 'You're right. But Steve and I have never been together in that way, not because I didn't want to, I admit, I more or less propositioned him but he wouldn't have it. It wasn't exactly that. But, the way I felt about Steve did cause Harry's death, Dad, and I couldn't admit it to myself. I don't want to talk about it but just take my word.' She leaned forward and rested her head on his bony shoulder. 'You have nothing to apologise for, you suggested nothing that I hadn't thought of a hundred times myself.'

He was quiet for a while, patting her hand absent-mindedly. 'You seem to be calmer now. Have you made it up with Faye?'

'Getting there. I just don't think I'll ever forgive myself for how I was with her.'

George lay still for a few moments and then squeezed her hand. 'Use it. Use how you feel, how you felt.'

'What do you mean?'

'Remember what it was like when you felt so guilty and remorseful – can you describe it to me?'

'Horrible. I hated myself - it made me want to hurt other people. There was a kind of vicious gremlin in me that was whirling a sword around and didn't care who got in the way. That's why I drank – to knock that nastiness into oblivion.'

'Think of your mother.'

Anna sat bolt upright in shock. 'My *mother*? Dad, the last thing I want to think about is my mother. She's been popping up in my mind like some cackling witch a lot lately and I'm certainly not going to dwell on that.' The image of how Lena had been the first time Anna had seen her in over forty years, leaped up. It was here, in this hospital, in a ward like this one, only a couple of years ago. Anna had looked at her own face rendered creased and blotchy with age and her own eyes, hard with malice. It had been her personal Dorian Gray moment and it had frightened the life out of her.

'Don't be angry with me, Anna. I need to say this. You've never come to terms with the way it was between you after meeting her for those last few weeks.'

'You mean I haven't come to terms with her insulting and rejecting me and then revealing to me that the only reason she had contacted me at all after forty years was to tell me to look after her darling Len? No, I haven't come to terms with that.' The harsh profile of her mother's face as the flesh fell from it in the last weeks before she died would never be forgotten. She felt the painful grip of her mother's claw as she had insisted that Anna make her that promise. She had refused and her mother had never spoken to her again.

In an odd twist, after Lena had died she had taken to Len in his grief and realised that he had suffered from the woman's callous self-centredness as much as she. More, in fact, since Lena's abandonment of her husband and baby daughter had meant a happy and secure life for Anna, albeit a lonely one for George. Len had not been lucky in his father or his mother.

Anna found that she had become angry and upset. Why on earth had her dad brought this up? What had this got to do with anything? A horrible thought struck her. 'Are you telling me that I was behaving like my mother?'

'Yes. In a way.'

'How could you say that to me?'

'Because we all do. We all can behave that way. Anna, the mother you knew was set in her character. She was a cruel and vindictive woman in her old age but I knew her long before that when she was young. She was always self-willed and, well, selfish, I suppose, but she wasn't a cold and nasty person, she was capable of love and affection just like you.'

Anna had a memory of George's poem at Lena's funeral – the magical moment of beauty and passion when they had been young lovers that it celebrated. 'You've been assuming, I think, that she left us at no cost to herself, just to be free in a kind of vague way that was fashionable then. But she did feel guilt, I'm sure she did. It couldn't be acknowledged or dealt with because people of our generation, hers and mine, didn't know how to do that. We were often blind to the dynamics of our own natures. So, that gremlin you talk about that mercifully you have experienced for such a short time, she carried with her until it *was* her. Think how Lena lived with that feeling almost all her life – burning and blaming. Now you know how bitter and confusing and lonely it was for her. Guilt corrupts and shrinks the heart. She would have laughed at me if I had suggested that, but it was so.'

Other visitors were coming in to the ward now and Anna drew her face closer to her father so they could speak quietly. 'I still don't understand.'

'You know now how guilt corrodes – how it brings out the worst in someone. You've experienced it and it horrified you. If you can understand that, you can forgive your mother so she can rest in peace in your heart, and if you forgive your mother, you can forgive yourself. It's just how these things work.'

They watched the pale young man opposite be greeted and gently hugged by a small bundle of family. He smiled and sighed with pleasure and sat up straighter in his bed.

'What about Steve, Dad?'

'I expect he's ready for a cup of tea, aren't you?' She was confused but then followed her father's eyes and turned her head. Steve had arrived at the end of the bed and was glancing nervously from father to daughter.

'Sit here,' she ordered. 'I'll get you one. I need to stretch a bit.'

When she got back Steve was telling George about a meteor shower that was expected soon and they were speculating on how the cloud cover would be and the exact orientation of George's bedroom at home for him to be able to see it. For a little while she was quiet, not trusting herself to join in the conversation, but it all felt so natural and easy that within a quarter of an hour she was teasing her father and smiling at Steve. She would say something to him as they left. It was the perfect opportunity to sound him out on how he was feeling and to convey to him how things were now with her.

But just as George was saying he could do with a nap, a text bleeped on Steve's phone. He read it and stood up. 'Sorry, got to go. I'll pop in again, probably, before you're discharged.' He glanced at Anna and the eyes were guarded again. 'Anna, take care.' He was gone.

When she drove up their street half an hour later she saw in Steve's front garden a For Sale sign from a local estate agent and Steve himself talking to a young couple with a little boy between them in his drive. She parked outside her own house and sat for a long time thinking until a football bounced on the bonnet and Mike and Ellis made faces at her through the window.

25

All day the skies had been cloudy in a moody and threatening way, great bullying banks of black vapour pushing over the city and making day into dusk. After the long weeks of heat and dazzling blue it was almost a relief despite the menace. They had had some brief downpours and even some dry thunder and lightning clashes over the weeks since Harry had died but this was looking like a proper wetting. Anna went out to the back garden and pulled the chairs into the garden tool-shed. She turned off the power at the sockets in George's writing shed, made firm the window latches and locked the padlock on the door.

Bobble had followed her out but seemed cowed by the darkening skies with their sickly green tinge and stayed close to her. She reached out for his head to stroke it reassuringly and noted that it his ears were now at her shoulder height even when he had all four feet on the ground. She put an arm round his rough neck. 'It's ok, we're going in. Just do a wee now if you want one, will you?' He panted adoringly into her face. She turned her head away from the meaty breath and flying gobs of saliva and as the first huge drops of rain fell pulled him towards the house. On her way in to the kitchen she picked up his outside water dish and a couple of pots of pelargonium cuttings and dropped them on the washing machine.

Before Maxon Blake had left he had asked Anna if he could Skype her and promised not to be a nuisance with it. Of course she had agreed. That evening after dinner she was sitting at the kitchen table with her laptop while Faye and Ellis banged about clearing up when the familiar dial tone started up. Outside the rain was pounding down like a military tattoo and it felt cosy and safe in the kitchen.

'Hi!' He sounded and looked cheerful she was happy to see. 'How's things? How's your father?'

They chatted as Faye made various excuses to pass behind her and have a good look at this cool American guy who seemed to know her mother very well. Finally, she could stand it no longer. She leaned forward, 'I'm Faye,' she said, 'the gorgeous and talented daughter you've heard so much about - ' Maxon laughed. 'So, who are you?'

'A client,' Anna said as Maxon said, 'A friend.' There was a brief pause and then Anna said, 'Friend,' and Maxon said, 'Client.'

Maxon was peering closely at the screen. 'Is this your kitchen at home? Oh, God, I'm sorry, I was forgetting the time. I just expected you would be at work.'

'No problem,' said Faye considerately, pressuring Anna to one side.

'Any excuse not to clear the dishes,' Anna laughed, pushing her away. 'Are you ok?' She motioned for Faye to carry on tidying up, she wanted to hear what Maxon's father had said. 'I'll just take this into the living room.'

'It's kind of neat to get a tour of your house, too,' Maxon said. 'I like it. It looks homey.'

'I'm not going to ask you what you mean by that,' Anna said, grimacing at him, 'but I'm dying to know how it went with your dad.'

'Well, that's the thing. It went better than I could have hoped. I got him after he'd just won a round of golf but actually I didn't need to worry, he was almost there before me.' Anna tucked her feet under herself on the big old sofa and balanced the laptop on a cushion.

'You mean he knew about the history?'

'No, not at all. But while I've been in England and he was, like, debating how to move forward financially, he went to a fund-raiser for a charity a friend of my mom is active with. It's not to do with housing, it's to help guys who've served time in jail, men and women, get back on their feet, mostly it's like a buddy system – you know, they connect with ex-cons who've gone straight. But while he was there he got talking to a bunch of them and realised how tough the housing issue is for them. Hostels are ok for putting a roof over their heads but they're violent places sometimes and the ex-cons that are hoping for a fresh start want to provide for their families, not be with low-life.'

'So he was open to your idea?'

'I didn't know he'd had this encounter so I just waded in and told him what I'd discovered about our family's grisly past and he went quiet, you know? I thought he was shocked, maybe angry with me, so I didn't push it and he said he needed time to think so it got left for a couple of days.'

Faye came in and energetically mouthed at her. 'What?' Anna asked. 'Sorry, Maxon, just give me a minute, please.'

'Steve's selling his house, Mum! I can't believe it! There's a board up, Ellis says, and that means I won't ever see Alice again! Mum, you've got to do something!'

'Can we just talk about this later, Faye?'

'No! It's your fault! You've been so horrible to him it's made him want to leave!'

Anna heard Maxon's voice and looked back at the screen. 'I can see you've got stuff going on, Anna. I'll email you.'

'No, don't go.' But the screen had gone blank. For a second Anna thought of being angry with Faye but this was, after all, her home and Maxon was work. Faye was standing by the fireplace with her hands on her hips in full affronted mode. The wind had eddied and the rain was now chattering against the front windows. Strands of unpruned wisteria waved frantically like maidens in distress.

'Make him stay, Mum! I'll never forgive you if Alice leaves – she's like my baby sister!'

Anna sighed and shut the laptop. 'If Steve wants to go I can't stop him. It's no use you getting angry with me and threatening me. It's his business – go and talk to him.'

'*You* go and talk to him. It's you he wants!'

Everything stopped. Time stopped. Anna couldn't believe what Faye had said. She and Steve had never shown the slightest intimacy in front of their families or hinted at anything other than a friendly, neighbourly relationship. 'Faye, you don't know what you're saying.'

In answer Faye swept out of the room and a second later the front door banged. Had she gone down to confront Steve? Surely she wasn't brazen enough to do that. But neither could Anna just let her go like a nuclear missile. Anna grabbed her raincoat and an umbrella from the rack and ran out just catching a glimpse of Faye, down the street, turning into Steve's drive.

But when Anna got there Faye was standing at the front door listening. 'There's no-one in – his car's gone. Phone him!' She was already soaked, her hair black with rain and dribbling rivulets down her face making her blink back the water. Anna stepped close to her and put the umbrella over her, rubbing her wet arms to bring back the circulation.

'No, Faye, I'm not going to phone him. Just come home with me and calm down and I'll talk to him tomorrow and see what his plans are. For all we know he may be moving locally if he's said nothing to you about it. You're round there often enough.'

They walked back to their own house clinging together against the driving sheets of rain. 'I'm not just being a brat, Mum,' Faye said, 'I really love Alice. I mean, Steve's all right, but Alice needs me. She always asks me to do stuff for her, not him. He's a man, isn't he? She wants another girl to do things with.'

'I realise that. He does his best, Faye.'

'I know. But please, Mum, please talk to him. Tell him he can't go.'

But the next day at work Steve was away and Anna didn't want to ask where and why.

Maxon emailed in the early afternoon and finished the story. In sum, he said, his dad had been shocked by the family history but not entirely surprised. He had sometimes wondered, it turned out, why the family had never visited England or looked up the legendary connections – many American families did. Why had they never known precisely where Albert Maxon came from in New England? These were vague questions, not worth following up, but they made sense in light of Maxon's revelations. To his son's delight he had become enthusiastic about Maxon's plans for low-cost housing and had got back to him the next day with the outline of how it could be managed: what tenancy criteria there might need to be, what safeguards and legal frameworks they might use, what building codes and federal and city regulations they might run up against and so on.

Maxon had thought that he was letting his father run things as an act of respect and deference but within a couple of hours he realised that his dad's expertise was invaluable. He and his dad would work together on the project and it seemed that the older man might be rejuvenated by it.

Anna sighed with satisfaction and sent a brief appreciative response. She turned to other work and the morning passed as usual but just as she was thinking about getting out of the building for lunch and wondering whether Suzy would come, her phone rang. It was the curator from the Art Gallery and Museum in Shrewsbury, John Lansdowne.

'Hello, Anna, I'm glad I've caught you.'

'Hi. How can I help?'

There was a slight pause as though the man was choosing his words carefully. 'Something has come up about the Blake family history. I can't go into it on the phone but there is someone who would like to talk to you. As it happens I'm coming into Birmingham for a meeting on Monday and could bring him. He doesn't drive any more. Could we all meet somewhere?' Anna thought rapidly.

'How about the Edwardian Tearooms at the BMAG?'

'Perfect. About 11.00?'

'Yes, I'll see you then. I'm intrigued.' As soon as she put the phone down Anna realised that she had not cleared this with Ted and, since Maxon's bill had been paid and his account closed, no money could come to Harts from this meeting no matter how interesting it might be. She got up and went down the corridor to Ted's office. He was immersed in a stack of manila files and there was a scatter of balled up paper on the floor around the overflowing waste basket. The paper recycling box was, as ever, empty.

'What?' he barked. 'Oh, it's you. Everything all right?'

'Yes, thanks. Dad's on the mend. In fact I wanted to talk to you about that. He'll be coming home very soon and I've got someone in for during the day to look after him but she has to leave at 4.00. Can I work from home for a couple of hours each day?'

'Hm.'

'It's only for a few weeks, Ted. But I am going to need an hour on Monday morning, too. It's personal.'

'It seems to me, madam, you're pretty much on permanent flexitime these days, anyway. Why ask? What does my permission matter?' She waited to see if he was serious. 'Oh, go on, then. Just don't flaunt it, I don't want all of them whining to me.' She backed out of the office giving the slightest hint of a genuflection.

At five o'clock she shut down her computer, stretched and pondered. For the next few weeks she would be either at work or at home or running errands. That was fine but there was one visit she wanted to make before it all started.

Joan answered the door wearing elbow length rubber gloves and a streak of dirt on her face. She let Anna in and they went out into the back garden. 'The outside drain's blocked. I put caustic soda down it yesterday but it's still bunged up.'

'Have you got a snake?'

'Of course I haven't got a snake – what are you talking about?'

Anna smiled at her. 'It's a plumbing wire that goes round the bend. You push it through and poke it about.'

'Oh. Well, no, I haven't got one.' She pulled off the gloves and stalked back into the kitchen to wash her hands. 'Do you want a lemonade or something? How's George?'

'Trying to tell Diane to back off, in the nicest possible way of course. He's not good at being nurtured.'

'No, I'm the same. It feels like being bossed about.'

'He's being discharged soon. I've got Rosa to come during the day.'

'That's a good idea. Just let me know if you want me to fill gaps.'

They took their drinks out to the garden and sat at the newly painted wrought iron table with its dainty chairs. 'It's probably leaves from that storm we had last night,' Anna said, looking up at the house gutters. 'You may have to get someone in. Did I see a removal van outside Briony's?'

'Yes, she's moving. Somewhere in the country she said. I got the impression she's found someone, and if she has, I'm pleased. Her mum would have been, too. She's got a lot of sterling qualities for any brave man who could take her on.' Or a brave woman, Anna thought, smiling to herself.

Joan squinted at her. 'You look better than you did. Diane and I have been a bit worried, love, you've not been yourself for a while. Understandable, of course.'

'Mm. I'm doing better.'

'So what did you come round for?'

'Can't I just come round to come round?'

'Of course you can, any time, but you haven't, have you?'

'You're a clairvoyant – I've always suspected it. You've got special powers.' Anna twitched her fingers in Joan's face and they laughed. 'Of course you're right. I wanted to ask you something.'

'Go on then.'

'You know what you told me – that day of the fundraiser – about having had an affair?' Joan nodded looking puzzled. 'Well, how did you deal with it, with the guilt, I mean? How did you go on?'

'Oh. Well, I never cared for the man, I didn't even like him really so it wasn't that I was in love – he was never a rival for Walter. I wondered whether to tell Walter but that seemed a cruel thing to do – it would only hurt him. I don't think I was being a coward. It was the fashion then to get everything out, to tell everyone everything, it was supposed to be healthier, but I don't think that's always right. No, the more time that went on, the more I thought of the affair as a virus.'

'A virus?'

'Yes. I had been taken ill, burned with a fever, not been myself, and then I got better.' Joan sipped at her drink. 'It felt just like that, actually.'

'Blimey.'

The doorbell went and Joan skipped off to answer it. A virus, Anna thought, no, it was not like that with her. With her it was love. That was the problem. Joan re-appeared with Diane in tow.

'Diane's says she's got a snake.'

Diane settled herself at the table while Joan returned with another glass. 'I'll come round tomorrow and see if I can shift it.' They sat for a moment enjoying the warmth and steaminess after the rain of the previous night that had refreshed the garden. 'Your dad's making a nuisance of himself again,' she said to Anna. 'He must be feeling better – he wants us to buy a campervan when he's back on his pins.' They sipped lemonade in silence for a few moments.

'I was just telling Anna about an affair I had way back,' Joan said easily, 'I said it was like a nasty virus.'

'I know what you mean,' Diane agreed, and Anna realised she knew almost nothing about Diane's past life. She had not married, she knew that, but not much more. 'No, I knew very early on that I didn't want to get hitched. I liked men and I liked sex but I knew I would never be able to settle with one.' She patted Anna's knee. 'This was a long time ago.'

'So you never had to worry about staying faithful?' Anna asked, half-amused, half-shocked at these uninhibited old women.

'Oh, I was faithful. Very faithful. Just not to a man. No, with me it's always been animals. When I went out to Africa as a student it just confirmed for me that that was my passion, my life's work. I even did a stint with Jane Goodall, you know, but my real interest wasn't wild animals at all. I just hated the way that people treated the animals that helped them, you know, donkeys, horses, cats, dogs. How can people abuse those poor creatures? That was what my life was about. I started a charity in Tanzania that set up refuges – very like Safe 'n' Sound, actually. We think we're so good to animals in this country but often we aren't, and Tanzania was no worse than Greece or loads of other places. Most places. I have been faithful to that. I think that's what loyalty is about. Sticking with what you really care about and being true to it.'

'Like dad and poetry,' Anna said, thinking also of Andrew Dunster.

'Yes.' They all sipped in silence for a moment. 'But, talking about sex,' Diane went on, 'I must admit I did have a very enjoyable threesome in Dar es Salaam in 1974.' Diane hooted at the memory and the others slapped at her, snorting lemonade down their noses.

26

It seemed to take for ever to discharge George. Nurses appeared, disappeared, insisted on putting him in a wheel chair and then left him in it for ages but finally, just at rush hour, he was given his meds and told he could leave. Anna almost ran down the corridor with him. She had decided to take him home in a taxi so she had got the train out to the hospital from New Street. 'Steady on, love,' he cried. 'If you were a jockey you'd be fined for over-whipping!'

As the black cab sat in traffic on the inner ring road George was texting. Diane had planned to come but an emergency admission of a fox with a crushed paw had diverted her. Anna was not sorry – she wanted her dad to herself for a little while. He seemed cheery but in the bright light of day he looked ashen and she couldn't wait to get him back into his own bed to rest. Faye was in charge of making a light and tasty meal which almost certainly would comprise the contents of a fistful of greaseproof bags from the deli being plopped out on plates. Ellis was on standby to help George up the steps at the front door but as the taxi pulled up at the curb of their drive, Anna saw that Ellis was not alone. He and Steve were putting the finishing touches to bunches of balloons trailing a rainbow of ribbons round the door. They ran towards the taxi and helped George out, supporting him on either side so enthusiastically that he nearly fell over.

When they got to the staircase Anna realised that they would have a hard job to get her dad up it. He was not tall and had lost weight but he was so weak that he had to rest after the first step and they all stopped to think it through, propping him from the side and the back. 'A block and tackle would come in handy,' he wheezed. Steve bent to say something quietly in his ear.

'Do you think you could manage it? I don't mind if it won't hurt your back. Don't worry if you drop me, my bed at the hospital should still be there.' They backed him down the one step he had climbed so he was standing shakily on the hall floor.

'Get me a cushion for my shoulder, would you, Ellis?' Steve asked.

Then Steve bent down and picked George up in a strong fluid movement lifting him from below his centre of gravity and placing him gently across his shoulder in a fireman's lift as easily as if he had been a rolled rug. 'Ok? Not hurting anywhere?'

'Only my dignity. Onward and upward, my good man!' George pointed up the stairs with his free hand as though leading a cavalry charge. Steve made a small balancing adjustment to his load and started up. Anna had both hands over her mouth watching them and Ellis' eyes were almost out of his head as Steve carried the old man steadily up the flight of stairs, turned on the landing and disappeared into his bedroom. Then they dashed up after them.

'That was awesome!' Ellis said. 'Can you teach me to do that?'

'Find another guinea pig,' George said, gasping. 'Lucky I'm not wearing false teeth.'

Faye appeared with Alice. 'What? What's happened?'

'Steve just slung Pops over his shoulder and ran upstairs with him! It was so cool.'

'Well, hardly ran -'

'Why didn't you tell me! I expect you all forgot I was slaving in the kitchen getting your dinner ready.'

Anna put her arm round Faye's waist, the shoulder was out of reach. 'Thanks, love, can you put something on a tray for Pops? He might need a minute to recover.' She plumped him up and tucked him in and stuck out her tongue at him when he protested that he could do all that for himself and to stop fussing.

Alice stared at the bed. She had never seen this room or George in bed before. 'Shall I tell you a story?' she asked, always keen to observe protocol.

'That would be very nice,' George said, smiling at her and breathing hard.

She went across to him and sat on the chair he used as a bedside table. 'Once upon a time there was a princess and she had a rabbit and the rabbit ate her up. The end.'

'Thank you,' said George gravely. 'That was a very nice story.' Faye took Alice by the hand giving her a squeeze of approval and they thumped down the stairs.

'Do you need a nap, Dad? You must be whacked.'

He looked around at the fresh day lilies on the window sill and the branches of the sycamore tree nodding in the breeze. 'It's very nice to be home.'

'Do you want your post?' Ellis asked. 'I can bring it up.'

'Thanks, Ell. I could get used to this.'

Steve had disappeared but now came back into the bedroom carrying a bottle of champagne and three glasses. George's eyes brightened. 'I am reliably informed that the upper echelons of society drink nothing else when a little bracer is required,' Steve said. 'The late Queen Mother swore by it.'

'And many other things, no doubt. Good lad. Just the ticket.'

In the end Faye's tray of food prettily decorated with nasturtium vines had to wait until George had had his nap which happened so suddenly that Anna only just caught the glass as it fell from his hand.

'Will you stay for something to eat?' she asked Steve quietly.

'Is that ok?' Now they were alone his tone was subdued and he didn't look at her. She felt very calm as she looked at him, seeing him clearly for the first time in months.

Now was the time. She stood up. 'First, please come with me, would you?' She walked along the landing and opened the big bedroom door. 'Please, come in.' Steve hung back, his face flushed. 'It's all right. Come in.' She closed the door behind him.

'Look, I -'

'Do you see that wall? All the photographs and letters and notes? They're all Harry. I did it right after he died. There's a hair of his stuck up there somewhere.' Steve stared, so surprised that he forgot to be embarrassed by where he was.

'I didn't know. Did it help?'

'At the time.'

'Why are you showing me this?'

Anna ignored the question. 'In this wardrobe are all his clothes and shoes. In that drawer is his sports gear.' She moved to the window ledge and touched the glossy green bag on it. 'This is him. His ashes.' Steve's face was now wary and concerned.

'Anna?'

She turned to face him. 'I want to tell you that this weekend I am going to take down everything on that wall and put it away. I'm going to bag his clothes and take them to the charity shops. Anything that isn't good enough will go out in the bin. Then I will paint every inch of this room and get a new bed and linens. When dad is well enough we will go up on to the Roaches and scatter Harry's ashes. Then, that will be the end of me and Harry as far as it ever can be.' She turned and faced Steve, looking calmly into his eyes. 'If you want, it will be the beginning of you and me.' She felt at peace and whole, drained of the tumult and chaos of the weeks since Harry's death. She would think of him every day and he would flit about her conscious and unconscious mind all her life but the hurricane was over.

Steve stepped forward and took both her hands in his. There was a moment of silence as they gazed frankly at each other. 'Tonight,' he said, 'I will email Sheffield University and refuse their job offer. Tomorrow, I will phone the estate agent and take the house off the market.' He bent down and kissed her gently on the lips. 'I do want. I love you more than I can ever tell you. When I thought I'd lost you, I felt as though all the colour had drained from the world.' She reached up to touch his cheek and let her hand rest on it.

They heard Alice's voice, as high as a bird's, calling, 'Steve? Anna? S'ready!'

John Lansdowne was seated at a table with upholstered chairs in the Edwardian Tearooms and Anna was happy to see that they had already been served. She walked across smiling at him and the man he was with, who stood up to greet her. She immediately liked him. He had that interested and alert air which characterises an outward looking mind and an open heart and which becomes more apparent and engaging with age. He twinkled at her much as George might have done, in fact she could imagine if the two of them met they would be chatting for hours.

'Thank you so much for agreeing to meet me,' he said. 'You must be wondering what this is all about because I asked John not to tell you.' He took her hand and shook it slightly. 'I like a bit of drama.'

Anna had mixed feelings about unscheduled dramas but let it go. 'Anna Ames,' she said, smiling.

'Felix Brown,' the man said, 'I'm Grace Thwaite's great-nephew.' He waited for the effect. Anna tried to make sense of this. 'I'm the grandson of Ruth who was her little sister.'

'Right.' Anna knew Grace had had younger siblings, of course, but had given no thought to them.

John Lansdowne had been watching this little scene play out with amusement and now rose to his feet. 'Let me get you something, Anna. Coffee? Cake?'

'Thank you. Coffee with just a spot of milk, please.' She sat down. 'I'm so sorry that you've just missed Maxon Blake who's a cousin, well several times removed, but -'

'Oh no, I know he's gone back to America, they said so in the article. I didn't want to meet him, you see. I waited until he had gone before I contacted John.'

Anna could see that Felix would want to tell his story, whatever it was, in his own way and had planned how he would do it. Her role would be to listen and let him. She didn't mind, but she wouldn't be surprised to find that he was a leading light in amateur dramatic circles in Shrewsbury. There was something charming about him, though, that made her want to indulge him rather than be irritated by him. Or was she feeling especially mellow? She realised he was already into the tale.

'The Smith family living on Chirk Street were terribly poor at the turn of the century, but Ruthie married a mine manager and in the next generation my father, their son, built up a good business selling cars. Poor man was quite cast down when I wanted to make my career in academia,' Felix was saying. 'He was handing me the company on a plate as he saw it but selling cars seemed so boring, don't you agree? The last thing I wanted to do was run a showroom for lumps of metal – heaven forbid. Much less money in my line of work, of course, but so much more fun!' He leaned towards Anna and grinned mischievously at her. She steadied herself and refused to be completely won over just yet.

'What is your field?'

'Same as yours! History, well social history. Not kings and queens and acts of parliament but what John Smith was doing in his village and how Mrs Smith fed her family and all that. Semi-retired now, of course. We, well, the university, set up a study centre for the Borders, the Marches, you know. So many people who went to the big industrial centres for work in the nineteenth century driven by rural poverty came from Shropshire, Herefordshire and so on. Conditions they were escaping were appalling. They were actually starving!' He slapped his thigh as though it was an outrage he had just discovered and was jolly well going to sort it out.

John Lansdowne returned with a cup of coffee for her. He raised his eyebrows sympathetically. She tried not to grin back. 'I'm afraid we're interested in rather more recent histories,' she said.

'Absolutely! Probate research – very fascinating. I met a woman the other day, young woman, at the Centre and her grandmother, I think, maybe great-grandmother, had grown up in one of the mud houses at the Lye! Can you imagine? They had nothing when they came in from the villages, they made their houses from packed mud. It's all astonishingly recent. Drink your coffee.'

Instead, Anna glanced at her watch. 'This is very interesting, Felix, but I only have an hour. Did you want some help with something?'

'Sort of. I will stop rabbiting instantly and come to the point.' To her surprise his whole demeanour changed. His shoulders slumped slightly, the jolly expression which had lifted his face vanished and in its place appeared a rather hang-dog look. 'I have something very unpleasant and sad to tell you. It's about Grace – you know, she married William Henry Thwaite and then when he left went off to America with little Jane.'

'Yes?'

John Lansdowne said, 'Felix found some letters.'

'Yes, I did. When my grandmother Ruthie died my mother and father didn't keep much, they naturally wanted their own modern things, but they did hang on to one of those old family bibles – you know the huge ones that births, marriages and deaths were recorded in?' Anna nodded. He dropped his voice confidentially. 'We weren't a religious family and I don't think it was ever opened - my mother gave it to me when I got my first degree in history. I remember being rather miffed – I'd been hoping for an MG sports car I'd seen on the lot.' He smiled briefly. 'She probably thought it had great sentimental value – family history and all that, so I would like it. I'm afraid I slung it under my bed at my flat in a fit of pique but I've never got rid of it.'

'But now?'

'When I read the newspaper article about your chap, Maxon Blake, being presented with the painting of The Mount, I wondered if the Grace that was mentioned was the one related to my family so I pulled out the monster book and looked at the names in the front. There she was, of course, Grace married to William Henry and then the date of her emigration. Nothing else. In fact, no generation after Grace and Ruth's parents ever made another entry.'

'So, you said there were some letters?'

'Yes, I'm just coming to that bit.' He took a swallow of cold coffee. 'When I tried to put the darn thing back it slipped out of my hands and out of it fell not just one or two but dozens of letters. They were written on very thin paper, do they call it onion-skin? They must have been there for over a hundred years some of them, and they'd got a bit stuck to the pages but they soon came free. Grandma must have used it as a filing cabinet. Knew no-one would ever look in it.'

Anna waited. Now he seemed reluctant to go on. The Tearooms were filling up with the lunch-time crowd and she inched her chair a little closer to spur him on.

'The letters were from Grace in America to Ruth, her younger sister. They started in 1895, July, I think it was, on the ship out to Philadelphia, the SS Warrington, and they finished just before Grace died in 1921. They were very close, the sisters. Grace confided in Ruthie.'

Anna couldn't help but wonder whether Grace had created a dream-life, a fantasy of her American experiences much as she had done of her English ones for Jane. But then, she hardly needed to. In many ways she had lived the American Dream – the rags to riches story.

Felix was looking at her intently. 'I'm going to sum up now what the letters revealed. It's shocking.' Both John and Anna were now listening closely. 'Grace's first husband, William Henry, was not a good choice. He was an officer in the Yorkshire Rifles and a lawyer so you can see why Grace was dazzled by him but she soon found out his Achilles heel. He was a gambler and such a dilatory and feckless solicitor that he lost his clients. They were desperately poor within a year of their marriage. Old James Thwaite wouldn't help because he was fed up with all the money that had already been wasted on his son. Robert, his brother, was doing very well in the bank and had even married money so William was the black sheep. Grace still loved him, though, and must have decided that the only way they could survive would be with a loan from Robert to tide them over.

'Grace was, by all accounts, a pretty girl and she no doubt made the best of herself to meet her brother-in-law and ask for help. He insisted on her meeting him at the bank in his own private office. I'm sorry to say this but he grossly took advantage of her desperate need. He raped her. I don't mean he asked if she would give him sex in return for money – she was quite clear to Ruthie that she was never asked. He just took what he wanted. She must have told Ruth when it happened but it had obviously traumatised her deeply. She refers to it several times in her letters home and how ashamed and defiled she felt.'

Felix frowned and passed a hand over his face as though wiping away a cobweb. 'Some money was paid – I don't know how much. Then she found she was pregnant and Jane was born. William believed the child was his, of course, but Robert told him about what had happened nine months before and lied that Grace had offered herself willingly, prostituted herself, in effect, since she had said her husband was such a useless provider. Shocking. In the fuss that followed Robert persuaded William to leave and paid his passage to Australia. That, of course, left Grace completely destitute and at his mercy.'

'So Jane really was Robert's daughter? It's on her death certificate and we didn't understand why.'

'I'm afraid it got worse. Robert knew full well Grace would be penniless and her family were not in a position to help her. He told her he was willing to have her be a servant at his house (presented, of course, as a noble act of charity) so she could keep Jane with her. She would have known exactly what that would mean.'

Anna nodded in agreement. 'How did she get the money to go to Philadelphia, then? Robert would have nothing to gain from giving it to her.'

'A stroke of luck. Her mother, Grace and Ruth's mother, was a very skilled seamstress and had a few wealthy clients. One of them died and left Mrs Smith a small legacy. Her mother, knowing only too well the situation her daughter had been placed in and how compromised she was, gave it to her so she could get away.' He sighed. 'Never saw her again, of course.'

Anna thought for a moment. 'But why would Grace tell Jane such a distressing thing when she told her who her father was?'

'She didn't. Jane was just a baby when they left England. All the certificates got lost in a fire, very conveniently. The families, I mean the Thwaites and Grace Blake's family were never in contact after she left and she told Jane, Grace did, that her father's name was Robert Thwaite which was true. Ruth must have said something about the wisdom of that but Grace felt it was the right thing to do.

She decided to not say what had happened - that they were not married - just that she had been widowed.'

'She edited the facts?'

'Yes, in a way. Jane must have believed that Grace had been married to Robert. It's possible that Grace never mentioned William Henry to Jane. Albert Maxon, you know, the American, was the man she regarded as her real father.'

'Maybe guilt played a part – women often were encouraged to blame themselves for their own victimisation then.'

'Well, of course, I don't know the answer to that. The letters stopped coming when Grace became bed-ridden a couple of years before she died so that's where it ends. The rape and its consequences were not referred to in letters after about 1900. Grace seemed content even if the marriage was not a love-match. Grandma never talked of it to my parents, I'm sure. She would have been ashamed of what Grace had gone through.'

Anna sat back and tried to make sense of what she had heard. She and Maxon, too, had never for one moment imagined that Jane had not known that Grace was married to William Henry and not to Robert. But now it seemed that Grace had simply not told her. It would even be possible that she had not ever actually lied – just told pieces of truth and let Jane make assumptions. 'My husband left us and then died.' 'Your father was Robert Thwaite.' No wonder she had no interest in returning to England to look up the family – such a visit would be explosive on at least two counts, setting aside Albert Maxon being on the run.

Felix could not know that Grace had made a bigamous marriage in America, that Albert Maxon was one of his grandmother's Chirk Street neighbours, that he was also a bigamist and not an American, and that he appeared to have funded his exploitative empire from theft. She had no right to tell him that and she had no plan to. That was Maxon's Blake's business.

She realised that John Lansdowne and Felix Brown were looking at her with some kind of expectation. 'This is very interesting and it solves a mystery but I'm not sure why you're telling me this, Felix. What do you want me to do?'

Felix sat back and smiled broadly. 'Advise me!'

'What?'

'I told you I waited until that nice young man had gone home? Well, I want you to advise me about whether it would be a good thing for him to know all this. You are under no obligation to tell him because your job is over, I'm assuming, but you must have got to know him quite well. He clearly wants to find out about his family history but he seems like a pleasant, rather innocent chap. Would it be a good idea or not for him to know that his great-grandmother was the result of a familial rape? Do you see what I mean? Not very nice, is it?'

'It certainly isn't,' Anna said to gain time.

'If you think he could cope I would send him the letters but if you think best not, then I won't.'

Anna pondered all the things that Maxon had finally managed to rise above and transmute to something good from his family's turbulent moral past and couldn't see one reason why he should need to know this.

'I don't think it would help,' she said, 'he's happy as things are.'

'Hoped you'd say that. You didn't mind me bending your ear?'

They all stood up. 'Not at all, it's been very interesting.'

'You just never know what's going to pop up out of the past and bite your bottom, do you?' Felix said.

Anna walked back to Harts slowly, reflecting on what Felix had said. She realised that over the weeks of working on Maxon's case she had developed a deep antipathy towards Grace and tried to remember when it had started. Maybe it was the fantasy about growing up at The Mount? That seemed so pretentious and dishonest. And yet, compared to her own fantasies, where was the harm? It was possible that she had profoundly misunderstood Grace – not just possible, likely, given her former febrile state of mind.

Looking at the facts, Grace had grown up in a poor family barely scraping by although everyone who could work, did. She was a pretty girl who would have been delighted when someone like William Henry paid court to her and why not? Why not want a way out of grinding poverty; maybe she would even be able to help her family? When he turned out to be a disappointment she didn't leave him, she tried to help him, but would have been powerless to prove her innocence when Robert made his accusations about Jane and so William Henry took the cowardly way out and left her in a terrible position.

What were her options at that point? Felix didn't know that Grace had begged James and Eliza to take her in so that she and her little girl would be safe and protected. That option failed. What Robert had suggested amounted to sexual slavery and she must have known it. What had popped up first at that critical moment, Anna wondered, Albert Maxon's plan or her mother's legacy? If she went to America alone and unfriended with barely enough funds to pay for her passage what would be the likely result? The best option would be some sewing work or as a live-in maid with a family who would take Jane, too, but they were long shots with no contacts and no financial buffer to tide her over. Prostitution would have been a very real hazard. So, sexual slavery at home or prostitution abroad would be the worst case scenario.

On the other hand, America might offer the twin blessings for someone like Grace of anonymity and opportunity away from small town gossiping, and Albert Maxon, someone she at least knew, could smooth the way. They may have been friends or childhood sweethearts before William Henry came along to dazzle her. In return he would expect to marry her. She had married once for love and that had turned out disastrously so why not marry for more practical reasons?

Anna had assumed, as the story unfolded, that Grace and Albert had had feelings for each other; to put it bluntly, that Grace had seduced her husband's brother *and* her neighbour and had probably tricked William Henry into marrying her in the first place. That she was, in the Victorian term, an adventuress. A flighty, immoral girl motivated by sensuality and greed. But what if the case was entirely different? She might have really loved William Henry and been abandoned by him with few choices. She could imagine whispered conferences between Grace and her mother and maybe even Ruth. What to do?

When Albert Maxon had seen that she was alone and desperate, he could have quickly planned a way that he could make his wildest dreams come true. A new life, with money, and with a woman he knew and found attractive, free from his own domestic ties which might have become irksome to him and perhaps were always second best. What was unknown was what Grace felt about him. But looked at logically, his plan was by far the best of her options. She would have a protector for herself and Jane and be able to put all the tangled, miserable mess behind her. The gossip about her would have already started and she would never want to expose Jane to that. Her mother's gift would make it possible to leave quickly to avoid scandal while Jane was still just an innocent and uninformed baby. She must have trusted Albert to be as good as his word and follow her. Did she know that he was planning to embezzle funds? Perhaps he spun her a line about that. It would be easy to make up a story about how he had come into money. She may never have known the source of it. On the other hand, she may have felt that the rich business people of Shrewsbury owed her something.

What would Anna herself have done under those circumstances? Perhaps Grace had not been narcissistic and selfish at all, perhaps she had considered her options very carefully and chosen the only one which might work out well. And so it had. No wonder she changed the back story for Jane. What would be gained by the girl knowing the sordid, shameful facts about Grace's involvement with the Thwaite family and her own genesis? Maybe Grace had looked at her life honestly and made the best decision she could. She must have known that Albert was at the very least a ruthless landlord in Philadelphia but she would hardly be in a position to take the moral high ground.

Anna felt a rush of compassion for the young woman who had been let down, violated, rejected and abandoned but had still had the courage to do what she believed best, no matter how risky, for the future of herself and her child. Anna hoped she would have had that kind of courage herself if she were placed in such a predicament.

27

Evidence of the storm was still lying around when Anna and Ellis picked their way along the tow-path from where they'd parked the car with a cool-bag slung between them. Plastic bags had been spiked by the hedge and all manner of paper trash had got blown into the roots. Fortunately, there were no tall trees by Rosa's boat but she pointed further up the canal to show where a branch had crashed down across a moored vessel. The Canal and River Trust was trying to track down the owners to tell them their boat was wrecked and had sunk on to the shallow underwater shelf near the path.

But today was fine and fresh with carefree little floccus clouds scooting about above and rain-soaked greenery flashing in the sun. Rosa had said it would be better if people just popped in to wish Len a happy birthday as the bank and boat couldn't accommodate crowds, so even Faye had allowed her arm to be twisted for a cameo exposure to her uncle. Besides, Alice wanted to come and see the boats and the ducks on the water and, of course, that clinched it.

The little girl was delighted by it all. 'It's a floating house, really,' Rosa said, lifting her on board, 'but it can move if you want it to.'

Alice immediately and predictably demanded, 'Make it move!'

'Look,' said Faye, 'there's one moving!' Down the canal came a hire-company narrow-boat leaving the Gas Street Basin and headed for the long tunnel a few miles ahead at Kings Norton. Alice stood and watched it pass but when the man at the tiller waved she jumped up and down and waved back.

She looked up at Steve who had arrived after parking the car. 'I want to go on it! Steeeve! Please, please, please can I?' Anna knew this politeness, instilled through many arduous drills, could in a second become a tantrum.

Rosa bent herself down to the little girl. 'You can have a look at mine, Leesha.' She began, with tantalising slowness, to open the little doors painted with castles to reveal the short flight of stairs down to the cabin. Alice peered through them, fascinated. Rosa leaned closer and whispered into the child's ear. 'Do you want to see the secret place where I sleep?' Alice was too overcome to speak but nodded violently.

Anna started to lay things out while Ellis and Steve set up the folding chairs they'd brought. Len had already booked the ones from the boat and was sitting in them with a friend from the band. He was wearing the red velvet waistcoat over his best black T shirt. Rosa had embroidered the musical refrain: '*You'll never know that you're my hero.*' Did Len know? Had one of his friends told him, or was it Rosa's typically low-key way of paying him a compliment? Anna caught her eye as she re-emerged with Alice and smiled, pointing back with her thumb to Len's wool-sack chest.

It had been arranged that this gathering would take place on the actual day and then there would be a Sunday lunch at home when George was up and about to which Diane and Joan would come as well. Anna could see that an acoustic guitar was now being tuned and that Len was wiping his flute under his armpit preparatory to raising it to his lips but she wanted to have a word before they got started.

'Here you go,' she said, giving him an envelope, 'happy birthday, little brother.' He tore the flap with his thick fingers and looked disappointed that there was no money inside. 'No, have a look,' she ordered. He drew out two tickets for Hellbent at the Town Hall the following week.

The guitar player leaned across to look. 'Hey, Len, that's so great of you to take me! Ta, mate!' Len cuffed him away.

'I didn't know you was into this sort of thing, Sis,' he said, 'but I am.'

Anna was standing and so was tall enough to hug him and whisper into his ear at the same time. 'Idiot! Ask Rosa.' Len's face flushed purple. 'Not now!' Anna immediately ordered seeing all kinds of teasing going on which Rosa might not care for. 'Wait until you're alone, ok?'

Len tucked the tickets into an inside pocket on the waistcoat which Rosa had thoughtfully provided and nodded, sweat breaking out on his upper lip at the thought of the chivalric challenge to come. Anna fetched her chair and sat in it next to him. 'Actually, Len, there was something I wanted to ask you.'

'What?'

'Do you ever,' she hesitated, not sure how to go on.

'Do I ever what?'

'Do you ever visit our mother's headstone – you know, where her ashes are buried?'

Len drew back a little. 'I might. I'm allowed. She was my mum.'

Anna felt a pang of remorse. Not only had she never been, but Len had never heard her say a good word about Lena. Well, had never heard her say a word of any kind but he knew how she felt. 'Of course. Only, I'd like to go with you some time if you don't mind.'

'Why? You couldn't stand her.'

'I think I was a bit unfair. Anyway, I want to – I want to put some flowers there. Roses from our garden, maybe.' Blossoms and thorns on the same stem seemed an appropriate choice.

Len grunted. 'Plastic ones are best – they last longer. You can get them from the pound shop.'

'Maybe another time, maybe when it's winter I'll do that.'

Anna watched Rosa moving calmly between people with offers of food and drink and a moment of chat. She stood now with her head on one side and two empty pint glasses in one hand smiling at Faye while the girl talked eagerly about something. Steve was lying in the grass while Alice sat on his chest and fed him scraps of lettuce, screaming with delight when he pretended to suddenly bite her fingers. She looked around for Ellis. He was hovering near the stern of the boat and when she caught his eye he glanced at his watch and made a swinging movement with his hand. She nodded and got to her feet.

'You could play something for her, too.'

Len turned and gave her his full attention. 'Yeah, I could.'

'Have a think what she might like.'

'I don't have to think. I know her favourite.'

'What?'

He looked at the flute he was holding and raised it to his lips and the melody of Lena's favourite song rang out. In a moment the guitar player had joined in and was singing the chorus, '*See that girl, watch that teen, she is the dancing queen.*'

Anna waved her goodbyes to Rosa, Len and the guitarist and when she kissed Faye and Alice, she kissed Steve too, and then walked off with Ellis to take him to his tennis tournament. Her dad had been right. For the first time in months she felt joy rise in her like a bird in flight and she couldn't resist pulling Ellis to her and hugging him whether he liked it or not. If she went before Len, she thought, he'd better not play 'Fat-bottomed Girls' at her graveside.

As the school holidays began the weather broke and late July merged into August in a soggy, sweaty muddle. George, nagged at by Anna and bullied by Diane, took refuge for hours each day in the shed but Rosa continued to come so that when he fell asleep in the old car seat in his sanctuary she could keep the world at bay.

Ellis lost the August junior tournament in the final but sufficiently impressed the selectors to make it on to the County Junior Team for next year's season. He was training Bobble to act as ball-boy while he practised serves in the back garden, which was not entirely successful because, although Bobble could clear the fences between them and the neighbours at an amble going after the ball, he had not yet grasped the concept of returning with it. Anna had to work all summer but John and Maggie Bryant took the boys to Cornwall for a few days to swim and surf and then to Dorset to look for fossils for which Anna was very grateful.

Faye took every shift she could at the Thai restaurant to save for a four-day girls' trip to Corfu before starting work at Mecklins. She arrived home tanned and exhausted and Anna didn't ask any questions at all.

Anna spent each weekend on the bedroom. She packed every scrap of memorabilia from the wall into a plastic storage box keeping only one photograph which she slipped into a little faience frame they had bought together in Italy. The clothes were the hardest to get rid of but Joan helped, moving her briskly along when she found herself sitting on the floor and saying, 'Maybe I'll just keep this?' Joan wouldn't let her do the shoes but sent her off to make them a sandwich. 'Shoes are very hard,' she said, 'they keep the shape. I'll do them, love.' Then, before she could weaken, the cardboard boxes were loaded into the Renault and Joan was backing out of the drive.

Once the clothes were done, Anna stripped the bed and put everything in the wash and when that had dried she took down the curtains and washed those. Then she pulled the clean things they had used for their king-sized bed out of the airing cupboard and made a pile of all of them – all the sheets, duvets, pillowcases and summer quilts. They all went into black bin bags for charity except for a couple of sheets which had been put aside years ago for decorating tarps as they'd become too scuffed for use. Only the mattress protector was left in place as the Salvation Army had said they would take the bed and she didn't want to spatter it.

The following weekend Anna put on an old T shirt and leggings and tied a scarf over her hair. She pulled the large step-ladders up the stairs and covered the furniture with the torn up sheets and then the real work began. Over two weekends she stripped the walls of paper, washed down the paintwork, and finally, after twenty-eight years of looking at the crack in the ceiling and planning to fill it, filled it. The job took seventeen minutes with another five the next day for sanding.

Ellis wanted to help with the re-decoration when he came back from his holiday and she was glad of the company. They took it in turns to choose music from their ipods and turned up the volume as loud as they dared. As Anna reached above her head to roller the ceiling and make it turn from a dull beige to sparkling white she felt a slow tide of renewal creeping through herself as well.

She consulted Ellis on the wall colour which was about as much use as consulting George. Diane suggested, in a surprise choice, lilac, which Anna instantly rejected and Joan thought nothing could better apple white everywhere. Anna pored over colour charts and designer's suggestions but in the end kept coming back to the same thing. *'You are the sunshine of my life,'* he had sung to her. She bought the paint.

The room glowed with light. The white of the trim and the windows, the freshness of the snowy panelled door and wardrobes all set against a glowing, no-holds barred, daffodil yellow was so satisfying she could hardly bear to leave it. She ordered white internal shutters, reckless about the expense, and then a new bed and a creamy carpet.

Faye came with her to choose the linens and they staggered home, footsore, with huge bags. They went up together to make up the room and place the lamps and rugs around and then stood back to admire the total effect. The last thing Anna put in place was the faience frame with the four of them, tousled and windblown, on a beach in Brittany. The children, as they were then, were all legs and grins and Anna was tucked up against him so he could easily circle all of them in his arms. The late afternoon sun slanted into his eyes, lit into relief the planes of his face and burnished his bright hair. Harry. It was on the bedside table where she would see it first thing in the morning and last thing at night. From start to finish the task had taken most of the summer holidays.

'So this is my room, right?' Faye asked, tenting her eyebrows at Anna. 'You *like* sleeping in the little crap room, don't you?'

'It looks good, doesn't it? I hadn't realised how dingy the old stuff was,' Anna said, putting an arm round her waist and letting her eyes travel round the room, resting with pleasure on the glass vase of sweet peas on the dressing table, the bright splashes of colour on the white duvet cover.

'What did you do with dad?'

'In my wardrobe.'

'So what –?'

'We need to talk about that. Maybe tonight after dinner. Pops is strong enough, I think.'

They sat on the bed and then flopped back against the bouncy new pillows. Faye put her head against Anna's. 'Mum?'

'Mm.' Anna half-closed her eyes and let the sunny room blur into soft brilliance.

'You and Steve.'

Anna opened her eyes wide and looked into Faye's chocolate irises. 'What?'

'I don't mind. I mean, he's all right.'

'For a wrinkly, you mean?'

'Obviously.'

Anna turned her head back and stared at the ceiling. The crack that had been there for so long had vanished. Not a trace of a lump or a change of plane remained – she had made a good job of it.

'Mum?'

'Mm.'

'Would it be like, totally crass, if we had that party? You know the one.'

'I know the one. No, love, it wouldn't be crass, it would be a really good idea. However, the bad news is I have spent the family treasure chest on this room so - '

'I'll ask everyone to bring stuff.'

'My thoughts exactly.' Anna looked back at Faye. 'Will Jason be coming?'

Faye snorted. 'Gone.'

'Really?' Anna considered this for a moment. 'Anyone else coming?'

'There might be,' Faye said, getting up and arching her back, 'if he behaves himself.'

28

When they drew in to the familiar car park Anna felt her stomach lurch with the power of her memories. She took a moment to gaze out over the sparkling reservoir. 'Shall we run there?' Harry had said and she had turned him to look up at Hen Cloud above them. 'No. We're going up there.' He had gazed up in delight. That was the time that she and Harry and Steve had climbed the path to the high ridge and found the tarn.

'Can we eat something first? I'm starving.' Faye was not good at early mornings and although Ellis groaned at her, Anna could see he was hoping the same. So, it was bacon sandwiches all round and hot drinks from The Roaches Tearooms and then they set off in a small single file, Anna carrying a bag and bringing up the rear with Ellis at the front since George and Faye had never been to this beautiful Staffordshire escarpment. Already a small team of climbers were busy on the rocky slopes to their left but they wound to the right up the easy path to join the ridge-top trail. The sky was messy as though a chalk had been turned on its side and scrawled across a blue page and then a careless stick of charcoal had scribbled over the top. It was a sky in transit, remembering and promising at the same time.

Anna stopped the group half way up to turn and admire the view over to Tittesworth Reservoir and give George a chance to catch his breath. She had wondered how hard it would be to re-visit this scene when the last time she had been here she had been kneeling by her husband's dead body. His blood would still be in the soil. But, although her heart beat fast with the memory, it was not as hard as she thought. Len had been right, this was a good place for Harry to die and it would be a good place to leave his ashes.

At the top they turned left and began the level walk along the trail, each head turning frequently to take in the magnificent spread of fields, forests and water below them. In some places they had to climb gingerly round rock outcrops but for most of the time the path was flat and even and in some parts, paved with limestone. Anna hoped she would remember. Every now and then she took a few steps off the trail to look around. The air was still and quiet – it was too early for the thermals to have started to rise from sun-baked rocks – and distant complaints of sheep and the calls of the climbers were all that broke the silence. The birds must be resting after their early morning foraging session.

Anna caught George up and said she would go ahead from here. 'What about a breather?' he gasped. Faye and Ellis threw themselves down in the grass and George lowered himself on to a boulder. Anna walked off to the upper side of the path and scrambled up a heap of rocks. At first she didn't see it but then she caught the glint of water not far ahead.

'We're almost there,' she said, sitting down next to George. 'It's only a little way ahead.'

'I hadn't realised how weak I've got,' George said gruffly. 'You can leave me up here if you like – save time later.' Anna smacked him on his shoulder.

'Mum?' Ellis was squinting at the boulders.

'What?'

'Are they millstone grit?'

'Um. I think so.'

'You are such a nerdy freak, Ell. No-one normal would think that stuff.'

Anna stood up and picked up the bag. 'Come on, we're nearly there.'

When they came to the little tarn everyone gathered in delighted silence for a moment. The surface of the water was just beginning to wrinkle as a light breeze stroked the reeds and grasses that fringed it so that they rippled glossily. Anna stood quietly smiling, remembering how Steve had shown them this and how he had knelt beside Harry and scooped the water into his hands for Harry to drink. How long ago had that been? Two years? More? She could see it as clearly as if it was happening right now; Steve's stook of burnt umber hair almost touching Harry's auburn tangle and then how both men had raised their heads and laughed at each other with the sheer exuberance of the moment.

Ellis was the first to leave the tarn and explore the mounds of rocks away from the path. Anna followed him while Faye sat on the grass and picked out stems of purple vetch to take back for Alice.

'Look, this is good.'

Anna peered between the rocks into what seemed to be a deep crevasse. 'Mm. Let's toss a pebble down – it could be deceptive.' But it wasn't. The pebble went a fair way before it struck another rock. 'Do you think Pops can get up here?'

They looked back down at the old man who was standing with his back to them looking over the valley, his hands on his hips. 'Let's ask him.'

Faye took her grandfather's hand and helped him scramble the short distance up the hill until they were all near the boulders. 'These rocks would have been at the leading edge of a glacier,' Anna said, feeling that Harry would want her to, 'they would have been scraped off the hills by the ice and got pushed this far before the glacier stopped and eventually melted. We're standing at the edge of the last ice age.'

'Good title for a poem,' said George. 'The Edge of the Last Ice Age.'

'Shall we do it?' Anna said, and they nodded solemnly. She took the plastic jar from the bag and loosened the top and then climbed another two metres to the edge of the rock outcrop. 'Goodbye darling,' she whispered and tipped the jar slowly down the space between the rocks until it was empty and only a small cloud of dust, like an exhalation from the earth, hung in the air.

As agreed, Ellis came up next as she stepped down. He stood for a while before he took from his pocket a folded piece of paper and pushed it into the darkness to follow the ashes. They each had written Harry a goodbye note, not to be read aloud but to go with him into the ancient rocks.

Faye had tears in her eyes when she came down and Anna held her close for several minutes until they heard George say, 'Goodbye, Son,' and then it was Anna's turn. She had spent hours writing a long message to Harry but had then torn it up. Instead, she wrote on the back of a photograph of the two of them taken at their wedding:

'My dear friend and lover, memories of you are stitched into my DNA and can never be unpicked. You were the sunshine of our lives, too, and we are forever warmed and comforted by what you have been to us. Rest in peace, sweetheart. Anna.'

When the path began to drop down towards the road Anna moved alongside her father. She took his arm. 'I don't know what to do about the rest of the money, Dad. Any ideas? I don't want it just to go into repairs and things like that. I know Gerald wouldn't care what we did with it but I'd like it to mark Harry's legacy in some way. I suppose that's why people buy benches but they aren't allowed up here.'

George pointed down the path to where Faye and Ellis were trying to kick each other's bottoms with backward flicks. The giddy silliness that often follows solemn occasions had set in and Anna was glad to see them horsing about and shaking off the sadness. 'There's Harry's legacy, love, in my view. Put it away for them. I think it's what he would have wanted although you shouldn't speak for the dead.'

Anna hugged his arm. 'No, you're right. I will.' They picked their way carefully down among the scree and rocks, Anna keeping a tighter hold on George's arm every time they slid. 'Just in case I never say it, I love you, Dad.'

'Likewise, Annie,' he panted, 'or, as J. M. Barrie had it, "Fame is nothing; daughters are the thing."'

By the time Anna and George got to the car park, Faye and Ellis had disappeared inside the Tearooms. George looked around scratching his knotty beard. 'I wonder if they let campervans stay overnight here?'

On the trip back home the first song on Radio Stoke was Reasons to Be Cheerful – Part 3, by Ian Drury and the Blockheads and they all shouted along until they were hoarse.

Thanks

Once again I want to thank Catharine Stevens not only for sharing her extraordinary knowledge of the art and science of genealogical research but also for our many pub lunches mulling over the hoops through which I might put some of my characters. For this book, it was an eye-opener to realise how the expansion of the British Empire (and more available transport) at the end of the nineteenth century meant that people from this country could give themselves a second chance abroad by manipulating their legal status. Also, thanks to friends who have read unfinished material and spurred me on. Encouragement from my sons and others in my family is deeply appreciated as are the kind reviews of readers.

Geraldine Wall has lived and worked in the UK, the USA and the Caribbean. She currently lives in Birmingham, England.

Email: geraldine.wall@blueyonder.co.uk

42713711R00171

Printed in Poland
by Amazon Fulfillment
Poland Sp. z o.o., Wrocław